May Not Appear Exactly As Shown

Gordon j. h. Leenders

ECW Press

Copyright © Gordon Leenders, 2003

Published by ECW PRESS
2120 Queen Street East, Suite 200, Toronto, Ontario, Canada M4E 1E2

All rights reserved. No part of this publication may be reproduced, stored in a retrieval system, or transmitted in any form by any process — electronic, mechanical, photocopying, recording, or otherwise — without the prior written permission of the copyright owners and ECW PRESS.

This is a work of fiction. The characters, incidents, and dialogues are products of the author's imagination and are not to be construed as real. Any resemblance to actual events or persons, dead or living, is purely coincidental.

NATIONAL LIBRARY OF CANADA CATALOGUING IN PUBLICATION

Leenders, Gordon, j. h.,
May not appear exactly as shown / Gordon j. h. Leenders.

ISBN 1-55022-608-8

1. Title.

PS8573.E359M39 2003   C813'.6   C2003-902198-X
PR9199.4.L435M39 2003

Editor: Jennifer Hale
Cover and Text Design: Tania Craan
Cover photo: © Paul Edmondson/CORBIS/Magmaphoto.com
Production & Typesetting: Mary Bowness
Printing: Marc Veilleux Imprimeur Inc.

This book is set in Frankie and New Baskerville.

The publication of *May Not Appear Exactly As Shown* has been generously supported by the Canada Council, the Ontario Arts Council, the Ontario Media Development Corporation, and the Government of Canada through the Book Publishing Industry Development Program. Canadä

DISTRIBUTION
CANADA: Jaguar Book Group, 100 Armstrong Avenue, Georgetown, ON, L7G 5S4

PRINTED AND BOUND IN CANADA

ECW PRESS
ecwpress.com

For my family:

*Henry,
Henny,
Sharon-Ann,
Yvonne &
Kevin*

Life's but a walking shadow, a poor player
That struts and frets his hour upon the stage
And then is heard no more. It is a tale
Told by an idiot, full of sound and fury,
Signifying nothing.
— *Macbeth*, Act 5, Scene 5

opening scenes

I'm southbound on the Yonge Street subway line trying to recall a day in the last fourteen months when the idea of suicide wasn't flickering through my frontal lobe — when I wasn't imagining my body being slit, stabbed, shot, shredded, burned, drowned, poisoned, hanged, crushed, exploded — and it's *before* I realize that such a day doesn't exist but *after* simultaneously smelling Miracle perfume by Lancôme and hearing two women plunk down in the seat perpendicular to mine that I

– open my eyes,
– steal a quick glance at the two women,
– casually retrieve my cousin Rebecca's diary from my canvas messenger bag, and
– (pretending to read the diary as a decoy) begin eavesdropping on the women's conversation, tuning in just in time to hear the slightly shorter, slightly chunkier one inventorying the line-up of *freak*shows (emphasis hers) she's dated since turning thirty exactly one year ago yesterday.

"I don't know why," she's now saying, "but ever since I turned thirty it seems like every *freak*show in Toronto wants to ask me out on a date."

Chuckling, the slightly taller, slightly thinner one says, "It can't be *that* bad."

"Trust me. It is."

"Oh, come on," the slightly thinner one says, nudging the slightly chunkier one's leather T-strap sandals with her satin wedges. "I've met some of the men you dated this past year, and they seemed fine, and they looked . . . my God, most of them looked amazing."

"I agree," the slightly chunkier one says matter-of-factly, "they *seemed* fine — and the package *looked* amazing. In fact, the packaging has probably never *looked* better. But that's not where the problems are. The problems are *inside* the package, in the actual *contents* — which is why I'm thinking of lobbying the government to make it mandatory for any man over twenty-one to carry a list of ingredients."

"A list of ingredients?"

"If the Food and Drug Administration requires food companies to place a list of ingredients on all food packages so consumers know exactly what they're eating, I think all men over the age of twenty-one should be required to carry a list of ingredients so we single women know exactly what we're dating, so we can decide if we want to put up with an Oedipus complex or a bipolar disorder or alcoholism or an 'I'll-always-love-my-lavender-Porsche-944-more-than-you' syndrome, so there's no more of this, 'Oh ya, P.S., I forgot to tell you, I'm already married,' or 'Oh, I'm sorry, I thought you knew I just wanted one last one-night stand before I proposed to my girlfriend,' or 'I thought you should know, I've got herpes. But don't worry, I made sure it was in its dormant phase before we had sex.'"

"*This* has happened to you?"

"To my friends. My stories are worse."

"Worse?"

"Trust me."

"Who *are* these men?"

"Not men, *f-r-e-a-k*shows. They're what men have become in the new millennium."

"I think it's time for some i.e.'s."

"Okay, without any further ado, let's meet our first nominee for 'Freakshow of my Thirtieth Year,' Mr. Michael Rawlings. Michael was twenty-eight, a fourth-year med student at the University of Toronto, had beautiful skin, a toned body, and was spectacular in bed."

"He sounds yummy."

"And yummy he was — right up until our fifth date when he informed me he was neither heterosexual nor bisexual nor homosexual."

"What was he?"

"*Try*sexual."

"Which meant?"

"Which meant he'd *try* sex with just about anyone — or anything."

"You mean even . . ."

"Yes, apparently even animals."

"Well, you have to admit, it certainly increases his chances of having a date on Saturday nights."

"Not to mention getting laid."

There is a moment — a very brief moment — when I think neither of the women is going to laugh, but then both of them burst out laughing and it's a few seconds later, while they're busy stifling their giggles, that I notice how unusually quiet the subway car is, especially considering the day (Friday), the time (4:07 p.m.), and the fact that we've been experiencing delays since Eglinton station (which, in itself, is usually enough to prick people into complaining), and for a moment I wonder if the reason everyone's so quiet is because they too are eavesdropping on the women's conversation and although part of me is tempted to raise my head and look at the other commuters, to survey and decipher their expressions, another part (my cousin Rebecca's part) is warning me *not* to look up from her diary in case my movements alert the two women to my presence and they end up PGing what they're saying.

"So," the slightly thinner one says after they've finished giggling, "what happened with '*Try*sexual man'?"

"The only thing that could; I told him there was no way I was having a ménage à trois if the trois was going to be a goat or his Labrador retriever. Besides, I've got enough to worry about without wondering if my date is going to give me 'hoof and mouth' disease."

When they laugh this time, I can't help myself and after tilting my head five, possibly ten degrees, I look up from Rebecca's diary and using only my eyes make three panoramic sweeps of the subway car realizing, after zooming in on the commuters closest to the two women, that no one seems to care what the women are saying — there's just a collage of tired bodies leaning against metal poles or slumped in stiff seats, their faces stamped with identical, 'I'd rather be somewhere else right now.com' expressions and —

the rest of this scene is momentarily displaced — obliterated, actually — by the sight of a petite Japanese woman boarding the subway at Bloor station where we've been stopped now for almost a minute (the conductor having already informed us we're waiting for a previous train to exit the next station) and initially I'm drawn to the dress she's wearing, which is blue — *turquoise* blue — and which, for a moment, reminds me of the dress Sarah Jessica Parker wore during a *Sex and the City* episode — the one where she's walking down the street and a guy tosses away a cigarette and it hits her in the arm — but more than the dress, although the dress is definitely part of it, it's the sight of the Japanese woman's shy, fragile eyes coupled with her unblemished skin — her perfect porcelain face — that gives me a jolt, that makes my stomach muscles tense and immediately rewinds my life until I'm back at our first appointment together when the two of us are in the living room of The Suicide Loft and I'm seated in the solid oak rocking chair watching her walking towards me, her blue — *turquoise* blue — silk robe slowly opening, sliding off her slender shoulders, slipping discreetly from her body, my eyes pursuing the robe's delicate descent to the carpeted floor before climbing back up her legs, passing swiftly over her ankles, her calves, her knees, her thighs, her — pausing at the sight of the five, six . . . seven! — seven wounds on her navel, all seven in various phases of healing, all seven the result of a knife's desperate attempt to plunge into her infertile womb, endeavouring to ease the shame of being unable to bear children, the pain of her husband divorcing her, the sight of him two years later holding hands with another woman, a *pregnant* woman, and as I watch her take hold of the knife, watch her bowed eyes slowly uncoiling, attaching themselves to mine, I notice the shy, fragile expression has vanished, has been replaced by a hopeless, borderline reckless gaze, a gaze that holds me captive, forcing me to watch as she re-enacts her suicide attempt, thrusting the knife deep inside her abdomen, violently stirring the handle, the serrated blade sawing through the porcelain flesh of her navel until her womb is a gaping hole, a butchered remnant of femininity and she suddenly stops, letting the imaginary knife slip from her quivering hands before once again bowing her eyes, her head, her body, then picking up her turquoise blue robe and quietly leaving the room.

It's been almost a year now and I'm still not comfortable seeing my clients in public like this — in malls, in restaurants, on the street, on subways — because I'm convinced they'll recognize me. Of course, they never do. But even though I know this, a wave of relief still washes over me when the woman walks by without noticing me and as soon as the train begins to pull out of Bloor station I return my gaze to my cousin Rebecca's diary and my attention to the two women, wondering how many men, I mean, *f-r-e-a-k*shows, I've missed.

"– forty-one, a chiropractor, married and divorced three times, no kids, two cars, and one beautiful house in High Park. During our first date — dinner at Auberge du Pommier — we're having a good time, telling jokes, laughing, really getting along when halfway through our second bottle of Chardonnay he leans over the table and says, 'Listen, before we go any further, there's something I think I should tell you.'"

"Still married?"

"No."

"Already engaged to someone else?"

"No."

"STD?"

"No."

"Bisexual? *Try*sexual?"

"No and no."

"What then?"

"He tells me he's on a quest."

"A *quest*?"

"For the perfect woman."

"Oh God, how original. And let me guess, he already knew exactly what Ms. Perfection looked like and it wasn't you."

"No, as a matter of fact, he said he didn't have a clue what she looked like. All he knew was that she would possess . . . now how did he put it? I used to have this line of his memorized. . . . She would possess — oh yes — 'She would possess a combination of mutually incompatible qualities that would attract and repel me at the same time, thus sustaining my interest forever.'"

"Excuse me? Can you repeat that?"

"A combination of mutually incompatible qualities that would attract and repel him at the same time, thus sustaining his interest forever."

"And your response to this was?"

"I told him I think I knew someone who fit this description."

"Who?"

"His mother."

Their giggles are almost immediately drowned out by the exchange of commuters at College Street station, by the awkward shuffling and repositioning occurring as the people left standing and the people now boarding scramble for the vacated seats and best places to stand. Seconds later the bell chimes and the train begins pulling us toward the next stop, the newly boarded passengers already wearing the same tired, dulled expressions as everyone else.

"After Frank was Jonathan — no, Ken. Yes, 'Ken but please, call me Kenneth.' Kenneth was thirty-seven, a chemical engineer, and wore nothing but Moore's suits even though he could easily afford Hugo Boss or Armani. During our second date, a Saturday afternoon at the Ontario Science Centre, Kenneth goes on a long-winded spiel about how relationships are like chemical reactions and that similar to two chemicals interacting, when two people get together the interaction can be quite boring, other times the interaction can be volatile, even explosive, while every so often two people mix together perfectly, creating a symbiotic union."

"And did you ask him what he thought the two of you were?"

"Of course."

"And?"

"And he said we fell into the boring category."

"He did *not* say that."

"He did."

"And what did you say?"

"I told him I agreed, though for a second or two I felt like bashing him with my shoulder bag just so he'd have to add 'volatile' and 'explosive' to his list."

They laugh again, this time drawing attention from a very short, very thin elderly man wedged between two obese girls — twins — wearing matching Nike T-shirts with the words JUST DO IT in blue lettering stretched across the place where their breasts will be in a few years.

(All three passengers boarded the subway at College station and, until the women's latest outburst of laughter were reading: *Harry Potter and The Philosopher's Stone* for the girls, *Barney's Version* for the elderly man.)

Presently, the two girls are watching the man who, in trying to locate the source of the laughter, now resembles the herky-jerky movements of *The Price Is Right* camera scanning the audience for the next contestant — his head bobbing and weaving, his eyes rummaging for an opening between the medley of shifting arms, legs, purses, knapsacks, and briefcases before finally giving up and reading the 'Poetry on the Way' advertisement above his head and it's just as he finishes reading the ad and is returning his gaze to his novel that my Bell Mobility pager starts vibrating, instantly inducing a slight spasm of panic in me because I realize I forgot to switch my cellphone to vibrate mode and since I don't want to draw any attention to myself by reaching into the front pocket of my non-pleated beige Dockers and retrieving the phone, I decide instead to cross the index and middle finger on my right hand hoping that no one, not Eriq or Nicole or Brad or Daphne — not even Rebecca — calls me.

The train slows, entering Dundas station, which is where I had intended to get off, wanting to go to HMV and buy *Revenge*, the second CD put out by the heavy metal band Wamphryi and then browse through The World's Biggest Bookstore before meeting Daphne, but when I see the two women aren't moving from their seats I decide to stay and listen to them, wondering if, like me, there are any other passengers who have elected to do the same thing.

At Dundas station, there's another flurry of incoming passengers — Chinese, Vietnamese, Pakistani, Somalian, Spanish, Italian (most unreservedly speaking their native tongues) — the aroma of languages immediately inflating the subway car, and I feel a twinge of regret at only being able to speak one point five languages (the point five being French), and it's as I'm giving some serious thought to learning more French, getting it closer to point seven, maybe even point eight before I commit suicide that I become aware of the fresh batch of smells now moving around the subway car — lavender, curry, CK One, vanilla, cinnamon, Polo Sport, cherry, apple, Chanel No. 5, garlic, coconut — but it's the cherry and apple that makes me think of the cyanide-containing sugar mygdalin located in the seeds of apples and cherries and which, when exposed to the beta-glucosidase enzyme in the human stomach, gets converted into cyanide and —

The women are laughing again, this time louder, more audacious, the raucous cackle ejected from the slightly thinner one's throat temporarily eclipsing the metallic shriek of the subway wheels grating on the tracks.

"Now Jonathan sounded like *a lot* of fun," she says after catching her breath.

"He was," the slightly chunkier one says, still chuckling. "But that was the problem, he was never serious. *Never.*"

Of course, in order for the seeds to be lethal, you have to ingest a substantial amount. Fortunately I've been collecting seeds for almost a year and now have two 500 ml preserving jars of apple seeds and four and a half 500 ml preserving jars of cherry seeds which I store in the freezer at The Suicide Loft and which, anytime I want, I can dump into a blender (the seeds need to be crushed or ground first in order to release the hydrogen cyanide), then stir into a glass of Kool-Aid and —

"And that brings us to — who?"

"That brings us to Matthew. Twenty-two — I know, a little

young, but after Jonathan I was still feeling very 'How Stella Got Her Groove Back,' and unlike Jonathan, Matthew was very progressive, especially in bed, not exactly the quality you'd expect from someone whose father was an orthodox Anglican minister and whose mother taught Sunday school."

"Kinky?"

"I'm not sure kinky even *begins* to cover it, but that's another story. Anyway, our first date was a visit to the AGO and dinner at the Zoom Café. Our second date was a visit to the ROM and dinner at Scaramouche."

"The Art Gallery, the Museum, and two dinners at two amazing restaurants? He sounded promising."

"He did, except I had a feeling something was wrong because he was always spitting."

"Spitting?"

"Aggressively. As though his spit was being repressed and needed to escape."

"Très bizarre."

"*Très, très* bizarre. Anyway, our third date, which he tells me on the drive over to his parents' place is going to be, 'Just a casual lunch at your nudge, nudge, wink, wink, ha, ha, future inlaws,' he —"

"Wait a minute. You went to his parents' place? On only your third date?"

"He told me his parents lived on this incredible farm, in this really quaint early 20th-century stone farmhouse, that they were harmless, and that his mother was a fabulous cook so I thought, why not? Besides, I'd never had sex on a farm before."

"How was it?"

"What?"

"Lunch."

"Oh. Well, the presentation was amazing. His mother had this incredibly beautiful spread of spiced minced lamb; shish kabobs of sliced portobello mushrooms, peppers, zucchini, and cherry tomatoes; puréed sweet potatoes and squash; home-baked sourdough bread; three kinds of chutney; and a large bowl of spinach and romaine salad — all served on this absolutely gorgeous antique oak table on their sun porch."

"It sounds amazing."

"It was. And the weather was incredible for April. Remember that great weekend in early April we had? It was really sunny and warm? Well it was the Sunday of *that* weekend and just after Matthew's father said grace, Matthew clears his throat and says he has an announcement to make and after his mother glances over at my left hand to see if there's a ring on it Matthew tells all of us he's getting a sex change, that he's felt he wanted one since he was twelve years old, maybe even ten, and then he spits, twice — once on the spiced minced lamb and once on the salad — and then walks out of the house."

"You're not serious. Tell me you're not serious."

"Ladies and Gentlemen, this is *not* a joke."

"Oh . . . my . . . God. What'd you do?"

"I told his parents it was really nice to have met them both but, seeing as I wasn't terribly fond of phlegm dressing, it was probably best I take a rain check on lunch."

"You didn't."

"I did."

"You're horrible."

"I know, but what was I supposed to —"

"Oh damn, this is my stop," the slightly thinner one says as the train enters the Queen Street station. "Listen, I desperately want to hear more. I'll call you tonight, say around 8:00, 8:30 — will you be home?"

"No date. I'll be home."

"By the way, I was going to tell you earlier — nice tan. Salon?"

"Bottled bronze. Estée Lauder."

"It looks amazing."

"I know. Remember how awful they used to be? All those orange blotches and streaks that suddenly appeared and made you look like a leper?"

"Yours looks completely natural, though."

"Thanks."

"It makes sense now too, with the ozone disappearing and the sun being so harmful these days."

"I know. I always carry an umbrella — rain or shine."

They give each other a quick hug while still sitting and then the slightly thinner one says, "Okay, I'll call you tonight," before popping out of her seat and rushing out the subway car door, nearly knocking my cousin Rebecca's diary out of my left hand.

recurrent? yes. intrusive? definitely not.

I'm now walking west on the north side of Queen Street, past the cluster of, as my friend Daphne calls them, 'Corporate Youth' (kids wearing Nike, Reebok, Roots, DKNY, Polo, etc.), milling about the rear entrance to the Eaton Centre, past the aroma of charcoal and sausages coming from the hot dog vendor's cart, past the man hysterically shouting, "Only Jesus can save you!" past the woman calmly chanting, "Allah knows best," past the temptation of running to the nearest phone booth and asking the person who answers the random number I've just dialled to give me one, *just one* good reason why I shouldn't kill myself right now, past the two teenaged girls wearing matching Catholic school uniforms, their dress shirts casually unbuttoned, exposing white see-through lace bras — after walking past all this, my pager starts vibrating again and using my new Kyocera cellphone I check my messages, both from clients calling to confirm their respective 1:00 p.m. and 2:30 p.m. appointments with me tomorrow at The Suicide Loft.

A minute or so later, while standing at the corner of Bay and Queen, I become so completely absorbed by the old City Hall — by the size and colour and burly shape of the blocks, by the building itself rising up solid and thick and making the nearby financial fortresses on Bay Street seem puny and brittle by comparison — that I miss the crosswalk light and have to wait for the next one, my eyes fast-forwarding in the process, taking in the sights of Nathan Phillips Square — the parked tour bus, the hot dog vendors, the ice cream trucks, the scrounging pigeons, the pockets of tourists taking pictures of the new City Hall — and it's as I pass the second ice cream truck that I notice a group of window washers on a platform near the top of the new City Hall and I see myself standing on the edge of the platform, preparing for my final dive, a forward *five* and one half somersaults with two full twists in the pike position (a dive with a degree of difficulty unmatched in competition, a dive that would've made Greg Louganis hesitate), and after giving several 'Tarzan of the Jungle' calls to bolster my courage and alert the media, I launch off the platform, quickly and easily completing the necessary rotations and twists in time to catch glimpses of the horrified-slash-surprised-slash-envious-slash-this-is-to-be-expected-given-our-current-poltical-and-economic climate expressions worn by the various politicians, secretaries, and office personnel inside City Hall watching my body carving an exquisite parabola — an *arc-en-ciel* — in the afternoon air before making a rip entry into the concrete directly in front of the dozens of spectators seated on the patio at Cafe on the Square.

I'm not, in case you were wondering, *obsessed* with suicide. It's merely something I've developed a keen interest in lately and, as such, end up carrying around with me wherever I go — the same way you probably carry snippets of dialogue from your favourite movie or lines of Shakespeare or quotes from Shaquille O'Neal or Bart Simpson or Ally McBeal around with you wherever you go, feeling compelled to introduce them into your conversations whenever they pop into your head, triggered by the scenery you happen to be passing or what someone else happens to be doing or saying at that particular moment.

The reason I say I'm not *obsessed* with suicide is because the DSM IV — the fourth edition of the *Diagnostic and Statistical Manual of Mental Disorders* — defines Obsessions (page 457 in Rebecca's copy) as 'recurrent and persistent ideas, thoughts, impulses, or images that are experienced as intrusive or inappropriate and that cause marked anxiety or distress,' and, although my ideas, thoughts, impulses, and images of suicide *are* recurrent *and* persistent, I *don't* regard them as either inappropriate or intrusive and they *certainly* don't cause me marked anxiety or distress. In fact, if anything, they're both a comfort and a source of inspiration. While others may take refuge in Prozac or marijuana, or require double espressos or daily shopping sprees or Double Stuf Oreos or *Seinfeld* reruns to get them through the week, I'm comfortably sustained by my inevitable suicide.

toronto's sidewalk citizens & the house that moses built

Moments later, while eyeing a rotating three-sided billboard of a partially naked model being driven around in the back of a cherry red Dodge Dakota Sport twincab, I almost stumble over a human exhibit sprawled on the sidewalk outside Osgoode

Hall, his rumpled beige silk suit smeared with what looks to be vomit, mustard, sauerkraut, and possibly a Reese's Peanut Butter Cup, possibly feces. The man's eyes, bleary and non-expectant, are rimmed with street grime while his mouth, camouflaged by a mangy beard, remains motionless as I skilfully sidestep him.

A second or two later, though, I hear a voice, garbled and chunky — as though being dragged through spit — say, "Spare some change, sirs?"

"Yes we can!" another sharper, overly enthusiastic voice says.

Surprised by the tone of voice, I half-turn, half-pause and see two young guys in suits stopped in front of the exhibit, now extending a used Starbucks coffee cup in their direction. One of the guys, the one closest to the exhibit, bends forward and, smiling cordially, says, with an undertone of barely contained hostility, "As a matter of fact, we can spare *plenty*," then rights himself and continues walking.

"*That* was cool," his friend says after a few paces, almost in front of me now because I've come to a full stop. "I'm going to have to remember that one: 'As a matter of fact, I can spare plenty,' and then just keep walking as if to say, 'But I'm not going to give a single cent to a shit-stained, scum-sucking, pseudo-silk-suit-wearing bum like you.' Very cool."

"Thanks," the other one says, trying to sound nonchalant. "I usually just ask them if they accept Visa but I thought I'd try something different today."

His friend chuckles. "Oh man, that's cool too. Mind if I use that one sometime?"

"Not at all," the other one says before shaking hands with his friend and entering the gate to Osgoode Hall.

After crossing University Avenue, I continue walking along the north side of Queen Street and ten, maybe fifteen seconds after I pass the native woman propped up against the thick cast-iron fence of the Historic Campbell House at the corner of Queen and Simcoe — the one who tells me I'm trespassing on native land, on *sacred* Ojibway land, and need to pay a toll — I feel the vibe of Queen West beginning to take over, the energy palpable, charging the air, transforming it into breathable electricity, and I instinctively quicken my pace.

On the opposite side of the street, a block, maybe a block and a half away, a group of twelve, perhaps fifteen girls are assembled outside the entrance to the City-TV building — a.k.a. the house that Moses Znaimer built. Seeing them dressed in funky club clothing and consulting their reflections in the glass windows every few seconds, I surmise the girls are auditioning for *Electric Circus*, which I've overheard twice in the last week and just read yesterday in the street magazine *Neksis* (but already knew) is the number-one TV dance music show in the world. A few metres past the *EC* hopefuls, another group of five girls — these ones wearing oversized cargo shorts, undersized tanktops, and carrying skateboards — is huddled around the *Speakers Corner* box.

The scent of sandalwood now wafting through my olfactory nerves continues to do so for five, maybe seven seconds before I'm able to locate its source: a burning incense stick stationed between three street youths seated on the sidewalk at the edge of the alley next to the Queen Street Market.

One of them, the girl, is holding a cardboard sign that has the words, **NEED MONEY FOR MARIJUANA** written in bold letters on it and when I get closer I see that in the corner of the sign the fine print reads,

> Now that we've got your attention, the truth is: <u>none</u> of us do drugs. Any money donated goes to food, shelter, clothing, and books. Thank you.

Slowing my quick pace, I examine them as I pass, inspecting them for signs of drug use, but even though their clothes, hands, arms, and bare legs are daubed with dirt, all three seem clean and lucid, their eyes (watching me from behind tangled curtains of dreadlocks) merely reflecting experience light-years beyond their age.

I pause a few paces past where they're sitting, pull a ten-dollar bill from my wallet — which is really an old burgundy Dyson computer disk case that Katelin, my *ex*-friend (emphasis and prefix hers), made into a wallet and gave me for my twenty-eighth birthday a few months ago — and, after I walk back and drop the ten-dollar bill into the upside-down Toronto Blue Jays baseball cap sitting beside a novel, *The Great Gatsby*, all three of them simultaneously give me incredulous, thankful looks before saying, in unison, "Thanks, dude. Thanks a lot."

queen west

Arriving at the corner of Queen and John Streets I don't see Daphne anywhere; I'd asked her to meet me on the patio at Starbucks, which she immediately told me was — and I quote — 'a stupid place to meet seeing as *you* hate coffee and *I* hate Star*fucks,*' but just as she was suggesting another meeting place I lied and told her I had another incoming call I had to take, adding, 'I'll meet you on the patio at 5:15 p.m. — sharp,' just before hanging up.

After quickly scanning the crowd inside Starbucks I
– take out my cellphone to call Daphne to find out where she is,
– realize, while looking at the time on my pager, that I'm

almost forty-five minutes early,
 – remember that I'd meant to stop at HMV and The World's Biggest Bookstore,
 – decide (instead of sitting on the patio and waiting for Daphne) to continue walking west on Queen Street to pass the time, noticing, as I have each of the last four times I've walked along this particular stretch of Queen Street, that the people and the clothing are more diverse, more eclectic here than anywhere else in Toronto — perhaps anywhere else in the world — the sidewalk on either side of the street morphing into runways of beautiful immigrants modelling a fusion of abandoned styles and resurrected colours, a mishmashed collection of the last century in fashion — the 1940s mixing with the 1970s, the '30s mixing with the '60s, the '20s mixing with the '90s. Even the '80s have come out of the closet again, pairing with the '50s to create captivating hybrids.

I continue walking, feeding off the eccentric vibrations swirling around me until, after pausing to read the line-up of bands playing tonight at The Horseshoe, I double back and end up sitting on a cement parking block between a hot dog vendor and a T-shirt vendor near the corner of Queen and Soho.
 Here I spend
 – a few minutes focusing on the blotches of ketchup and mustard staining the concrete around my feet in an effort to determine how old each blotch is, dating them anywhere from fifteen minutes to fifteen days (though some of them look as though they might have survived the winter), then
 – a few moments with my eyes closed, sniffing the confederation of fragrances being carried about on the slight breeze, the pineapple and watermelon scents escaping through the open door of Lush mingling with the aromas of

sausage grease, exhaust fumes, and the scent of spilled motor oil being slowly released from the hot asphalt, then

— a few seconds enjoying the warm prickling sensation of the raw, unfiltered UV rays expanding the pores on my skin until the words of the slightly taller, slightly thinner woman on the subway intervene and I subtly reprimand myself for forgetting to wear sunblock, then

— a few minutes watching the puddles of people evaporating into the various stores across the street — The Gap, Aldo, VICE, Pam Chorley, Silver Snail, XOXO, Guess, B2, Urban Mode, Club Monaco — the shop doors incessantly opening and closing, alternately absorbing and discharging purchase-laden consumers, then

— a few moments debating whether or not to get up and run after my sister Jennie who just walked out of VICE until, just as I'm about to get up, I lose sight of her and after trying unsuccessfully to locate her for almost a minute decide to stay put, my gaze continuing on, drifting lazily towards downtown and I become increasingly fascinated by the buildings interrupting the skyline, by the 'Towers of Babel' as Daphne calls them, their mirrored skins reflecting, then swallowing, a few sluggish clouds.

a hundred thousand exits

"I'm like just dying for you to see him. He's like *soooo, soooo* gorgeous."

A couple, early- to mid-twenties, are standing beside the T-shirt vendor and one of them — the woman wearing black leather fuck-me boots, mesh stockings, a black felt mini-skirt, and an undersized pink T-shirt with the words *Attention: Gardez hors de la portée des enfants* emblazoned across her ample chest — is talking on a neon pink cellphone, while the other one — the guy dressed in Dolce & Gabbana running shoes, flared low-rise stretch jeans and a violet rhinestone-edged T-shirt that says, *'I am Gaynadian'* — is alternately smiling at her and taking light drags on his cigarette.

"He's playing tomorrow night at The Rivoli. . . . Uh-huh. I think he's like their bass player or something. He's like *soooo, soooo* hot. What? . . . Ya, we're on Queen West. . . . We just got the tickets like ten minutes ago. . . . Ya, he's already seen him play like about a thousand times. He says he's hung like a horse. . . . I don't know, hang on, I'll ask. She wants to know if Blaine is, like, bi?"

The guy dressed in Dolce & Gabbana running shoes shrugs, then makes a face like he's not sure if Blaine is bi but that if he had to guess, he'd say he was.

"He's not sure. He thinks he might be. Why? Do you care? Me neither. I mean when someone's like *that* hot, it's like, who cares? Besides . . ."

I continue listening to her with my eyes closed and before long I'm editing her, taking out the pauses, tightening her sentences, limiting her use of the word 'like,' toning down her over-emphasis on the word 'so,' giving her a Brooklyn accent — no, something more incongruous, a Pakistani, no, a *German* accent, even though she looks Filipino — changing her clothes, dressing her in something elegant, perhaps a pantsuit by Liz Claiborne or Marc Jacobs, switching the set design from 'beside a T-shirt vendor on Queen Street West in Toronto' to 'inside a McDonald's restaurant in Boise, Idaho' or maybe 'inside a brownstone in New York City' or 'sitting beside an elderly woman on an airplane destined for Amsterdam' or . . .

It's a technique I picked up from my cousin Rebecca who wrote (on page 4 of her diary) that by her seventeenth birthday,

'My suburban, two-parent, two kids, two SUVs in the two-car garage life had become so tediously monochromatic — my parents' lives so fucking boring and annoyingly predictable, my girlfriends already locked into "I want to be beautiful, thin, rich and famous" mode, my brother, at 16, already on auto-pilot: go to university, join a fraternity, get laid a few times, graduate, backpack through Thailand and Indonesia for six months and get laid a few more times, come home, get an MBA, get a job, find a spouse, buy a house, and start recreating the same suburban, two-parent, two kids, two SUVs in the two-car garage life that our parents have — I found all of this so *disastrously* dull and ordinary that it forced me to begin mentally editing reality, to begin viewing it through a different lens, one that automatically modified people's lives, their dreams, their words, replacing them with more tolerable, liveable ones, ones that were more colourful, more entertaini —'

A streetcar, the 501 Neville Park, the one I usually take back to my apartment in the Beaches, rumbles through the intersection, temporarily overwhelming the woman's voice, and when sparks fly as the connector passes through one of the overhead wire junctions, I imagine myself up there, pinned to the wires, jolts of electricity surging through my spastic body, my eyes bulging, internal organs liquefying, skin smouldering, melting, fusing to the wires before I spontaneously burst into flames, the smell of cooked human flesh descending on Queen West and I pull the notepad from the back pocket of my Dockers, quickly jotting down the scene, adding it and the platform dive off the new City Hall to the list of possibilities.

Although I've had the day of my suicide planned for nearly a year now, it's the method — the *way* I want to die — that continues to elude me. Like Montaigne said, 'Nature has given us only one entry into life, but a hundred thousand exits' and deciding on what exit I'm going to take is more difficult than it may seem. There are a lot of factors to consider, not the least of which are a) the type of corpse you want to leave behind, b) who, if anyone, you want to witness the event, c) who, if anyone, you want to find your body, and d) who will be affected by your suicide.

For instance, a dive off a window washer's platform near the top of City Hall on a Friday afternoon that will not only be witnessed by the general public (including tourists), but also leave behind a soggy, pulverized corpse for everyone (including children) to gawk at and may result in injuring, maiming, possibly even killing other people should you land on them, is *one* way to do it. Waving goodbye to your parents who are leaving on a two-week Caribbean cruise then saying 'See ya later,' to your brother who's leaving to go snowboarding in Whistler, British Columbia, and then going into the house and slicing your wrists while taking a hot bath like my sister Jennie did, is an entirely different way to do it.

open-air confessions

"I don't believe it — are you serious?"

"Totally serious."

Two guys slightly older than me are now walking away from the hot dog stand towards one of the cement parking blocks carrying hot dogs, Diet Cokes, and matching Club Monaco tote bags. One of them, the one wearing the canary yellow silk print shirt, lime green cotton slim-leg trousers and beige lace-up loafers, is listening to the other one, the one wearing the brown V-neck jersey top, off-white double pleated shorts, tan leather sandals, and Polo Sport cologne, telling him, "I've been getting more sex than I can handle these days," and as they draw nearer I instinctively go into eavesdropping mode, my hand already inside my messenger bag, reaching for Rebecca's diary.

It's another technique I picked up from Rebecca.

'The secret,' she wrote (on pages 17 and 18 of her diary), 'to eavesdropping is to look as benign, as *physically innocuous*, as possible, which isn't nearly as easy as it sounds. It's only through trial and error and by spending hours and hours practising as well as keeping detailed notes on my successes and failures, that I've become almost chameleonlike, capable of blending into nearly any environment. It's got to the point where nowadays, if this is my intention, a person's gaze will pass over me as though I'm merely part of the decor, a piece of furniture or a nondescript painting which, by virtue of its banality, never arouses interest or even subconsciously suggests to the persons speaking that they should modify the content of their conversation.'

One of Rebecca's favourite accessories or eavesdropping aids while on the street, aside from sometimes wearing a disguise or bland, unadorned clothing like I'm wearing now (I've removed the Dockers' tag from my pants), is a book or a literary magazine — 'something to make it appear as though you're in another world.'

Of course, as she's quick to point out on page 19, 'It also helps that an increasing number of people [such as the slightly chunky woman on the subway, the young woman on the neon pink cellphone, and the Polo Sport cologne guy] are quite willing to talk out loud in public about virtually anything.'

"I'm telling you," the Polo Sport cologne guy is now saying to the beige lace-up loafers guy, "women are just looking for Mr. Relatively Normal."

Both guys are now seated on a parking block ten, maybe only eight feet from where I'm sitting.

"If you've got a good apartment, a half-decent car, and can hold down a job, you're set. There are so many fucking wackos out there right now that all these hot women are jumping at the chance to be with a guy who's relatively normal. I'm dating models, lawyers, doctors, all of them hot, all of them making way more money than I am, and all of them wanting to take *me* out to dinner. I've even had two offers to go on vacations — on them."

"Unbelievable."

"No kidding. When my wife and I got divorced last year I thought being thirty-six and single was going to be hell, but it's awesome. And you know what the best part about being in your thirties is? You get to fuck the mothers *and* the daughters!"

When the beige lace-up loafers guy starts laughing, then coughing, probably from inhaling a piece of his hot dog, I commit an eavesdropping faux pas by looking directly at him and it's as I'm watching ketchup seeping from the corner of his mouth and tiny bits of food being ejected from his mouth that I consider asking him what kind of corpse *he'd* want to leave behind, if he'd want to be electrocuted, his organs liquefied, the smell of his burnt flesh rather than the smell of his friend's Polo Sport cologne wafting through the nostrils of the pedestrians walking along Queen West but then, after reconsidering, I decide to return my attention once again to the blotches of ketchup and mustard already embedded in the sidewalk.

there's only one thing worse

In the Middle Ages you were considered insane if you sat around pondering suicide; engaging others in conversation about it was regarded as a sure sign of madness. Of course, the ones spreading these ideas were the clergy — priests, ministers, and pastors — who, even though the Bible doesn't directly condemn suicide nevertheless made certain their congregations believed suicide was the work of a diseased mind. In an attempt to purge people of any desire or empathy they may possess for suicide or a suicidee, persons who committed suicide were deemed insane, had their corpse publicly cursed, condemned to everlasting damnation, tortured, dragged through town, refused burial on hallowed ground, and were sometimes impaled on stakes at well-travelled intersections.

Nowadays, although people who commit suicide aren't tortured or dragged through town posthumously, suicide is still a very taboo subject, rarely discussed, with the overwhelming majority of persons still believing it inconceivable that a sane or healthy person would consider taking his or her own life. But they do.

In fact, in my fairly informed opinion, if the idea of suicide *hasn't* crossed your mind by the time you're sixteen or seventeen I'd say you're either in denial or you're lying. If you're honest, you'll admit to not only thinking about suicide, but considering it. In fact, at one time or another you've probably even imagined yourself hanging from a noose (like Mamaengaroa Kerr-Bell in *Once Were Warriors*), drinking yourself to death (like Nicolas Cage in *Leaving Las Vegas*), jumping off a building (like Michael Douglas in *The Game*), getting run over by a steam-roller (like the Coyote in *The Bugs Bunny Roadrunner Show*), driving your car off a cliff (like Susan Sarandon and Geena Davis in *Thelma & Louise*), or being suffocated (like Staffan Kihlbom — assisted by Leonardo DiCaprio — in *The Beach*). Most people have.

And, as with most subjects — even notoriously taboo ones like suicide — people are always willing to voice their opinions. Take, for example, the guy I spoke with last night: after dialling a random number from a payphone and hearing a man in his late forties/early fifties answer, I asked him if he ever thought of suicide and, if so, what method he'd use and when he asked me if this was a joke and I told him that no, it wasn't, that in fact I was sincerely interested in what he had to say on the subject, he said that yes, he'd thought about suicide a few times in his life and that if it came down to it he'd probably buy a shotgun, put the barrel in his mouth and Boom! end of story. When I asked him, 'Why a shotgun?' he said, 'It seems like the best way to do it if you're serious. Besides,' he added, 'I'm a big fan of Hemingway, and that's the way he went.'

He was right, of course, on both counts: Hemingway used a shotgun to commit suicide and, if you're serious about committing suicide, if you're not just making a suicide *gesture*, guns are a very effective way to kill yourself. Not foolproof, mind you. In fact, guns only have about an eighty percent success rate, which is yet another thing to consider when choosing your method: effectiveness.

Unless you jump from a very high place (and even then it might not be high enough since people have survived falling out of airplanes at 25,000 feet) you might just break your back or your neck or shatter all the bones in your legs and be confined to a wheelchair or a coma, or, if you decide instead to take pills or poison yourself with cyanide or drown yourself or shoot yourself in the head, you might only end up with irreversible brain damage to show for your efforts. As author and suicidee Arthur Koestler said, 'There's only one thing worse than being chained to an intolerable existence. And that's the nightmare of a botched attempt to end it,' which is one of the main reasons why the method I'm going to use to commit suicide remains undecided.

suicidE-mails & henry david thoreau

The two guys are gone now, having left behind a few fresh mustard and ketchup splotches and after subjecting the blotches to time-lapsed videography, seeing them slowly soaking into the concrete, I realize that instead of my cousin Rebecca's diary I'm holding a copy (upside-down) of my friend Eriq Desjardins' as-yet-unpublished collection of short stories, tentatively titled *Identity Crisis*, which I printed up for him on my laser printer and had bound and jacketed in a navy blue felt cover — the same material as Rebecca's diary.

I smile, thinking of how intent I was on listening to the conversation between the two guys that I hadn't even bothered to notice what I was pretending to be reading, or even that I was holding it upside-down, then abruptly wipe the smile from my face when I realize that Rebecca wouldn't have been impressed with my eavesdropping performance, that if she had been one of the guys beside me she would've recognized my ruse and modified her conversation, undoubtedly telling some outlandish, borderline unbelievable story for the benefit of the eavesdropper — which is actually something she said she started doing just after her seventeenth birthday — bringing the imagined or modified versions of her parents' lives, her brother's life, her friends' lives out of her mind and into her conversations, reinventing them on almost a daily basis until the lines between the stories and the reality blurred, became indistinguishable. . . .

After replacing Eriq's collection of short stories in my canvas messenger bag, I pull out a duo-tang containing the latest batch of suicidE-mails I received at The Suicide Loft's e-mail address.

It's one of the services I offer at The Loft, giving people another medium through which to communicate their thoughts/feelings/ideas about suicide.

The suicidE-mails I receive are
- always dated,
- sometimes located — as requested on The Suicide Loft Web site — either by province or state or country (city/town is optional), and
- usually only a paragraph or two in length, though they've been as short as one word — 'Goodbye' — and as long as 152 pages, both of which, incidentally, were written by confirmed suicides. (I know because they enclosed their real names and addresses in the e-mail and I checked.)

After looking around to make sure no one's watching me, I close my eyes and begin fanning through the e-mails (probably one hundred in all) readying my index finger.

It's a habit I picked up from my sister Jennie.

She'd walk into a library or a bookstore, pluck a book off the shelf at random, close her eyes, start fanning through the pages then arbitrarily insert her index finger between two pages, open her eyes, and start reading. I was with her one day in Indigo when she did it with the Ontario Criminal Code, her eyes falling on Section 444 and the following week I saw a McDonald's employee throwing out several dozen make-shift placemats that had a copy of Section 444 printed on it.

After inserting my index finger between the pages of the logbook, I open my eyes and start reading:

> *Every night I play the same game: I convince myself tomorrow is not today. Tomorrow I will wake up and realize the life I've been living has been a dream. Tomorrow everything will be different. But tomorrow is always today and today is always the same and today my life, just like it has for the last two years, choked me, hit me, beat me and threatened me until I promised not to dream of anything different.*
>
> *June 4, 2001. (Georgia, USA.)*

Close eyes, flip through pages, insert index finger, open eyes, and

> *Aren't we all killing ourselves? For instance, you could argue that smoking is a form of suicide, albeit not exactly a quick return on your investment, as are a lot of other activities — such as driving a motorcycle or riding a bicycle (especially in a city), eating non-organic fruit and vegetables or greasy, fatty McFoods, or deciding to spend your spare time on a couch instead of exercising. Aren't these all just milder forms of suicide? And if so, aren't we all trying to kill ourselves?*
> *27/05/2001/Los Angeles/California/USA.*

Each time I read a suicidE-mail I'll inevitably hear a person's voice — a voice with a distinct tone, pace, cadence — embroidering the words. Sometimes the voice is assertive or desperate or self-righteous; other times hurried, confident, scared, pitiful; other times disillusioned, depressed, intoxicated, indignant, pleading.

Close eyes, flip through pages, insert index finger, open eyes, and

> *Thoreau went to the woods, to Walden Pond, to live deliberately, to suck the marrow out of life. But where can I go? Where is my sanctuary, my retreat? Is there a place that can suck these thoughts of death out of my head?*
> *May 23, 2001 Whistler, British Columbia*

Close eyes, flip pages, insert finger, open eyes, and

> *In the middle ages and later on, people had access to duelling*

> contests, jousting tournaments, wars, noble causes — ways of getting rid of the ennui, the boredom, the violence in them, ways of risking their life or getting rid of their lives in so-called honourable ways: but what do we have?
>
> 05/2001, Dieppe, France

Close, flip, insert, open, and . . . already read that one, repeat steps, and

> I'm surrounded by people who are killing themselves slowly, a little each day, from the lack of purpose, the lack of meaning in their lives, the lack of having something to do, to believe in, to direct their lives.
>
> June 1, 2001 Montreal, Quebec, Canada

Close, flip, insert, open, and

> My mother used to threaten me and my brother with suicide all the time, telling us she couldn't stand us — it was passed on to my brother, who never talked about it, he just did it. 'Why don't you go and kill yourself if you think your life is so bad?,' my mother shouted at him last summer. That same afternoon I found him hanging from the rafters in the garage.
>
> 30/05/2001/Canton, Connecticut

I'm about to close my eyes and flip to another e-mail when I notice a camcorder looking in my direction and instinctively duck, as though someone just hurled a rock at me. When a woman's voice behind me asks the man holding the camcorder, "Are we recording?" I'm instantly back in my parents' house watching my sister Jennie commit suicide, watching her on the two Sony 32" Trinitron Wega Stereo TV monitors, the monitors being fed by two Sony Digital8 camcorders:

— Cam 1, mounted on a Sony Tripod, providing a steady, wide-angle, full-body shot remains stationary while
— Cam 2, handheld by my cousin Rebecca and providing close-ups and quirky angles, is now zooming in on Jennie as she calmly slides a Wilkinson razor blade along her right wrist, making one . . . two . . . three . . . four . . . five — five deep, longitudinal cuts, the blood quickly oozing from each cut, drooling down her arm, momentarily pooling at her elbow before falling off, the large globules alternately PLOPPing and POINGing on the surface of the bath water and then
— Cam 2's angle and focus adjusts, tracking Jennie's right hand as she slices her left wrist (four times) before setting the bloodied blade in the soap dish container and then
— switching to the TV monitor fed by Cam 1, I watch Jennie easing her arms into the hot water, the blood now flowing gracefully, generously from the wounds like two ethereal umbilical cords, coiling playfully around her legs, the water slowly changing colour, as though red dye were being added to it and then
— switching back to the other TV monitor, I see Cam 2 tracking slowly up Jennie's naked body to her head, now resting peacefully on the edge of the porcelain tub, before zooming in on her eyelids (rhythmically opening and closing like two fish mouths gasping for water), on her breathing (growing increasingly faint), on her life (drifting slowly into unconsciousness, into death) . . .

two scenarios

My cellphone rings, causing me to realize that not only have I been vigorously sawing away at my left wrist with my right thumbnail hard enough and long enough to draw blood but I'm also rocking back and forth and mumbling under my breath, all of which has attracted the attention of a young woman standing beside the hot dog stand wearing a white University of Toronto tanktop and a 'What the hell is wrong with you, buddy?' expression, forcing me to

– acknowledge to myself (since this is the third time in as many days it's happened) that these previously private displays are now being made available to the general public and
– try (since this acknowledgement more than mildly disturbs me) to normalize my behaviour, to somehow translate my wrist sawing, torso rocking, mumbling under breath display into something that will dissuade this young woman from relating the story of a 'really weird, I mean, really, really, weird guy I saw at the corner of Soho and Queen West' to her friends, and just as I'm about to start quoting Shakespeare's *Macbeth*, specifically Act 5, Scene 1, where Lady Macbeth is vigorously scrubbing her hands and saying, 'Out damned spot, out, I say!' in an attempt to get the imaginary blood off her hands, the first or third or ninth ring of my cellphone interrupts me and when I answer I hear Daphne's voice on the other end, her tone already borderline impatient, saying, "Where *are* you?"

"Not far," I reply, my eyes still on the woman with the white University of Toronto tanktop who is now wearing a 'Was that just all an act?' expression.

"I've been sitting here for *five* minutes already. You know I hate this place."

"What place?" I ask, trying to sound confused.

"*Starfucks* — where you, for reasons beyond my comprehension, wanted us to meet."

"Oh ya. I'll be there in two minutes," I say, finishing the sentence even though I've hung up after only saying, 'I'll be there in . . .'

Ten minutes later, after I've ignored Daphne's first two callbacks while continuing to watch the woman in the University of Toronto tanktop slowly making her way west (she's already looked back at me four times), I answer Daphne's third call and am about to say "Hello?" when I realize she's already in the middle of a sentence,

"— giving you exactly one more minute to get here and then I'm leaving," she's saying, her tone now definitely impatient.

Arriving back at the corner of John and Queen exactly seven minutes and forty-eight seconds after she hung up on me, I see Daphne seated beside the railing near the back of the Starbucks patio and think she's looking directly at me so I wave and when she doesn't smile or wave back I'm instantly reminded of a character in one of my cousin Rebecca's made-especially-for-TV videographies who finds himself in a similar predicament. At this point the character narrates, 'There's a split second during which two scenarios present themselves: in the first one a slight spasm of embarrassment grips me and I hear myself saying, "She must be blind," aloud, for the benefit of the two guys waiting on the corner with me who have noticed what's happened and, in the second scenario, I'm not at all embarrassed, don't say anything for the benefit of the two guys, but just watch to see what their reaction will be.'

I choose to act out the second scenario, the same one Rebecca's character did, and as the two guys glance at me then look at each other and smirk, I hear myself say, "Two scenarios emerged in my mind and I took the one Rebecca's character did and that, *that* has made all the difference."

preferably a stun gun

After winding my way through the tiny labyrinth of 'Make-eye-contact.quickly-look-away.he's-not-important.com' types cloistered on the patio and adjusting the position of my chair to give me a slightly better P.O.V. (point of view) before sitting down at Daphne's table, one of the servers — a Sarah Polley look-alike wearing Birkenstock sandals, beige khakis, and a white polo shirt under her green Starbucks apron — smiles at me while clearing a nearby table and says "Hi" in a surprised, yet friendly I-sort-of-know-you-already way because I'm fairly certain she lives in the Beaches and that we said "Hi" to each other last month while in line at The Fox to watch *Bridget Jones's Diary*.

When she finishes clearing the table and walks back into the café I turn to Daphne and am about to ask her if she wants to switch seats with me (since she's got the better P.O.V.) when I notice she's now wearing her 'Super Annoyed Look' which, even though Daphne gets annoyed quite often, for some reason makes me realize that she's been wearing it a lot more since my cousin Rebecca left five weeks ago.

A moment later Daphne shushes me as though expecting me to ask her something and then says, her words tinged with moderate hostility, "What's *wrong* with this picture?" nodding her head at a woman seated alone at a table roughly fifteen feet from ours.

The woman — probably in her early forties though obviously trying to young-down her appearance by wearing a tan, the latest

Jennifer Aniston haircut, a fuchsia scoop-neck crop top, fuchsia Skechers running shoes, and what looks to be the exact same pair of low-slung black leather pants as Eliza Dushku was wearing on the cover of last month's issue of *Maxim* — is talking in a loud voice on a fuchsia Motorola cellphone.

Although the woman's clothes and hairstyle might be enough to annoy Daphne, I'm not completely convinced it's what's wrong with the picture, but since Daphne's so annoyed she doesn't allow me more time to figure it out and, now clenching her fists and gritting her teeth, says, "Ms. Recycled Teenager over there hasn't stopped talking since she sat down. Ten. Bloody. Non-stop. Minutes."

I watch the woman for a few seconds — talking loudly, gesturing theatrically, abruptly over-laughing, her one-woman show siphoning attention from most of the patio patrons and a few pedestrians waiting on the corner for the light to change — and it's while I'm watching this that I play one of my favourite games, guessing what method a person would use to kill themselves, and I'm guessing this women would be what Rebecca refers to as an MSG — a Multiple Suicide Gesturer — someone who attempts suicide either as a cry for help or, in this woman's case, probably just to get attention — and I imagine her leaving about a dozen notes around the house saying what brand of pills she took and a P.S. that says, 'If you care about me, you'll call 911 right now,' before taking less than half a lethal dose of aspirin or Valium or ibuprofen fifteen minutes before her husband or teenage daughter came home, making sure it wasn't a holiday because hospitals are usually short staffed on holidays and not on a Friday or Saturday evening because Emergency rooms would be too busy.

"Look at her," Daphne snarls. "She's sucked the life right out of this place. When I first sat down there were at least half a dozen other conversations going on. Then *she* comes in and within twenty seconds she's the only person anyone can hear.

She's like a goddamn TV — turn it on and it gobbles up all the real conversations."

When the woman over-laughs again the guy sitting at the table next to her wearing spiked black hair, a black sleeveless Harley-Davidson shirt, blue jeans, black 8-hole Doc Martens and reading Alice Munro's, no, Jane Urquhart's novel *The Underpainter*, actually stops reading, stares at the woman for at least ten seconds like he's about to rip out her tongue, then shakes his head, and after slapping his book closed, sighing loudly and mumbling something about there being "Too much goddamn ear pollution in this place," he gets up and walks briskly out of the patio, leaving a three-quarters full Frappucino on his table which, as soon as he's out the gate and on the sidewalk, is snatched up by a street kid who seemingly materialized out of nowhere.

"It'd be one thing if she was saying something of *value*," Daphne seethes, so completely focused on the woman that she's oblivious to what just happened with the Harley-Davidson guy or his Frappucino, "but she's talking complete *garbage*. Christ, it's like being forced to listen to The Home Shopping Network."

At that moment the Sarah Polley look-alike returns to the patio to wipe down the table she's just cleared and when she passes by us Daphne asks her if Starbucks sells earplugs or stun guns — preferably stun guns — and when the Sarah Polley look-alike gives her a confused look I tell her Daphne's just kidding and Daphne says, "No, I'm not."

analogies

While tracking someone who I'm fairly certain is Mike Bullard walking west on the opposite side of Queen Street, several slices of sunlight ricochet off a chrome-filled SUV, stabbing me in the eyes, and several seconds later, after blinking and squinting and trying to wipe the stars from my eyes, I notice Mike has disappeared and Starbucks suddenly looks like the café set of *Friends*, filled with extras walking around, surveying the menu, ordering, drinking coffees, talking, laughing, checking each other out, waiting for Chandler and Monica & Co. to arrive on the set, and when I see the Sarah Polley look-alike inside the café waving at me, I instinctively smile and wave back, only realizing after she continues smiling and waving that there's a cloth in her hand and she's actually cleaning the inside of the window with a semi-strained expression on her —

"I'm starting to feel like David in John Wyndham's book *The Chrysalids*," Daphne says, interrupting my thoughts, placing her hands over her ears.

Daphne loves analogies, especially ones that a) align her with her favourite literary characters and b) expose other people's ignorance of literature.

When I don't respond with a knowing laugh or an appreciative comment, choosing instead to affect an 'I'm-sorry-but-I-haven't-the-slightest-idea-of-what-you're-talking-about' expression, Daphne delivers the expected eyeroll-slash-sigh combination before continuing the analogy, her voice now assuming an irritated, 'Christ-I'm-tired-of-always-having-to-explain-shit-to-people' tone.

"*The Chrysalids* is about people who can communicate via thought-pictures and it's the part in the book when Petra, the narrator's little sister, sends him her first thought-picture and he says it feels like a fishhook tugging at his brain, like he's powerless to ignore it and it forces him to run to her."

I remain on MUTE, making it appear as though I'm mulling over the analogy, debating whether or not it makes sense.

Five seconds later, Daphne, nearing exasperation, sighs again and says, "Just like the narrator and his inability to ignore his sister's thought-picture, I feel completely powerless to ignore this woman. Her voice just keeps tugging at me, forcing me to listen to her."

I pretend to get it, making a clichéd facial expression to mark the occasion (picture a light bulb going off) and then, a second or two later, after furrowing my brow and moving forward a bit in my chair, ask, "What book was that again?" causing Daphne to groan, then nearly shout, "Can't you hear her?" before reburying her ears in her hands.

changing the course of yourstory

I'm smiling — and in case you're wondering why, it's partly because I'm imagining how Daphne would respond to knowing that I do drink coffee, that I especially enjoy Starbucks coffee, but mostly because I'm thinking about cause and effect and how if I didn't ignore Daphne's phone calls and I arrived at the patio sooner than I did or if I decided to wait for her on the patio instead of sitting on the parking block near Queen and Soho — things probably would've been a whole lot different. I mean, would we still be sitting here? Would Daphne have insisted we go someplace else? Would she be paying as much attention to this woman as she is now? What thoughts would we, she, I, be thinking now? As Rebecca wrote (on page 23 of her diary), 'The smallest decision, the slightest action or inaction, can change the course of his/her/our/ their/my/yourstory.'

more analogies

"Maybe she's a goddamned ventriloquist," Daphne says sharply, leaning forward over our table, momentarily regarding the woman with suspicion before her expression morphs into a look of contempt and she says, in a considerably louder voice, "Or *maybe* it's just that she insists on using a VIP voice because she thinks it'd be a sin to deprive the rest of Toronto from hearing what she has to say."

Noticing several patrons have now turned their attention to our table, as though a microphone boom had been placed over our table the second before Daphne delivered her last line, I start to say, "Maybe we should —," but Daphne interrupts me, saying, "Ah, forget it," and flicks her hand at the woman as if banishing her from her thoughts and then, turning to me, the look of contempt on her face now completely gone, lifts a glass of half-melted ice cubes and asks, "So, you enjoying your time off work?"

She's referring to the two-week holiday I started three days ago. I'm a rehabilitation therapist for people with ABI, an acronym for Acquired Brain Injuries. I did it full time for four years before switching to part time about a year ago. Though the work is both interesting and challenging — trying to rehabilitate people with all sorts of maladaptive behaviours resulting from traumatic injury to the brain — it's not my vocation. My vocation (what people might say is my passion or the thing I'd do even if I didn't get paid for it) is something neither Daphne nor Eriq nor Nicole nor Brad nor anyone else except Rebecca and my landlady, Jo-Jo, knows about. It's the reason I decreased my hours as a rehab therapist from full to part time and decided to move to Toronto last summer: The Suicide Lof —

"These people are pathetic," Daphne hisses.

Four, maybe five seconds after Daphne asked me how I was enjoying my time off work, I noticed her attention had already begun to wander away and a few seconds later, after scanning the remainder of the Starbucks' crowd, her face slowly bunching into a tight scowl, I knew she was no longer interested in my reply.

Still scowling, she says, "I feel like I'm at a bloody casting call for some TV show and everyone's sitting around expecting Egoyan or Scorsese or Spielberg or Spelling to discover them, to say that they *desperately* need them, that their next film or mini-series or episode of *Beverly Hills, 90210* won't be a success unless they're in the leading role and —"

Though I agree with her analogy, I'm about to remind her that a) Atom Egoyan and Martin Scorsese make films, not TV shows and b) Aaron Spelling isn't producing new episodes of *Beverly Hills, 90210* anymore, when two groups of motorcycles — four Harley Softtails and three Kawasaki Ninjas arriving at opposite sides of the intersection — begin revving their engines while waiting for the light to change, the resulting noise obliterating Daphne's voice.

pebble in a pond

After spending a second or two watching Daphne's now muted mouth moving maliciously in the direction of the cellphone woman, I pan slowly left, passing over ten, perhaps a dozen, nondescript faces until, through the window of the café, I catch a glimpse of my sister Jennie typing away on her laptop.

Zooming in, I see a young woman seated at the window counter working on an IBM Thinkpad and even though (upon closer inspection) I realize she only vaguely resembles Jennie, it's already too late. I've already replaced her and her IBM Thinkpad with the image of my sister Jennie typing a letter on her Apple Notebook computer, the letter absolving me, Rebecca, my parents, her friends — everyone — of any responsibility for what she's about to do, and instead of stopping or fast forwarding the memory, I decide to let it play at regular speed, continuing to watch her finish typing the letter, proofreading it, then printing out four copies before selecting one and reading it while facing the camcorder and holding up that day's newspaper, her expression serene, her voice calm, much calmer than it was an hour earlier when . . .

– I returned home to find Green Day's song 'Time of Your Life,' coming from the open door of the upstairs bathroom and after walking upstairs and seeing Jennie's portable CD player, a bottle of wine, a half-full wine glass, and several patchouli-scented candles positioned around the tub I thought that Jennie was going to be having a nice, relaxing bath, until I noticed the camcorder sitting on the tripod next to the vanity, and then

– I saw my cousin Rebecca backing out of Jennie's bedroom, pointing another camcorder at Jennie who I could see was wearing the white terry cloth bathrobe I'd bought her for Christmas a few months earlier, and then

– I noticed Jennie was carrying a red plastic cafeteria tray full of paraphernalia that I later learned via my own research consisted of more than three times the lethal dose of aspirin, a mickey of Canadian Club whiskey (to increase the lethality of the pills), two new Wilkinson razor blades (two, in case one broke in the process of slicing her wrists), a bottle of sleeping pills (to knock her out, help her cope with the body's shock response to the loss of blood), and that the hot water wasn't going to be used for a nice relaxing bath (it would be an anti-coagulant), and then

– I heard her say, her eyes leading the camcorder's lens toward the paraphernalia on the tray, 'As you must all be aware of by now, this isn't going to be a suicide gesture or a suicide attempt or a cry for help or attention. I am going to kill myself, I am going to —' and then

— Jennie saw me, abruptly stopped talking in a calm voice, began waving at Rebecca, yelling, 'Cut! Cut! Stop recording! Stop recording!' brushing past Rebecca, past her bewildered expression, past her two questions, 'Why?' and 'What's wrong?' and then

— Rebecca whirled around and saw me instinctively duck, attempting to get out of the way of the still recording camcorder, before both of us heard Jennie — in an annoyed-slash-surprised tone — ask, 'What the hell are you doing here, Ryan?'

'I forgot . . . my . . . the lift . . . tickets and my . . . ,' I stammered, feeling like an intruder, an interloper, like I was about to be tossed off a movie set. 'I'm sorry. I didn't know you two were doing . . . this, I thought you said you were going out to a party or —'

'Don't even *think* about trying to stop me.'

'I won't,' I said, starting to back away, still in a daze until I suddenly realized that unless Jennie was about to do something really twisted she wouldn't have told me not to stop her, and so I asked, 'Stop what?'

At this point my cousin Rebecca stepped into the picture, her back initially toward me and, in retrospect, I imagine her making a face to Jennie, something that said, 'I've got an idea, so just play along with it, okay?' because Jennie's facial expression went from seriously annoyed to relatively calm almost immediately and then Rebecca turned to me and proceeded to tell me what they were doing, that she and Jennie were filming something like a snuff film, 'You know, like the movie *8MM* with Nicolas Cage and Joaquin Phoenix and how they discovered some of the snuffs were fake, only we're not filming someone getting killed, we're filming Jennie committing suicide and, and *may*be,' at this point

Rebecca's voice became considerably more excited, as though she'd just hit upon an even better idea or an extension of her original idea and was about to play it out, using me and Jennie as her test audience, '*May*be Ryan here,' she said, pointing at me while simultaneously raising her eyebrows and holding up a finger for Jennie to hang on a sec and hear her out, 'maybe Ryan could be in the film too. Maybe, just like what's happening right now, we could film Ryan coming back to the house, unexpectedly, of course, because an hour earlier we filmed him telling us he was flying out to Whistler, B.C., to go snowboarding with his buddies for two weeks, but he forgot his wallet or his lift tickets, so he comes back, runs into the house, is about to go downstairs to retrieve his wallet or the lift tickets from the coffee table in the rec room, when he hears the music coming from the bathroom upstairs, walks upstairs, sees the wine, the candles around the tub, the steamy bath, the camcorder set up on the tripod and then sees his sister coming out of the bathroom carrying this tray of god-only-knows-what and hears her saying something about suicide, about it being the real deal, and then Jennie sees you, yells, "Cut! Stop recording!" at me, then asks Ryan, "What the hell are you doing here?" and then Ryan'll stammer something like, "Um, I . . . I forgot my lift, my lift tickets and my, um, my wallet," and the reason Ryan's unable to form a complete sentence is obviously because his head is reeling from trying to figure out what's going on, like why his cousin is filming his sister and why his sister is talking about suicide, and then Jennie'll say, "Don't even *think* about trying to stop me," and Ryan'll say, "I won't," and then, because it suddenly dawns on him that his sister probably wouldn't have told him not to stop her if she was only *acting*, if she was only *pretending* to commit suicide, he asks, "Stop what?" and then Jennie, realizing that she might have given herself away, says, "It'd be nice if you left now," and then the camera will zoom in on you Ryan, on you standing there, looking like you're still in a bit of daze, and you'll start shaking your head, slowly at first, then more vigorously until finally you say, in a really I'm-totally-fucking-serious tone of voice, "Listen, I'm not going anywhere until I know *exactly* what the hell is going on here," and at this point, right here, is where I'll come into the picture and start explaining things, start telling you that your sister is planning on committing suicide and she wants me to film it, document it, that this is not a test, that this is really going to happen, at which point you Ryan, you'll interrupt me and say, "What? You're serious?" and when you realize we are serious, you'll start shouting, "You guys are sick, you know that! Totally fucking sick!" and I'll say, "Ryan, we are *not* sick!" and Ryan'll say, "Oh ya, well I guess you won't mind if I get a second opinion? I guess you won't mind if I call a psychiatrist to see whether or not my diagnosis is correct?" Or, better yet, you might, while turning and grabbing the portable phone, say something like, "I could dial 911 right now, prevent *both* of you from leaving, and wait for the cops and emergency response teams dispatched from the 911 call centre to investigate an emergency call made at this address and easily get *you*" — pointing at Jennie — "committed to a psychiatric hospital and *you*" — pointing at me — "charged with assisted suicide," at which point, I'll start protesting and say something like, "Bloody hell! I'm not *assisting* her. I'm only *filming* her. Besides, she *wants* to do this; I'm *not* forcing her to do it," and Jennie will say, "If you love us Ryan, if you love me, you won't try and stop us. You won't call 911. You'll just leave and let us do this in peace," and then Ryan, you'll stand there for a few moments shaking your head and maybe gritting your teeth before saying, "Listen, this is *not* going to happen," and Jennie will say, "Why not?"

'"Because it's not," you'll say.
'"Why?" I'll ask.
'"Because it's not."
'"What do you want?!" Jennie'll ask.

'"I don't want you to do this!" you'll shout and at this point I'll intervene again, telling you and Jennie that I've got an idea, that maybe Ryan can stay and watch or, *better yet*, help us film —'

'That's *not* how we planned it,' my sister said at this point. 'This is precisely why I didn't want to film it in the first place — there are too many variables to take into consideration. Too much shit that can go wrong. I'm going back to my original idea of —'

'No, no, no,' Rebecca said, interrupting Jennie, her voice suddenly very calm, very reassuring, very convincing. 'I realize this wasn't part of the original script, Jennie. We're just doing a little improvising here, okay? No big deal. Besides, this way, if Ryan helps us film it, we can get another angle, an overhead full frontal shot, and if we, I mean, if I don't like it, I can always edit it out later and —'

'I don't want Ryan filming me. I don't want him anywhere near me when I'm doing this . . . scene.'

'Okay, okay, no problem. He doesn't have to be, he can . . . he can . . .'

At this point Rebecca got that look in her eyes again, that same 'I'm-so-full-of-another-great-idea-I-could-just-burst' look she'd had before and she said, 'Okay, I think I've got something here, I think we can work this out. How about after I suggest Ryan helps us film your suicide he stares at me in disbelief and says, "You're a sick twisted bitch, you know that Rebecca? A sick, twisted, psychotic bitch! I should report you to the police right now," and then, as Ryan is making a move towards the phone, Jennie'll jump in front of the phone and say that maybe there's something he *can* do and then Ryan will say, "I'm not doing anything Jennie! This is fucking insane. In-*fucking*-sane! And I'm not going to be part of it," but then I'll start talking really fast, throwing out ideas, storylines, all kinds of possibilities, and each one in turn will get rejected by one or both of you until I hit upon an idea that Ryan likes: he gets to keep all copies of the videotapes, every single one, as well as anything to do with the production — the script, Jennie's suicide letter, her journal, all the video equipment — everything except the memories, for a period of one month. "It's like a patent," I'll say, "and during that time you can do whatever you want with the tapes, whatever you see fit to do, except destroy them or let anyone else see them." Of course, initially Ryan'll suggest something a lot longer, like five years, saying that one month isn't long enough and then Jennie and I'll say five years is outrageous, that this isn't what we'd planned and Ryan'll say, "I don't give a shit about your plans. This so-called plan is insane, anyway. In fact, it's the most insane thing I've ever heard of," and then we'll start bartering and finally Ryan'll say, "Okay, no more bartering — two years is my final offer. It's either two years or 911," and then Jennie and I'll mull it over for a few seconds and then Jennie will give in and agree to the terms, "Providing, of course, he doesn't destroy the tapes, agrees not to be in the bathroom, doesn't do any filming, and promises to stay in the bedroom watching the TV monitors during the *entire* scene," which Ryan agrees to and so then we'll just carry on from there. Like after filming everything up to this point right here, I'll film Ryan retiring to the bedroom and — oh ya, I almost forgot, only Jennie will use her real name and stay as she is right now, both of us' — pointing at herself and me — 'will use phony names and be in disguise, nothing quite as elaborate as Bryan Brown's character in *FX* or Tom Cruise in *Mission Impossible* but enough so that we're not recognized — and so after Ryan retires to the bedroom and I close the door, Ryan'll start watching the rest of the action on the two TV monitors being fed from the tripod-mounted camcorder in the bathroom and my handheld camcorder, the whole time being filmed by a third camcorder which will be capturing his reaction to Jennie staring at him through the TV monitors and saying, "As I'm sure many of you already know, suicide is never a private matter. Like a pebble in a pond the ripple effect can cause dozens, hundreds, possibly even thousands of people to feel the effects of a suicide long after the person is —'"

"— I mean, would you *listen* to the crap she's spewing."

The motorcycles are gone and Daphne's voice, once again audible, interrupts my memory, making me realize a) my knuckles are white from squeezing the plastic arms of the patio chair, b) my jaw muscles are burning with fatigue from grinding my teeth, c) I can actually hear the blood pulsing through my temples despite Daphne and all the other noises along Queen West, d) I'm not breathing, and e) I'm starting to stand up, am about to hurl my chair into the street and stampede through the rest of the patio in an Incredible Hulk–like rampage — and it's just as this is about to happen that I instinctively close my eyes and begin flooding my occipital lobe with images of me lying in a blue felt-lined coffin, resting in peace, my dead body no longer capable of feeling, of remembering, which has the immediate effect of calming me, of assuaging my guilt and I sink back down into the chair, start breathing, stop grinding my teeth, release my grip on the chair, and it's maybe a second or two after the sound of the blood pulsing through my temples begins to fade into the background that I hear Rebecca's voice say, 'Aren't you getting just slightly ahead of yourself here, Ryan? I mean, before you "off" yourself and go rest-in-peace there's this not-so-small thing that has to happen with me and Daphne which, incidentally, unless you get your ass in gear will more than likely postpone not only your rapidly approaching expiration date and your R.I.P. status but also our —'

"Christ, why can't she just hurry up and die?"

"My thoughts exactly," Daphne replies, causing me to stop breathing again, my jaw immediately clenching, hands regripping the arms of the patio chair, realizing I've just spoken out loud and am now wondering if I've also narrated Rebecca's words out loud until, a second or two later, when Daphne says, "I mean, she shouldn't be allowed to *speak* let alone *live*," I realize Daphne thinks my comment was directed at the cellphone woman and not at her and I breathe a slow, sizeable sigh of relief while scanning the café to see if anyone else heard what I said.

Moments later, still more than slightly unnerved because of my two 'incidents' in less than an hour, I'm about to suggest to Daphne that we get going when she grabs my arm while still looking at the woman and says, "Wait, just listen," and I listen to the woman who is now telling her cellphone in a matter-of-fact, borderline professional tone (like a travel agent listing an itinerary) what she's going to be doing this summer:

"A sailing trip in the Florida Keys next week,

a white-water rafting trip on the Ottawa River the weekend after,

two health spa retreat weekends,

a week, maybe two at our cottage in the Muskokas in early July,

a trip to San Francisco in late July,

a weekend at The Stratford Festival in early August,

a week in New York in mid-August . . ."

Daphne rolls her eyes and mutters "Fucking VAP" which, depending on the context, is either a) short for 'vapid,' b) an acronym for 'Very Annoying Person,' or c) both, and then gestures as though she's about to get up and leave but stops when the woman's voice becomes overly excited and she says, "I couldn't agree more. It just amazes me what we're capable of building nowadays. Space stations, stealth bombers, satellites, CD players, palmcorders, cellphones, DVD players, smart cars, smart roads, smart bombs and —"

Like a lobbyist for technology the woman continues listing high-tech products until, when she starts cataloguing all the wonderful gadgets on her 2001 Pontiac Grand Prix Special Edition Sport Coupe, commenting on how intelligent the car is, how if she locks her keys in the car it can be unlocked via satellite, Daphne says, "Alright, I've had enough," and gets up and starts heading for the exit.

high standard of living?

We're almost outside the gate when Daphne abruptly turns around and, pushing past me, walks directly over to the cellphone woman and asks her, "Excuse me. Have you ever heard of Abraham Maslow?"

Startled, confused, the woman first looks at Daphne then glances at the non-existent person sitting behind her to see if Daphne might be talking to someone else then back at Daphne and says, first to the cellphone, "Hang on a sec," then to Daphne, "No, I'm sorry. I've never met him."

"Well," Daphne says, quickly taking a seat beside the woman, causing her to recoil slightly, "Abraham Maslow was the man who came up with the Hierarchy of Needs and at the very bottom of the hierarchy were things like food, shelter, clothing, clean water, clean air — the basics of life."

The woman is now looking past Daphne to me, possibly wondering if we're together, possibly wanting an explanation as to why Daphne is talking to her, possibly expecting me to tell her Daphne comes with a muzzle or a medical bracelet or an off switch, possibly hoping I'm going to intervene on her behalf, but then Daphne places her arms on the table between a set of car keys and a bottle of Evian, which immediately redirects the woman's attention away from me and back to Daphne who, while leaning in very close to the woman, says, her tone of voice stern, almost reproachful, as though she was a teacher scolding an impudent student, "Now I realize that all our politicians and economists and CEOs like to boast about how technologically advanced we are nowadays, focusing on how we're so well off, how our standard of living is the highest it ever was, how we're capable of building all sorts of remarkable gadgets and machines like laptops and smart cars and smart roads and cellphones and space shuttles and satellite TV and stealth bombers and space stations, but the thing I always marvel at is how even with all these remarkably intelligent gadgets and our so-called advancement in technology, we're no longer able to provide the basic needs of life here in North America."

The woman, completely speechless, has seemingly forgotten all about the person on the other end of the cellphone and is giving Daphne a confused, borderline bewildered, expression. Then, just when it appears the woman has snapped out of it and is about to bring the cellphone back to her ear, Daphne (and I'm not making this up) puts her right hand over the cellphone and using the same stern, scolding tone of voice says, "When you consider the millions of people right here in North America who are prevented from having adequate shelter, food, or clothing each day, how we buy our water from bottles and can't swim in our rivers and lakes because they're too polluted, how the air is becoming so contaminated with sulphur and carbon monoxide that it's becoming lethal to breathe, how is it possible for anyone in their right mind to believe we're rich or developed or advanced or have a high standard of living?"

Without waiting for a response, Daphne, after patting the woman's hand, stands up and walks out of the patio.

our vision

A block later, I hear a jingling noise and notice Daphne is playing with a set of GM car keys that she calmly deposits into the garbage can outside The Black Bull restaurant on Queen Street.

"Were those . . . ?" I start to say, then stop, knowing they belonged to the woman in Starbucks.

"Let's see if her car is smart enough to start without a key," Daphne says, smirking, then, a few strides later, her expression changed, the smirk replaced by a sad, yet hopeful gaze, she asks, "Heard from Rebecca yet?"

I shake my head. "You know Rebecca," I say, trying to sound casual. "She's either here or she's not here, no word in between."

"Has she ever been gone this long before?"

"I don't think so," I say, lying, then, after recalling Daphne phoning me in a panic five weeks ago, telling me Rebecca hadn't shown up at Book City in the Beaches where they were supposed to meet, that she wasn't at our apartment either that afternoon, that night, or the following morning, that neither Brad nor Nicole nor Eriq nor anyone else had seen or heard from her in several days, that Rebecca had gone and done it to her again, taking off without telling her where she'd gone or when she'd be back, after recalling all this I'm about to add, 'I wouldn't worry about it, Daph, she'll probably show up at the restaurant where we're having dinner tonight' (which is something Rebecca is notorious for doing — showing up at a place where we're all at without any of us telling her in advance), when Daphne asks, "Where do you think she is?"

I shrug. "No idea," I say. "She could be anywhere. India. Columbia. Montreal. California. Scarborough —" and then, thinking of the suicidE-mail I read earlier, I add, "Walden Pond."

"Walden Pond?"

"I was talking figuratively," I say. "She might just need a sanctuary, you know, a place to go to get away from it all, like Thoreau and how he went to the woods to live deliberately, to suck —"

"I *know* the quote Ryan," Daphne says, her tone condescending.

Silence for a few strides during which time (in retaliation for her condescending tone) I imagine myself saying, 'You know Daph, the truth is, Rebecca never started taking off like she does until she met you' (which is actually true) then, depending on Daphne's reaction, adding, 'She was always the kind of person who was content to just stay in her apartment and sketch and paint and write all day' (which isn't true) and possibly even, 'In fact, before she left this time she told me she does it just to get away from you' (which she didn't, but which *might* be true).

Instead of me saying any of this, however, Daphne is the first to break the silence by saying, "Did I tell you I'm seriously considering going to live in Southern Russia for a while?"

I smile.

Last year Daphne found an old article (maybe in *Harper's*) on how the people who live in the Caucasus Mountains in Southern Russia, the Ecuadorean Andes, and the Hunza Valley in Kashmir are not only the healthiest people on Earth, they also live the longest. She called me from her friend's place that afternoon, her voice bursting with optimism and told me that (I'm paraphrasing here, so bear with me), 'the reason they're the healthiest and live the longest is because they exercise regularly, live in extended families, never experience loneliness, live at high altitudes where there's little air pollution, eat a high-fibre, low-salt, low-fat, low–refined sugar, no preservatives, no artificial flavours diet that's loaded with fresh fruit and vegetables, drink water from mineral-enriched mountain streams, hardly ever drink alcohol or smoke, and believe in promoting a sense of community over the pursuit of individual wealth or success.'

Every time Rebecca leaves and is gone longer than a few days Daphne mentions this. In late December, when Rebecca disappeared for a week, Daphne said she was moving to the Caucasus Mountains in Southern Russia. The next time Rebecca left, in early February for ten days, Daphne was determined to set off for the Ecuadorian Andes. The next time, in April, when Rebecca left for almost two weeks, Daphne talked about Kashmir, and now she's back to Southern Russia.

"I'm seriously considering it," Daphne says, sounding serious, as we're crossing over to the south side of Queen Street. "I've already done a ton of research on the Caucasus Mountains and on Southern Russia," she continues, and then, after we've reached the sidewalk and are walking past the Peter Pan Bistro, she abruptly stops, spins around to face Queen Street, her hands now forming tiny fists as she scrunches her long, thick blond hair, and says, her voice straining to remain calm, "I've got to get out of here and live some place sane. I've got to get away from all this traffic, these blaring car stereos, this noise, these billboards and highrises and concrete and bloody disinterested, disenfranchised, *sealed for protection* people.

"For Christ's sake, look at this, will you?" she says, raising her voice while emphatically gesturing to the surrounding cityscape. "Like take ten bloody seconds and look at what we've *created*. *This* is our *vision*, our Eden. This is what thousands of years of civilization, creativity, and mastery over nature has spawned!"

It's during the next few moments — as Daphne continues shouting, speaking in exclamation marks while flinging her hands into the air, gesturing wildly, her joie de vitriolic erupting over Queen West — that I'm reminded of why Rebecca agreed to select Daphne, why Rebecca and I have been 'working on' Daphne for almost eight months now; in Rebecca's words (on page 131 of her diary), 'Here is someone who exists to make others question the validity of their existence, whose raison d'être is to take away everyone else's raison d'être and who, because of her unbridled misanthropy, is seemingly destined to live forever. Knowing this, how can anyone not want to take up the challenge of getting her to question the validity of her existence, of taking away her raison d'être, of changing her destiny?'

"And it's spreading!" Daphne is now shouting at a group of terrified tourists, drawing dozens of reproachful-slash-disturbed-slash-curious looks from other passersby. "This *vision* of ours is *spreading*. Like a malignant tumour it's *infecting* every corner of the goddamn world! The Amazon Rainforest is being destroyed! They've found mercury poisoning in the Inuit! An acid raincloud the size of the United States is hovering over the Indian Ocean! People in Patagonia, Ethiopia, and Mongolia are wearing Levi's and Ray-Bans and dreaming of eating Big Macs and Supersized fries while driving in their Lexus SUVs to the Disney World theme park that just opened last week. And every day more satellite dishes are installed, more TV channels are created, and more movie theatres are built so they can get the vision out there. Pretty soon there won't be a single inch of the Earth or a single neuron in the human brain that's not infected with it!"

I'll be fine!

Two minutes later, after we've walked down Peter Street, made a left on Richmond Street, and Daphne has a) given the finger to the building where they film the TV show, U8TV's *The Lofters*, b) shouted, "Do you have any idea where the hell this place is?" referring to the restaurant we're heading to, c) immediately thrown her arms in the air in frustration when I shrug, shake my head, and say, "No, not really," and d) abruptly crossed over to the south side of Richmond, cutting in front of oncoming traffic and causing two cars — a white Cavalier and a black Civic — to screech to a stop and both drivers to blare their horns and shout "Stupid bitch!" and "Fucking idiot" respectively, I catch up to her and say, using a stern, almost accusatory, voice (you have to know how to manage the talent), "Maybe you shouldn't go to dinner, Daph. I mean, it seems like you're not even in the vicinity of being in the right frame of mind to be good company at Nicole's birthday dinner," adding, after a brief pause, "I'm sure Brad and Eriq — even Nicole — will understand. I'll just tell them you weren't feeling well."

It was Nicole's birthday last week and though all of us (Nicole, Brad, Eriq, Daphne, and myself) are supposed to be having dinner tonight to celebrate, since Daphne's tirade in front of the Peter Pan Bistro I

– fast-forwarded the evening (inserting Daphne's present mood into the dinner scene) and decided she was not capable of delivering anything but an exceptional performance,

– became instantly euphoric at the prospect of directing Daphne in this frame of mind, immediately crossing my fingers in hopes that Rebecca would neither show up nor call me with her usual list of detailed instructions regarding what direction she wanted to take Daphne and the rest of 'the gang' tonight, giving me poetic licence to create whatever *scenes* I saw fit to create,

– sensed, however, that it was just a matter of time — a few minutes, perhaps only a few seconds — before Daphne told me she'd rather pull out her fingernails with a pair of pliers than spend another evening with the four of us at some nouvelle cuisine restaurant,

– thought about giving her the letter Rebecca left for her — the one I've been hanging onto now for almost five weeks — but, knowing that a) I wasn't permitted to give Daphne the letter until instructed to do so by Rebecca and

b) even if I was, the letter would undoubtedly alter Daphne's mood which, in turn, would significantly alter her performance at dinner which, in turn, would alter my present state of euphoria, and so I

– concluded that instead of giving her the letter I needed to suggest (in order to guarantee her attendance) that she *not* attend dinner tonight, citing her present frame of mind as the excuse.

"I'll be fine," Daphne snaps at me and then, moments later, as we're walking past the front entrance of the Chapters bookstore, she screams — a very loud, very demonic-sounding scream that so completely terrifies the three young girls carrying Gap bags and exiting Chapters that all three yelp and reflexively retract the bags to their chests like protective shields.

daphne's vision, that's life!

Two seconds after pointing a crooked, threatening index finger at the three stunned girls and snarling, "All homogenized label consumers shall be excommunicated," Daphne says to me, her tone now matter-of-fact, "Did I already tell you I haven't finished reading a book in almost two months?"

I smile, momentarily marvelling at Daphne's capacity for changing topics and moods so abruptly, then say, "No," and she says, "I've probably started more than thirty books in the last year — *The English Patient, She's Come Undone, Angela's Ashes, The Cider House Rules, The Blind Assassin* — and I haven't finished a single one."

"Why?"

She shrugs, "I don't know. Whenever I sense the end coming

my eyes just stop working, they blur."

"Maybe there's something wrong with *your* vision," I suggest.

"Ha. Ha. Very funny, funny man," she says, punching my right shoulder hard enough for me to consider punching her back. "But there's nothing wrong with *my* vision."

While rubbing my shoulder I eye the small, Lake Michigan –shaped birthmark on Daphne's left shoulder for a few seconds, imagining the middle knuckle of my right fist hitting the birthmark with enough force to severely bruise her bicipital tendon and after I've spent another few seconds imagining her face cringed with pain, I say, "So, what's the problem then?"

This time she thinks about it for a while, her eyes momentarily retreating into Chapters, browsing the dozen or so people sitting on the windowsill bench reading a magazine or flipping through a book until, sounding slightly unsure, as though she hasn't quite figured out if what she's about to say is true or not, she says, "I disagree with conclusions."

"Why?"

"Because conclusions just don't make sense anymore. They're anachronisms. Nothing is concluded anymore. Nothing stays the same. Everything changes. Everyone is *under construction* nowadays."

"And what does this have to do with not being able to finish reading a book?"

"Because a book *has* a conclusion," she says, using her 'You-should-have-already-known-this-you-bloody-moron' tone of voice. "Because a book is no longer *under* construction. It's completed, finished, an island unto itself. It never changes. It's always the same."

Two scenarios converge in my mind:
– in the first, I tell her that a character in one of Eriq's short stories would disagree with her, that this particular character, an elderly woman, believes books — their words

and meaning — change all the time, that literature is always evolving, always moving, always morphing into some other creation depending on what she's doing or where she's at or what's happened to her since the last time she's read it

– in the second, I tell her that's why relationships with TV shows — especially soap operas — might be better for her since not only are soap operas always around, readily accessible via cable and satellite seven days a week, they're also always changing, the storyline always evolving, the characters always under construction, which might make for the perfect relationship but

– since Daphne doesn't even know Eriq writes and Eriq would kill me if I told her and since Daphne despises TV and would kill me if I even *attempted* to suggest that a TV series — especially a soap opera — is better than a novel, I decide to not say anything and that results in Daphne asking me, "You know what trait I despise most in people?"

"I don't know," I say, after a few moments, shrugging my shoulders. "Apathy?"

She shakes her head.

"I don't give a damn about apathy. It's certainty. The idea that we know what's going to happen from one moment to the next, that we know what someone's going to say, what they're going to do, what they're going to think."

A tow-truck towing a lavender Porsche 944 hits a pothole on the street in front of us setting off the 944's car alarm, momentarily interrupting Daphne's rant. After *it* makes a left on Adelaide Street and *I* make a quick survey of the patiophiles sitting across the street in Al Frisco's and *we* make a slight detour around a middle-aged man seated on the sidewalk outside Playdium scanning the young and the listless eating in Milestones café with a nostalgic, 'Been there-had that.com' expression tattooed on his face, Daphne continues.

"Politicians, economists, religious leaders all sit there trying to project this image of certainty, trying to convince us they know what's going to happen, that they've got it all figured out well in advance of it actually happening, which is pure bullshit. The truth is not a single person in this entire city, in this entire world of six billion people has a fucking clue what's going to happen from one moment to the next. Oh sure, you might be sitting there thinking you've got it all figured out, that your life is going the way you planned it, that it's pleasantly predictable — that is until you're supposed to meet her at a bookstore and instead of meeting her you find out she's gone, that she's taken off to god-knows-where and you may never see her or hear from her again and it suddenly hits you that 'That's life!' and you better get used to it in a bloody hurry!"

We remain silent for the remainder of the walk to the restaurant.

rain & eriq

The restaurant we're going to is called Rain and is located on Mercer Street. Though I didn't tell Daphne it was Nicole's choice I'm certain she already knows since Nicole has been pestering us to have dinner at Rain since the end of April.

In early May, while eating dinner at our usual Friday evening spot — Jump Café — Nicole once again started discussing her desire to have dinner at Rain, trying to gain support by assuring us that Rain was 'the hottest, hippest restaurant in Toronto,' that 'there are occasional near-riots to get in,' and as she continued talking I noticed she sounded less and less like herself and more and more like a restaurant review. So the following day I decided to spend an afternoon in the city library browsing old copies of the *Globe and Mail*, the *Toronto Star*, and the *National Post* and eventually found an article on Rain in the April 23 edition of the *Toronto Star* — noting that Nicole had done an admirable job of regurgitating Judy Steed's review.

Since the restaurant doesn't have a big golden arch piercing the skyline above it and neither Daphne nor myself have ever remembered being on Mercer Street we walk too far east, then too far south, then finally, once again at the corner of John and King, decide to stop and ask a hot dog vendor for directions — a woman with reading glasses, lots of freckles, and a pleasant smile — and she points to a small street on the other side of a nearby parking lot.

Entering Rain through a revolving frosted-glass door, I'm immediately struck by the coolness of the place; the unadorned concrete floor, the stainless steel/frosted-glass host station, and the shivering water sliding down two large wall panels. The ambience of the place sends a pleasant chill through me.

The hostess, a young woman shrinkwrapped in a two-sizes-too-small black stretch cotton dress and wearing a Visa Gold smile on top of her considerable make-up approaches us and says, perkily, "Hi! Welcome to Rain."

I pause for a second, allowing Daphne the opportunity to respond but she's busy staring at something — possibly the scooped seat bar stools, possibly the tall buff bartender pouring what looks to be a scotch, possibly the . . . well, possibly anything — so I smile at the hostess and say, "Hi. I believe we have a reservation for 6:00 p.m. We're with the Wellington group."

Daphne snorts and says something inaudible when I say "Wellington group" and the hostess, still smiling, lifts an eyebrow at Daphne before placing her unpainted index fingernail at the top of the reservation book and quickly scrolling down the page.

"Party of five?" she asks a moment later, looking up at me and when I nod, she picks up two menus and says, "Please follow me."

She leads us through a lounge area where several thirtysomethings are seated on a few of the dozen or so retro style black padded benches arranged around a large vinyl-covered circle couch that occupies the centre of the room. One of the thirtysomethings — a woman wearing a black pantsuit with a chartreuse-coloured chemise and a bouquet of thick, auburn curls falling past her shoulders, is gazing longingly at a twentysomething — a blond-haired, blue-eyed guy dressed in brown leather Aldo shoes, khakis, and a navy blue dress shirt and who, until a moment ago, was staring at the chandelier of clustered raindrop-bulbs above the circle couch but who is now giving Daphne a quick once over, his eyes lingering on her sandals.

"Is this your first visit to Rain?" the hostess asks, half-turning, half-pausing, as we leave the lounge area.

I nod, then direct the hostess's attention to Daphne by glancing at Daphne in a manner that suggests her response might be different from mine, giving me the opportunity to focus on the aroma of curry and coriander and what I think is ginger wafting into the dining area from the open kitchen before glancing back at the blue-eyed, Aldo-shoed guy in the lounge area to see if he's still looking at Daphne's sandals, which he's not; he's now tenderly caressing the ringless left hand of the chartreuse-chemised woman while gazing at the water panels.

"This section here," the hostess says, continuing to walk, gesturing to six or seven attached frosted-glass/stainless steel tables stretching almost the entire length of the area, "is our communal dining experience. People enjoy it because they can share everything — conversation, food, even plans for the evening."

A couple, a man and a woman in their early twenties and dressed in matching cherry red Tommy Hilfiger T-shirts, flared corduroy pants, and leather flip-flops, are seated in the middle of the long dining table exactly two place settings away from a woman in her late thirties wearing a red floral chiffon dress, red satin-beaded mules, and sipping what looks to be Hot Pot soup from a porcelain spoon.

Walking past the woman, the hostess leads us around the far end of the sectioned dining table then through an opening in a bamboo partition, and I see Eriq in the corner, his back to us, seated on one of the three black vinyl padded chairs pulled up to our table, staring intensely at the frosted plexiglass window which more than likely will be incorporated into one of his short stories.

Most of the stories he writes are about us, about these little get-togethers we have; he told me a few weeks ago that his writing productivity has increased about fivefold since we started meeting every Friday night at Jump Café, which is one of the main reasons he shows up every week.

Initially, Eriq doesn't see us but just as I'm about to say 'Hi' he turns his head and, immediately looking past the hostess and me to Daphne, says, his expression already a not-so-subtle blend of irritation and amusement, "Well, well, well. If it isn't Petite Misère and the —"

"*Street of Riches*, Gabrielle Roy, 1957," Daphne says, interrupting him in mid-sentence to footnote his reference, "And just how is our little narcissistic Patrice-wannabe today?"

"*La Belle Bête*, Marie-Claire Blais, 1964," Eriq says, footnoting Daphne's reference before adding, "I'm well, thank you. Well enough to see Morag is still without her lover."

"*The Diviners*, Margaret Laurence, 1974," Daphne says quickly, before adding, "And if only you, like Patrice, gained the quality of being mute you would be *so* much more attractive."

Both Eriq and Daphne were raised on literature, much of it Canadian, much of it French-Canadian. They were born to different French mothers and the same English father on the same day in the same hospital — which is how Daphne's mother found out her husband was also the father of her best friend's baby boy. Born less than five minutes apart on October 5, 1970, an hour before the British Trade Commissioner in Montreal, James Cross, was kidnapped by the FLQ, inspired the mothers to declare that Daphne and Eriq were the progeny of the Quiet Revolution. A week after giving birth, coinciding with the date of Cross's assassination, Daphne's mother filed for divorce and moved in with Eriq's mother and by the time Daphne and Eriq were three months old, they were already falling asleep to Eriq's mother and waking up to Daphne's mother reading aloud pages, sometimes entire chapters, of Tolstoy and Atwood, Hemingway and Roy, Fitzgerald and Laurence, Salinger and Blais, Faulkner and Richler, Chomsky and Steinem — at times rendering them unable to sleep or unwilling to go to school, refusing to leave the comfort of their bed, the reassurance of their mothers' voices, their minds alternately comforted and aroused by the words floating like pollen around the room.

The hostess, completely baffled by the exchange between Daphne and Eriq, has placed our menus on the table and, after whispering to me that our waiter will be with us momentarily, is now backing away slowly, allowing us to seat ourselves.

"Hey, Eriq," I say, offering him my hand, noticing his cologne — CK Be — has already displaced the smell of curry and coriander and ginger wafting through my nostrils. "Good to see you."

"Nice to see you too, Ryan," he says, shaking my hand while gesturing with his other hand for me to sit down, something I'm already in the process of doing having previously noticed that the corner seat (the one with the best overall P.O.V.) was still vacant. "And just how is my favourite tourist?" he says as I slide over, making room for Daphne.

He's referring to the fact that I've been a resident of Toronto for less than a year. In Eriq's mind it requires five years just to be considered a mildly capable Torontonian. He's right, of course. Though I've done my best to 'see the sights,' I'm only, to paraphrase Eriq's description, *mildly capable* in certain sections of the city and feel very much like a tourist everywhere else.

"I'm well, Eriq," I say, smiling. "And you?"

He smiles back and says, "I'd be a whole lot better if you weren't always accompanied by my troll of a sister. We really must arrange a Daphne-Free Night Out."

Eriq is the only person I've met who talks to Daphne like this; of course, excluding Rebecca, he's probably also the only person I know who can match wits with her. In fact, if she and Eriq weren't related, I'm almost certain they'd be lovers.

"Screw you, Eriq," Daphne snaps, adding, after plopping down beside me on the padded, black vinyl bench across the table from Eriq. "It must be sheer torment for you to leave your reflection unattended for so long. How ever are you managing?"

Eriq smiles, then says, "I'm consoling myself with the fact that I'm not depriving my fellow Torontonians of the pleasure of seeing me and my —"

"Vanity, thy name is Eriq," she says, cutting him off and, then, turning to me, says, "When he was younger he would spend hours, sometimes entire days in the bathroom admiring himself. He'd stare at his reflection on the back of his spoon, in his glass of Kool-Aid, and every time we went anywhere he was always looking at himself in car windows, shop windows, office buildings. He even started carrying a compact when he got to high school."

Within two hours of meeting me for the first time, Eriq told me he's only ever wanted to be two things: a writer and very good looking. Although he's still looking for a publisher for his two collections of short stories, he *is* good looking. *Very* good looking. In fact, he's so good looking that whenever I spend an afternoon with him walking around Toronto there's about a seventy-five percent chance someone — usually someone in their teens or early twenties — will come up to him and say, "Aren't you someone famous?"

Before Eriq can conjure an equally incriminating childhood memory of Daphne, a rather androgynous-looking waiter wearing black dress shoes, black leather pants, and a thin black cotton stretch shirt that both reveals and enhances his very erect nipples arrives at our table and is about to speak when Daphne says, "Triple scotch, two ice cubes."

Smiling, the waiter opens his mouth to speak and is again cut off — this time by Eriq — who says to Daphne, his tone suddenly light, his eyes glittering with a joie de vivre, "Now *that's* the spirit, sis. To hell with the puritans!" and then, to the waiter, who has handled both Daphne's abrupt dispensing with formalities and Eriq's interruption remarkably well, Eriq says, "Well, in honour of my sister once again falling off the Mayflower and into the proverbial drink, I'll have a Heineken, in a chilled glass, if that's possible."

Still smiling, the waiter, instead of verbally replying, bows his head (which I suppose indicates that a chilled glass *is* possible) and then, tilting his still bowed head in my direction, he raises his eyebrows and his eyes ask, 'And for you?' and when I say, "A bottle of Evian please," he says, "Of course. Thank you," as though knowing all along this was what I was going to order.

After the waiter leaves and Eriq has commented on his cute butt and his *very* erect nipples, Eriq says, his eyes still attached to the waiter's butt, "I take it there's been no news of Rebecca's whereabouts?"

"What?" Daphne snaps, her tone menacing, her eyes looking as though she's about to pounce.

Undaunted, Eriq calmly returns his gaze to our table, looks at Daphne for one-thousand-and-one, one-thousand-and-two, one-thousand-and-three full seconds before saying, "Why else would you be drinking again? You never drink when Rebecca is around."

"As if," Daphne replies too quickly, too unconvincingly.

Smiling smugly, Eriq flicks his gaze over to me and says, "I do so like it when Rebecca performs one of her disappearing acts — I get my old sister back. Not only does she drink far more liberally but she loses that nauseating *Better Than Chocolate* expression she has whenever Rebecca's around."

"It's *half*-sister," Daphne hisses. "And speaking of nauseating things people wear — nice suit. Another Armani?"

"Prada," Eriq corrects, adding that it's the same one Harry Connick Jr. was wearing in April's edition of *GQ*.

"A gift from one of your *sugar daddies*, I presume?" Daphne asks.

"I prefer to call them *patrons*."

"Semantics. You're still a whore, Eriq."

"What *I* am is none of *your* concern," Eriq snaps back. "You are not your *half*-brother's keeper."

"No, that job belongs to any man or woman with a large enough bankroll."

In his late teens Eriq discovered he did not possess a preference for either gender, concluding it was the result of having a left-handed French mother and a right-handed English father. 'I'm am*bi*dextrous and *bi*lingual. It's only natural I would be *bi*sexual.'

"You're beginning to bore me, Daphy-dear," he says in response to Daphne's last comment, his head now swivelling, eyes skipping around the restaurant, shuffling through the patrons, assessing them like hockey cards, like he's visually playing a 'Had him/Need him/Don't want him' game, adding, as his eyes come to rest on a handsome man in his late forties wearing what looks like to be an Armani suit and Prada shoes, "Fortunately I have other ways to occupy my attention."

After learning of the 16th-century Roman courtesans who, by virtue of their physical charms, savoir-faire, and ravishing intelligence, were able to attract and secure the patronage of wealthy noblemen, Eriq, putting a late 20th-, early 21st-century entrepreneurial twist on this 16th-century custom, quickly discovered that with his physical beauty, intelligence, social decorum, and ability to perform *extraordinarily well* (emphasis his) in bed with either men or women, he could receive not only free room and board in some of Toronto's more exclusive neighbourhoods but also enough leisure time and spending money to pursue his two passions: writing and looking good.

"I wonder who designed this place?" Eriq is now saying, his eyes tracing the wall of bamboo separating the two dining areas. "It looks like the work of someone I just —"

"Blew?" Daphne says, finishing his sentence.

"Possibly," Eriq says, smiling wryly.

A few minutes later, just when it looks as though Daphne might get up and leave, our waiter — his nipples no longer quite so erect — returns with our drink order and Daphne immediately orders another triple scotch with two ice cubes before downing her drink in one gulp, making me think Eriq was right; since Rebecca's departure five weeks ago Daphne has been drinking more at our little get-togethers. Much more.

and the 'ifs' played on . . .

The clientele in Rain is, for the most part, late twenties to early fifties, ethnically assorted and predictably trendy.

Except for myself and the young twentysomething in the cherry red Hilfiger T-shirt and the blue-eyed, Aldo-shoed guy now sitting at the end of the frosted-glass/stainless steel dining table section, all of the men in my F.O.V. (field of view) are suited and tied; the women, with the exception of Daphne and the leather flip-flop girl, are wearing dresses, skirts, or pantsuits, and are mounted on a wide selection of mules, wedges, pumps, platforms, and classic stilettos, and it's as I'm admiring the open-toe leather T-strap heels on the auburn-haired, chartreuse-chemised woman that two women walk into my F.O.V. and although one of them looks a lot like Mia Kirshner (whom I've been infatuated with ever since seeing her in the movie *Exotica*) it's the clary sage essential oil the other one is wearing that overwhelms me, that reverses my thoughts, instantly pulling me back to my sister's funeral and the scent of clary sage swirling around the funeral parlour, as well as the sight of my parents huddled tightly together in the front pew, my mother's face poking over my father's shoulder, her eyes suddenly opening, blinking away the tears, looking at Rebecca and me with a half-surprised, half-frightened expression on her face long enough for me to wonder where the surprise part of the expression is coming from until I realize that Rebecca and I are laughing, not loudly, but still out loud — Rebecca in response to the clary sage scent that is designed to evoke happiness and, in some people (in this case Rebecca), can cause spontaneous laughter; me in response to Rebecca's laughter and the fact that the funeral home is actually using clary sage — and so I reflexively change my expression to something more appropriate but it's too late and later on, on the way to the cemetery, in the lead car, my father, having heard of our breach of etiquette, is now saying to me, 'How anyone could be laughing during a funeral, let alone their sister's or cousin's funeral is beyond me,' while my mother adds, 'I'm going to have to live with that image for the rest of my life. What kind of *monsters* are you two?'

It was immediately after I told Rebecca what my parents had said regarding our behaviour at the funeral home that she decided we weren't ever going to tell my parents what really happened, that we would merely sit back and observe how they responded to Jennie's death without knowing the things we did, wondering if they'd blame themselves, each other, us, society; if they'd think they could've done something to prevent it, that if only they didn't go on their two-week cruise until the following year or if only they'd departed a day later Jennie wouldn't have done it. She wanted to know if they'd try to figure out why Jennie had done it, if they'd invent theories or plausible explanations, if they'd arrive at any false conclusions to make themselves feel better; she wanted to see if they'd start lying to themselves, if they'd start to believe it wasn't a suicide or if they'd start talking to people at random, seeking solace in the company and conversation of strangers or if, when someone asked them, 'How are you?' they'd immediately blurt out, 'Horrible, my daughter just committed suicide'; she wanted to know if, like her, they'd start making up stories, if either of them would tell people there was a 'suicide gene' in our family, that several people on both sides of our family had committed suicide, and that it was probably a bad idea that my parents — two people whose mothers had committed suicide — decided to start dating, get married, and have children; she wanted to see if either of my parents would become suicidal or if they'd look at me as though I was next . . . if, if, if. . . .

obsession, for men

Ten minutes later Brad Wellington, unescorted by the hostess, strides into view wearing his usual 'shiny-happy-people-holding-hands' grin.

Brad and I have known each other since university and even

though we've been friends for almost ten years, were roommates for two years at university, kept in semi-regular contact after university and he's just recently asked me to be the best man at his wedding in three months, I've never really considered him to be my *best* friend.

"Hello everyone," Brad says, now at our table, still wearing the same grin. "Wow, this place sure is . . . it's quite, um, different, huh?" he says, half-turning and making a quick visual sweep of the restaurant. "I . . . I like it, though."

"Thank you for your exceedingly articulate critique," Daphne says, her mocking tone instantly dissolving Brad's goofy grin. "I'm sure the designers are thrilled Beamer Boy approves."

Daphne sometimes calls Brad 'Beamer Boy' because he made the mistake of telling us once that his high school friends referred to him as Beamer Dude after discovering that the three initials in his name were BMW.

Brad's full name is Bradley Manfred Wellington and (fortunately, for Brad) what Daphne doesn't know is that he actually enjoyed people calling him 'Beamer Dude' or 'The Big Beamer' until 1995 — the year Brad Pitt was voted Sexiest Man Alive by *People* magazine — at which time he started telling everyone to just call him 'Brad.' Since then, depending on Pitt's reception by the critics, he subtly lets people know whether or not they should add or subtract the 'l-e-y' from his current name. For most of 1998, all of 1999, and some of 2000, he introduced himself to people he didn't know as Bradley but after Pitt's performance in the movie *Snatch* in late 2000 and his recent renaming by *People* magazine as the Sexiest Man Alive, he once again began telling people to call him 'Brad.'

"Nice shoes, *Brad*," Eriq says, emphasizing the name without a trace of sarcasm while glaring at Daphne. "They're so . . . *vintage*."

Eriq — who adores Brad and desperately wants to have sex with him before Brad marries Nicole — spent the ten, perhaps twelve, seconds prior to his shoe comment assessing Brad's clothes and I could tell by his expression the assessment was proceeding well, that he was quite pleased with Brad's recent haircut, the amount of hair gel he'd used, that he liked the Harrington jacket, the blue/green geometric print cotton shirt and the navy double-pleated cotton trousers Brad was wearing — and it was only after Eriq's gaze travelled towards Brad's shoes and I noticed Eriq closing his eyes, taking a deep breath, and clasping his hands together as though he was praying, that I recalled Eriq telling me last fall, 'It's so incredibly disappointing to see a person, especially a man, wearing bad shoes — or worse, wearing shoes that don't match the rest of his outfit. It's like seeing De Niro or Cruise or Bono in person and realizing they're so much shorter than you've imagined them. It ruins everything.'

The moment Eriq opened his eyes, however, I knew he wasn't disappointed. A perfect blend of relief, approval, and admiration spread across his face, the expression hanging there for a moment or two until he looked up, said, "Nice shoes, *Brad.* They're so . . . *vintage*," patting the chair beside him twice, gesturing for Brad to sit on his side of the table.

"Thanks," Brad says, referring to Eriq's compliment on his shoes, "They're Prada. Nicole bought them for me when we were in L.A. last weekend."

"Really," Eriq says in a somewhat deflated tone — probably due to the mentioning of Nicole's name.

Even though Eriq is bisexual and Nicole is *very* attractive, he's never once expressed an interest in Nicole sexually. (In fact, if anything, I get the feeling that the thought of being with her repulses him, perhaps because he, as I do, suspects Nicole has had sex with Daphne.)

"How was L.A.?" I ask Brad.

"It was alright," he says, sliding into the chair beside Eriq. "We must've met about a dozen people who said they envied us living here in Toronto. Ever since *Forbes* magazine voted Toronto as the best city in the world to live in, everyone raves about it."

"Speaking of raves," Eriq says, lightly tapping Brad's arm, "there's one happening later tonight."

"Where?" Daphne asks, "Church and Wellesley?"

"I'm not sharing that information with you," Eriq says haughtily, then, after stealing a quick glance at Brad's crotch, adds, "Besides, Daphy-dear, you're not *dressed* appropriately."

"Another '*Members* Only' party," Daphne says, rolling her eyes.

"Something like that."

"I'm not sure I'm up for a rave tonight," Brad says, seemingly oblivious to what Daphne and Eriq have been talking about.

"Don't worry," Eriq says, patting his arm. "There'll be plenty of Viagra circulating."

In the last thirty seconds or so — since Brad slid into the booth beside Eriq — I've been aware of his cologne (Obsession for Men) encroaching on Eriq's CK Be. At first it seemed like the two scents were going to remain separate, distinct, but within seconds they were playfully mingling and now, less than a minute later, they're indistinguishable, having already melded, creating an entirely new scent.

nicole's tommy

After our waiter, arriving at our table a few moments ago, gives Daphne her drink that, this time, thankfully, she starts sipping (it's substantially more difficult to manage the talent when they're intoxicated), and Brad orders a cranberry juice with no ice that makes Eriq sigh and say something about there being far too many teetotallers in Toronto, which makes Daphne laugh and the waiter smile, Nicole — escorted by the hostess — approaches the table wearing her hair up, silver earrings, a beaded silk halter dress with flared hem, a set of matching silver bangles on both wrists (to cover the scars), a silver satin clutch purse, a new pair of what look to be Steve Madden shoes, and a pair of bra inserts that nicely accentuate her wasting breasts.

"Hey, there she is," Brad says, his 'shiny-happy-people-holding-hands' grin reappearing when he sees Nicole. "Just in the *Nic* of time. What would you like to drink, honey?"

After glancing quickly at Daphne's drink, Nicole says, "I'll have a sco — a gin and tonic, please," and our waiter who, for the last eight seconds has been staring at Nicole's long, thinning neck and too-defined cheekbones while probably thinking 'She looks like a thinner version of Audrey Hepburn in *Breakfast at Tiffany's*' (which she does), smiles and nods his head before spinning on his heel and walking away in the direction of the bar.

"Hi, Nicole," Eriq says, trying to sound cheery but obviously disappointed that Brad's fiancée has shown up and he won't be as inclined to flirt. Then, noticing her shoes, he perks up a bit and says. "Love your shoes. Steve Madden?"

Before she can respond to Eriq's question, Daphne, not looking up from her drink, says, "Love your inserts, Nicole. Sensual Shapers by Victoria's Secret?" to which Nicole responds by giving Daphne an icy glare that Daphne doesn't notice because she's still staring at her triple scotch but which gives me the chance to notice not only how skinny Nicole has become since I last saw her — which was only last week — but that her eyes have changed colour as well, from an olive green to a Caribbean blue.

After realizing Daphne is not going to notice her glaring at her, Nicole turns to Eriq, smiles, and says, "Hello Eriq. Thank you. And yes, you're right. They're Steve Madden. Brad bought them for me in L.A."

By this time Brad is standing beside Nicole and is now attempting to give her a kiss on the lips which she promptly rejects, offering him her cheek instead, whispering, "Lip gloss."

Brad obeys, dutifully planting a light kiss on her cheek, and says, "You look great, honey" and after Nicole air-kisses him and says "Thank you, so do you," Brad makes a sweeping gesture toward the table while half-bowing his head and saying, "Now, where would the beautiful lady from Rosedale like to sit?" After eyeing both sides for a moment or two, Nicole, ever so slightly, leans in the direction of Daphne but before the lean becomes a step Daphne points to the other side of the table and says, her tone as caustic as possible, "The section for *coloured* contacts is over there."

Eriq smiles. "Ignore her," he says, "She's suffering from chocolate withdrawal," before pointing to the chair on the outside of the table.

Before thanking Eriq, Nicole glares at Daphne who, after giving Eriq the finger, is now stirring her drink with the same finger.

"At least *someone* has manners," Nicole says, before slowly seating herself in the chair between Eriq and Brad, her Tommy Girl Cool Spray perfume by Tommy Hilfiger immediately separating Eriq's and Brad's cologne, once again cleaving them into two distinct scents.

inspired

"Isn't this place fabulous?" Nicole says excitedly after taking a quick sip of her gin and tonic. "It's so, so —"

"Clean, simple, elegant, understated, not over-designed," I

suggest, directly quoting one of the owners (Michael Rubino) that appeared in the Judy Steed article in the *Toronto Star*.

Gleefully impressed with my statement, Nicole says, "*Exactly*, Ryan. That's *exactly* what I was thinking."

I smile, add, "It's sort of got that whole L.A. vibe to it."

"Have you ever been to L.A.?" Daphne asks me sternly, not liking that I've made Nicole happy, oblivious to the fact that I was actually poking fun at her.

"No," I say, shaking my head.

"Well then, how would you know it has an L.A. vibe?"

"I don't know," I say, shrugging. "It just feels that way," thinking of adding that the reason it *feels* that way is because I've read almost every possible review of restaurants in North America in the last two or three years and therefore have a pretty good fucking idea as to what kind of vibe a particular restaurant gives off.

"Do you guys *realize* how many famous people have eaten here?" Nicole says excitedly.

"Like who?" Eriq asks, sounding interested, edging slightly forward in his seat.

"Like Robin Williams, Denise Richards, Michael Douglas, Harrison Ford, Danny Devito and —"

"And now they can add the not-so-famous-yet-infamously-unstable Ms. Nicole Chambers to their list of distinguished guests," Daphne sneers, causing Nicole to blush, her lips immediately tightening, beginning to quiver.

I'm not sure when the hostility between Nicole and Daphne started. It's been there since we've started hanging out, which is almost eight months now, though it still surprises me Nicole puts up with Daphne to the extent she does and often makes me wonder if she's indebted to Daphne in some way, if absorbing Daphne's animosity is a penance of sorts.

"Have you seen the menus, Nicole?" I say, trying to insert

something between Daphne's last remark and Nicole's reaction to it, something to stop Nicole's lips from quivering, to prevent her from deciding to run out of the restaurant. "They're so . . . delicate," I say, and then, even though I know the menus are made of rice paper, but knowing Nicole will probably correct me and feel better for doing so, I add, "I think they're made out of recycled paper."

Almost immediately Nicole's lips stop quivering, her mouth breaking into an affectionate smile before saying, her voice now cheery, light, "Actually, if I'm not mistaken, Ryan, I believe they're made from rice paper," and then, after passing a menu between her fingertips for a few seconds, she scans it and adds, once again plagiarizing Judy Steed, "it's so obvious the food is Japanese-inspired."

Brad, a comparison between two possibilities

After we've ordered both our appetizers and main dishes and I've initiated a discussion about Toronto's downwardly mobile and how some of them are now wearing silk suits, albeit smeared with feces or Reese's Peanut Butter Cups, which predictably embroils Daphne and Eriq in a debate about what should be done about *the homeless epidemic* (Daphne's phrase), I tune them out and — after conducting an unsuccessful visual search for Rebecca, fully expecting to see her sitting somewhere nearby, eavesdropping on my performance — I end up focusing on Brad, on why almost every time I see him I can't help thinking he's a pathetic loser.

When I first met him — while he was looking at and subsequently renting a room in the student house in which I was staying — he was what Eriq would call *a riveting character*, riveting in the Holden Caufield/Will Hunting sense of the word, in the sense that the best characters, the most memorable characters, are the ones who have a shadow side, a side full of hidden, often quirky details, usually inconsistent with other parts of their character, which ends up distinguishing them from the rest of the herd, making them more colourful and more intriguing.

Probably the most intriguing thing about Brad was the fact that no one, not even his closest friends or family, knew that
– even though he'd had plenty of offers to play basketball and football in the States he actually loathed these sports because they didn't contain enough *inherent risk*,
– all the BMOCs at university — mostly the football, basketball, and rugby jocks who paraded around campus like they were heroes and called Brad a 'chickenshit pussy' because he wouldn't try out for any of their teams — wouldn't even attempt *one tenth* the things Brad had been doing since he was sixteen,
– when he took off nearly every weekend during the school year, he was rarely going to stay with his grandparents so he could really focus on his studies like he said he was; instead he was travelling all over North America to go sky-diving, white-water kayaking, bungee-jumping, parasailing, cliff diving, glacier snowboarding, big wave surfing, street luging, tower-diving, rock climbing — anything that involved the possibility, sometimes even the probability, of dying, and
– after he asked me to do him a favour once and we'd driven to a storage shed where he stored all his equipment, packed some jump gear, flew to Arizona, rented a van, drove to a jump tower in the desert and I filmed him jumping from the tower, watching his chute opening only a second, maybe a second and a half before he hit the

ground and after seeing that he was okay and shouting how insane he was, how absolutely in-*fucking*-sane he was, he turned to me and said, 'Hey, like Freud said, "Life is impoverished when the highest stake in the game of living, life itself, is not risked."'

Of course, the truth is, none of this is true.

It was just a story Rebecca made up to get Eriq to come to dinner one night, to join what she referred to as 'the cast of faux friends' she was in the process of assembling.

Rebecca and I were at Toronto's International Festival of Authors last fall and during an intermission Eriq came up to Rebecca and I and started talking and eventually we found ourselves discussing the makings of an interesting character, a riveting, page-turning character, and after Eriq revealed to us what he thought were the necessary ingredients, Rebecca told him that that sounded exactly like my friend Brad, that Brad had this enormous shadow side, this risky-slash-adventurous-slash-cerebral side that no one else knew about, that no one else could know about because, 'To tell you the truth, Eriq, it's a secret and before I say what it entails you've got to promise Ryan and I that you won't mention or even let on you know *anything* about it — to anyone, but especially to Brad,' which was enough to hook Eriq and get him to meet us for dinner two weeks later at Jump Café.

Of course, like Rebecca, I've also come to realize that just because it's not true doesn't mean it's not real; I mean, just because Brad was never recruited by any U.S. colleges or he's never actually been bungee-jumping or white-water kayaking or cliff diving or quoted Freud, he *could have*, and it's this possibility — the possibility that he *could've* done these things and, more specifically, the comparison between these two versions of Brad — that is making me look at him right now like he's a pathetic loser.

progeny

I tune back into the conversation when I see Brad's lips moving. He's saying something — something that causes Daphne to slam her fist down on the table and shout, *"What?"*

"I said," Brad says, timidly, "not *all* of them are that hard off."

"How the hell would you know?" Daphne snaps.

He shrugs, then, less timidly, says, "Some of them have places to stay, places where —"

"You mean bus shelters? Alleys? Doorways?"

"No, I mean there are places where people who take them in and give them food and clothing and —"

"Homeless shelters?"

"No, other places, other people — just regular, ordinary people who —"

"You mean the regular, ordinary, 'I'll-give-you-a-bagel, a hot bath, and a sweater if you give me a blowjob' kind of people?"

"No, nothing like that. I mean, there are a lot of street people who just need a place to stay occasionally or a fixed mailing address, while the rest of the time they prefer to live on the street, enjoy the sense of community they get from hanging out with other street people and —"

"Do you *realize* what you're doing?" Daphne says, looking at Brad like he's a complete idiot. "You're romanticizing homelessness. You're making it seem like this is a good life, like they're not that bad off, like —"

"Maybe they're not," Nicole says, interrupting Daphne. "On my way over here I saw a bunch of kids with a sign saying they needed money for marijuana."

Daphne gives Nicole an exasperated, 'You-can't-be-serious' look, then says, "It's a joke, you moron. They did it —"

At this point I interrupt Daphne and, using a polite, though corrective tone, state that I saw the same sign but that the fine print said they'd just written 'Need Money for Marijuana' to get people's attention and that none of them actually smoked marijuana and any money they received was going towards food, clothing, and shelter.

"Ha," Daphne says, grinning triumphantly. "Always read the fine print, Nickelhead. You should know that — your father's a goddamn lawyer for Christ's sake. Besides, who cares what these kids are spending their money on? Who cares if they're using the ten bucks they get begging on the street each day to buy clothes or marijuana?"

There is a momentary lapse of silence before Brad says, "I care," surprising me because a) he said he cares and b) by him saying 'I care,' it sounds as if he's challenging Daphne.

"*You* care?" Daphne nearly shouts. "Christ. Why on earth would *you* care what these kids spend their money on?" and then, leaning over the table towards Brad but not lowering her voice, she says, "You want to care about something, care about what you and your father's Bay Street cronies are doing with the money people give them. Care about the fact that when some banker or mutual funds rep or flashy billboard urges you to invest in their company what you really might be investing in is a multinational corporation responsible for the destruction of a rainforest or a tobacco company responsible for the deaths of thousands of people each year or a waste disposal company responsible for contaminating drinking water and destroying wildlife. Why is it that because these kids live on the street instead of in Rosedale or Beverly Hills, ride skateboards instead of drive SUVs, wear eyebrow rings and torn khakis instead of Rolexes and $1,500 power suits, and use handwritten cardboard signs instead of a Web site or a massive electronic billboard, they're deemed scum, eyesores, and their motives are constantly called into question?"

"Maybe because they *are* eyesores," Eriq says, barely able to contain a smile.

"And all the billboards and neon signs and office buildings plastered around this city aren't?" Daphne says.

"That's different," Eriq says.

"How so?"

"They're *generating* money."

"So are the street kids."

"No," Eriq says, "they're *begging* for it."

"No," Daphne counters, "they're *advertising* for it — the same as any investment or financial group or bank or other business in this city is. These kids are just being entrepreneurial."

"But they're being deceitful," Nicole insists, "they're using false advertising to —"

"Oh for Christ's sake, Nicole, wake up. These kids are the *progeny* of false advertising. They were raised on it. They know it works because it's worked on them from the moment they were born and. . . ."

has this happened?

Daphne's, Eriq's, and Nicole's debate on the social evils versus the capitalist benefits of advertising stretches beyond my attention span and I end up tuning them out again, this time focusing on the group of six — three men and three women, all from London, England, and all in what I would guess to be their late forties — being seated at a nearby table. One of the men is now telling the hostess he had no idea that Toronto had the third largest theatre district in North America behind L.A. and New York, and my interest piques when I note that between the word 'Wales' and the word 'Theatre' in the statement, "We're going to see *The Lion King* at The Princess of Wales Theatre," spoken by the same man to the hostess — right smack dab in the middle of these two words, several caramelized prawns — a moment earlier travelling securely on a slab of broken slate carried by our waiter but then suddenly bumped from the slab by a young guy wearing a tuxedo who, without checking his blind spot, backed his chair into our waiter — land on one of the women.

By the time the tuxedo guy looks up, one of the prawns has already slithered down the woman's chest and now looks to be tunnelling into her cleavage, another is clinging to the scooped neck of her evening gown, while the remaining two have just rolled (slowly at first, then gaining momentum) off the ledge provided by the woman's breasts onto her as yet un-napkined lap.

The disbelieving-slash-denying expressions now etched on everyone's face — the guy wearing the tuxedo, the waiter's, the hostess's, the woman's, the other five members of her group — all suggest this *hasn't* happened, that this incident is just a figment of their imagination. Yet, despite the collective disbelief, the denial, it *has* happened, it *is* real and the only thing that can be done is to admit it and deal with it and as these words are zipping across my visual cortex like a stock market readout they connect me with the scene of Barry, my father's friend and a specialist in grief counselling, sitting beside my mother in the loveseat of my parents' living room and squeezing her hand with a 40–60 split of compassionate warmth and clinical detachment while utilizing his years of training and experience with grieving persons to gently, yet confidently, propose, 'a model, a paragon, a paradigm, if you will [his words, not mine — trust me], to deal with the question that all of us will undoubtedly be asking ourselves in the months ahead, which is, "Why has this happened?"'

And as I'm listening to this slick, pseudo-sympathetic baby booming New Age aficionado telling us that nothing in life is certain, that it is only our (false) belief in the certainty of anything that causes us so much misery and grief, that if we could only destroy the 'Myth of Certainty,' if we could only realize that certainty is elusive and fleeting and not a thing we can ever hope to possess, we would be instantly free of pain — as I'm listening to this, part of me has to admit I'm more than a little impressed with this 'paragon,' this 'paradigm,' of his and wants to ask him to explain it in more detail, but another part is seized by the urge to start laughing, to tell him he's full of shit, that certainty is neither elusive nor fleeting, that a person *can* possess it, and the way to possess it (as Rebecca wrote on page 1 of her diary You. Stupid. Fucking. Moron.) is through suicide, in deciding when, exactly when, and by what method, you're going to die. I mean, what can be more certain than that?

here we are now, entertain us

"Another *moveable* feast, Nicki?"

We've just finished eating the appetizers and our main courses, some of which were served on slabs of broken slate, all of which, our waiter suggested, "should be consumed communally since the food at Rain is arranged by our chefs to be a cumulative digestive experience that's almost guaranteed to give you a palate orgasm."

After having two charred scallops, three nibbles of sugar cane skewered lamb and nearly a dozen forkempties of banana onion cake, Nicole spent the rest of the time alternately watching, rearranging, and transferring food from her plate to Brad's, suggesting the rest of us try combinations of this or that, topping up our water glasses with Evian, commenting on how 'succulent,' 'sumptuous,' and 'tantalizingly tasty' the roasted tandoori duck breast, the miso black cod, and the roasted pork loin stuffed with dried pineapple, lychee, and papaya in a mango-chili chutney *looked*, occasionally drawing our attention to the various elements of the restaurant, the wall of water, the circle couch, the scooped bar stools, the bamboo poles, the fact that at one time this building was Toronto's first prison for women, as well as twice insisting that our waiter promise to give her *personal* compliments to chefs Guy Rubino and Michael Pataran, which, until Daphne reminded us that their names appeared at the bottom of the menus, I was impressed Nicole had remembered.

Finally, after a suitable enough time had elapsed and using the waiter's arrival to remove the final few plates from our table as a decoy, Nicole politely excused herself to the washroom and when she arrived back at the table wearing freshly glossed lips, Daphne, now midway through her third triple scotch, said, "Another *moveable* feast, Nicki?" causing Eriq to almost spit up his sip of Heineken.

"I am *not* bulimic," Nicole is now insisting, glaring at Daphne.

"You shouldn't be," Daphne snaps back. "The amount of food you eat doesn't exactly warrant a purging."

"Well, unlike you, Ms. Naturally Skinny, I unfortunately have to watch what I eat."

"Well, unlike *you*, Ms. Bile Breath, I fortunately don't have to watch what I puke."

"I said, I am not —"

"Having dessert? I know, what's the point if it's just going to end up being part of the *toilet's* cumulative digestive experience?"

While Daphne and Nicole continue bantering I'm occupied with the image of myself throwing up in my apartment in Hamilton.

It was roughly a week after Jennie's suicide and I was alone, watching the video for the first time and when I saw myself on screen, just sitting there, calmly watching Jennie slicing her wrists I suddenly vomited. A week later, unable to hold down food longer than a few minutes, I'd lost almost ten pounds. By the end of the second week, after losing another three or four pounds, part of me thought it was punishment for what I'd done, that God or karma or something had ordained that my carnivorous body feeding on itself, my hair falling out in clumps, my teeth rotting, ribs protruding, my immune system and organs deteriorating and eventually failing would be the type of slow, excruciatingly painful death I deserved and —

"Are you okay, Ryan?" Brad says, interrupting my thoughts as well as Daphne's and Nicole's bantering.

I freeze, realizing I've been daydreaming, wondering if it's happened again, if I've been talking out loud, if I've —

"Look at him," Brad says to the others, pointing at me. "He looks like shit. Look at those rings around his eyes. Is he on something?"

Daphne and Eriq laugh and Eriq says, "Just the opposite, I'm afraid. He's not *on* anything. I keep telling him he should be, though."

"You're suggesting he do *drugs*?" Nicole says, her mouth dropping open as though this were the most incredulous thing she'd ever heard.

Eriq nods his head.

"Why not?" Daphne says, "They work wonders for you, Nicole."

"I do *not* do drugs," Nicole says sternly.

"Nicole," Daphne says, putting down her drink, then, speaking slowly, enunciating each syllable, "In the eight years I've known you you've been addicted to caffeine, TV, fashion magazines, make-up, Paxil, cigarettes, shopping, the Internet —"

"You just described ninety percent of the people in North America," Eriq says, cutting Daphne's list short.

"And I wouldn't exactly classify shopping as an addiction," Brad says.

Ignoring Eriq's comment, Daphne turns to Brad and says, "Oh

you wouldn't? Well, Beamer Boy, seeing as addiction is defined as anything a person can't do without, have you ever known your fiancée to go two days *without* shopping for shoes or clothes or jewellery or any one of a dozen other things she doesn't really need? Have you ever seen what your fiancée *looks* like when she hasn't had her RDA of shopping? She suffers withdrawal symptoms that are comparable to any heroin or cocaine addiction. Why don't you *try* to prevent her from shopping for a week? Why don't you *discontinue* her drug for seven days and see what happens?"

"That suggestion," I say, slightly raising and deepening my voice while lightly pounding the table with my fist, "is nothing short of an abomination, a direct affront to the eleventh commandment."

"Which is?" Eriq asks, right on cue, the line perfectly delivered.

"'Thou shalt shop,'" I reply.

Daphne scowls, gives me a 'Ha. Ha. Very funny, funny man' look but before she can say anything, Eriq, now using his BBC radio reporter's voice — complete with English accent and cadence — says, "It's not only a commandment, my good man, it's in our very genes, part of our evolutionary make-up."

"You don't say?" I say, trying to mimic Eriq's English accent but not quite pulling it off.

Nodding, Eriq, continuing to use the voice, says, "Scientists working on the Genome Project discovered the shopping gene almost one year ago today. Dormant for thousands of years, the gene — thanks to several decades of increasingly clever and intense advertising — has been irrevocably activated."

"And just in time, too," I say, my accent somewhat improved this time around. "What with the economy slowing down and all."

"Oh yes, thank God in heaven for giving us a *buy*-ological urge to shop, even when there's a recession."

"There's certainly nothing recessive about this gene."

"Oh, far from it, far from it. They're calling it the gene of the new millennium, the saviour of consumerism, the protector of capitalism."

"Vive la capitalisme!"

At this point, Daphne, who, for the last few seconds has looked as though she can't decide whether to toss her drink in my face or Eriq's, opens her mouth to say something — something I'm certain is going to be far worse than being doused with scotch — but doesn't say anything because Nicole is now saying, "It's not a joke, you guys, it's a *disorder*. It's called CSD — Compulsive Shopping Disorder — and they're recommending it be included in the next psychiatrists' manual and —"

"For Christ's *sake*, Nicole," Daphne says, almost shouting, "where the hell did you get this from?"

"Dr. McPhilsly. She said —"

"Poutain de merde," Daphne says, this time definitely shouting, drawing momentary attention from the three couples in their late forties as well as the chartreuse-chemised woman and the Aldo-shoed guy. "Don't *tell* me you're being treated for this?! Don't *tell* me —"

"So," I say, using a casual-yet-firm, easy-yet-intrigued tone to redirect Daphne, deflect her attention away from Nicole (who is on the verge of tears for the third time this evening), "what kind of drugs do you suggest *I* take?"

Daphne looks at me — glares at me, actually — but is only slightly miffed that I've cut her off in the middle of what might have turned into a good rant because two seconds later she smiles and says, after glancing at Nicole, "I'd start you off on the basics, the pillars of modern western civilization: TV, caffeine, fast food, and shopping for unnecessary items."

Eriq, who, while Daphne was speaking, tipped his imaginary hat at me in appreciation of my successful redirection of Daphne, is now laughing in response to her suggestions.

"Of course, if you didn't respond well enough to these drugs," he says, still chuckling, "I'd recommend supplementing them with alcohol, the Internet, cigarettes, and refined sugars. Lots of refined sugars."

This time it's Daphne who laughs, giggles actually, her eyes suddenly alive, dancing, like they are whenever she's with Rebecca and she says, "I'd also suggest daily consumption of marijuana, video games, sleeping pills, and child pornography, in order to produce the desired effect."

"And what exactly," Nicole says sarcastically, "is the *desired effect?*"

"The *desired effect,* Nicki dear, is to make our friend Ryan here human."

"And what is he now?"

"Less than human."

"Or, perhaps," Eriq says, raising an eyebrow at me, "more human than human."

"Hey," Brad says, snapping his fingers excitedly and pointing at Eriq, "that's a line from, from, from *Blade Runner,* when Harrison Ford is —"

"Oh, for Christ's sake, Brad," Daphne says, cutting him off. "Just once I'd like to go an evening without you referencing a TV show or a movie."

"May I remind you Daphne that *you* watch TV and movies too," Nicole responds haughtily.

"May I remind *you* Nicole that I don't spend my time relating everything someone does or says to something I saw in a movie or on some TV show. I'm sick of always hearing you and Brad say things like, 'Her hair looks like Winona Ryder's' or 'Your lips are exactly the same as Angelina Jolie's,' or 'He looks like James Gandolfini from *The Sopranos,*' or even worse is when someone's talking about something and one of you cuts in with, 'Hey, that reminds me of that *Seinfeld* episode where Kramer was —,' or

'Hey, that's like on *Friends* when Monica goes out and —,' I mean, do either of you have any idea how refreshing it is to have a conversation where someone isn't constantly retrieving metaphors from mainstream media?"

"Everyone does that," Nicole says.

"If a billion people believe in a dumb idea Nicole, it's still a dumb idea. We're already inundated with enough pop culture mind candy that we don't need your fiancé infecting our conversation with it every time we get together. I mean, read a fucking book for a change, Beamer Boy. Get thee to a bookstore and expand your view of the world beyond the bloody TV or movie screen."

"Brad already has *plenty* of books."

Daphne rolls her eyes. "We're all aware of Beamer Boy's infamous book collection, Nickelhead. But I'm *not* talking about a *collection* of books sitting on some bloody over-priced antique shelving unit. I'm *not* talking about having something pretty to look at when you pull your eyes away from the TV screen for a few seconds. I'm talking about shutting off the TV and actually taking the books off the shelf and *reading* them."

At this moment our waiter stops by the table to take another drink order and when he leaves, Nicole, using her matter-of-fact voice, states, "I don't have time to read."

"Of course not," Daphne snaps, her face hardening, eyes seething with disgust. "You're too busy browsing through all your adult *picture* books."

Nicole, worried that others may have heard Daphne, makes a furtive, anxiety-ridden visual sweep of the surrounding tables before replying, resolutely, "I do *not* read pornography."

"I was referring to your subscriptions to *Cosmo, Glamour, Vogue, Victoria's Secret, J. Crew, L. L. Bean* —"

"I think Nicole's right," I say. "People are too busy nowadays to read. Besides —"

"Too busy?" Daphne sneers, interrupting me. "Doing what? Surfing the 'Net for something to buy on eBay? Sipping cappuccinos in some café hoping to be discovered? Being entertained by some insipid TV sitcom or movie-of-the-week?"

"Here we are now, entertain us," Eriq says.

"Thoreau?" I ask, smiling.

"Cobain," Eriq corrects.

I smack my forehead. "I feel so stupid."

"You know something," Eriq says, his face now gripped by a severely confused expression, "I think it's, I think it's c-o-n-t-a-g-i-o-u-s."

Daphne gives Eriq the finger again before quickly rotating her wrist in my direction, prompting Eriq to say, "You know, it would save time if you held that finger up permanently and just rotated your wrist in the direction of differing opinions," to which Daphne responds by mouthing the words 'Fuck. You. Eriq.' and rotating her wrist in his direction so she's now giving him the finger before saying, out loud, "If a million words stand between you and the truth, isn't the time and effort required to read the million words worth it?"

"Thoreau?" Brad asks.

"Nietzsche — paraphrased," Eriq answers.

"How many pages is a million words?" Nicole asks.

"Roughly four thousand," Eriq says. "The length of about fifteen novels."

"Fifteen novels?" I say, whistling. "I think I'll wait for the mini-series."

Eriq, who I'm now focusing on, shifts his attention immediately to Daphne who, when I look at her, looks as though she's about to have an aneurysm — either that or tear off one of my arms and beat me silly with it — prompting Eriq to say, "I think Ryan's right. There's nothing better than watching a good book. Besides, reading is so passé."

"And I suppose watching TV is for the *avant-garde?*" Daphne snaps at him.

"That's *not* what I'm saying."

"Then what *are* you saying?"

"I'm saying," Eriq says, pausing to take a long sip of his Heineken, long enough to create the dramatic pause effect but short enough not to diminish the attention span of his audience, "I'm saying that when Gutenberg invented moveable type in 1454 people feared the oral tradition of storytelling would be replaced, lost, or regarded as a lower form of communication. They were upset that information previously communicated by word-of-mouth was now being written, coded in text, and that access to this information would be restricted to only those persons who could read — which, in many cases, is exactly what happened. Now book people, the *literati*, are upset because the world is adopting a more image-based communication system, because we're telling stories and sharing information via pictures, because more and more of our would-be novelists are opting to write ad copy or sitcoms or screenplays or TV commercials, because more and more of the novels and short stories that *are* published nowadays are being formatted in advance to fit the TV or movie screen."

"The TV has become mightier than the pen," Brad says, grinning foolishly, over-pleased with himself.

Daphne groans, is about to offer a rebuttal when I say, "It's true," coming to Brad's defence. "If you want something to enter into public discourse, if you want a topic, an issue, an idea — even a book — to be on everyone's minds, to become part of the collective consciousness, it *has* to appear on TV."

"Just like Oprah's Book of the Month Club," Nicole says, looking at me for confirmation.

"A perfect example. Thank you, Nicole," I say, smiling with appreciation at her before turning back to Daphne and saying,

"Oprah's done more for the book industry than any one person in history, and how has she done it? By having the number-one rated *TV* talk show in the world. I'm telling you, if you want an idea, an invention, or a book to infect the people of the world faster than the bubonic plague, get it on TV, preferably on Oprah, MTV, or CNN."

"Just remember, morons," Daphne says, "that something gets destroyed when something is created."

"And what, may I ask, is getting destroyed by watching TV?" Nicole asks.

"Duh, gee Nicole, let's see. How about deep thought, contemplation, reflection — you know, the three things you and TV are incapable of because just like your brain, the medium of television can't sit still long enough for these things to take place. TV — especially TV news and TV talk shows — doesn't allow for any in-depth coverage or dialogue or debate on issues because it's too busy zooming off to the next scene, the next image, the next commercial, the next hot topic, the next whatever. Television can't sit still. In fact, it can't even slow down, which makes any sort of deep understanding or involvement in issues almost impossible because the average person requires time to contemplate issues like education or the economy or the environment or health care in order to fully understand them. And *that's* the problem. Because what most people don't realize is that contemplating or reflecting deeply gets you to insights that you can never get to if you're just rushing through a question or an issue or from one topic to the next. If all you've got to go on are fifteen-second news fragments, entertaining image-based commentaries, and two-minute pre-packaged 'in-depth' reports, how can you possibly be informed, how can —"

"You ever wonder what got destroyed by books?" Eriq says, interrupting Daphne.

"You mean aside from things like irrational thought, soothsaying, conjecture, speculation, myth, assumpt —"

"Books," Eriq says, again interrupting her, "forced our lives, our thoughts, our experiences onto the page, into words, relegating our other senses such as taste, smell, and hearing to second-, third-, or fourth-rate status. Pre-alphabet cultures never did this. They incorporated all senses into an experience. They didn't try to confine experience to words, to reduce life to the printed page. Books have segregated our senses, severed us from our environment —"

"Books," Daphne snaps, returning Eriq's interruption, "have the ability to *extend* and *amplify* our senses. And as for severing us from our environment, that's probably not only a good thing, but a necessary one. Have you looked around at this world of ours lately? Tell me we don't need some type of severance from our environment, from this constant attack on our senses by hyper-electronic media? Now more than ever we need the solace of a book."

"The word *solace*, Daphne," Eriq says, "isn't that far removed from the word *isolation*, which is my point: reading is an isolating activity. And since Gutenberg's invention we have become physical and mental extensions of books — insular, isolated beings with —"

"Better than becoming an extension of TV," she snaps back. "Better than having a brain that's unable to sit still or contemplate anything longer than a nanosecond because it's too busy flicking around, wondering where the next oversensationalized, undercontextualized tidbit of information is going to . . ."

Before I continue narrating Daphne's rant, I'll mention (in case you were wondering), what everyone's doing at the moment:

- Nicole has taken out her cigarette case and with her eyes closed (as though she's reading Braille) is alternately running her emaciated fingers over the design of the Hindu god, Vishnu, and the scars on her wrists,

– Brad appears to be genuinely interested in what Daphne's saying but seems also to be slightly put off by the fact that he's being scolded in the process,
– Eriq is slowly massaging his left temple with his left index finger and wearing a furrowed brow, making him look quite contemplative which, if I didn't know him better, might make me believe he was seriously thinking about what Daphne is saying right now but since I *do* know him better, I know he's probably only giving the *impression* that he's seriously thinking about what she's saying and that what he's *really* doing is thinking of a witty remark to throw back in his sister's face while,
– I am imagining an overhead cam shot, momentarily suspended above our heads before abruptly swooping down, the screen dividing into five parts, one camera on each of Daphne, Eriq, Brad, Nicole, and myself, the camera that's on me situated just behind me, watching me watching the four others on the divided screen, while a) wondering if it's possible to create any more drama, any more tension in this particular scene and b) being reminded (as I watch Daphne preaching) of my uncle Jack, a priest, who seemingly had an answer for every situation prepared well in advance: locked, loaded, ready to Fire! just waiting for the right question or the right circumstance to trigger its release.

The only time I saw my uncle Jack delay his response was when I asked him if Christ's crucifixion wasn't really just a rational suicide.

It was Easter Monday, three days after my sister Jennie's suicide on Good Friday and three hours before her funeral would start and Rebecca, just prior to our families sitting down to lunch at my parents' place, told me to ask our uncle Jack the question immediately after he said grace and when I did there was more than a temporary or thoughtful delay as he considered my question; in fact, judging by the 'deer-caught- in-headlights' expression he was wearing the moment after I posed the question, it seemed likely that, just like Rebecca predicted, he quickly accessed his inventory of prefabricated responses and realized there wasn't a response waiting in storage for him, which is probably why (as Rebecca also predicted) he then switched to the 'How dare you ask such a question at this time,' expression being worn by my parents and Rebecca's parents before eventually getting rid of it and saying, after reassuring our parents it was okay, that it was something he and I would discuss at another time.

Of course, throughout dinner, I noticed — by the way he was now looking at me from across the dinner table — that it wasn't okay, that he was seeing things from a place, an angle he hadn't known existed; that though it may have been God's will, Christ still had a choice, and that given the condition of the Earth and its people, Christ's choice was to take his own life.

very little direction

Daphne is still talking at us and I notice Eriq's left index finger, though still making small circles on his temple, has slowed considerably and, after Daphne says, "which is probably why every time you open your mouth what comes out sounds more and more like a beer ad — 'Sounds Great, Less Filling,'" the finger stops circling and Eriq says, his voice edged with sarcasm, "So, if what's coming out of our mouths sounds like a beer ad, are we to assume that what comes out of your mouth resembles a cough syrup ad, 'Sounds awful, but it works'?"

The comment causes Brad to chuckle and prompts Nicole to stop caressing her scars and say — whisper, actually — "I agree, they do sound awful," and then, after her fingers are once again on the cigarette case, tracing the design, add (almost as an aside to herself, as though the rest of us are no longer here and she's sitting alone at the table talking to the case), "I wonder why that is? I wonder why Daphne's topics, her *remedies* are so difficult to listen to, so upsetting, so . . . so disturbing?"

"You know what disturbing is, Nic-o-tine?" Daphne says, snatching the cigarette case out of Nicole's hand, causing Nicole to recoil in fear-slash-confusion and the rest of us to watch Daphne punctuate her sentences by repeatedly jabbing the cigarette case at Nicole each time she says the word 'Disturbing' in the following rant:

"*Disturbing* is the fact that we're a culture of people who know the names of all the actors, supermodels, and sports figures but if you ask us the name of the trees or plants or neighbours we pass by every single day we'll shrug our shoulders and say, 'I don't know,' or 'I don't care,' or something equally as brilliant. *Disturbing* is how many people can watch a thirty-second segment on *Headline News* or a two-minute 'in-depth' report on CNN and suddenly feel qualified to give their opinion or debate issues like the economy or health care or terrorism or the environment. *Disturbing* is how TV thoroughly consumes our lives. *Disturbing* is how we've been raised on TV, how there are entire generations of people out there right now who get their news, their leisure, their style, their thoughts, their values, their conversations from TV, from whoever and whatever the TV decides is hip or cool or awesome or newsworthy or relevant at that particular moment. *Disturbing* is how I can't even begin to tell you how many times I've heard you and Brad talking — for hours — about TV people. *Disturbing* is listening to the two of you go on and on about what Jennifer Lopez wore to the Grammys, who's been kicked off *Survivor*, what Shaquille O'Neal or George Clooney said during an interview, who Carmen Electra is supposedly sleeping with or what Courteney Cox and Matthew Perry discussed during the latest episode of *Friends* as though it was absolutely *vital* to your existence. *Disturbing* is that you are *capable* of talking about TV people to this extent. *Disturbing* is that you actually know more about the lives of TV actors — *people you've never even met before* — than you do about the lives of your own friends. *That's* disturbing."

It now seems as if the entire restaurant has been sucked into silence and we're all looking at each other, waiting for someone to say something and it's not until Nicole gives Brad a 'Well, aren't you going to say something' look that he says, "Not *all* TV is bad," which, although he's right and I'm thinking about saying so, maybe even providing Daphne with a list of examples — not only of good TV, but also of why some TV is good — I don't, mainly because I want to hear Daphne's immediate response.

"No, Brad, you're right," Daphne says, "not *all* TV is bad. But the fact is, ninety-five percent of what's on TV doesn't do anything to elevate the mind. It's all for *entertainment*. And because we're so busy being entertained, no one — including you — ever stops to wonder, 'Why are we being so *entertained?*' Is being *entertained* by five hundred channels, by twenty-four-hour sports stations, shopping stations, talk shows, and soap operas the raison d'être of humanity? Is this the pinnacle of our existence? Is this what we're all striving for? Or is it just that our lives are so pathetic, so empty, and our current economic and political systems have failed us so miserably that we need this to cope, to help us forget what we've done to ourselves and the rest of the planet?"

Again there is a momentary pause as everyone remains silent — perhaps too stunned to speak, perhaps formulating a convincing rebuttal, perhaps realizing that they're all rhetorical questions — until Eriq breaks the silence by saying, "And that, Ladies and Gentlemen, is the reason people should continue watching TV and rarely, if ever, pick up a book. I mean, can you imagine walking around with that sort of logic in your head? You'd probably end up bashing everyone over the head with it any chance you got."

As Daphne slowly uncoils her middle finger while glaring at Eriq, it suddenly occurs to me that I've done very little directing tonight. 'Most of the time,' Rebecca wrote (on page 21), 'reality needs constant direction in order to be liveable, let alone filmable. However, every once in a while you'll assemble a group of people who seem to require very little direction, which is probably why finding the right cast of characters is more than half the battle for a director. With the right cast, direction becomes virtually unnecessary; you merely sit back and allow the cast's inherent antagonisms, conflicts, and motivations to direct the narrative, develop the characters, create the storyline, and advance the plot.'

Before Rebecca and I brought everyone together eight months ago at Jump Café,
– Daphne and Nicole hadn't spoken to each other in four years,
– Eriq and Daphne hadn't spoken in over five years,
– Eriq and Brad had never met, nor had Daphne and Brad or Nicole and Eriq and although it took a considerable effort to bring them all together, Rebecca and I discovered it required considerably less to get them to continue meeting as regularly as we do. From the outset they seemed to be enchanted by the friction, the drama, the *scenes* produced by the mixing of their personalities and, like a good TV audience, kept coming back week after week, unable or unwilling to miss an episode.

making another scene

"You know," I say, after pretending to clear my throat to attract everyone's attention, "I think we should make TV producers do what food producers are required to do on food packages — list the ingredients of their programs, the percentage of fat and sugar and protein, like the total nutritive value of each program, so we all know what we'll be putting into our minds if we decide to watch it."

For a moment I actually think Daphne might like the idea, thinking it isn't so far-fetched, but then Eriq lurches forward, nearly knocking over his glass of Heineken in the process, and starts laughing and so does Brad, and then Nicole, who's not laughing yet but is trying to, says, sarcastically, "That's a wonderful idea, Ryan," and Eriq adds, "Yes, absolutely wonderful. Let's call the networks tomorrow and tell them of your plan."

When Daphne looks at me (probably to see if I was joking) I'm wearing a dismayed-slash-bewildered look that suggests I was serious and have no intention of laughing along with the others and after she glares at the other three for a few seconds she says, "Laugh it up, morons. Keep sucking on your TV sets. Keep inhaling all the mind candy despite the warnings and soon there'll be a cavity where your brain used to be and Ryan here will be taking care of you."

"Oh, really? Now *that* seems like an interesting proposition," Eriq says, winking at me. "Will you take care of me Ryan dear?"

"I'm pretty sure a person can't get an acquired brain injury from watching TV," Brad says, "in fact —"

"Really?" Daphne says, cutting him off. "Well, judging by the collective idiocy and lack of common sense sitting across from me at the moment, I'd beg to differ."

At this point in the conversation our waiter returns and it's as I'm watching the waiter place our drinks on the table that I glimpse a flash of flame leaping out of a pan in the open kitchen and instantly see myself on fire, engulfed in flames, the image immediately merging with the framed photograph of the Buddhist monk who set himself on fire in protest of the Vietnam War (on display in the bathroom at The Suicide Loft) — and as I picture myself serenely burning I try thinking of a cause I would want to attach my suicide to. The homeless? The destruction of old growth forests? Tibet? East Timor? AIDS? NAFTA? Bill 101? The fact that we have the technology to build a space station but can't or won't feed people? The policies of the WTO? And it's as I'm realizing these are all reasons stated by various people in their suicidE-mails as to why they can't possibly go on living that Brad, after our waiter leaves, continues what he was going to say before being cut off by Daphne, telling us that he believes TV has actually raised everyone's level of intelligence, that we're far more knowledgeable than we were fifty, even twenty years ago.

"And what have we done with this increase in TV-derived intelligence and knowledge, Beamer Boy?" Daphne snorts. "We've merely become more intelligent polluters and more knowledgeable consumers of unnecessary products. Everything we've learned has been lost on us, wasted. It's what Alfred North Whitehead called 'inert knowledge,' knowledge we have but don't use because we haven't the capacity or the willingness to do anything with it. What TV has done is increased everyone's level of passivity. We're no longer the producers or directors of our lives; we're the viewers. Our minds have dried up and we're all residing in a mental nursing home being fed our lives, our ideas, and our values by TV, accepting everything without scrutiny, without investigation, without analysis, without a mental fight because *that* part of our brains has either shut down or become inaccessible since the neurons regulating these activities have fallen into disuse. . . ."

At this point in Daphne's rant I notice Eriq is completely

riveted to her, as is Brad; in fact, she's got everyone's attention, even the people sitting at the nearby tables (including the chartreuse-chemised woman).

"I mean, what's the sense in learning something if you aren't going to use it?" Daphne is now saying. "What's the point of knowing that The Gap or Nike or some other retailer is using sweatshop labour if we continue to buy their products? And not only that, what's the point in having an idea if there was no mental fight involved in its formation? Common sense implies that there be a mental fight involved in the formulation of our ideas. But with TV there's none of this. We're allowing this stuff access to our brains, to *children's* brains, without a fight, without scrutiny, without a challenge, and it's making us increasingly dependent and increasingly controllable and —"

For a few moments I consider asking Daphne to stand up and take a bow, crowning her this evening's debating champion, but Eriq does her an even bigger compliment by saying, without a trace of sarcasm, "So, what you're saying is what's going on today is, instead of Pavlov ringing the bell and the dogs salivating, we've got someone like Oprah speaking and the rest of us automatically listening, Oprah saying, 'It's true,' and the rest of us obediently nodding our heads, Oprah shedding a tear and the rest of us reaching for our Kleenex boxes, Oprah telling us to buy this book and the rest of us stampeding to the bookstore to buy it?"

"Exactly. I mean, can you imagine what would happen if Oprah cancelled her Book Club? People wouldn't know what to read anymore. The sad truth is the more we continue handing control of our lives, our minds, our decisions, our ideas over to Oprah, to CNN, to MTV, to technology, to whatever, the more chance we have of winding up like . . . like —"

"Like in *Terminator* 2 when —"

Daphne growls, actually growls, before shooting Brad a look like she's about to rip out his tongue and stuff it down his throat.

"What?" Brad says, a wounded expression on his face. "It proves your point about humans depending too much on machines and losing control of their —"

"Sometimes dependency isn't such a bad thing," Nicole says softly, placing her hand quietly on Brad's right wrist and beginning to caress its unscarred surface. "In fact," she continues, doing her best to ignore Daphne who is now looking at her like she's completely crazy, "I think dependency is natural. It's part of being human and people shouldn't be made to feel inadequate or idiotic because they feel they need help from others. There's nothing wrong with reaching out to other people for help or receiving advice and counselling and —"

"We interrupt our regularly scheduled program to bring you this special News Bulletin sponsored, in part, by our Patient of the Millennium, the woman who's reached out to more therapists than an Oprah audience, the one who flew *into* the Cuckoo's Nest and liked it so much she decided to stay, the always-dependent, always-a-patient, Ms. Nicole Chambers," Daphne says and then, after donning a sceptical expression, she says to Nicole, "You wouldn't happen to be the spokesperson for Dr. McPhilsly's, would you?"

"Dr. McPhilsly is a smart woman."

"Smart enough to trick you and your Master's Degree in Psychology into believing the whole world should be in therapy, Nicole."

"Speaking of the good doctor," I say, my tone nonchalant, non-threatening. "When *are* we going to meet this psychologist friend of yours? She sounds so, so —"

"Manipulative?" Daphne says, but I shake my head and, trying to look as harmless as possible, say, *"Intriguing."*

"Well," Nicole starts to say, then pauses, making me wonder if she's picked up on my intent, then, just as I'm crossing my fingers, she continues, saying, "she'll be at the wedding."

"You've invited her?" Brad says, not angry or put off, just surprised.

"I'm thinking about asking her to be one of my bridesmaids."

"A bridesmaid!" Daphne nearly shouts, momentarily drumming her fingernails excitedly on the table before continuing to speak in exclamation points. "Christ! You've known this woman for what, four months, and she's already your bridesmaid! In another five sessions she'll be your Maid of Honour! In ten, she'll be your groom! You better watch out, Beamer Boy, I think your fiancée's true colours are beginning to shine through!"

Nicole blushes — deeply this time, the skin along her jawline tightening, becoming increasingly pale, her lips once again starting to tremble.

"What's the matter, Nicki dear," Daphne says, raising an eyebrow and giving her a knowing look. "Did I hit a *soft* spot?"

Nicole starts crying, her face crumbling into tears, and, after grabbing her purse and pushing Brad out of the booth, she runs out of the restaurant.

"Happy?" Brad says in a hushed, borderline angry tone while leaning toward our table, looking like he's about to sit back down but remaining standing.

"Happy? Why should I be happy?" Daphne says, waving her hand dismissively at him. "Nicole's the one who should be happy. Nearly everyone in the restaurant noticed her. I did her a favour. She was seen making a scene. What could possibly be more rewarding for her? Now she and her damn psychologist Dr. McPhilsly can talk about how this incident has irreparably traumatized her. Hell, she'll probably get diagnosed with post-traumatic stress disorder and get her daily dosage of Paxil increased."

"Why do you insist on punishing her?" I say.

"Punishing her?" Daphne says incredulously, not picking up on my mock chastising tone because of the amount of alcohol she's consumed. "You think that's what I'm doing?"

"You know she's ill," I say.

"She's *not* —"

"Ill?!" Daphne shouts, interrupting Brad. "For Christ's sake, Ryan, her family doctor said she might — *might* — be suffering from Seasonal Affective Disorder because five months ago, just like nearly everyone else living north of the 49th parallel, she was feeling a little *down* because of the weather and the shorter days. And, in case you haven't noticed, it's the beginning of June now and we're only a couple weeks away from the *longest* day of the year. What started out as *one* season of Affective Disorder seems to have migrated into all *four* seasons."

"I'm sure she has other . . . issues," Eriq says, nearly bursting.

"Of course she does, there are always more *issues* with Nicole. *If you label it, Nicole will become it.* But excuse me if I don't care to indulge her manufactured illnesses."

"They're *not* manufactured," Brad says.

"Well if they're not, Beamer Boy, then how come Nicole never knew she had them until she started seeing a psychologist?"

"That has nothing to do —"

"Bullshit! If Nicole didn't have any money this Dr. McPhilsly woman wouldn't have even seen her. It's all about money, about creating a dependence."

"I think it might be time to change the channel," I say, realizing the situation (in other words — Daphne) is in jeopardy of getting out of control.

"Yes, please, let's drop this," Eriq says, perhaps agreeing with me that the drama in this scene is too much, too over-the-top, perhaps voicing the opinions of the other dinner guests who have stopped glancing at our table every few seconds and are now staring at us, or — and this is probably closer to the truth than the previous two — perhaps realizing that if the subject matter doesn't change and change soon it's going to destroy his chances of sleeping with Brad tonight.

Daphne, however, has no intention of changing the channel or dropping anything.

"Ever wonder why it's only the people who can *afford* therapy who are *in* therapy?" she says.

"There's more to it than that," Brad says, "a *lot* more."

"I know there is," Daphne snaps. "And the *more* is that your fiancée has fallen in love with her *perceived* dysfunctions *and* the woman who gave them to her."

"Nicole is *not* in love with her psychologist."

"How do you know? Have you asked her?"

"Daphne, you're so far off base —"

"Am I? I've known Nicole for more than eight years. You've known her for what, two and a half? Before you start telling me how far off base I am, you might want to find out what she was like *before* you met her. Nicole's life did not start, nor is it likely to end, with a ride on the big Beamer."

Brad opens his mouth, starts to say something, then shakes his head and turns to leave.

"No, don't," Eriq says, taking hold of Brad's arm, "don't leave. At least not without me. We can go to the rave."

"I'm sorry, Eriq," Brad says, gently breaking free of Eriq's hold and starting to walk away from the table. "I have to go, really. Maybe next time."

Eriq sighs, shakes his head while watching Brad leave. "Great, just great," he says. "La Petite Misère strikes again."

"Oh, go stare yourself into a catatonic stupor, Patrice," Daphne replies before swallowing the last mouthful of scotch left in her glass.

open relationship

When I get back to my apartment just after midnight, Renaldo, the superintendent, is closing the door to the third floor hallway, something he normally does every night at 11:00 p.m. for fire safety.

Dressed in a baby blue satin housecoat and flip-flops, he jumps when he turns around and sees me, his hands reflexively clutching his heart.

"Oh my God you scared me," he says, before exhaling forcefully. "I almost had a heart attack."

I apologize and with his right hand still over his heart, he waves his left hand and tells me it's okay, "I'm probably still a little jumpy from the dream I just had. I dreamt the building was on fire and I couldn't get out of my apartment." Then, after telling me he can actually feel his heart pounding in his chest he motions to the door and says, "I forgot to close the doors at 11:00. My subconscious must've known it."

Since I'm not in the mood for conversation I forge what I think is an agreeable expression for the circumstance, hoping this will be enough for me to get by him without further comment, but it's not.

"Rebecca back from vacation yet?" he asks, reaching for the door handle but not opening it.

Renaldo, who is gay and was thrilled to hear that I was (I'm not), had no problem with Rebecca moving into my one-bedroom apartment with me about six months ago because I told him (whispered, actually) that Rebecca was a transsexual (she's not) and that we were lovers (we're not), then asked Renaldo, made him swear, actually (which he did), to not let on he knew anything, that Rebecca hadn't told anyone yet, that her parents were *very* Catholic and would be *absolutely mortified* if they knew. By this point, I'd been watching Rebecca concoct 'impromptu screenplays' for almost three months and I remember thinking at the time that I'd concocted a slightly outrageous, yet still believable screenplay of my own for Renaldo — a screenplay that I was sure Rebecca would not only enjoy but also admire — but when she heard of it, she shouted 'Bloody hell!' about a dozen times and then proceeded to tell me I'd overstepped my bounds, made use of a poetic licence I hadn't yet earned and it was only after I reassured her that Renaldo would never say anything to anyone and informed her I was charging her only $200 a month for rent *and* letting her use the only bedroom in the apartment that she stopped reprimanding me about my impromptu screenplay.

Anyway, every time I run into Renaldo he asks me about Rebecca and two weeks ago I told him she was vacationing in Colombia and was due back in a couple of weeks.

"No," I say, "he's, I mean, *she's* not back yet. In fact, she called yesterday to say she's extending her trip a few more weeks."

"Must be nice. Where is she again — Colombia?"

"Costa Rica," I say, causing Renaldo to scrunch his face and give me an 'I thought for sure you told me she was vacationing in Colombia' expression, which, by the time I'm finished saying, "When she called yesterday she said the beaches and the rainforests and the people in Costa Rica were so gorgeous and full of life she couldn't bear to tear herself away just yet," has been replaced by an envious, 'Costa Rica sounds like *so* much fun' expression.

"Costa Rica sounds like *so* much fun," Renaldo says. "I'll bet you wish you were there."

I shake my head. "Not really. All those bugs and mosquitoes and snakes and spiders and crawly things — yuck. I prefer the city." Then, after sighing, I say, "But, to each his or her own — that's my motto."

"You're very understanding, Ryan," he says, batting his eyes at me. "If my boy — I mean, *girl*friend — went off on a two-week vacation to Costa Rica and then called to say she was extending it a few weeks, I'd be *insanely* jealous. I couldn't help myself from thinking what she was up to."

"Well, we have a pretty open relationship."

"Is that so?" he says, suggestively, slowly opening the door for me.

I smile, say, "Thanks," adding, as I pass him, "Hope you sleep better now," and he giggles, then coos, "I'm sure I will," and a few seconds later I hear his flip-flops flopping down the stairs.

the apartment . . . rewinding, replaying, reviewing

I'm now sitting in the living room in Jennie's padded rocking chair — the one I sat in while watching her commit suicide — and after I hit rewind on the VCR (I want to rewatch an episode of *The X-Files*) and chase three Smarties with a swig of Lowenbrau and two puffs of my Colt Mild wine-tipped cigar while gazing out the window overlooking Queen Street, my thoughts begin rewinding, replaying the conversations we had at Rain, instinctively editing the dialogue, re-arranging who said what, doing a quick rewrite, making it more suitable for a TV audience, before reviewing what happened after we left the restaurant, which was:

– Eriq inviting me to the rave,
– me declining,
– Eriq hailing a cab at King and John,
– Daphne and I continuing up John Street together until hearing someone, a man, frantically calling her name from across the street — at which point she hailed an approaching cab, quickly getting in and zipping away

before the man could make his way across the street,
– me standing there, slightly dumbfounded, alternately watching the cab heading west on King Street and the man approaching me,
– the cab disappearing from sight,
– the man, now beside me, extending his hand, introducing himself as Josh Sebring before asking, politely, if that was Daphne Garceau who just got into the cab,
– me replying that it was,
– Josh wondering why Daphne hadn't stopped to say 'Hi,'
– me making an excuse for Daphne, telling Josh that she had a very urgent engagement across town that she was already too late for,
– Josh sighing, saying that it was unfortunate he'd missed her, that he hadn't seen Daphne in months and would've loved to speak with her, that he was certain he had something that she'd be interested in, providing she was still in the business,
– me, after promising Josh that I would give Daphne his business card, walking alone up John Street, past Hooters, past the same middle-aged man sitting in the same place on the sidewalk wearing the same expression, past the sight of a young woman with lollipops glued to her clothes being paraded around in front of Al Frisco's restaurant, her friends requesting passersby — men and women — to pluck the lollipops off with their teeth while one of her friends film the action with a camcorder, past the two girls kissing aggressively beneath the Public Parking sign on Richmond Street,
– me pausing then stopping near the entrance to Fluid nightclub when I see the auburn-haired, chartreuse-chemised woman from Rain watching the blue-eyed, Aldo-shoed guy talking to one of the bouncers, a big burly

black man weighing at least 250 pounds who is telling the Aldo-shoed guy he's not allowed in because of what he's wearing and the Aldo-shoed guy, after looking at his leather loafers, khakis, dress shirt and then giving the bouncer a 'You *can't* be serious' look, saying, "Do you realize how ironic this is, that you're denying me *access* to this club, that I'm being *discriminated* against because of my *clothes*? What's next, body fat percentages? All doormen will be equipped with fat callipers and take measurements before letting people in?" and the bouncer telling the Aldo-shoed guy he should get moving — *"Right fucking now bud, if you know what's good for you"* — and the auburn-haired, chartreuse-chemised woman taking hold of the Aldo-shoed guy's arm and leading him across the street to Whiskey Saigon,

– me walking up Duncan Street to Queen Street and making a phone call to someone at 10:32 p.m., asking the woman who answers what method of suicide she prefers, listening to her, instead of answering my question, asking me in a reasonably concerned tone if I need help and without waiting for my response giving me the Suicide Hotline number and then hanging up,

– me wandering around Queen Street, thinking about rooting through the garbage can in front of The Black Bull Restaurant for a set of keys to a Pontiac Grand Prix,

– me getting on the 501 Neville Park streetcar at University and Queen and moments later, at Yonge, seeing the Sarah Polley look-alike from Starbucks getting on, her not noticing me, thankfully, because I'm seated near the back,

– me reading another five or six suicidE-mails then closing my eyes and listening to the Sarah Polley look-alike talking to the driver, her voice soothing, comforting, hopeful, drifting back to me, embroidering my increasingly vacant thoughts until it's gone and I wake with a start realizing

that the streetcar is empty and is now pulling into the loop at Neville Park — the end of the line — and I've missed my stop,
– me, after dropping a few business cards for The Suicide Loft on several seats, getting off the streetcar and walking to the Hasty Market convenience store where I buy a big box of Smarties and a pack of Colt Mild wine-tipped cigars,
– me arriving at my apartment building and scaring Renaldo, the sight of him clutching his heart, telling me he could feel his heart pounding in his chest, that he felt like he was going to have a heart attack and,

it's at this point when I stop and think about the possibility of this, of having — what's the term, sudden cardiac death? — that I begin recalling the times when I thought I was going to have a heart attack: last fall on the Peace Bridge in Niagara Falls when Rebecca and I had a gun pulled on us by two guys in a souped-up Toyota Celica; five summers ago in Oregon, in Eugene-fucking-Oregon during the Oregon County Fair, when a bunch of neo-conservative right-wing hippie-haters wearing (and I'm not making this up) three-piece business suits and brandishing scissors and metal-tipped canes told me they were going to cut off my ponytail and cane me; the time I was on a solo hiking trip along the West Coast Trail and walked around a large clump of trees and saw this grizzly bear sniffing the wind probably only fifteen feet from me; the time when I was at a party in Hamilton and some guy (after consuming about a dozen beers) decided it'd be a good idea to retrieve the chainsaw from the back of his pickup truck and come running into the living room with it on full throttle screaming 'Here's Johnny!' which may have been funny *if* he didn't trip and the chainsaw *hadn't* come flying out of his hands, forcing some girl I didn't even know to yank me out of the way at the last possible instant, the chainsaw embedding itself deep into the section of the couch where I'd been sitting, gashing and shredding the fabric while bucking and snarling and flailing around like it was possessed, like something out of a Stephen King movie; at McMaster University during my first year when Brad and I and a couple of other guys were driving to Daytona Beach for Spring Break and it was Brad's turn at the wheel and after Brad had finished passing an 18-wheeler at eighty miles an hour but hadn't yet returned to our lane despite the fact that there was a mini-van rushing at us in the oncoming lane, I grabbed the steering wheel and yanked it, the car, us, into our lane just in time; the first time I saw Jennie after her suicide, waving to me from a street corner as I rode past on the 501 Neville Park streetcar; the first time I heard Rebecca's voice talking to me without her actually even being there. *In each one of these situations* I thought I was going to have a heart attack, could feel my heart pounding, stretching, reacting to the external event and so I spend some time wondering what types of things could induce enough fear, enough fright, for me to suffer sudden cardiac death, before pulling out my notepad and adding 'Sudden Cardiac Death' to my list of possibilities.

the top five kids

A while later, after I've eaten all but two of the Smarties, drunk two beers, smoked one cigar, and called four random numbers — getting three immediate hang-ups and one, 'Because I said so, psycho!' in response to me asking them to give me one good reason why I shouldn't kill myself right now — I find myself in the middle of fast-forwarding through the third set of commercials on the *X-Files* episode when I hear two people talking and immediately recognize the voices: it's the Top Five kids.

At least twice a week, usually on Fridays and Saturdays and usually after midnight, these two surprisingly cerebral and well-spoken teenagers sit on the stoop of the pharmacy below my apartment, pick a topic and then give each other their top five answers. Past topics have included naming the 'Top Five Places in Canada you've visited,' the 'Top Five Rumours you've started' (one of my favourites), the 'Top Five Things you thought you'd be before you were ten years old,' the 'Top Five Places in Toronto to read a book,' the 'Top Five Moments of regret,' the 'Top Five Things you'd do exactly the same even if you could do it over again,' and the 'Top Five Things you'd do if there were no consequences.'

After turning off the VCR and TV, I scooch the rocking chair closer to the open window and begin eavesdropping on their conversation, tuning in just in time to hear the boy say,

"Alright. I've got one. List your Top Five Moments of Amazement."

"Defined as?"

"Defined as moments where you have, I don't know, like an epiphany or something. When you've experienced something that totally blows you away, that like thoroughly stuns you."

"Good and bad?"

"Sure."

"Okay, well, once again, in no particular order — number one would definitely have to be discovering all these 'How to Raise Your Child' cassettes and videos in my parents' closet when they went away for holidays last year and me like realizing after listening to them and watching them that I'd been raised by other people's ideas and not my parents' ideas."

"Wow. That must've been — I don't know, weird, I guess."

"It was. All the things they said, how they said it, when they said it, even things we *did* came from these cassettes and videos. It was thoroughly bizarre."

"Sounds like it."

"Next would have to be my thirteenth birthday when I saw a truck plough into the kid across the street and kill him. He was coming over to my birthday party and me and several of my friends were in the window laughing at him because it was raining and he was standing at the intersection getting drenched. Then the light changed and he started walking and this truck, this big green 4 x 4, ran a red light and just completely creamed him."

"Holy crap. You never told me that."

"I've never told anyone that."

"Did you know the kid?"

"Not really. The only reason he was invited to my party was because we were neighbours and his older sister used to babysit me. She saw it too."

"His sister saw it happen?"

"Ya. She was standing in the front window of their house."

"That's sick."

"I know."

"So, like, was the kid . . . did he, like, die right away?"

"Instantly. Poof. Gone. The End."

"And what did his sister do?"

"I think she went into shock or something. She didn't even move from the window for like five minutes. She just stood there, watching. It was totally bizarre."

"What about the person driving the truck?"

"I think he got charged with reckless driving or something."

"That's it?"

"Ya, well, the guy just ran a red light. It wasn't like he was actually trying to kill the kid."

"I know but —"

"Okay, I don't mean to interrupt but I think we should move on to a lighter example. The next in my Top Five Moments of Amazement would be when I was ten and watching my baby sister being born. Seeing her come out of my mother like that was absolutely amazing. There she was, my baby sister, all gooey and pink and slimy and alive. A life. I think everyone should be a part of something like this. Every time I get mad or frustrated with her I just think about that moment, seeing her being born. It was amazing."

"That's cool."

"Next would be last week when I was standing in the cereal aisle at Sobey's completely stunned by the sheer number of choices. I mean, have you ever counted how many different brands of cereal there are? It's insane. Anyway, I stood there for a long time until one of the stock fillers tapped me on the shoulder and asked me if I was alright."

"No way."

"Yep. He was pretty cute too."

"Did you tell him what you were doing?"

"Ya, sort of. I told him I was so torn between Count Chocula, Frosted Flakes, and Froot Loops that it had rendered me catatonic."

"What'd he say?"

"He told me I should buy all three and mix them together."

"Count Chocula, Frosted Flakes, *and* Froot Loops together? That's gross."

"Don't worry, I didn't buy any of them. I like yogurt and granola for breakfast. Anyway, rounding out the Top Five would be realizing that I am a part of everything that's come before me and everything that will come after me."

"You sound like my uncle."

"It's true. I've been reading this big coffee table book at my grandmother's. It's *The National Geographic Society's* 100 *Years of Adventure and Discovery* and near the end of the book is — here, wait a sec. I made a photocopy of the page because I thought it was so cool, I put it in my purse. Here it is. It's an excerpt from an article written by this John Boslough guy and it's called 'Worlds Within the Atom': 'Some 2300 years ago the Greek philosophers Democritus and Leucippus proposed that if you cut an object, such as a loaf of bread, in half, and then half again and again until you could do it no longer, you would reach the ultimate building block. They called it the atom.'"

"They figured out the atom that long ago?"

"Yep."

"That's incredible."

"I know, but that's not even the best part. Listen to this: 'The atom is infinitesimal. Your every breath holds a trillion trillion atoms. And because atoms in the everyday world we inhabit are virtually indestructible, the air you suck into your lungs may include an atom or two gasped out by Democritus with his dying breath.'"

"Holy shit, can you imagine?"

"That's all I've been doing since I read it yesterday. I mean, if you think about it — Hitler's breath, Northrop Frye's, Susanna Moodie's, Bill Clinton's, Julia Hill's, Saddam Hussein's, Laura Secord's, Louis Riel's, Che Guevara's, Conrad Black's; as well as the smoke from SUVs, factories, cigarettes, the gas given off by building materials, by plants, animals, and birds — we breathe *all* this in, *all* of it goes into our lungs, gets absorbed by our bloodstream, becomes part of our cells, part of who we are — it's so friggin' mind-boggling. . . ."

Five minutes later, after waiting for one of them to speak, I quietly poke my head out the window and, looking down, see them gazing in opposite directions, one southeast, the other southwest, seemingly lost in their own thoughts.

Thirty minutes later, after watching them not speaking and not moving, I withdraw my head from the open window and retire to Rebecca's bedroom.

if I could turn back time

While lying in Rebecca's bed, which is something I've been doing since she left (it's considerably larger than the futon in the living-room-converted-into-my-bedroom I usually sleep on, plus there's a little less street noise in her room), I reread the last suicidE-mail I read while riding on the streetcar tonight before once again closing my eyes, flipping through the pages, inserting my index finger, opening my eyes, and

> *I feel so relieved at what I'm about to do; I've never had such clarity; it's as though the fog has lifted and I know what I must do; by the time you read this, I'll be dead; I'm pressing 'Send' and then, after confirming the message has been received, pulling the trigger on my father's shotgun . . .*
> *04/06/2001, Duluth, Minnesota*

It took my parents nearly three days to get back home from their trip; they had to wait until their cruise ship docked at a port in Puerto Rico. Sixty-eight hours after Jennie's death they were at the morgue, watching the attendant sliding her out of her temporary grave, my father almost immediately collapsing in a crumpled heap on the floor beside her frozen corpse.

Close eyes, flip pages, insert index finger, open eyes, and

> *Sometimes I pretend I'm just like everyone else.*
> *But I'm not.*
> *Everyone doesn't think about suicide nearly every minute of every day.*
> *I do.*
> *Everyone doesn't see themselves dying a hundred times a day.*
> *I do.*

Everyone doesn't want to be like me.
I do.
Everyone wonders why I don't want to be . . .
I don't.

June 5, 2001, Meaford, Ontario

 A few minutes after reading this last suicidE-mail the feeling that I'm being watched by Rebecca, that she's filming me with her camcorder, begins circulating through my body and before long I feel like she's actually in the room and after checking under the bed, I walk casually over to the closet door, yank it open, and after a few seconds of punching and pushing aside Rebecca's clothes and making sure the large vertical trunk where she keeps her disguises is locked I start chuckling at my paranoia until I hear a noise coming from somewhere in the apartment and after quietly opening the bedroom door and peering down the hallway I notice the flickering blue light from the TV casting shadows on the living room wall and, thinking it may be Rebecca, slowly tiptoe down the hallway and am just about to yell, 'Boo!' when I see my parents sitting on the loveseat and I'm so happy to see them together again that it's almost a full minute before I notice Rebecca is there too, sitting in the rocking chair, and that all three of them are watching TV, their eyes riveted to the scene of me sitting in Jennie's rocking chair calmly observing Jennie picking up the razor blade and bringing it towards her left —

 Lunging into the room I snatch the VCR remote control out of my mother's hand, jabbing the STOP button just as Jennie is about to make her first slice.

 "A little late for that, isn't it?" Rebecca says, her tone thoroughly sarcastic.

 "I can't believe you would do this," I shout, wheeling around to face her. "I can't believe you would actually do something like —"

"Careful, Ryan," she says, nodding her head in the direction of my parents, "you're upsetting our guests," and when I look I notice they haven't moved, that their eyes are still glued to the now blank screen, that they're still wearing the same horrified expressions they were a few moments ago and so I move closer to them, explaining as I approach, reassuring them that it wasn't my fault, that it was Rebecca who orchestrated the whole thing, that she directed me to do —

"I don't think they can hear you, Ryan," Rebecca says, interrupting my explanation. "Besides, even if they could, are you sure you'd want them to? I mean, do you really think there's a good enough explanation for what you did — or should I say, *didn't* do?"

"Rebecca, I swear. If you don't shut up, I'm going to kill you."

"My, my. First an assisted suicide and now a murder. You certainly are making your parents proud," she says. Then, smiling, she begins to sing, "'If I could turn back time. If I could find a way. . . .'"

Returning my gaze to my still catatonic parents, I begin pleading with them to snap out of it, my voice getting louder and louder, discharging volleys of apologies and excuses into the air — which is when I suddenly wake up, the sound of my screaming voice ringing in my ears, my hands instinctively wiping away the tears streaming down my face. . . .

a neat story

In the shower a few hours later I still feel more than slightly spooked, not by my dream or the fact that I woke up screaming and crying, but at discovering that the TV was actually on when

I was certain I'd turned it off prior to going to bed. Unable to find a rational explanation, I decide to put it down to fatigue and/or forgetfulness and begin mentally mapping out my morning, seeing myself wandering around Queen Street, browsing the store windows, pausing to read the menu at Satay, my favourite Thai restaurant in the Beaches, scanning the marquee to see what's playing at The Fox Cinema, stopping in at The Wholesome Foods Store to grab a couple of samosas and some hemp lip balm and then, after walking down to the lake, closing my eyes and opening my ears and nose and mouth and trying to form a mental picture of my surroundings from the various sounds and smells and tastes before getting ready for my first client at The Suicide Loft at 1:00 p.m.

While towel-drying my hair in the bedroom, I turn on the stereo and when Sarah McLachlan's 'Building a Mystery' comes on CBC Radio a few seconds later I tell myself I want to be dressed and ready to leave the apartment before the song is over, which is something I occasionally do since reading in my sister Jennie's journal that she's been doing it nearly every day since she turned sixteen.

She wrote that none of her friends could believe it only took her three songs (four at the most) from the moment her alarm clock went off to be showered, dressed, and out the door. 'I wish I had your hair,' they'd tell her. 'Mine's so unmanageable. It takes me twenty minutes just to product, style, and blow dry it,' or 'I wish I were like you and didn't need to wear make-up,' or 'I have so many clothes — it usually takes me an hour just to decide what to wear.' Although Jennie offered them her advice — 'Cut your hair, throw away your hair products and blow-dryers, don't wear make-up, and only buy clothes you actually need' — none of her friends ever took the advice.

Dressed and ready to go as Sarah is singing the last chorus, I'm about to leave when the phone for the outside apartment door rings and after sneaking up to the kitchen window, peering around the refrigerator and out the half-opened window to the street below I'm only mildly surprised to see Daphne standing there, looking up at Rebecca's bedroom window.

"Hey, what's this?" I hear Daphne shout from the living room.

"What's what?" I ask, coming out of the bathroom and starting to walk down the hallway towards the living room.

"This," she says, and I see she's pointing down at the box of Smarties, the three bottles of Lowenbrau, and two plastic Colt cigar tips in the ashtray.

"Oh, that? That's Renaldo's."

"Who?"

"Renaldo — he's the superintendent of the building. When I came home last night he was pacing around outside the building, smoking a cigar. He told me he couldn't sleep — hasn't been able to sleep, actually, since his lover left him. I kind of felt sorry for the guy so I invited him up and when I told him I didn't have anything to drink he asked if I'd be offended if he stopped by his apartment and got a few things and five minutes later this is what he showed up with."

"Your superintendent?"

I nod.

"Weird."

"Ya, I know. The really intriguing part was he'd eat three Smarties, then chase them with a swig of beer, and two puffs on his cigar. Always in that order: three Smarties, one swig of beer, and two puffs on the cigar."

"Are you serious?"

I nod.

"What happens if there's only one or two Smarties left in the box?"

I point to the box. "Pick it up."

She does, dumping two Smarties out in her hand. "He left them?" she asks, shaking her head.

I nod. "I think he said something about not wanting to disturb his karma."

"His what?"

I laugh. "Ya, I know. I thought the whole thing was a little odd at first too, but then I asked him about it and he said it was something he and his boyfriend used to do on Friday nights. The two of them would go out to dinner with their friends, usually some place downtown, some place expensive, then take the subway back, all the way to the end of the line, then walk to the Hasty Market just down the street here, buy two big boxes of Smarties, a pack of Colt wine-tipped cigars, walk to his apartment and sit in their matching Lazy-Boy chairs watching *The X-Files* and chasing three Smarties with one swig of Lowenbrau and two puffs on their cigars."

"You're *not* serious."

I nod.

"People. Are. Fucked. Up."

"Really? I thought it was a neat story. Kind of outrageous, but believable at the same time, you know? I mean, can't you just see the two of them sitting in their matching Lazy-Boy chairs, eating Smarties, drinking Lowenbrau, smoking cigars, and —"

"I get the picture Ryan — and trust me, it isn't worth another word."

I chuckle, and then, while walking out of the living room and heading back to the bathroom, say, "If I'm not mistaken, he brought over a six-pack and I think there's still three bottles left in the fridge. Help yourself if you want one."

"I think I'll pass."

"Not a fan of Lowenbrau?"

"Something like that."

unfortunate coincidences

"I really do miss her old wallpaper," Daphne says, suddenly, veering more than slightly off topic.

We've been sitting in the living room for about ten minutes now; Daphne on the padded rocking chair, me on the couch; Daphne (while gazing disapprovingly at the blank walls in the living room) giving me a lengthy synopsis of the first article she remembered reading at Rebecca's old place, explaining how U.S.-led UN sanctions in Iraq were responsible for the deaths of over a million people, more than half of them children, since the Gulf War; me (while watching her reflection in the blank TV screen) recalling how the after-image of Gillian Anderson had remained on the screen, glowing, for almost half a minute after I'd turned off the TV last night which, of course, made me think, 'See, I knew I'd turned off the TV before going to bed last night' and just as I was about to start replaying my dream, Daphne said, "I really do miss her old wallpaper."

She's referring to the wallpaper in Rebecca's old apartment. I took Daphne over there in early December (at Rebecca's request) four days after Rebecca took off the first time. The apartment was actually the one my sister Jennie used to live in and when she died, Rebecca took it over, the landlord allowing her to do so without raising the rent since she was Jennie's cousin.

Like growth rings on a tree, the walls in the apartment were plastered with layers and layers of poems, aphorisms, journal articles, essays, and short stories that Jennie had either collected or written over the years. Most of the articles were about what was happening to the Earth and to the people and animals and plants inhabiting Earth, and it wasn't long afterwards that Daphne began to take more than a passing interest in these sorts of things, bringing these issues with her to our Friday dinners at Jump Café and introducing them into our conversations.

"You know," she says while gently touching, then vigorously rubbing the beige painted wall beside her, perhaps hoping to uncover a poem or an aphorism, "I asked Rebecca a couple of months ago how long she thought she was going to be in this Blank Phase."

"And what'd she say?"

"She said she preferred to call it her 'Ode to Robert Motherwell,' phase."

"Who's Robert Motherwell?" I ask.

"That's exactly what I said."

"So who is he?"

"An artist — a painter, I think. And a writer."

"And why did Rebecca call it her 'Ode to Robert Motherwell'?"

"Because Motherwell said if you're going to create something — whether it's a painting or a novel or a movie — the challenge is not to diminish the original loveliness of the blank canvas."

"And what'd you say to that?"

"I told Rebecca I preferred her Idea Phase."

Almost exactly eight months ago, Rebecca and I were at the city library near Yonge and Bloor; Rebecca was doing some research on how to direct and produce videographies, I was reading a book about acquired brain injuries, when we both smelled the sweet scent of patchouli drift by us on the way to the book stacks.

Though Rebecca told me she'd always found the smell of patchouli extremely arousing, borderline erotic — and I agreed — she also told me she no longer bothered to see who the scent belonged to anymore because nine times out of ten the wearer — whether a man or a woman — turned out to be some neo-treehugger wearing hiking boots, khaki shorts, hairy legs, and a beard.

A few minutes later the smell drifted by again and this time Rebecca slid a piece of paper over to me on which she'd written,

'While other spirits sail on symphonies/Mine, my beloved, swims along your scent.'

"Keats?" I whispered, after reading it.

Not looking up from her work, Rebecca shook her head.

"Shelley?"

Another head shake.

"Poe?"

After shaking her head a third time I was about to whisper, 'Byron?' when a patchouli-scented hand snatched the piece of paper off the table and a moment later a voice stated, "Baudelaire."

Both the scent and the voice were attached to a soft, strikingly sensual face — a cross between Angelina Jolie and my sister Jennie — wearing a J. Crew spaghetti strap top, capri pants, leather mules, and a scorpion tattoo on her left ankle.

"Glad you like it," the woman said, referring to her scent, then, dropping the piece of paper on the table between us, she added, "though, the *beloved* comment might be a bit premature, don't you think?"

Slightly embarrassed at being caught passing notes about her, I smiled 'Hello' which she ignored, then said "Hello," which she replied to with, "Let me guess, you're an out-of-town grad student working on his Master's, right?"

"Actually, I'm an in-city therapist working with —"

"A *therapist?*" she groaned, cutting me off before I could tell her I worked with people who had acquired brain injuries. "How depressing."

"Excuse me?"

"Never mind," she said, waving her hand at me dismissively before turning her gaze on Rebecca and asking, "and what about you?"

During our brief exchange I'd noticed Rebecca hadn't yet looked up from her books, that she'd remained in her usual unobtrusive, 'I'm-trying-to-blend-in-with-the-furniture-while-eavesdropping-on-your-conversation' mode — except for one exception, she'd stopped reading, her eyes on PAUSE, frozen at a spot somewhere near the top of the page.

"Are you mute or just a fan of silent cinema?" the patchouli-scented woman asked her.

"Neither," I replied.

Groaning loudly, the woman turned back to me and said, "I take it you're either a *speech* therapist or just someone with the irritating habit of answering questions not addressed to you?"

Before I could respond she looked away and this time, while pointing at the collection of books surrounding Rebecca said, slowly, "And. What. About. You?" using her hands and fingers as though she were communicating in sign language while continuing to speak. "Are you a) a Master's student? b) a Ph.D. candidate? Or, yawn, yawn, c) just another dreary therapist?"

Thinking back on it now, it was probably the combination of her knowledge of poetry, her obvious dislike of therapy, and her ability to use sign language — all in the same minute — that caused Rebecca to take her eyes off her book, smile like I'd only ever seen her smile at my sister Jennie, and, while looking at the patchouli woman for the first time, use her hands in a similar fashion as the woman had and reply, "d) none of the above."

"You wouldn't believe how turned on I was the first time I saw her old apartment," Daphne says, now sticking her head out the open living-room-converted-into-my-bedroom window. Then, a few seconds later, after pulling her head back in, she adds. "I mean, I had a multiple mental orgasm right on the spot. I just kept coming and coming and coming," she says, giddily, breaking into a playful laugh. "I remember I had to close my eyes just to stop *feeling* so much."

She's never told me this before. She only mentions things about Rebecca, about how she feels about her, when Rebecca's not around. Whenever Rebecca's gone longer than a week, Daphne becomes confessional.

"I felt like Jamie Lee Curtis in *A Fish Called Wanda* when she's writhing and humping the railing because John Clease is speaking Italian to her."

"Did you just say what I think you said?" I say, poking my head into the living room. "Wait until I tell Brad and Nicole you used a reference from a movie."

"Don't even think about it, Ryan Brassard," she says, moving towards me, her fists already up, ready to box. Then, after shadow boxing with me for a few seconds and telling me she'll disown me if I tell Brad and Nicole she used a movie reference, she stops and says, "I'm serious, though, about Rebecca's place being a turn-on. It was always so depressing to walk into someone's apartment and see reprints of Van Gogh, Picasso, and Dali or black and white photos of Marilyn Monroe, James Dean, and Humphrey Bogart in Ikea frames. It was all so . . . predictable. But when I walked into Rebecca's place it was so . . . so . . ."

She doesn't finish her thought, opting instead to start a new one. "And to think I was actually considering going out to dinner with a guy that night."

"Like on a date?"

She nods.

"Who?"

"The guy from last night."

"Which guy from last night?"

"The guy who was frantically calling my name on John Street."

"You mean Josh Sebring?"

"You know him?"

"Not until last night. He introduced himself."

"What? Are you serious?"

"Yep."

"What'd he say?"

"He said he wanted to talk to you, that he had something you'd be interested in, providing you were still — quote-unquote — *in the business*. In fact," I say, noting the completely baffled expression on Daphne's face while retrieving Josh's card from atop the TV, "he gave me his card to give to you."

Two seconds after I hand it to her she starts chuckling.

"What's so funny?"

"This card says he's a producer for some indie film company based in Montreal."

"And?"

She laughs again. "And he's not."

"He's not?"

"No, he's not."

"How do you know?"

"Because he's a bullshit artist, that's how I know."

"What do you mean?"

"Just that. Josh Sebring is the biggest bullshitter I've ever met. In fact, Josh Sebring's not even his real name, it's like Joey Selwigg or something like that, and when I first met him he was handing out business cards that said he was the founder and CEO of some dot-com company worth almost a billion dollars."

"So Josh — or Joey's — a bit of a player then?"

"Understatement. Anyway, him giving you his card to give to me is nothing more than an attempt to add me to his list of 'Conquered Women' — which he probably would've already accomplished months ago if you hadn't invited me to dinner with you and Rebecca the same night I was supposed to go out with him."

She's referring to when Rebecca excused herself that day in the library (for five minutes, to allow me to determine what kind of first impression she'd made on Daphne) and as soon as she was out of earshot Daphne had said, "So, what's the deal with your friend?" her eyes trailing after Rebecca.

"What do you mean?" I said.

"I mean, is she available?"

"For what?"

After an annoyed sigh, she said, "Can you please remove your therapist's hat for a second and stop answering a question with a question?"

"Sure. But before I do, can I just clarify that I'm a therapist for people with ABI — Acquired Brain Injuries — and not another, 'yawn, yawn, dreary therapist'?"

"Well, well, well," she said, giving my shoulder a playful punch, "aren't *you* the sensitive type," and then, before I could say anything else she started talking about Rebecca again, reassuring me this wasn't some Florence Nightingale thing. "I'm not interested in *fixing* her or putting a light in her dark, damaged, and brooding soul. I have no intention of playing nurse or spiritual healer."

"Then what *is* your intention?" I asked.

"I just want to fuck her brains out," she replied and then, a few seconds later, after giving me a playful jab in the chest with her fist and saying, "Ha. Made you choke," in response to the fact that I was now coughing after almost inhaling the piece of Wrigley's spearmint gum I'd been chewing, she laughed and said, her tone much softer, more serious, "Listen, all I want to know is, is she going to break my heart? I can't handle another heartbreak."

"Who, Rebecca?"

"Yes, Rebecca."

"No. Never. Of course not. She's . . . she's Rebecca," I said, which seemed to satisfy her and when Rebecca got back from wherever it was she'd went, Daphne introduced herself as 'Daphne Garceau' and within two minutes she and Rebecca were chatting, the kind of intense, exclusive, 'RSVP Only' chatting that makes a third person keenly aware they're a third person and just after saying, 'I'm going to grab a bagel, you guys want anything?' (which they either didn't hear or chose to ignore) I noticed Rebecca was wearing a very animated-slash-intrigued expression, something I hadn't seen since she and my sister Jennie were in conversation.

As I expected, when I returned from grabbing a bagel, Rebecca was already gone and Daphne, who at that point told me she volunteered at the library twice a week, was waiting for me near the entrance and informed me that she'd been paged to the front desk and when she returned to our table a few minutes later, Rebecca was already gone.

I reassured Daphne that that was just Rebecca and told her that if she gave me her number I'd arrange something in a week, maybe less than a week, and called her five days later, telling her that Rebecca and I were having dinner at Jump Café that night and that Rebecca had asked me to ask Daphne if she'd like to join us.

"Of course," Daphne says, now seated on Jennie's rocking chair in my living room, "in hindsight, maybe I should've gone out with that guy. I mean, seeing Rebecca again didn't exactly come without a price," she says, referring to the fact that she ran into her half-brother Eriq, as well as her old friend Nicole and Nicole's fiancé Brad — all of whom, along with Rebecca and myself, were already seated at the table when she arrived. "I mean, talk about unfortunate coincidences."

daphne, modified

"What were you like before you met Rebecca?"
I'm now in the kitchen, retrieving a 500 ml bottle of Evian from the fridge.

"What do you mean, what was I like?" Daphne says, still seated in the rocking chair in the living room.

"I mean, did you have . . . was there ever someone else who . . . who, I don't know, *affected* you the way Rebecca does?"

When she hasn't responded by the time I've opened the Evian and taken two swigs, I consider telling her to forget it, that it was a silly question, then, thinking I'd better get an answer for Rebecca, I say, trying my best to sound both sincere and apologetic at the same time (a classic Rebeccian approach), "Hey, I didn't mean to pry or anything, Daph. I was just wondering if like, I don't know, if she —"

"She inspires me," Daphne says, quickly, softly, her voice barely audible above the street noise coming in through the open windows, and when I look over at her, from the kitchen, I see that her head is bowed and she's fidgeting with her hands, clasping and unclasping them like 'Jason' (not his real name), a sixteen-year-old autistic boy who suffered a mild head injury in an MVA.

Like Daphne, 'Jason' could only be inspired by one person — in his case, a small Portuguese woman who worked in the cafeteria where he was receiving rehabilitation. It took the rehabilitation staff a while to realize the connection, that during the week, when the woman was in the building, 'Jason' behaved as though he had a purpose, a raison d'être, but on weekends or during holidays when the woman wasn't working, he either retreated into an almost vegetative state or became hostile and uncooperative. The tragedy occurred when the woman went on maternity leave for six months and the separation anxiety became too much for 'Jason.' He killed himself one month into her leave.

For the duration of a thirty-second commercial, I've been watching Daphne from the kitchen, watching her being modified, altered by the memory, by my mind's analogy of 'Jason' and the cafeteria lady.

"In what way?" I say, making eye contact with her reflection in the TV screen as I enter the living room.

"What?" she says, looking at me as though she hasn't understood the question.

"You said Rebecca inspires you. I was just wondering in what way?"

Daphne hesitates, thinking, then says, "She has this . . . I don't know, this unrestrained, spontaneous, curiosity."

Well, two out of three ain't bad, I think to myself. I mean, Rebecca is *curious* — curious to see how far she can push people, what she can get them to do — and she's definitely *unrestrained* in her approach — she'll do whatever it takes to get the person to do it — but *spontaneous* is never an adjective I'd use to describe Rebecca. I mean, aside from Jennie's funeral when she burst into spontaneous laughter from inhaling clary sage essential oil, I don't think I've ever seen her lose control. In fact, I don't think I've ever met a more calculating person in my entire life.

"She has this childlike thirst for knowledge," Daphne is now saying. "She's always wanting to know 'Why?' or 'How come?' which is so rare nowadays because nowadays an adult with this kind of curiosity is made to feel naïve or foolish. People regard her as silly or too innocent . . ."

As Daphne's sentence fragment dangles there, it strikes me — for about the twentieth time, but this time far more poignantly than the previous nineteen times — that she's actually trying to protect Rebecca, to preserve Rebecca's innocence, and it's at this point that I feel my stomach muscles tighten, cringing with a 50-50 split of envy-slash-admiration for not only Rebecca's storytelling, but her incredible acting abilities, for her ability to fool someone like Daphne so completely.

"Have you . . ." Daphne's voice cracks, the remaining words stalling somewhere in her throat.

"Heard from her yet?" I say, finishing her sentence. Then,

while shaking my head, I try to imagine what Daphne'd be like if I told her where Rebecca really was, if I confessed to her right now what Rebecca and I were planning, have been planning ever since we'd met her and a few moments later, I ask (as per Rebecca's instructions), "Would you kill her?"

Daphne is now staring at me, horror-stricken.

"What?"

I insert a pause here, not speaking for a few seconds to allow the shock of what I just asked her to wear off slightly, then, using a matter-of-fact tone of voice that suggests this is a perfectly normal question I've just asked her, say, "Euthanasia, you know, mercy killing, assisted suicide. If, say, Rebecca was on her death bed, if right now, at this very moment, she's in some hospital in North Dakota or Mexico or Manitoba or Jakarta, hooked up to a life support machine, beyond saving, beyond recovery, and you knew that her wish was to never be in this situation, that she'd asked you if she *was* ever in this situation to help her die, would you be willing to pull the plug or smother her or administer a lethal injection of morphine or potassium chloride?"

The shocked look Daphne is now wearing suggests she's actually picturing Rebecca on her death bed, that she is imagining herself pulling the plug or smothering Rebecca and though I'm tempted to take it further, to ask Daphne if she'd agree to a suicide pact if that's what Rebecca really wanted (which she does) but, using the horrified expression she's still wearing as a hint that she's not quite ready for this question, I instead say, "You know, Daph, I'm fairly certain Rebecca isn't on her death bed in some hospital in North Dakota."

"Then what's wrong with her?" she says, "Where is she?" and her tone is so desperate, so discouraged, I decide she's ready for the next piece of the puzzle and say, "I think she might be looking for her 'Perfect Place.'"

"Her what?"

"Her 'Perfect Place.'"

"What's that?"

"Ever since Rebecca was, I don't know, like sixteen or seventeen, she's been trying to find the perfect moment to [dot, dot, dot; please insert your dramatic pause here] die."

"What?"

"Ya, I know, it sounds slightly bizarre and, judging by the look you're giving me right now, I'm thinking I probably shouldn't have said anything so we'll just forget I did and move on to something —"

"Like hell we're forgetting about it," Daphne snaps, and then, just as Rebecca said she would, she starts insisting that I tell her.

"Listen. I'm sorry. I really shouldn't, I mean, I thought it was something Rebecca and you already discussed but if you haven't it probably means Rebecca hasn't said anything about this to anyone but me which means she'd be really, I mean, *really* upset if she found out I told you, so maybe we should —"

"Ryan, you can't do this to me."

I insert another dramatic pause at this point, allowing myself enough time to properly construct an appropriate facial expression, one that suggests I'm having an internal debate, wrestling with the decision to either go against Rebecca's wishes or with my desire to assist Daphne.

"Okay," I say a few moments later, "but you're going to have to promise me you won't say anything to anyone, I mean, *anyone*."

"I promise."

"Cross your heart."

"Ryan, I'm *not* crossing my bloody heart. We're not ten years old. Just tell me about Rebecca's Perfect Place."

"Okay, well, you know how in the movie *Thelma & Louise* when they drive the car off the cliff together? Well if you freeze that scene and isolate it, if all you saw was that particular scene without anything else, you'd wonder, 'Why the hell are they doing this?' It wouldn't make any sense to you, right? But if you start rewinding the tape and getting the background information and complementing that particular scene with other scenes, you'll slowly start to see why they did it. In fact, if you keep going back you'll see that their whole lives were in preparation for this one scene, that every decision they'd ever made, every conversation they'd ever had, every molecule of air they'd ever breathed, every right turn instead of a left turn they'd ever taken led them irrevocably towards this particular scene, to the point where it seemed like there was no other decision for them to make, that doing what they did — driving the car off the cliff, together, into the Grand Canyon — was almost pre-ordained, that they had arrived at the perfect place, that this was the perfect moment for what they did and —"

"Ryan, stop. What does this have to do with Rebecca?"

"I'm getting to that. I was just trying to give you some context, some — oh hell, never mind, forget it. What this has to do with Rebecca is ever since Rebecca was sixteen or seventeen she's felt that everything she was doing in her life was a preview, a rehearsal to this perfect moment, that it was just a matter of finding the right person to be with and once she'd found her Perfect Partner, sooner or later the two of them would arrive — just like Thelma and Louise — at the perfect place and it would be the perfect moment for her to _____."

I leave the rest of my sentence blank, hoping Daphne will fill it in and in less than two seconds she says, "Are you saying that right now, at this moment, she's looking for the right place, the right moment to . . . to die?"

I nod my head. "I think so."

"Well, what if . . . what if she finds it before I get a chance to talk to her?"

I shrug.

"Does she already have . . . has she found her 'Perfect Partner' yet?"

Another shrug. "I'm not sure," I say. "Maybe. Maybe not."

"Well, do you think she would've told the person if she did find her? I mean, would she have already let the person know?"

"Again," I say, shrugging. "I'm not sure. Maybe. Maybe not."

"Well, what if her 'Perfect Partner' isn't . . . what if she's found someone and she's planning on — Ryan, what am I going to do?" Daphne sputters, her eyes filling with tears and when she asks me again, "Where is she?" her tone so pleading and panic-stricken that I consider a) making up some story like I did for Renaldo, the superintendent, telling her that Rebecca is in Costa Rica or Colombia and will be back in a couple of weeks, b) letting her read the suicidE-mail I read yesterday on Queen West about someone needing a figurative Walden Pond to retreat to every once in a while and telling her it was from Rebecca, c) giving her Rebecca's letter — which I'm forbidden to do, d) telling her that although Rebecca and I 'interviewed' four other applicants for the position of Rebecca's 'Perfect Partner' prior to meeting Daphne (which we did), Daphne should know that all four of them were only under consideration for a combined three weeks whereas she has been in the top spot for almost eight months now — but before I can do either a), b), c), d), or even think of an e) my cellphone rings, startling me, and after four rings Daphne says, "Are you going to answer that?" in a tone that suggests she's hoping it's Rebecca and when I answer it and hear Jo-Jo's voice on the other end, I shake my head and watch Daphne's expression go back to being desperately worried before tuning back into Jo-Jo, who is now asking me where I am and what I have planned for the next couple of hours and while walking towards Rebecca's bedroom I tell Jo-Jo that I'd planned on doing some grocery shopping and then, after I'm in Rebecca's bedroom and I've closed the door and I'm certain Daphne can no longer hear me, I tell Jo-Jo that I have two clients this afternoon at The Suicide Loft but that I *may* be able to come by afterwards — "say, around 4:00 p.m.?" — and then Jo-Jo's voice changes to a girlie, borderline whiny tone and she says that she "Really, really, *really* could use some company," and wants me to "Please, please, *please* come over for a visit right away," adding she's not getting off the phone until I say I will and when I promise her I will she then asks me to pick her up three 2-litre bottles of Evian water, a bottle of co-enzyme Q10, a bottle of Swiss brand B-complex vitamins, and a box of PowerBars at the Optimum Natural Food store and while I'm agreeing to this I hear my apartment door open and close and a few moments later, from Rebecca's bedroom window, I see Daphne burst from the building and begin running down Queen Street.

appointments within twelve hours

Twenty minutes later I'm standing in the Optimum Natural Food store on Queen Street, eavesdropping on the conversation between two women standing in front of the organic cereals. One of them, the one dressed in a plain white cotton T-shirt, denim short-shorts, and Dolce & Gabbana running shoes, is telling the other one, the one dressed in a plain white cotton T-shirt, denim short-shorts, and Dolce & Gabbana running shoes, how hyper-organized her life is.

"I feel as though I spend every minute of every day trying to establish a sense of order and predictability in my life, in my relationships, in my job — in everything."

"That sounds pretty normal."

"But I'm completely stressed out. And not only that, as soon as I think I've got everything organized the way I want I end up complaining how boring my life is, how there's no spontaneity and I want a change. And then, as soon as there's a bit of spontaneity or change in my life, I start trying to get rid of it, to organize it. When did I get like this? When did I turn into this neurotic nutcase?"

Her friend laughs, causing her to laugh, and when the one wearing the tattoo of what looks to be a caterpillar crawling out of her short-shorts and into her belly button turns and looks at me I consider asking her what method of suicide she would use but before I can my pager goes off and when I don't recognize the number I call in and it's a message from the same woman who's called me at least five times in the last three weeks — the one who has made four appointments for interviews and hasn't shown up for one of them. This time her tone of voice seems slightly more urgent as she tells me she'd really like to schedule an appointment-interview for tonight sometime between 7:00 and 10:30 p.m., if possible, adding that although she knows it's early notice, my business card did say 'Appointments available within twelve hours.'

jo-jo's five star demographics & economics

Joanne Fielding, or Jo-Jo as she likes to be called, lives a couple of streets west of my apartment — on Scarboro Beach Boulevard — in one of two homes she owns in Toronto. Aside from not being able to find suitable companionship, Jo-Jo's greatest fear is of getting old.

It's been two years since her divorce and a year and a half since she started working out in a gym six times a week, drinking two litres of Evian water each day and consuming vitamins, co-enzyme Q10, ginseng, and PowerBars as though each were a separate food group — a regime that caused Rebecca to describe Jo-Jo once as 'one of those forty-one-year-old women trying to Stairmaster-Evian-PowerBar-ginseng-facialscrub-hairdye-kiddy-clothe herself back to twenty-five.'

After I hand Jo-Jo the bag containing the items from her 'grocery list,' she tells me I look good, really good — quite handsome, in fact — then asks me my age, which she already knows is twenty-eight and says, "That's too bad. I'm not dating anyone older than twenty-four at the moment," and begins walking towards the kitchen.

After her divorce and the subsequent discovery that her ex-husband was dating much younger women, Jo-Jo found herself attracted to increasingly younger men. Like runner's categories for a marathon, she began dividing men into age groups and started dating men in the thirty-five to thirty-nine category. A few months later, she dropped down an age group to the thirty to thirty-four-year-olds and then, last year in June, after experimenting with the twenty-five to twenty-nine-year-olds for most of the spring, she turned forty-one and felt she needed to date men almost half her age.

Today, Jo-Jo is wearing her Naturalizer border-stitch sandals, a blue stretch denim miniskirt, and a scoop-neck striped cotton crop top that shows off her abs which, I have to admit, look pretty good for someone her age — as good as her legs — but not quite as good as her breasts which, courtesy of what I'm certain is one of Victoria's many Secrets, have been elevated and squished in such a manner as to look absolutely edible.

"Can you stay for long?" she asks when she reaches the kitchen, looking back over her shoulder and smiling suggestively.

After feeling a slight stir in my groin that's accompanied by the thought that Jo-Jo would like me to walk into the kitchen, bend her over the table, hike up her stretch denim miniskirt and . . . I say, "For a while," then walk through the living room and out onto the front balcony, immediately noticing the sun isn't nearly as ambitious as it was forecasted to be and that a slightly cool, northwest breeze carrying almost no humidity with it is blowing, possibly alluding to a coming rain shower.

Standing with my hands on the wooden railing of the balcony, eyes closed, head tilted towards the sun, listening to the soothing sound of the breeze tickling the maple leaves, I suddenly smile, thinking how much I enjoy being here, in the Beaches, hanging out with Jo-Jo on her balcony before one of my appointments at The Suicide Loft.

Contrary to Edwin Sneidman, one of the leading researchers and so-called experts on suicide who stated, 'No one commits suicide out of joy, no suicide is born out of exultation,' Rebecca wrote (on page 77 of her diary) that it's during moments like this, during a spasm of joy like the one I'm having right now, that she would love to end her life. 'Imagine dying in the middle of an orgasm or while experiencing the adrenaline rush of skydiving. Imagine if Thelma and Louise were doing each other as they drove off the cliff? Now *that* would've been a perfect ending.'

Although part of me has to admit she makes sense, I tend to side with Sneidman on this one. I don't think I could do it while I'm feeling like this. Of course, I also know that my current state of happiness is ephemeral, that much sooner than later the memory of what I have done will overwhelm my happiness and immediately send me into a state of self-loathing, reminding me that my only remedy, my only real solution, the only way I can really be assured of everlasting happiness is to kill my —

"How's business?" Jo-Jo shouts from somewhere inside the apartment.

She's referring to The Suicide Loft, the business I run out of the apartment beside hers. She — we — call it a business but it's really, as I mentioned before, my vocation, my passion, what I would do even if I didn't get paid for doing it, which I do, sort of.

"Business is good," I say.

"Good enough for me to start charging rent?" Jo-Jo hollers back.

I laugh. "I wouldn't go that far," I say, knowing that she's only joking, that she'd never accept money.

Though I don't officially charge anything for my services, I do accept whatever people are willing to give — and some people are willing to give a lot. Since I opened The Suicide Loft nine months ago, I've seen almost five hundred people. Presently, I have roughly twenty-five clients who see me at least once every two weeks and who never leave without dropping a minimum of $50 into the 'Donations' box by the door; another twenty or so bi-monthly clients who leave no less than $20 and another thirty or so bi-monthlies who usually leave at least $10. When you do the math, and I'm sure you will, my so-called 'not-for-profit' vocation makes me a lot of money.

"Well then," Jo-Jo says, walking out onto the balcony with two tall glasses of Evian water, each with three Evian ice cubes, "how about a nice birthday present for your darling landlady then?"

"Birthday present?" I say, feigning ignorance, knowing it's Jo-Jo's forty-second birthday in two days.

"Don't tell me you forgot?"

"I didn't. You're going to be twenty-nine, right?"

After handing me one of the glasses she gives my bum a playful squeeze and says, "Twenty-eight," before sitting down on one of the two Henry Jacobus & Sons balsa wood chaise-lounges she has on the balcony.

"Thanks," I say.

"Thank *you*," she says, winking suggestively at me. "How much do I owe you?"

"For what — the stuff at the health food store? Nothing."

"Oh, come on now, are you sure?"

"All I ask is that you continue being the most understanding landlady in Toronto."

"I think I can manage that," she says, smiling, then adding, "And remember, Ryan, I'm not *just* an understanding landlady, I'm also a client."

I laugh, stretching out on the other Henry Jacobus chaise-lounge, my thoughts tumbling back to the first time I saw Jo-Jo.

I was still living in Hamilton then, had just gotten off work — an evening shift — and was walking home when I saw a black Jaguar XJS paused at the intersection of Upper Paradise and Scenic Drive. It was facing the escarpment, engine revving, headlights illuminating the 'Dead End' sign at the end of Upper Paradise.

As I drew nearer, the automatic sun-tinted driver's side window slid down and instead of the woman asking me for directions like I assumed would happen, she poked her head out and asked me if she could please drive me home.

I thought about it for a second or two, then told her she could and when I got in the car and we started driving along Scenic Drive she told me if I hadn't accepted her offer she would've driven her car off the escarpment.

On the way to my place she told me she'd been visiting friends of hers, a couple that she and her ex-husband had known since they were all at the University of Western Ontario together, adding that the four of them had been going on annual spring vacations for over twenty years and that part of the reason for her visit was to apologize that they'd be missing out on their trip this year until she saw the tans her friends had and discovered they'd already gone — with her ex-husband and his new girlfriend — and she said she'd suddenly felt more alone than she ever had in her life, told her friends she had to leave, got in her car, and started driving towards the escarpment.

When we got close to my apartment on Locke Street, I invited her to have a drink with me at the West Town Bar & Grill and, once inside, I started talking to her about suicide, telling her about my sister's suicide, how ever since that day I'd thought about ending my own life, had even planned on doing so a few weeks after Jennie's death, in fact, but how my cousin Rebecca had intervened at the proverbial eleventh hour and how she told me if I went through with it I'd end up being an 'ignorant suicide' which, according to her, was the worst thing anyone could be. According to her, if a person is required to spend seven or eight years at university studying to become a doctor, learning how to save someone else's life, it seemed only logical that a person would want to spend at least a few months learning how to take their own life which, for some reason, ended up making perfect sense to me and so, even though I still thought about committing suicide, I decided to commit myself to the study of suicide and during the next couple of months of researching it I developed a radically different perspective on the subject.

"It's definitely *not* something you want to rush into," I urged her. "It should *never* be an impulsive act. If it is, it usually means you're depressed, that there's something else going on, and that if this depression or whatever was removed from your life, you'd be fine."

After a couple more drinks, I invited her to my apartment to have a look at some of the suicide paraphernalia I'd collected during the past couple of months and after I showed her most of my stuff and she said something about me definitely having more than just a passing interest in suicide, I told her that, "Suicide has become my passion, my raison d'être. It's the reason I get up in the morning," before going on to tell her how I was actually thinking of converting my apartment into a type of sanctuary for similar-minded people, a place where people could go to understand their suicidal tendencies, to show them that they were normal, that, like the psychiatrist Karl Menninger said, 'There's a little suicide in all of us.'

"It would be like an alternative to suicide," I told her. "A place where people could go to commit virtual suicide. A place that neither glorified or horrified suicide. A place where the curious, the serious, even the delirious could visit."

"Well, why don't you do it then?" Jo-Jo asked.

"It's a question of demographics and economics," I said. "If I'm going to do something like this I'd like to be in a better area, that is, an area that has the greatest number of suicides and attempted suicides in Canada, which is in metropolitan Toronto. I suppose I could live with my cousin Rebecca — she's living in my sister's old place in Toronto — but it's only a bachelor apartment, which is a little too small for what I had in mind. But even if it wasn't, and even if my cousin didn't mind me converting her apartment into this sanctuary for suicidal people, I still don't have the money right now to renovate it the way I want because I'd want it to be really nice. I mean, the *last* thing I want is to have some seedy, decrepit, nondescript clinic where people get depressed just by sitting in it. I want the place to be original, uncommon, almost archetypal. I want people to be reassured and inspired, intrigued and comfortable, all at the same time, which, like I said, given my current financial situation is impossible. Besides, even if I did have the money to renovate it like I want to, I'd still need a pretty understanding landlord, so, unless you know someone who can help me out with all this. . . ."

After checking my watch and seeing that I have almost an hour before my first client shows up, I take another sip of Evian, then close my eyes again, once again listening to the leafy wind chimes tinkling away, once again feeling very content, borderline non-suicidal.

forbidden fruit

"By the way," Jo-Jo says sometime later, after I've returned from wherever it is I've drifted off to for the last while, "how have you been sleeping lately? Do you need any more sleeping pills?"

In my current state of contentment I almost tell Jo-Jo she's got things mixed up, that it's not me but Eriq who uses her sleeping pills — which he does, but no one but me knows that.

"Why do you ask?"

"Can I be honest?"

"Of course."

"You look like you haven't slept in about a week."

The truth — and it's obviously getting more and more difficult to hide — is I probably haven't had more than two or three hours of sleep per day for the last year or so because I'm terrified of dreaming which, since I'm so REM-deprived, is what usually happens as soon as I close my eyes.

A couple months ago I was dining at Sen5es — a restaurant on Bloor Street West — and overheard a woman saying that every time she took a sleeping pill she didn't dream, that normally she had loads of dreams every night but each time she went 'on the pill' it acted like a dream-blocker. That same night I tried some over-the-counter sleep aid and for a couple of nights it seemed to work. But when my dreams re-appeared on the third or fourth night as lucid and haunting as ever I asked Jo-Jo if she could get me some stronger pills — the stuff she used — and she did, but after a few days they too were unable to block my dreams and so I ended up passing the pills on to Eriq.

Apparently he too had developed a bit of sleeping problem in the last year or so; not because he was afraid of his dreams, but because most of the short stories he writes are about the environment's effect on humanity and although it doesn't seem like it on the surface (probably because Eriq's such a good actor) these environmental effects often get him so worked up he literally thinks himself into insomnia.

When I haven't responded in about ten seconds or so to Jo-Jo's comment about me looking like I haven't slept in about a week, she asks, "So, will you be needing any more pills?"

"Um, not right now, thanks," I reply, thinking that Eriq has enough Imovane to last him another few weeks. "Maybe in another couple of weeks or so."

"Well, just say the word. My doctor has a crush on me and can't deny me anything."

"How old is your doctor?"

"Too old. He's almost forty and —"

At this point Jo-Jo stops talking and, when I open my eyes to look at her, I see that she's craning her neck to look at something on the street below.

"Oh God, there goes three more," she says, her tone a perfect blend of disgust and disappointment, referring to the three women pushing baby carriages in the direction of the lake. "I see them everywhere. Can't get away from them. It's a bloody epidemic. A plague. Someone should do something."

Unlike most women, Jo-Jo has never been burdened by the instinct to bear children. 'Not once,' she's told me, 'Not even for a second.'

The idea of being surrounded by bottles and baby food ('I would never breastfeed'), constantly changing diapers, having spit-ups ruin her designer outfits, the endless wailing and demands on her attention at all hours of the day — her life would be over, it wouldn't be hers anymore. She even has recurring nightmares about pushing a baby stroller along the boardwalk and being forced to watch, in horror, as passersby gawk and coo at the baby without so much as noticing the vessel from which it came. "Plus the stretch marks. Some of these women swell up like a hot air balloon. Your skin can never recover from something like that. And your breasts, my God, they're never the same."

After watching the three women for a while longer, Jo-Jo turns to me and says, "And what are your plans for the rest of the afternoon and evening?"

"I'm off to visit a friend," I say, stretching.

"Male or female?"

"Male."

"And does this male friend of yours have a name?"

"He does. But he's rather a private fellow and doesn't like me to share these sorts of things with everyone."

"He sounds mysterious. May I have his number?"

"Unfortunately it's unlisted and I'm forbidden to give it out."

"You know I love forbidden fruit. Is he good looking?"

"Very."

"Describe him."

I think of Brad and Eriq and after a moment's debate decide to describe Eriq, thinking he's the more tantalizing of the two options. "He's tall — almost 6'2", about 180 pounds — very fit, works out a lot, eats really well, has dark hair, blue eyes —"

"Oh my, he sounds exquisite. Does he come with a brain?"

I nod. "He's quite brainy, in fact."

"Really? What's he do?"

"You mean what's his job or what's his vocation?"

"Jobs are boring. What's his vocation?"

"Writer."

"Published or unpublished?"

"The latter, so far."

"Is he any good?"

"I think so. I have a copy of his latest short story collection with me."

"Really? May I read it?"

I consider it, even though I know Eriq would never approve, that he's far too protective of his characters, too afraid to let them out into public by themselves, that, in his words, 'They're not strong enough,' which is kind of ironic seeing as most of his main characters are just thinly veiled versions of himself who, like Eriq, are afraid to let their friends and families know they have the types of concerns and feelings and thoughts they do.

"Well?" Jo-Jo asks, and in the second or two that follows I convince myself that the chances of Eriq and Jo-Jo meeting are slim, very slim and that even if they did meet, Jo-Jo would never betray my confidence and so I say, "I suppose I can let you read it while I'm occupied with my appointments."

"By the way," she says, tapping her Swatch watch, "isn't it about time you got into make-up?"

the suicide loft, in make-up

The Loft is silent, entombed in darkness.

One of the first things I did to The Loft was completely seal off all the windows, making it impenetrable to the outside world. The only way to illuminate it now (excluding the two skylights — one in the main bedroom, the other in the living room — both of which are also currently sealed) is by artificial lighting.

After flicking on a light, stepping inside, closing and locking the main door, I realize it's quite warm in the apartment and there's a faint odour of my last client's Cucumber Baie perfume lingering about so after turning on several more lights and switching on the central air and setting it to 69°F, I begin deodorizing the apartment with a lilac scent that my incoming client, during her interview three days ago, said she enjoys.

Excluding roughly ninety percent of the suicide paraphernalia, nearly everything in the apartment was paid for by Jo-Jo. The living room, where I conduct most of my interviews, contains a gallery day bed, a side table, an avonne bench by Roy Banse as well as a Hampton sofa and chair by Daniel Perez (all acquired at Fluid Living on Queen Street West); an atelier mirror, a coffee table, a small sofa; and a large oak entertainment unit by Henry Jacobus & Sons that is equipped with a VCR, a 2001 Sony 32" widescreen television set, and a Denon AVF-100 audio system with DVD player.

The dining room is furnished with a secretary's desk, an oak dining table with four matching oak chairs, and an oversized oak rocking chair (all by Henry Jacobus & Sons), as well as a small oak bookcase that used to belong to Jo-Jo's niece and is now filled with dozens of videotapes of actual suicides and suicide attempts, stacks of issues of the *Hemlock Society*, dozens of pamphlets and books on suicide including classics like, *Survivors of Suicide* (1972), *How to Die with Dignity, Let Me Die Before I Wake, A Guide to Self-Deliverance, Why Survive? Being Old in America, The Awakening,* and *Suicide, Mode D'emploi* (which caused quite a stir in France when it first came out in 1982), as well as several movies about suicide that include *Leaving Las Vegas, Soylent Green,* and *The Thread.*

The walls in these two rooms, coloured in a soft taupe, are adorned with what I consider to be an interesting blend of unframed mirror pieces; framed C. Laframboise paintings (all originals); assorted photographs of suicides; a chronological chart of suicide with the names, dates, and places of notable and not so notable suicides, including my sister Jennie's; another chart depicting the various methods people have employed to kill themselves, ranging from the usual suspects — guns, knives, pills — to the bizarre — putting their head in a vice and tightening it until it crushed their skull, sawing their head off with a table saw, driving a nine-inch nail into their right ear, drinking a bottle of bleach.

As well, on both the living room and dining room walls there are two large glass display cases containing all sorts of poisons, pills, and various instruments of suicide including an authentic circa 1750 French guillotine blade (which must have cost Jo-Jo a fortune). Though I have the words, 'In Case of Emergency — Break Glass!' stencilled on the glass, the cases are actually made of bulletproof plexiglass.

I've had many people say they initially came to The Loft thinking it was a place to go if you were interested in assisted suicide but, once they'd arrived and spent some time in The Loft, these same people admitted that confronting suicide in this manner ended up generating such comforting/peaceful/ life-affirming sensations that it made it virtually impossible to continue to consider committing suicide — at least while they were here.

The main bedroom is furnished with a large, hand-forged iron Alexandria canopy bed by Charles P. Rogers, two oak night tables and another oversized oak rocking chair by Henry Jacobus & Sons, an entertainment unit housing a 24" RCA TV with DVD player and a portable Samsung stereo system with detachable MP3 player, a small oak computer desk holding a Cassius wireless PC with Internet hookup and, in the corner, a foldable balsam-pine massage table, also by Henry Jacobus. In addition to the room being equipped with special lighting, including several spotlights, the room has been completely soundproofed and, unlike the other rooms, the walls are unadorned.

The second bedroom I have turned into an office where I record, simultaneously on audio and video, detailed notes of each session as well as store — in the two large armoires, one dresser, one oversized trunk, one small refrigerator, and one medium-sized safe — all the paraphernalia associated with my vocation, such as all Rebecca's video and audio equipment, several changes of clothes, a dozen different knives (including a Sabertooth Dagger, a Viking U.S. Marine sword, and a Samurai sword), two rifles (a Sako Finnfire Hunter and a Tikka Sporter), two live grenades, a variety of pills (including Valium, Seconal, Prozac, aspirin, Tylenol, and Imovane), several bottles of wine (Chardonnay), two bottles of whiskey (Crown Royal), a case of beer (Lowenbrau), the 500 ml preserving jars of apple and cherry seeds, a 500 ml container of potassium chloride, my grandfather's 12-gauge shotgun, a copy of Rebecca's diary, several copies of Jennie's original suicide letter, her journal, her suicide tapes, and a living will.

Though, as mentioned, I do keep detailed notes on each of my clients, I never request their names, occupations, or any personal information such as their addresses or home/business numbers. A client, if he or she wishes, may give me their real name, a false name, or remain unnamed.

For example, my 1:00 p.m. client, during her interview, said she wished to remain unnamed and would prefer to go directly to the main bedroom which I am now in the process of preparing — laying down an impermeable nylon sheet (which doesn't produce the distracting noises of the typical plastic hospital bed sheet), then two cream-coloured cotton sheets, and finally, a cream white top sheet.

After boiling some water in the kettle, I pour the water into a ceramic bowl, place a squeeze bottle containing one hundred percent pure coconut oil in the water, carry the bowl to the bedroom and set it on the nightstand beside the bed. Then I take out the *Last of the Mohicans* soundtrack CD from its case, place it in the portable Samsung stereo, pre-select the 'Repeat' option, then arrange the spotlights and lay the control switch on the bed before going to the office and getting disguised.

During all Suicide Loft interviews and sessions I wear a disguise; nothing quite as elaborate as Bryan Brown's character in *FX* or Tom Cruise in *Mission Impossible* but convincing enough that I've never been detected — and I've seen dozens of my clients throughout Toronto without being recognized.

Before each session I put in chestnut brown coloured contacts, darken my eyebrows with a CoverGirl Perfect Point Plus Espresso 210 eyebrow pencil, put a Cindy Crawford mole on my left cheek with the same pencil and then, after working a large dollop of Sebastian Molding Mud into my hair, I slick it back with a fine-toothed comb and hairspray it into place with Vidal Sassoon Ultra Firm hairspray to make it appear much darker and straighter than it really is.

The clothes I wear for each session are all black, all expensive, and all things I've never worn in public: black Ralph Lauren dress socks, black Hugo Boss loafers, black Calvin Klein boxer shorts, black Armani dress pants, a black Ralph Lauren cotton T-shirt, a Seiko Kinetic Auto Relay watch, a pair of black-rimmed, non-prescription Gucci glasses, and Eau de FCUK No.1 cologne for men by French Connection. Excluding the watch — and the loafers and glasses, of which I only have three identical pairs — I have seven identical outfits, the idea borrowed from my sister who borrowed it from Einstein who had seven identical outfits so he didn't waste any mental energy each morning deciding what to wear.

Each of my outfits, if you include the glasses and loafers, costs $943.27; $1158.76 if you include the watch.

client #1

After getting changed, groomed, and cologned, I wait for client #1 in the living room while listening to Rage Against the Machine's CD *Battle in Los Angeles*.

Halfway through the song 'Guerrilla Radio,' I hear the bell and after turning off the CD with the remote, I flick on the TV, turning it to channel 101 (which is the channel fed by the camera located in the vestibule) and, after confirming it's her, I buzz her in, unlock the two deadbolts to the apartment door, and walk into the dining room, remaining out of her sight until I hear her open and close the door to the main bedroom and then I relock the apartment door, walk silently down the hall, and sit on the felt-padded barstool outside the main bedroom, waiting for her to call me.

I wait for almost five minutes before the door opens a crack and she calls me in, asking me to keep my eyes shut until I have closed the door behind me and when I open my eyes the room is dark and suffused with the smell of lilacs and all I can do is listen to the sound of the *Last of the Mohicans* soundtrack and breathe in the scent of lilac until one of the spotlights is abruptly turned on — the beam concentrated on a small section of her stomach, just below her belly button — and I notice her right hand is moving, tracing the spotlighted section with a blood-red lipstick, carefully following the edge of the light, slowly separating it from the rest of her body.

When she's done, her voice — as though coming from the highlighted body part — asks me to look at her, to *really* look at her, which I do for over a minute before she abruptly switches off the light, once again sending the room into complete darkness. Fifteen seconds later, the spotlight is on again, this time the beam encircling part of her left breast, and she begins moving the lipstick along the edge of the light, slicing over her breast, again asking me to look, *really* look at her once she's finished the outline, which I do for approximately a minute before she again switches off the light.

Though this pattern continues for nearly three-quarters of an hour, I begin to see the effect after about ten minutes: each time she switches off the light after I've spent between thirty and sixty seconds staring at a highlighted section of her body, I'm left with a residual imprint — the negative — in my brain. Like turning off a TV in an already dark room, the body part remains behind, glowing, pulsing, floating around in my head like a snapshot, a reverse Polaroid, the image slowly fading, almost disappearing before I'm exposed to another one and then another one and then another one, and soon my head is filled with a dozen fractured, orphaned body parts drifting around, bumping into one another, momentarily fusing, occasionally forming bizarre, sometimes grossly incongruous figures.

At last she puts on the secondary spotlight, this one illuminating her entire body which now, in full view, resembles a cow's body marked into sections, ready to be butchered, and she asks me to look at her, to put her back together, to stare at her until the she becomes whole and

– when she switches off the light this time I hear water sprinkling (the sound of her removing the bottle of coconut oil from the ceramic bowl?) then the smell of the oil reaches my nostrils, momentarily dislodging the lilac scent, then making me more aware both of it and a slightly musky odour and

– she flicks on the light, her body now speckled with drops of coconut oil, each glistening globule acting like a tiny prism, splaying the concentrated light from the spotlight into a rainbow of colours that shoot off and around her body like searchlights seeking out the perimeters of the room and then she begins massaging herself, slowly smearing the lipstick lines, blurring them, the sectioned parts swirling, mixing, converging, merging, and then – she tells me to close my eyes one more time and when I do I hear the spotlight being turned off and my mind is immediately drenched with the image of her body, no longer sectioned or malleable, but whole, staring at me . . . the image embroidered by soft moans, by moist breath coming in gasps, by muffled whimpers, by a soft eruption, by sighs of completion and unity and then by her saying, "Thank you" and asking me to leave the room.

client #2

In preparation for my 2:30 p.m. client, I remove the old sheets on the bed, put fresh ones on, remove the coconut oil and bowl from the room, turn on the outside fan to remove the air in the room, place a few drops of sandalwood and lavender oil in the aerator, turn it on, uncover and open the skylight, lay Leonard Cohen's book of *Poemes et Chansons* on the chartreuse-coloured felt pillow of the rocking chair, the bookmark between pages 54 and 55 (in my copy) before quickly showering, changing into a fresh set of the same attire, and waiting in the living room, lying on the gallery bed while listening to *Puddle Dive* by Ani DiFranco and reflecting on Client #1, on her donation of $100 and her accompanying note that said, 'Thanks. You're a lifesaver — literally,' which, instead of making me feel good, has the effect of reminding me why Rebecca dislikes The Suicide Loft, of her belief that I'm doing people a disservice by creating a dependency in them, that instead of Prozac or daily shopping sprees or *Seinfeld* reruns, they now rely on The Loft to get them through the week.

Of course, while I do see her point, I also know Rebecca well enough to know that the real reasons she doesn't like The Loft are probably because it's something I did on my own, without her approval, and also because The Loft is an antidote to suicide — which is a constant reminder that suicide, although definitely a final solution, is not always the best solution for everyone.

At 2:28 p.m., I hear the bell and after checking to make sure it's him I buzz him in before turning off the CD manually, unlocking and opening the door to The Loft.

Once we're in the main bedroom and I'm seated in the oversized felt-padded rocking chair and he's lying on the bed with his back to me, I read the poem "You have the lovers," to him, slowly, and then, when I've finished reading, push PLAY on the remote and when Guns N' Roses song 'November Rain' comes through the speakers I move in behind him and once he's nestled in my arms, once this 6'2" 240-pound, fifty-seven-year-old man whose wife committed suicide four months ago by jumping in front of a train while they were vacationing in Spain is nestled in my arms and the lyrics and music of Guns N' Roses envelops him, he begins to cry and less than a minute later he's sobbing as though his heart has been punctured by a pain so intense, so lonely and inconsolable, that it makes me feel as if it's only my embrace that prevents him from shattering.

a writer in residence

Before cleaning up The Suicide Loft I give Eriq a call.

Last night, as we were leaving Rain, I motioned to my messenger bag and (so Daphne wouldn't hear) mouthed the words,

"It's done," referring to his book being printed and bound and ready to give back to him and he shook his head and mouthed the words "Tomorrow. Call me."

Of course, that's not the only reason I'm calling Eriq. The other reason is due to Rebecca's long-standing instructions to either call or visit the rest of the gang the day after one of our get-togethers — as a sort of check up to see what's going on inside their heads which I then relay to Rebecca so she can plot-slash-direct the gang's next move(s).

Anyway, after the fifth ring Eriq answers the phone with an aphorism: "TV atrophies a person's capacity to read."

"Neil Postman?" I ask.

"Faulkner," Eriq corrects. "William-fucking-Faulkner."

"You should've used that one during last night's 'TV vs. the Book' debate."

"I thought about it, but . . ."

"But?"

"But I was having too much fun listening to 'The Sound and the Fury.'"

I laugh. "Wasn't she something?"

"A real piece of work."

"Speaking of which," I say, "get any new material off her last night?"

"Not really. I'd already heard most of it. She's missing her muse."

"You think so?"

"To tell you the truth, I'm worried about her."

"About Daphne?"

"I've never seen her like this."

"Like what?"

"Dependent."

"Dependent?"

"Daphne's always made a point of letting others know she's

not one of those people whose happiness or life depends on another person. She used to say it made her physically ill whenever she'd hear of people who couldn't be happy without their partners or spouses, who couldn't stand to be separated from them. It's why she's always despised *Romeo & Juliet*."

The mentioning of *Romeo & Juliet* automatically makes me think of Rebecca and how she believes Shakespeare to be the author of her suicidal ideations ('To be, or not to be, *that* is the question'), noting (on page 49 of her diary) that 'there are 52 characters in Shakespeare's plays who commit suicide for a variety of reasons, including (as Eriq has just mentioned) the idea of not being able to live without a partner' which, naturally, makes me think of what I tried to get out of Daphne a few hours ago — whether she'd choose to commit suicide with Rebecca rather than living without her — and, as if reading my thoughts, Eriq says, "That's precisely who Daphne seems to have become, though. She's become Juliet, unable to function, *to be*, without her Rebecca."

I sit in silence for a few moments thinking of Rebecca's prediction nearly eight months ago that she was certain she could break someone as strong as Daphne, that she could change Daphne's modus operandi, that she could convince her to take her own life and, more importantly, that it now looked as though her prediction was going to come true — and even though I'm more than slightly stunned by this, I'm still able to realize what this means, that Daphne and Rebecca's mutual suicide means I'll finally be able to commit my own suicide and, with the image of myself resting in peace now almost palpable, I hear myself saying, "Ain't love grand?"

"This ain't love," Eriq says and even though I know he's right, especially when you consider what Rebecca and I have done in the last eight months, I still want to try and make Eriq believe it's love.

"You don't think they're in love?"

"Hell no."

"Then what would you call it?"

"For Daphne I'd call it a one-way ticket to misery. She's a thinker, not a feeler. She doesn't like emotions — at least not the ones she can't control and use to her advantage and it's obvious she has no control where Rebecca's concerned which is why I think that —"

At this point he abruptly stops talking, making me wonder if perhaps he thinks he may have said too much and a moment later he says, "Ah, forget it. I've got my own problems to worry about."

"Such as?" I ask, deciding to pursue this line of dialogue even though I'd rather continue exploring the subject of 'Daphne and Rebecca.'

"Such as trying to write about something I haven't had any real experience with — contentment," he says, then, chuckling, adds, "It's like you trying to write a novel about life in Toronto."

"Almost impossible?"

"Exactly."

"Well, why don't you just write a tourist's impression of love then?" I suggest.

He laughs and after we talk for a few more minutes and I agree to give him his book tomorrow night at Brad's dinner party, I hang up and make my next call, this one to Nicole, knowing that because of what happened last night at Rain I'll probably have to smooth things over a bit in order to ensure her attendance at the dinner party, but her mother tells me she isn't home and when I ask her if she's at Brad's her mother says she might be — either there or out shopping — but can't really say for certain.

"You know Nicole. She's always doing something."

After deciding to wait a bit before calling Brad's place, thinking I may want to visit him and Nicole instead of talking to them on the phone, I clean up The Suicide Loft, have a quick shower, change back into my regular clothes, and go back down to Jo-Jo's with the intention of getting Eriq's book before leaving for Brad's but Jo-Jo talks me into letting her continue reading it, promising that she'll have it finished and will gladly give it back to me after my 3:30 p.m. appointment tomorrow so I can return it to Eriq tomorrow evening.

"Well what do you think of it so far?" I ask, gesturing towards the book.

"He's talented."

"That he is."

"His writing reminds me of Timothy Findley's."

"Hey, Findley's his favourite author," I say, almost reflexively, surprised — both by the ease with which I divulged the previously secret information and the fact that I continue to do so — "his favourite and his most feared."

"You can tell. They have a similar style, and since I expect your friend is considerably younger than Findley, my guess is he's been influenced by Findley, hence the favouritism and the fear."

Here she pauses and, intrigued by the look in her eyes, by the admiring, borderline enchanted expression she's wearing, I decide not to interrupt the pause, opting instead to have her continue, which she does a few moments later, stating, "It's not blatant, however. And it's certainly not borrowed or copied. 'A borrowed style is a bad style,' as François Mauriac, the French novelist said. He's just been influenced. The good thing is he's far enough along in his own writing that it merely gestures in Findley's direction and, unless you're a connoisseur of Findley, you probably wouldn't even notice."

Again she pauses.

Again I don't interrupt.

"Of course, the content is different from Findley's. Quite different. It's not a very comforting view of humanity. His main characters are so ambiguous. They seem to always be wearing a guise, as though they're afraid to admit who they really are — even to their closest friends and family. Everyone behaves as though they were merely acting their way through life. And the act, my God, the act is so well done, so convincing, that you actually get used to the idea that everything they're doing is an act, that there doesn't exist an authentic emotion in any of them until, suddenly, you're confronted with an image of these same characters weeping uncontrollably in their condos or breaking down in a restaurant washroom or on the drive home as they try to deal with the fact that their lives are nothing more than performance art."

If you were watching me right now you'd see me looking at Jo-Jo with slightly more than mild curiosity.

"I bet he doesn't use a computer," she's now saying, flipping through Eriq's book. "I'll bet he writes his stories on a typewriter or longhand and gets someone else — you perhaps — to type them out on a computer and bind them for him. Am I right?"

I only realize I'm nodding my head after three, possibly four nods, then say, "I mean, no," before retracting the statement by saying, "How'd you know?"

"Just a hunch. My guess is he's not a quick writer, either. He's far too concise, too exacting. He's probably a bleeder."

"A what?"

"A bleeder. It's what people in the writing industry refer to as someone who writes slowly, who can't churn out a short story in an afternoon or a novel in two weeks. The opposite of someone like Georges Simenon or Stephen King."

"Eriq told me he can spend an entire weekend worrying about whether or not to use a particular word or deciding whether he should use a semi-colon or a comma."

Jo-Jo laughs. "He's definitely a bleeder. I think there's even a line in one of Findley's short stories about a writer who spent the morning putting in a comma and the afternoon taking it out."

"I can't imagine . . ."

"Has he tried writing a novel yet?"

"Why?"

She shrugs. "My guess is he'd probably have a difficult time of it. It's not just that his material is more suited to the short story — I'm thinking that maybe his temperament is better suited to it as well. A novel requires commitment, whereas short stories are more like little affairs. A fling here, a fling there. Is he the type of person who likes to have affairs or is he more inclined to have a committed, enduring relationship?"

"He's actually said he's been trying to write a novel for several years now but just can't seem to —" I abruptly stop talking. "How do you know so much about this stuff, Jo-Jo?"

She laughs. "Women's intuition."

"Jo-Jo, you're starting to make me speculate."

Probably realizing that I'm referring to the fact that she's the only other person besides myself who has access to The Suicide Loft and to my office where I do all the transcribing for Eriq, Jo-Jo, after placing her hand on mine, says, reassuringly, "Don't worry, dear, it's not what you're thinking. I used to be a manuscript reader when I lived in England is all."

I look at Jo-Jo for a while, giving her time to smile, laugh, say 'I'm just joking,' or 'Gotcha' but she doesn't, so I say, "Bullshit."

"Young man," she says, quickly withdrawing her hand from mine, pretending to be offended, "it is *not* bullshit. There are plenty of secrets in my various closets."

I smile. "Really? Care to share?"

"Not right now. But I was wondering, aside from the characters in his stories, is your friend involved with anyone at the moment?"

I laugh, consider telling her about Eriq's numerous flings,

then reconsider and say, "I believe he's living with someone."

"Ahh, a writer in residence. It's always been a dream of mine. Is he subject to temptation?"

"I suppose like everyone else he has his weaknesses."

"Would I be one of them?"

"I don't know. Perhaps if I had a chance to sample the merchandise."

Laughing suggestively, appreciatively, she asks, "How old is he?"

"Slightly out of your range, I'm afraid. He's going to be thirty-one in October."

"Well, I can always make an exception."

"Does that mean *we'll* be retiring to the bedroom soon?"

"If you were a 6'2", 180-pound, dark-haired, blue-eyed, as-yet-unpublished-but-quite-talented writer, you probably wouldn't have to ask me that question."

nothing compares 2 u

On the subway ride over to Brad's place I call him (five times) since in the last year or so he's been insisting people call him before they come over because (surprise, surprise) he's not overly fond of surprises and he doesn't like being disturbed when he's doing work (he's a lawyer in his father's firm), but each time I call I get his answering machine and when I get out of the Spadina subway station I think about calling him again but decide not to, saying, out loud, "Fuck it. I'll be at his doorstep in less than five minutes anyway."

Less than five minutes turns out to be an exaggeration because a moment later I've decided to stop off at Noah's Natural

Foods store on Bloor West and it's while I'm waiting in the checkout line after picking up an organic yogurt and the hemp lip balm I forgot to buy this morning before visiting Jo-Jo that I try to figure out where it is I've met the cashier, noting that even though her head is shaved she still looks incredible — even better than Sinéad O'Connor looks in the video 'Nothing Compares 2 U' — so incredible in fact that I barely notice she's not wearing a bra and that her breasts and exposed midriff are perfect, and even though she can't be more than seventeen, nineteen tops, I still find myself thinking that I may have gone on a date or had sex with her and after she says, "Thank you. Bye now," to the woman gathering up her groceries and smiles (warmly? knowingly? naughtily?) at me while reaching for the yogurt and the lip balm, I'm tempted to ask her where it is we've met, am actually about to ask her this, when — in a searing flash — I realize she's the exact physical replica of a character in Eriq's short story, 'New and Improved,' which is something he sometimes does — uses real people's physical features for his characters — and I hear myself chuckling a) in admiration of Eriq's descriptive powers, of his ability to get me to identify so strongly with the narrator of 'New and Improved' that I had myself convinced it was actually *me* who had sex with this girl instead of his main character and b) for the thought that's now traipsing through my mind which is that, despite her age, I should ask her out on a date to see if she's actually as good in bed as Eriq wrote she was but just as I'm about to, the store phone rings and two seconds after the other cashier answers it she hands it to the Sinéad-O'Connor-look-alike, saying, "It's your lover," and the Sinéad-O'Connor-look-alike grabs the phone and says, while smiling at me, "Hi gorgeous" (into the phone's receiver), then "That'll be $4.29, please," (to me) and after paying for the items, eating the yogurt, and applying some lip balm, I go to the nearest payphone, dial a random number, and ask the person who answers — an elderly lady — if she's ever thought about suicide and, if so, what method she thinks she'd use and she tells me I have the wrong number and hangs up, so I dial another number, get someone's voicemail, don't leave a message, dial a third number and the young guy, after I've asked him the same question, says "Fuck off, Andrew, you fucking idiot," and hangs up and it's not until my sixth call that I get someone who is willing to answer the question — a young woman, probably in her mid to late twenties, with a very soothing, almost familiar voice — but she's having a difficult time deciding what method she'd use and after saying, "Hmmm, that's a tough one," twice in the span of thirty seconds, she then says, "You know, I used to think about this a lot, I even had the method picked out and everything but then something happened a while ago that made me stop thinking about it so much and so when you asked me the question I realized for the first time in a long time that my answer wasn't the same anymore, that I've changed, and so now I don't know how I'd do it even if I wanted to do it and since I know it's an important question I don't want to just give you my *old* answer, so if it's alright with you I'd like to give it some more thought," and then she asks me if I can call her back tonight after 11:00 p.m. if that's not too late, and I tell her I'll call her around 11:30 p.m. and she says, "Great. I'll talk to you around 11:30, bye," then hangs up and it's while I'm entering her number into my cellphone and replaying our conversation while walking up Brad's street that her voice becomes even more familiar and after the second replaying I begin to see a face forming around the voice, and it's just as I think I'm about to recognize whom the voice belongs to that the nearly formed face is abruptly replaced by the sight of three people walking down Brad's driveway.

donation

"Who is it?"

I've already rung the doorbell three times before Brad's voice comes through the intercom beside the front door.

"Ryan," I say.

"I'll just be a minute. I'm on the throne."

"Take your time," I say, picturing Brad seated on the toilet and talking to the monitor above the toilet paper dispenser while

– thinking that you'd probably have to be near-royalty to be able to take a dump and still acknowledge the person at the front door

– surveying the security bars on the windows, the drawn curtains, the motion detector lights on the front porch and over the garage

– smiling when the description, 'Fort Bradley' (Daphne's), pops into my head

– opening the mailbox and finding six letters in it, two addressed to Brad M. Wellington and four others addressed to four different people, which strikes me as odd, seeing as Brad has lived here, alone, for nearly five years.

A couple minutes later he opens the door and I'm immediately surrounded by the scent of vanilla, the air overly dense, almost opaque with the smell, causing me to step back outside for a few moments.

"What the hell is that?" I say, using the envelopes in my hand to swat at the space in front of my face in an attempt to breathe some vanilla-free air.

"*That*, is a mask for the *odeur de naturel* coming from la salle de bain," Brad says, pointing to the bathroom in the hallway.

"Is it that bad?"

"Five stars," he says, beginning to walk down the hall towards the kitchen. "At least."

"Hey," I say, stepping back inside and closing the door. "These are for you," holding out the envelopes. "Or, at least two of them are," I say, as he walks back and takes them from me. "The rest are addressed to some other people."

"Thanks," he says, adding, as he starts walking down the hallway again, "I think this place must have been a commune or an orphanage or something before my father bought it. I get other people's mail here all the time."

When he's nearly down the hall I remember what I was going to ask him and holler, "Hey, who were those three kids leaving your place?"

"What three kids?" he asks, coming to an abrupt stop.

"I just saw three kids in your driveway," I say, kicking off the 714 New Balance running shoes I bought last week at the Runner's Den in Hamilton while visiting a friend. "About two minutes ago. They were walking away from the house."

"*That* must've been who that was," he says, snapping his fingers. "I was replacing a lightbulb in the basement and thought I heard the doorbell but when I got to the front door there was no one there and then, well, then nature called and — did you talk to them?"

"No," I say, shaking my head, "but I'm almost positive they were the same three street kids I saw on Queen West yesterday — the ones with the dreadlocks and the 'Need Money for Marijuana' sign — remember?"

After scratching his head for two or three seconds, he says, "Oh ya, now I remember. You said you saw some fine print on their sign about them actually needing the money for food and clothing, right?"

"Exactly. The only thing was they looked a lot different today."

Brad gives me a puzzled look. "Different? What do you mean, different?"

"Well, for starters, not only did they look a lot cleaner, they also looked like they were wearing some of your old clothes."

He laughs. "Ya right."

"I'm serious. The two guys were wearing the same kind of beach volleyball shorts you wore last summer and the girl was wearing the exact same pair of mauve cargo shorts you wore last summer and that T-shirt you got when you were down in Georgia a few years back, the one that has 'Model Basketball' in big letters on it?"

"Whatever."

"I'm totally serious. I mean, besides you, I think I've only seen one other person wearing a 'Model Basketball' shirt before and that wasn't even a T-shirt, it was a sweatshirt."

"Well, I *did* give all my old summer clothes to The Salvation Army about two weeks ago, so maybe —"

"Wait a second," I say, cutting him off. "Are you telling me you *donated* last year's entire summer wardrobe — *including* those volleyball shorts, the mauve cargo shorts, *and* the 'Model Basketball' T-shirt — *to The Salvation Army?*"

"Ya, so?"

"So? You got those cargo shorts at VICE on Queen West and those volleyball shorts at Overkill in the Beaches, right?"

"Ya?"

"And they cost you like what, seventy bucks a pair?"

"More, actually. What's the big deal?

"The big deal is, how about asking your so-called best man here if he wants first dibs on the stuff? I'm serious," I say, responding to the, 'Ya right, whatever,' expression now on Brad's face. "I mean, why the hell do you think I called you last year and started hanging out with you again — for your stimulating conversation?"

"You're trying to tell me it's because of my clothes?"

"Ladies and Gentlemen, we have a winner," I say, clapping my hands a few times before raising them above my head and cheering. "I mean, what's the use of having a rich, ultra-stylish friend who's constantly buying new clothes because he just has to be on the cutting edge of what's in style if he's going to donate all his nearly new, just-entering-the-mainstream-as-stylish clothes to The Salvation Army instead of passing it along to his best buddy?"

"I hope you're not serious."

"About wanting your old clothes or the reason I got back in touch with you?"

"Both."

"Well, I am joking about the reason I got back in touch with you, but I'm not joking about the clothes — those I want."

He laughs, shakes his head. "I don't know what you're worried about, Ryan. I'm sure you can afford to buy your own shorts."

"Well contrary to what you may believe Mr. 'Obviously-too-rich-for-his-own-good,' ABI therapists don't make *that* much money."

"Well," he says, mimicking and exaggerating the tone of voice I was using, "I'm sure ABI therapists make considerably more money than street kids do. But, if you want to deprive the really needy of some nice clothes, I'll try to understand."

"Thanks," I say, patting him on the back as we continue walking down the hallway, "that's real swell of ya, bud."

a big fucking house

"Doing some entertaining?" I ask when we're in the kitchen.

While passing the closed French doors that lead into the living room, I noticed several things scattered about inside the room — two newspapers (the *Globe and Mail* and the *Toronto Star*) laying on the sofa, a book *(The Great Gatsby)* resting on the arm of the Lazy Boy, several dinner plates, a few glasses, two coffee mugs, and one large orange juice carton (Tropicana) sitting on the coffee table — which made me think the place actually looked like a regular home instead of the latest ad for 'TidyHouses.com' — which is extremely unusual for Brad since he likes everything to be neat and tidy.

It was one of the things I didn't like about him when we roomed together at university — the fact that he was overly tidy. That and the fact that he didn't like anyone using or borrowing his stuff.

"What?"

"I said, 'Doing some entertaining?'" flicking my thumb in the direction of the living room. "Glasses. Dirty plates. Orange juice carton. Sections of newspaper all over the living room. Not exactly a typical scene in Brad Wellington's residence."

"Oh, that. No. No visitors. Just me and Nicole — she spent the night here last night."

"Who's reading *The Great Gatsby*?"

"Me."

"Decided to take Daphne's advice?"

"Advice?"

"About reading instead of watching TV."

"Oh, ya," he says, "right," then opens the refrigerator and pulls out a bag of carrots, two tomatoes, a zucchini, an eggplant, and a few celery stalks from the crisper.

"So you're sure you didn't talk to those street kids, huh?" I ask him again, this time studying his face for a reaction.

"Yes *Dad*, I'm sure."

"Weird. I wonder what they were doing here?"

"Who knows?" he says, shrugging, starting to rinse off the carrots. "Maybe someone told them this was a good neighbourhood to go door to door asking for donations for marijuana?"

I laugh. "Well, they wouldn't be far off. Isn't this area full of nostalgic ex-hippies?"

"Hey, nostalgia's *in* nowadays," he says, now retrieving some onions and several cloves of garlic from the cupboard below the sink and setting them on the ceramic countertop near a large cutting board. "It's one of the most lucrative commodities right now. Just ask my father, he'll tell you. Everyone's trying to capture that feeling of a bygone era — fashion designers, appliance makers, antique dealers, car manufacturers — even housing developers."

"Speaking of houses," I say, putting into words what always goes through my mind whenever I'm here. "*This* is a big fucking house."

It's true, it is a big fucking house, but even though I'm always surprised by its size and the fact that only Brad lives in it, even more surprising are the security systems he has in place — the alarms, the barred windows, the deadbolts, the sensor lights. He even has a note on the front and back doors reminding himself to '<u>Always</u> *Lock the Door When You Leave — even if it's just for a few minutes.*'

"Don't even think about starting that shit," Brad warns, his tone stern, responding to my 'This is a fucking big house' comment.

"No. No," I say quickly, "I wasn't even thinking about *that* — honest."

When Rebecca told me about having to move a few months ago,

I approached Brad with the idea of letting her rent a room here — thinking he'd immediately go for it since I suspected he liked her, but he refused, telling me he enjoyed having the space to himself, that he sometimes enjoyed sleeping in the other bedrooms, which was when I called him a 'liar' and we ended up getting into quite a heated argument.

"I am *not* lying, Ryan," he replied.

"Yes. You. Are," I said. "And the fact that you just used the excuse that you sleep in all five bedrooms confirms it."

"*That* confirms nothing."

"It confirms that you won't help out Rebecca. She's your friend for fuck's sake."

"I know *what* she is."

"Well then why won't you help her?"

"I already told you. I use the rooms."

"Bull-fucking-shit you use the rooms, Brad. Why don't you tell me the real reason?"

"And what would that be?"

"I don't know, maybe that you're a selfish, anal bastard who doesn't like to share anything?"

"Ryan, it's obvious you don't have a clue as to what you're talking about."

"Well why don't you *enlighten* me then," I said, thinking if he wasn't five inches taller, forty pounds heavier (Brad is 6'4", 210 pounds), and could kick the shit out of me in less than five seconds I would've told him I felt like grabbing the 'Carlos Delgado' autographed baseball bat from the wall mount above his entertainment unit and take a Barry Bonds swing at his Nakamichi Soundspace 9 audio system followed by a Sammy Sosa swing at his 32" Sony widescreen television and a Robert De Niro (as Al Capone in *The Untouchables*) swing at Brad's left frontal lobe with enough force to crush Broca's region and give him expressive aphasia for the rest of his life and probably enough retrograde memory loss that Rebecca could move in and tell him she'd been living there for months already and he wouldn't know the difference.

the real voyage of discovery

Brad has finished cutting the onions and garlic and is now informing me, while placing the onions and garlic into a sauce pan with some olive oil, that, as usual, all the ingredients are organic. He's preparing ratatouille — from Peter Gzowski's *Morningside Cookbook* — for tomorrow's dinner party and it's while he's cutting the zucchini, the celery, and the carrots that I notice, then stare at, then become fixated on the twenty-three-centimetre WUSTHOF-TRIDENT high carbon stainless steel knife he's using, enchanted by this beautiful soulless metallic creation slicing quickly-slash-meticulously-slash-matter-of-factly through the vegetables and I hear myself asking Brad where he bought it and when he tells me I make a mental note to go to the Eaton Centre tomorrow to buy one, the whole time imagining it's me instead of Brad cutting the carrots, that I continue to advance the knife past the last piece of carrot, slicing the nibs off my index finger, then down to the first joint, then the entire finger, then the rest of my fingers, my thumb, perhaps even my entire hand, watching the blood drooling from the open wound, flowing past the pieces of carrots and fingers before spilling over the sides of the cutting board onto the countertop, then over the countertop to the floor, then think that maybe, if I first administered a local anaesthetic — either in the shoulder or just above the elbow — it would completely numb the pain and I could observe the entire scene as though it were someone else's fingers or hand I was dismembering. Of course, I'd probably also need an anaesthetic for my mind since the loss of blood usually induces a shock response in the body which is why my sister Jennie —

"So, what brings you around, Ryan?"

"Um, I was . . . I was actually hoping to find Nicole here. I called her place and her mother said she might be here."

"You after my fiancée?" he says, his tone mock-serious.

"Actually no. I just wanted to see how she was doing after last night. She seemed pretty upset."

He stops cutting and looks at me, really looks at me, for maybe five seconds, then says, sincerely, "That's nice, Ryan," which makes me think he probably wouldn't think I was so nice if he knew the only reason I wanted to know how Nicole was doing was because Rebecca always wants a full report on everyone's emotional frame of mind after each get-together so she knows how much damage control is required to convince everyone to continue getting together and in what direction to steer 'the gang' during our next get-together.

"She's fine, though," Brad says, beginning to cut the eggplant into thin slices, "She just believes in the 'I feel, therefore I am,' theory and gets a little emotional sometimes."

There are a few moments of silence during which just the sound of the knife slicing through the eggplant and whacking against the oak cutting board fills the kitchen and then I ask, "What made you want to be with her?"

"Who, Nicole?"

I nod.

"Where'd that come from?"

"I don't know. I guess maybe I've always wondered why her, why Nicole? I mean, you always said you only fell for women who were — what was the word — *unique*? So I was just —"

"You don't think Nicole's unique?"

I think about it, about Nicole's many addictions, her neuroses, the tiny scars on her wrists, her over-emoting. "Sure," I say, then, reconsidering, thinking she's actually quite typical, a template for the average thirty-year-old woman in today's society, I add, "Just not in a way . . . not in a way that's easily definable."

"Well, that's certainly true," he says, smiling, seemingly pleased with my analysis.

"So then, what made you want to be with her?"

He stops slicing the eggplant, smiles, shakes his head, chuckles (to himself), then says, "You know, I don't think I've ever told you this before but Nicole reminds me a lot of Jennie."

"My sister?"

"They're very similar."

"You think Jennie and Nicole are . . . *similar*?"

He nods his head, continues slicing the eggplant. *"Very."*

"In what way?" I ask, thinking he's tweaked, that he's totally misinterpreted Jennie and Nicole, that except for maybe the wrist scars, there couldn't possibly exist two more *dis*similar people on the planet.

He stops slicing again, smiles again, this time gazing up at the ceiling for a few seconds before saying, "For one, Nicole is an intelligent woman. Far more intelligent than she lets on. And I'm not talking about intelligence in the Stanford-Binet IQ test sense of the word. I'm talking about her empathy."

"Her empathy?"

"Ya, you know, the ability to enter into another person's —"

"I'm aware of the definition, Brad."

"Well, that's Nicole. She's incredibly empathetic. And so was your sister."

Swilling about my visual cortex at the moment is an image of Nicole obsessing about her nails, her hair, her clothes, her makeup, being far too preoccupied and self-absorbed to spend a moment trying to understand or connect herself with another person and I'm comparing this to the image of Jennie who spent the last few years of her life really helping people but instead of asking Brad, "Are we talking about the same Nicole?" I say, "I hope that's not the *only* similarity?" thinking that if it is, if he can't provide me with any more evidence — at least a hint of a connection between Nicole and Jennie that I don't see — I'm going to call him a fucking deluded moron.

"No, that's not the *only* similarity," he says.

"Well then?"

He pauses, smiles — again at the ceiling — and says, "I don't know. Sometimes I just look at her and marvel at her strength. I mean, the things she's gone through, the thing's she's *done* since I've known her, just makes my head spin."

"Really?" I say, trying hard, maybe a little too hard, to sound intrigued. "And what sorts of things has she done since you've known her that just makes your head spin?"

"Listen, Ryan, I can't — shouldn't — say anything else."

"Why not?"

"Because, and I know you're going to hate the cliché, but I'm not at liberty to say."

I look at him for a few moments, watch him finish slicing the eggplant, wondering if he's bullshitting me, if he's just making it up, creating this line of question-and-answer to either get information or a reaction out of me and ten seconds from now is going to burst out laughing and say something like, "Gotcha!" or "You should've seen the expression on your face when I said Nicole and your sister were 'very similar'!" which is something Rebecca used to do to me all the time, until I finally caught on.

"So why exactly are you — quote, unquote — 'not at liberty to say'?" I ask, trying to make it sound like I know what he's up to, that I'm on to him.

"Because at this point I'm just speculating."

"So? I don't mind. Go ahead and speculate. I'm not going to sue you if you're wrong."

"Ya, but if I'm wrong it would suck. I hate it when I tell someone something I'm not one hundred percent sure of and then the person starts imagining things. Like say I told you something about Nicole that I swore was true and you believed me and it severely altered the way you looked at her from that point on, and then, like a week or a year later, the story turns out to be complete bullshit. I hate that. Secrets I don't mind, but I hate when people speculate, when they invent all these possibilities out of only tiny bits of information. Things always end up getting blown to hell."

"Well, if it's any consolation, I don't mind a good story, even if it's *not* the truth."

"Ya, but we're talking about my fiancée here."

"Well, what if you're right? What if it's not just a story and your speculation turns out to be what's actually going on?"

"Well, if I'm right, I'd want her to be the one to tell people, not me."

Genuinely intrigued now, both by the things Nicole may be doing and by Brad's unwillingness to provide me with any more details, I ask, "How about a hint?" and he sighs and then looks at me as though there's a mini-battle going on in his frontal lobe.

"A hint, huh?" he says, pausing — more battling, more battling, more — "Okay," he says, a few seconds later, whacking the cutting board with the knife and then, squinting his eyes to make himself look more serious, he points the knife at me and says, "I'll give you *one* hint of what I *think* she's doing — deal?"

"Deal," I say, backing away from the knife and raising my hands in the air.

He smiles at my antics. "I *think* she's conducting an experiment."

"What?"

"Con-duct-ing an ex-per-i-ment."

"What kind of an ex-per-i-ment?"

He looks at me as if to say, 'Ryan, I just gave you the one hint.'

"Come on," I say in a mock-pleading tone, bringing my hands together as though I'm praying, begging him. "Just one more hint."

He laughs, says, still pointing the knife in my direction, "If I give you one more hint, do you promise not to ask me any more questions?" and when I say, "I promise, cross my heart and hope to die," while crossing my heart with my right index finger, he says, after retracing my cross in the air with the knife, "I think it was Marcel Proust who said, 'The real voyage of discovery is not in seeking out new lands, but in seeing with new eyes,' and when you figure out how a person can see with new eyes, you'll not only figure out what the experiment is, but also why I think your sister and Nicole are very similar."

heaven on earth

I'm southbound on the Yonge Street subway line
 – watching an elderly (possibly Greek, possibly Portuguese) woman slumped in the seat across the aisle from me, sleeping, the fingers on both her hands curled tightly around the straps of a black faux leather purse,
 – listening to the classical music (Bach?) pumping out of some grade school kid's Sony headphones,
 – smelling the pepperoni from the upside-down pizza slice melded to the subway car floor a few feet from me,
 – feeling the blood draining from my arm, my fingers starting to tingle as I grip the cool metal rail above my head even tighter, while

— thinking about what Brad said, about the quote from Marcel Proust, wondering if he's ever read Proust or if he only knows this one particular quote or if the quote is part of some elaborate scheme he's been planning for days, weeks, months — maybe even since he met me for dinner with the gang that first time at Jump Café?

I leave these thoughts for the moment and begin speculating as to what Nicole's experiment could be, what she could be doing that would make Brad compare her to Jennie and after putting Nicole into increasingly outrageous scenes, her experiments becoming more and more extreme, for some reason, I begin replaying the mini-sermon my uncle Jack — the priest — delivered to me after stopping by my apartment in Hamilton a month or so after Jennie's suicide, informing me he'd had some time to, as he put it, pray and consult the Bible on why Christ's crucifixion wasn't, as I had put it during Easter Monday dinner, really just a rational suicide.

While he sat there across from me, telling me that a) Jesus was the physical embodiment of purity and goodness, b) Jesus was the *only* earthly vessel capable of absorbing humanity's sins, c) by Jesus absorbing these sins and then dying he would, in the process, cleanse the earth of our sins, and d) the disciples allowed it to happen because not only was it what God commanded and what Christ wanted but bearing witness to this event charged the disciples with spreading the word, with communicating what Jesus had sacrificed for humanity — the whole time I was sitting there listening to him I was overlaying his mini-sermon with the image of Rebecca sitting beside Jennie's dead body, talking directly to Cam 1, informing the audience that, just like Jesus Christ, Jennie Brassard had committed rational suicide, that, just like Jesus, Jennie was totally disillusioned with a world gone mad and would rather die than continue to be a part of it and that, just like Jesus, Jennie knew killing herself was what needed to be done, that not only was this *her* will but that she too, in a sense, was dying for our sins and wanted Rebecca and I to bear witness and spread the word of why she had decided to take her own life.

When I come out of these memories I realize I've retrieved the copy of Jennie's journal from my messenger bag, my eyes already on the section I've read dozens of times before and, as though I was still back at my old apartment in Hamilton, sitting across the living room from my uncle Jack, I hear myself saying, 'I will now read an excerpt from my sister's journal.'

> I was sitting on the bumper of the garbage truck watching as each one of the pores in my skin turn into a garbage can and things were being dumped into me — polymers, plastics, Pepsi, Coke, Bud Lite, Quaker State motor oil, caffeine, TV commercials, aspartame, next month's fashions, Starbucks coffee cups, last month's fashions, sitcoms, PowerBars, Ikea furniture, Prozac, Club Med vacations, cosmetics, talk shows, cigarettes, recovered memory therapy, MTV, exhaust emissions, the Internet, refrigerators, CNN, lawn pesticides, leftover Pad Thai — everything imaginable. At the bottom of each can was a garborator and everything that was dumped into my pores was chewed up, puréed, and the resulting liquid ended up leaching into my bloodstream and began circulating through my body. At first, I was okay with it, my body adapted, but after a while there was just too much stuff, the concentrations became too high and that was when all my body hair started falling out and tumours started forming inside me and some of my organs — such as my lungs and kidneys and brain and liver — started malfunctioning. But the stuff kept coming, to the point where it actually started displacing my blood and lymph and oxygen and since I couldn't

absorb or process anymore I ended up choking and gagging and then all this gunk started oozing out of my garbage can pores and spilling out and before long a team of experts arrived to inspect me and I was classified as a BIOHAZARD and they erected a massive fence around me and no one was allowed to come near me for the next million years and that was when I 'woke up,' my eyes filled with tears, my brain throbbing with the question, 'Why do I want to continue being a part of this?'

Instead of reading on — reading the part where Jennie stated that the only rational thing to do was to remove herself from the equation, to take as much of the *stuff* she'd absorbed as possible with her to the grave — I decide to tune into the conversation a guy and a girl are having about the upcoming Gay Pride Parade, the guy wondering if it would be as good as last year's parade, the girl saying it probably wouldn't be seeing as last year was the Millennium Parade and when we enter Dundas Station a feeling of déjà vu strikes me and I remember wanting to buy the Wamphryi CD at HMV and so I get off at Dundas station and now I'm walking through the Eaton Centre, following a middle-aged man wearing a T-shirt that says, *'Attention: ce contenant peut exploser s'il est chauffé'* through the main level of the Eaton's store while listening to the young woman he's holding hands with telling him that they'll soon be closing the Eaton's store for good, that it's going bankrupt, which makes her wonder if they'll end up renaming the Eaton Centre and it's as I'm casually surveying the overly made-up men and women stationed behind the cosmetic counters that I bump into the memory of one of my sister Jennie's poems, this one entitled 'Escort Service,' which I begin reciting while walking.

*I weave my way through the
labyrinth of cosmetic counters,
each one neatly arranged with
despots of
lipstick,
mascara,
nail polish,
eyeliner;
each one embroidered with a
Cindy,
a Christy,
a Tyra,
a Halle,
an Elizabeth —
or some other member of the Official Opposition, smiling
beside a vacant mirror.*

It's what nearly ruined my friend.

*She had them everywhere,
spent hours in front of them,
consulting her reflection,
constantly comparing and contrasting it with the model examples staring back at her from
the pages of Vogue, Cosmo, Glamour,
magnifying her inadequacies:*

*hair too thin & straight
nose too wide & crooked
lips too thin
breasts too small
hips too big
legs too short*

feet too —

the improvements to be made appeared endless . . .

*Once,
when she wasn't home,
I got rid of them;
disconnecting them
from the walls, the doors, her vanity — even the ones in
her Ford Escort —
taking them to the city dump along with her
collection of creams, shampoos, conditioners,
sprays, gels, lotions, perfumes, and back issues of
Cosmo, Glamour, and Vogue.*

*I thought that would be the end of it —
out of sight, out of mind —
but it wasn't that simple;
I didn't realize the model examples were already indelible,
that they'd already left a permanent mark . . .*

It's as I'm passing the last counter — the Eaton's store opening up into the rest of the Eaton Centre, into 'the cathedral of consumerism' as Daphne called it last week — that I notice a woman carrying what appears to be a handcarved canoe paddle, which immediately gets me thinking about travelling and I'm once again gripped by the idea of leaving, of rushing back to my apartment, packing a few things and heading to some place I've never been, a place where no one knows me, where I can create a totally different life than the one I have now, but before I become overly enamoured with this possibility the realization hits me that no matter where I go — whether to Alaska or Nova Scotia, Portugal or Provence — I'll never be able to recreate my memories or control my dreams, which is probably why, moments after I see the sign, I enter the House of Knives and begin admiring the twenty-three-centimetre WUSTHOF-TRIDENT high carbon stainless steel knife in the display cabinet, envisioning what I'm going to do with it until (despite the fact that I'm wearing a 'Do Not Disturb' expression) the salesperson asks me if I'd like to take a closer look, which, for some reason, instead of taking a closer look or buying the knife like I'd intended, causes me to think she knows what I want to use it for, what I'm envisioning doing to my fingers and I decide to leave without replying to her question, heading straight for Indigo Books and walking immediately to the Travel section, my eyes quickly browsing a variety of travel books until one marked 'British Columbia' urges me to pull it off the shelf and look up The Sunshine Coast, specifically Hornby Island, where my sister Jennie said she dreamed of moving to, often referring to it as 'Heaven on Earth.'

potential

"It's one of our best knives."

I'm back at the House of Knives, listening to the salesclerk giving me her spiel about the twenty-three-centimetre WUSTHOF-TRIDENT high carbon stainless steel knife I'm now holding in my left hand while replaying the dream about Jennie I had after falling asleep in the bookstore.

It started off with me being at Brad's house, with Brad saying that he couldn't believe that Jennie was gone, that it was such a tragedy, that he wondered if maybe the reason she did it was because she stopped taking her medication and it was at this point the dream shifted, and I was suddenly back at my parents' house in Hamilton, walking in on Rebecca filming Jennie coming out of the bedroom, only this time, instead of listening to Rebecca, instead of allowing her to persuade me to go along with what she was proposing, I actually picked up the phone and called the cops and got them to arrest Rebecca and take Jennie to the hospital, and it was just as I was getting in the ambulance with Jennie that I woke crying, realizing immediately that I'd fallen asleep in the Travel section of Indigo, that I'd been dreaming again, and that instead of getting into the ambulance with Jennie I was watching my tears falling on the pages of Hornby Island, on Jennie's version of 'Heaven on Earth,' which was when I made up my mind about my particular method of suicide and the fact that, despite my promise to Rebecca to remain suicide-free until after her and Daphne's mutual suicide, I was going to bump up my expiration date and kill myself tonight, and I got up and started walking back to the House of Knives to get the knife.

"It's capable of cutting through almost anything," the salesclerk continues. "A butternut squash, a porterhouse steak, even an index finger."

"Excuse me?" I say, not sure if I heard her correctly.

"Don't worry," she says, giving me a knowing wink and a slight nudge. "Your secret's safe with me."

"Secret? What secret?"

"Oh, come on now. No need to be coy."

"Lady, I have no idea what you're talking about."

The saleswoman sighs, then, sounding slightly annoyed, says, "I was just trying to be supportive."

"Supportive? By telling me with a nudge-nudge, wink-wink, that this knife is capable of cutting through my index finger?"

"I merely thought you'd be interested in knowing the knife's potential."

"The knife's *potential*? Is this the kind of sales approach you use with all your customers?"

"I was only trying to —"

"Ya, I heard you the first —"

"Oh for Pete's sake!" the woman suddenly hisses, interrupting me and quickly stepping forward, moving to within inches of my face before speaking again, this time through clenched teeth. "I was only trying to be supportive in your choice of exits."

"My what?"

"*Exits*. You know, 'One entrance, a hundred thousand exits.'"

"Who . . . how do you know . . . where . . . ?" I stammer.

"I mean, think of it," she continues. "Now that you've decided to do it you won't have any more disturbing dreams or voices in your head or any of those weird public displays you've been having recently. You'll be guilt-free. In fact, you'll be feeling-free. Which is why I'm sure you can't wait to get home and do it, right?"

It was after she spoke the word 'displays' that I realized something was wrong with this picture, that this so-called saleswoman knew far too much about me and so I start nodding my head and say, "Well, ya. I guess. I mean, all that's true, but I can't do it. At least not yet, anyway."

"Why not?"

"Because I've got something to do first."

"What?"

"Something."

"Ya, well, whatever it is, I'm sure it's nowhere near as important as having that peace of mind you want, right?"

"Actually it is. And besides, I promised."

"Who?"

"Someone."

"Well, whoever this person is I'm certain they'd understand if you broke the promise. I mean, look at you, you're coming apart at the seams. Why don't you just end it now?"

"I told you, I promised. I gave someone my word."

"Oh please, *'I promised. I gave my word.'* How corny is that? I mean, really, who cares about these things anymore?"

"I care," I say and then, after saying, "Besides," I insert a dramatic pause until the saleswoman responds with, "Besides what?"

"Besides, you'd probably kill me if I did it before fulfilling our agreement."

"You're goddamn right I would," the saleswoman says, abruptly snatching the knife out of my hand and placing it on the counter before walking briskly out of the store, out of the Eaton Centre and it's not until she's almost at Nathan Phillips Square that she slows down enough for me to confront her.

"Rebecca, what the *hell* are you doing?"

She shrugs. "I just had to be sure."

"Sure? Sure of what? This is bullshit."

"Hey," she snaps, suddenly stopping and poking my chest with her index finger. "This is *not* — I repeat, *not* — bullshit. I've got a lot of time and effort invested in you and I don't want you offing yourself before we do what we agreed we'd do."

I'm so pissed at her, so incredibly angry at the lengths she's willing to go to to ensure that I follow through on our agreement that for the first time since the mock-yelling I did at Jennie's suicide I start yelling at her, calling her a fucking psychotic, manipulative bitch from hell who deserves to be burned alive at the stake like some fucking —

Five minutes after an Indigo employee woke me up and I realized a) that I'd actually *dreamt* I woke up from my dream, b) that I'd actually dreamt I confronted Rebecca in Nathan Phillips Square, c) that I was actually seated in a chair in the Travel section of Indigo Books the entire time, and, d) thanks to the Indigo employee who not only woke me up but, as I was leaving, politely informed me that I'd been talking in my sleep, that she even let it go for a while because people sometimes fall asleep in the store but then, when I started shouting and swearing, she had no other option but to wake me — and so, five minutes after realizing all this, I find myself exiting the Eaton Centre, walking past two buskers energetically beating plastic pails with drumsticks just outside the doors, past the woman handing out 'Shop 'til You Drop' pamphlets, past the guy saying that this summer is going to be 'Hot. Really hot. *Scalding* hot. The hottest summer on record is my prediction,' past the man dressed in a winter parka, blue jeans, and workboots standing in front of The Gap at the corner of Dundas and Yonge handing out 'Satan — the god of this world' flyers, past a guy handing out flyers for the Aldo retail outlet which makes me smile, thinking of the blond-haired, Aldo-shoed guy from last night, past — as I'm crossing Yonge Street — a young Pakistani man whom I think I recognize as a one-time visitor to The Suicide Loft but, after crossing the street and looking back at him decide, for whatever reason, that it wasn't.

Once inside HMV, I search for almost ten minutes without finding the Wamphryi CD and then decide to ask a salesclerk, a girl woman wearing a black T-shirt with the words 'ACCESS RESTRICTED TO THOSE PERSONS OVER THE AGE OF 29' in white lettering and who, before I can even ask her about the CD, smiles at me like she sort of knows me and says, "How's your wrist?"

"Excuse me?"

"Your wrist," she says, pointing at my left wrist. "That was you the other day wasn't it? On Queen West? I was standing by the —"

"By the hot dog vendor," I say, remembering. "You were wearing a white University of Toronto tanktop and watching me sawing —" (I stop before adding 'my wrist with my thumbnail while I was replaying the memory of my sister Jennie's suicide').

"Yep. That was me," she says, smiling. "You looked like you were rehearsing for a play or something. I was trying to figure out what it was and I kept thinking I should ask you, but I was too chicken."

I laugh. "So what'd you settle on?"

"What do you mean?"

"What play did you think I was rehearsing?"

"Oh. I thought it might've been Shakespeare. And if it was, then it was probably *Macbeth*. And if it was *Macbeth* then I thought it was probably the part where Lady Macbeth starts scrubbing her hands like crazy and saying, 'Out, damned spot, out!'"

I smile. "Well, you certainly have an active imagination."

"So does that mean I was right?"

Still smiling, I shake my head and say, "Unfortunately, no. I was just thinking."

"Really?" she says, and then, pointing to the fresh scab on my wrist, she says, "Does that always happen while you're thinking?"

"Only when it's serious."

"Well, maybe you should stick to lighter topics or one of these days you're going to think too hard and end up committing suicide."

I laugh, chuckling at the irony.

"What's so funny?" she says.

"Nothing," I say, adding, "You're probably right," and then, before I say something that I probably shouldn't, I say, "You wouldn't happen to know if you have any CDs from the band Wamphryi in stock right now, would you?"

"No way," she says. "Are you serious?" And when I nod, she says, "Okay, like how ironic is this? I just ordered ten copies of both their CDs not even thirty seconds before you came up to me. They're only like my favourite band in the world."

"Really?"

"Ya, their music kicks ass."

"Ever seen them live?"

"Four times. I only started listening to them a couple of years ago, though. My sister got me into them. She started listening to them since they first got together in like 1995."

"Really?"

"Ya. She was dating the lead guitarist for a while."

"Scott E. Dee?"

"You know him?"

I nod. "I went to high school with his younger brother, Ronnie."

"Oh my God, I know Ronnie. Tall, long hair, great smile, kind of quiet?"

"That's him."

"He plays guitar too, right?"

I nod. "Ya, but not in a band, though. I thought maybe he'd hook up with Wamphryi."

"Is he into the same kind of music?"

"Ya, I think so. He likes the harder, in-your-face stuff."

"That's Wamphryi."

I nod. "So, does your sister still listen to the band or was it more because she was dating Scott?"

"Ya, she's still a die-hard fan. She always said it was their music that got her. Of course, dating Scott I'm sure helped. But she still goes to all their concerts and Scott and her are really good friends."

"Speaking of concerts," I say, giving her my 'FYI' expression, "did you know they're playing at Lee's Palace next month?"

She smiles. "Yes, I did. In fact, I was just about to say that," and it's at this point, just as I'm about to say something about the last time I saw Wamphryi in concert, that the kid behind me clears his throat for the third time (this time much louder than the previous two, this time in such a manner as to indicate that although he's, like, totally thrilled that the salesclerk and I enjoy the same music he'd really rather pay for his CDs right now so he can get the hell out of the store) and so after making a whiny face in response to the kid's fourth throat clearing, which makes the salesclerk giggle, I tell her, while pointing at her T-shirt, that, "You know, Ronnie just turned twenty-nine," adding that I'll give him a call and maybe he and I will meet her and her sister at Lee's Palace next month and she blushes, ever so slightly, is about to say something when the kid clears his throat at us for the fifth time and so I turn around, quickly — in time to see the kid swallowing the phlegm he's just coughed up — and say, "I see you prefer to swallow instead of spit," then walk away, the sound of the salesclerk's giggles lightening my step.

designer

After exiting HMV, I start walking north on Yonge Street then turn right onto Gould Street, smelling the sweet odour of marijuana exactly six seconds before noticing the girl across the street sitting on the ground behind the vending booth smoking a joint and grazing the men, mostly middle-aged and mostly East Indian or Asian, playing chess on the outdoor chess tables, her head slowly turning in my direction until, just before we make eye contact, I avert my gaze and walk into The Salad King, my favourite restaurant in all of Toronto.

It's where my ex-friend Katelin and I first met.

Actually it's the second place we met.

She'd been to The Suicide Loft the day before.

In her interview at The Loft she told me she'd broken down in the washroom at Ryerson in January, immediately after her first class of her last semester of her final year. She was taking Interior

Design and it suddenly hit her that she didn't know if this was what she wanted, if she wanted to become — like the dozens of people in her field told her they'd become — either a glorified shopper for corporations or spending her talent designing *different looking* furniture for so-called avant-garde retailers, offices, and restaurateurs, while manufacturing desire for an ever-increasing array of non-essential, superfluous products.

Sitting in the bathroom stall she said she began to question the enormous amount of waste involved in the design industry, in the need to constantly innovate, to change, redo, replace what had just been labelled 'the best, most essential, most stylish piece of whatever' with something supposedly even better, even more essential, even more stylish. The fact that everything in the design industry seemed to be about style and obsolescence, not about substance and longevity, depressed her — *really* depressed her — as did knowing, as her professors had often mentioned, that longevity does not yield a continual profit — *and* generating a continual profit is what keeps designers employed.

She told me she'd tried talking to her brother, her mother, her friends about it — even a stranger on the streetcar — but no one seemed to understand; they all looked at her like she was crazy, like she had some sort of disease.

Only her boyfriend SJ understood.

He told her to get out, to quit, suggested they go someplace, anywhere, just get away from it, telling her she could always come back and finish her degree if she changed her mind, which is when they decided to go to Portugal and stay with SJ's aunt — a widow, who, each time they spoke on the phone, gave SJ an open invitation to come for a visit and stay as long he wanted.

Four days before they were supposed to leave, a week after SJ had purchased the airline tickets, two weeks after Katelin had quit university, telling her classmates and her professors what she really thought of design and designers and design school, SJ told her he was in love with someone else, that he was taking her to Portugal instead of Katelin, that he was sorry, very sorry. 'It all happened so fast, the day I got the airline tickets, in fact,' and so here she was, at The Suicide Loft — on the verge of. . . .

The day after Katelin's appointment at The Suicide Loft I saw her in HMV buying U2's CD *The Joshua Tree* and followed her into The Salad King, ordered what she did — the Golden Tofu Curry — then sat at the table next to her to see if she would recognize me, which she didn't, even after I'd made eye contact with her several times, even after she asked me to join her, stating that she didn't want to eat alone, even after we ended up hanging out for thirteen hours — until 6:00 a.m. the following morning — during which we finished our dinner in The Salad King, went for a long walk through Chinatown, sat on a bench for a couple of hours in Queen's Park, had a late-night dessert at Sen5es on Bloor Street West, watched a band at Lee's Palace, and I finally walked her back to her apartment near Bloor and Bathurst.

Not once during our thirteen-hour walk and talk did she mention anything she did the day before during her first session at The Suicide Loft, nothing about quitting her Interior Design course at Ryerson, or that she hated design in general, or that she'd been dumped by her boyfriend for another woman four days before they were supposed to leave on a year-long, possibly life-long trip to Portugal. In place of all this information, Katelin created a completely different picture of herself, an entirely different character, which was why I invited her to join the rest of us for dinner the following weekend at Jump Café, thinking she'd not only bring more than just a certain je ne sais quoi to our cast, she might also, if things didn't work out with Daphne, tickle Rebecca's fancy. . . .

moments

"Wait. I give candy. Candy for the children."

I'm third in line at The Salad King now, listening to the woman working the cash register talking to the mother of a family of five as she retrieves a large clear plastic bag filled with candy from beside the cash register and dumps three or four candies into each of the three children's cupped hands.

"That was nice of you," says the young man standing in front of me when the woman returns to the cash register.

The woman shakes her head. "I give candy to kids and kids say to parents, 'Let's go to Salad King.' I'm smart businesswoman."

After ordering the Golden Tofu Curry, taking my number, picking up a *NOW* magazine from one of the newspaper trays, walking to the back dining area and finding the seat with the best possible P.O.V., I begin focusing on the aroma of curry and coconut and coriander and onion embroidering the sounds of sizzling frying pans, the steam billowing over the plastic partition between the dining room and kitchen, the various people smiling, eating, tasting each other's food, and scurrying to the pickup window when their number is called over the intercom.

"That's just it, that's the point."

A couple has just sat down at the table next to mine and the guy, the one wearing black low-rise jeans, a plain black T-shirt, and black Airwalk sneakers, is the one who just made the preceding comment.

"What's the point?" the other one, the young woman wearing black low-rise jeans, a black lace-trimmed camisole, and black Steve Madden shoes, says.

"The point is we're all trying to make it fit, to have the job, the movie, the stock market, the marriage, our lives, make sense."

I've been trying to do it for years. But maybe it's not supposed to make any sense, maybe reality is only momentary."

"You mean situational?"

"Sort of. I guess what I mean is maybe only parts of our lives make sense — and only for a moment — and when that moment changes, we change, and when we change the part that made sense goes out of focus and is replaced by another part that makes sense and so on and so on. Only sometimes what makes sense to us at a particular moment can end up changing our lives forever because it leads us to do things we wouldn't even *conceive* of doing during other moments."

Which is almost exactly what the psychiatrist said had more than likely happened to Jennie. He said that since she was depressed, since she was experiencing a, quote-unquote, 'down' phase in her bipolar cycle, she was much more inclined to commit suicide. 'At that moment, what she did made sense to her,' he told us. 'In fact, it probably seemed like her only option. And, this being so, you must take some consolation in the fact that being in the frame of mind she was in, unless you were by her side the whole time or had her physically restrained, there would've been nothing you could've done to save her.'

suicidal separations

I've already had three appointments this afternoon — at 2:30, 4:00, and 5:30 p.m. — all of them regulars, all of them wanting to just sit and chat about recent developments, anomalies, epiphanies they've had in their suicidal thinking patterns.

The only thing of real interest came from my third client, a woman in her mid fifties and a ten-year member of The Hemlock

Society who gave an interesting twist to Socrates' dictum, 'The unexamined life is not worth living,' by suggesting that 'The possibility of death is always worth examining,' adding that people often accuse her of being obsessed with her own death even when she insists she likes life, that she doesn't want to end her life, and that the reason she talks about death so often is because most of us walk around like we're immortal, like nothing can harm us, but when you realize that at any moment, anyone, including yourself, could end up taking your life, life becomes very real and very, very precious.

My 7:00 p.m. appointment is a woman who is here for her fourth visit. During her interview, after she had a look around The Loft and I'd informed her of the various services I offer, she told me that during her first session she'd be interested in seeing a simucide.

In the same way some hair salons offer computer-generated simulated hairstyles and plastic surgeons offer simulated breast augmentations or rhinoplasties, I offer simulated suicides for my clients, illustrating (via footage from the Internet and lifelike footage from a computer program that Rebecca, a graduate of the medical illustration program at the University of Toronto, designed for me) what happens when a foreign object such as a bullet or a knife blade enters the heart, or substances such as cyanide or potassium chloride or Liquid Drano are introduced into the stomach, highlighting the impact on the various organs, the amount of pain involved, time until unconsciousness, until death, what can go wrong, etc., etc.

After she'd watched her first few simucides, I suggested that whenever she felt like committing suicide she mentally replay the simucides, imagining herself dying over and over again using these various methods, which may give her enough relief and comfort (and distraction) that the urge to really kill herself would pass. Since that first time, she's been back twice, both times to watch more simucides and augment her inventory of ways to imagine herself dying.

For tonight's appointment the woman has brought a CD with her and asks me if I wouldn't mind listening to it while she watches the 'simucides' — which I don't, it's her time — but after watching two simucides — of a hanging and an overdose of sleeping pills — I find myself so increasingly distracted by the CD, which, to me, sounds like a collaboration of Ani DiFranco's quirky guitar work, Sarah McLachlan's vocal stylings, and Gord Downie's rambling, curmudgeonesque lyrics, that I pause before beginning the asphyxiation simucide and ask her who this is and when she tells me it's her, I ask her if the CD is for sale, if she's a performer, and she says that, "No the CD is not for sale and no, I'm not a performer," adding, "Does this face, this body, do *I* look like I'm marketable?" which causes me to realize that neither her face nor her body is marketable. In fact, she's not even in the same vicinity as marketable, but her music is — and I tell her so — and we spend the next half hour talking about how many times she's reared her ugly head against societal expectations and lost.

In the end, just after she's booked another appointment at The Loft, we joke about her getting someone to be her front woman, the girl on the poster or the CD cover, a female version of Milli Vanilli, or maybe she could wear a costume or make-up like the rock group KISS or Darth Vader or some of the performers in the WWF and never reveal her true identity, calling herself 'The Artist Formerly Known As Deb,' which would not only add to her mystique but probably increase sales of her CDs and concert tickets.

My 9:00 p.m. appointment (the woman who has called me five times in the last three weeks and who called today while I was in the Optimum Natural Food store and said she *really* needed to have an appointment) is late again, so I decide, while waiting for her, to watch my sister's suicide — this time in German.

I've already translated the entire suicide, including our voices, into eight other languages — French, Spanish, German, Greek, Italian, Urdu, Japanese, Mandarin — and still have yet to translate it into Norwegian, Ojibway, and Dutch, as well as a Closed Caption version for the hearing impaired.

Roughly twenty-five cents out of every dollar I've made from The Suicide Loft has gone towards the documentary film Rebecca and I are making of Jennie's suicide. We've been working on it for over a year now, translating the dialogue as well as excerpts from Jennie's suicide letter into different languages, narrating and renarrating various scenes, inserting, deleting, and reinserting excerpts from Jennie's letter, her journal, various novels, other films — the editing process has been endless.

In addition to the Closed Caption and foreign language versions, we also have a version that is just audio, another 'Video Only' version, another with classical music — mostly Bach and Vivaldi — instead of dialogue, another done to '80s retro music, and another one interspersed with photos and film footage of every war of the 20th century.

> (FYI, *as you've probably already guessed, these were solely Rebecca's ideas. She said that she had that right, that [as she wrote on page 142 of her diary] 'when you hand over responsibility of production to someone else, you have to expect some changes to be made.'*)

Anyway, because it's the first in a trilogy, Rebecca wants the first episode to be really good. Episode 2 (Rebecca's suicide) will start off with footage from Episode 1 — of her in my parents' house, being filmed by Cam 1, sitting on the tub beside Jennie's lifeless body, holding Cam 2, then unmasking herself, wiping off her make-up, taking off her wig, removing her disguise, and revealing who she really is.

If things continue to unfold along the present timeline (fingers crossed), I'll probably end up filming Rebecca and Daphne's mutual suicide some time in the next couple of weeks, unmask myself beside Rebecca's and Daphne's dead bodies, complete all the necessary editing, translating, and production work myself — unless I have a one hundred percent trusted assistant by this time (which I think I may have) — and then, as soon as Episode 2 is ready (providing I've decided on the proper exit), I'll have my assistant film Episode 3 (my suicide) with detailed instructions on what to do with all three episodes.

Of course, none of this was supposed to have happened.

Jennie's original idea was to commit suicide alone, to leave behind only a letter and her journal for my parents and me to read, but Rebecca convinced her to film it, convinced her that a video would make more of an impact, would give her more exposure, that simultaneously sending copies of the suicide to NBC, CBC, ABC, CTV, CNN, and the BBC and having them saturating the airwaves with it would not only be the perfect ending to Jennie's life, it would also virtually guarantee that Jennie, her suicide, and her reasons for committing suicide would be ingrained in people's consciousness forever.

Which is precisely what happened to me the first time I viewed the tape. I couldn't think of anything but Jennie, couldn't erase the images of her or her suicide from my mind. No matter what I tried — alcohol, drugs, denial, a vacation, TV, Prozac, daily shopping sprees — nothing could make me stop thinking of it; it became the backdrop for everything I looked at, everything I thought about and even, starting that same night, everything I dreamed of, which was why a couple weeks later I decided I would, after sending my parents a package containing the original video tapes, Jennie's letter, and her journal, take a Greyhound bus up to Lake Superior, paddle far out into the lake and, after placing the barrel of my grandfather's 12-gauge shotgun in my mouth, simultaneously jump out of the canoe and pull the trigger.

Of course, like I told Jo-Jo that night in the bar in Hamilton, Rebecca got to me first. After telling me there was nothing worse than being an ignorant suicide, that I shouldn't be too hasty or premature in my decision, she gave me her diary, telling me it would not only help me cope but would also give me a different perspective on suicide and life in general. A month or so later, after I'd had time to read the diary and reflect on what was written, she suggested that while I was continuing to research suicide and find the right exit, we could do something else — and presented me with the idea of the trilogy, of how we could make all our deaths mean something special, starting with Jennie's.

I'm now sitting with my eyes closed, automatically translating the dubbed German into English, hearing Jennie's voice patiently answering Rebecca's scripted questions — why she chose this particular method, this day, this place; what led her to do this; if she had any regrets; if she felt any responsibility for the people she was leaving behind; what she was thinking — picturing Jennie's movements/gestures/facial expressions, seeing Jennie make the first longitudinal slice on her right wrist before hearing Rebecca ask her how she was feeling, the camcorder zooming in on the Wilkinson razor (which Jennie had instructed Rebecca do, to show my father that it wasn't his razor, that it was a different brand than the one he used, so he wouldn't think it was his fault, that if only he had used a Bic razor or the electric shaver she'd bought him for Christmas last year, she wouldn't have killed herself, which is precisely the kind of logic family members of suicide victims are prone to employing).

Of course, it didn't matter that my sister used a Wilkinson razor; my father blamed himself anyway. He said he should've known she was depressed, that he should've picked up on the cues she was suicidal, that he should've had his brother Jack (the priest) or his friend Barry (the grief counsellor) or the psychiatrist talk with her before he and my mother left on their vacation.

In his quest to rid himself of his guilt my father became so obsessed with trying to find out why she'd done it that twice in the first month after Jennie's suicide I found him lying in the empty bathtub, a bottle of Crown Royal, a bottle of wine, a fresh package of razor blades, and a container of pills (all unopened) sitting on a cafeteria tray, like he was repeating the sequence of events in an effort to get inside my sister's head and understand why.

My mother was the exact opposite and avoided the question 'Why?' altogether, refusing to talk about it, unable to bear the sound of my sister's name, yelling at me and my father whenever we spoke it. In the end, their conflicting methods of grieving drove them so far apart so quickly that they were separated less than four months after Jennie died, divorced after eight.

At 10:27, after rewinding the tape and putting it back in the safe, I decide the woman isn't going to show up again and, after showering, changing, and making certain everything's locked up, I leave — walking down to the basement of Jo-Jo's apartment and out the back door — heading for Hasty Market where I buy another box of Smarties and a package of Colt Milds before arriving back at my apartment in time to wave 'Goodnight' to Renaldo who is closing the exit door at the far end of the hallway.

the perfect place

Once inside my apartment I'm confronted by a mass of heavy, stagnant air and immediately switch on the oscillating fan perched on the coffee table, recalling the guy outside the Eaton Centre predicting it's going to be the hottest summer on record.

After standing in front of the now swirling hot air for a few moments, I retrieve a bottle of Evian from the refrigerator before returning to the living room and sitting down in the rocking chair beside the open window, looking west along Queen Street.

At 11:47 p.m. I check for messages on my cellphone and discover I have three — one from Brad telling me that he and Nicole are having brunch at Brasa in The Beaches tomorrow around 11:00 a.m. so why don't I join them, one from Eriq wondering if he can hook up with me some time before Brad's dinner tomorrow night — 'I need to get your advice on something' — and one from Rebecca saying she has found the 'Perfect Place' and that she'll call back later for an update on Daphne's condition.

After leaving a message on Eriq's voicemail to meet me at Brasa tomorrow morning at 11:00 a.m., I remember I promised the woman I talked to this afternoon in the phone booth outside Noah's Natural Foods store — the one with the soothing, more-than-vaguely familiar voice — that I'd call her back and so I press *67 to block my call and after we talk for a bit she tells me she'd like to meet me, have a tête-à-tête, and when I suggest 'the Starbucks on Queen West across from the City-TV building at say, 1:00 p.m. on Monday?' she hesitates, then accepts when I agree to make it 3:15–3:30 p.m., and after finding out what both of us will be wearing so we know who to look for, she says, "I guess I'll see you around 3:15–3:30 p.m. on Monday then."

the top five kids

"What are the Top Five Problems in Today's Society?"
 – Twenty minutes after hanging up the phone,
 – fifteen minutes into a taped episode of *Friends*,
 – halfway through my second bottle of Lowenbrau,
 – all the way through my first Colt's Mild wine-tipped cigar and,
 – roughly, say, two-thirds of the way through the box of Smarties, I realized I forgot to ask the woman I'm supposed to meet Monday at Starbucks for her name and just as I hit PAUSE on the VCR and was about to hit REDIAL on my cellphone, I heard the voices of the Top Five Kids.
 "The Top Five Problems?"
 "Yep."
 "Defined as?"
 "Whatever you consider to be a problem in our modern day society, preferably something that like totally disturbs you."
 "Hmmm. That's a good one. And a tough one. And I can see from the look on your face that you've already given this some thought so why don't you go first. It'll give me time to think."
 "Okay, and, as always, this is in no particular order but I'd say one of them is the fact that it almost doesn't pay to care about anything."
 "Why?"
 "Because a lot of the times you end up being totally duped."
 "I don't know. I think I'm going to have to disagree."
 "Really? Okay, how many times have you cared about someone and then they turned out to be a big phoney? I mean, look at your ex. He told you that he totally loved you and wanted to be with you forever and then it was like only *three days* after he told you all this when he said he didn't think he was ready to have a relationship with you, and only *two days* after that when

you found out he was dating someone else?"

"That doesn't mean we should stop caring."

"I didn't say that. I said that it *almost* doesn't pay to care because a lot of the times you end up caring about something or someone that's phoney which leads me to the next problem plaguing today's society, which is advertising, and how its sole purpose seems to be to convince you that you're a total loser if you don't buy their product."

"Okay, I totally, one hundred percent, agree with you on this one. I hate how advertisers try to make you feel like you're sub-human or something if you don't have a certain pair of shoes or the right car or the latest cellphone or the latest hairstyle or whatever. It's totally insane."

"You wanna know what's twice as insane?"

"What?"

"The fact that nowadays people are so desperate to be seen with the latest 'whatever' that they'll buy almost anything, which is exactly what that Fiona Jack woman proved when she got some billboard company in New Zealand to start advertising this totally non-existent product called, 'Nothing.'"

"What? I never heard about this."

"Ya, this Fiona Jack woman designed these billboards that said, 'For the person who wants nothing,' and tons of people actually ended up calling the billboard company and asking where they could buy Nothing."

"That really happened?"

"Yep."

"That's like totally, one hundred percent insane."

"I know."

"I can't believe that. I'm actually getting upset just thinking about it. Quick, I need something to take my mind off it — what's the next problem on your list?"

"Okay, I'm not sure it's going to make you any less upset but the next problem on my list — which my grandmother actually pointed out to me and I totally agree with her — is how people have lost the ability to be shocked."

"You mean like . . . wait, what do you mean?"

"I mean like I was sitting on the subway the other day listening to a bunch of grade school kids — like they were maybe eight years old — and this one kid was telling his buddies what he'd been doing the night before and he was going on and on about it, and they were some pretty insane things he was saying he'd done, really, they were, but the really disturbing or, to use your favourite phrase tonight, the totally, one hundred percent *insane* part about this whole thing, like the thing that really got my attention, was how the kids that were listening to him were all wearing these like tranquillized expressions, you know, like as if they weren't even *remotely* bothered or surprised by what he was saying, and seeing this, like seeing their response made me think about how nothing really shocks anybody anymore, how like pretty much everything is conceivable nowadays, you know? I mean, nowadays you'll hear about something really deplorable and instead of stopping dead in your tracks and being unable to move or speak or comprehend it because of the sheer inhumanity, you just accept it as normal."

"'The trouble with normal is it always gets worse.'"

"Exactly. Hey, isn't that a line in a song by . . . oh, what's his name?"

"Bruce Cockburn."

"Ya, I thought so. Anyway, that night I was talking to my grandmother about it and she said that she was listening to CBC radio one night and heard some guy talking about it. I think she said it was that George Steiner guy again. He's like her favourite philosopher or whatever. Anyway, she said that he said that up until World War I there was always the idea that people were acting within certain limits, that even during a war there were still certain things that people couldn't conceive of ever happening. But then, during the first World War, something changed. And what changed was the sheer number and speed of people being killed. Like for the first time in history thousands and thousands of people got killed and gassed and blown to bits — daily. *Daily.* Sometimes even *tens* of thousands. And in battles like Passchendaele and Verdun, something like half a *million* people ended up getting killed — half a million — and so once people started hearing about this and seeing this, their idea of limits and what was normal or conceivable drastically changed. Which is why Steiner said it was basically World War I that paved the way for the possibility of other totally deplorable things happening — like what guys like Stalin and Hitler and Pol Pot did and what happened in Vietnam and Rwanda and Bosnia and Kosovo and how all this has led to where we are today and how undisturbable we all are, like how being undisturbed has actually become a normal response, which I think is like way more awful than someone like Pol Pot or Pinochet or Suharto. Like sure, these guys were pretty bad and everything, but the thing is these guys would've never been able to do the things they did if other people didn't decide to just go along with it, you know? I mean, we always like to point to these sorts of guys and say how evil and cruel and cold and abnormal or unjust they are and how if it wasn't for them none of these atrocities would've happened or whatever, but the truth is, these atrocities have more to do with the rest of us so-called normal, sensible people *letting* them happen. And, I mean, we might think this isn't the case but, like my grandmother said, if you just take a few minutes and think about all the really disturbing stuff that's gone on or is still going on in the world or in your country or your city or your neighbourhood or even in your own home and the fact that you ignored it or let it happen, you'll realize what I'm talking about. Like I'm not so sure how normal or humane you can say you are when you're aware of all this stuff and you just sit there and allow it to happen, you know?"

For the first time since the appearance of the Top Five Kids beneath my window nearly three months ago, I leave before they do, unplugging the oscillating fan and bringing it with me to Rebecca's bedroom where I get undressed and go to bed.

yugen

"You're probably asking yourselves," I say, casually, quickly scanning the jurors. "'How the defendant could just sit there and allow this to happen?'"

The jury has just finished watching the videotape (in English) of Jennie's suicide and most of them are now looking at me (the defendant) with the same expression my mother gave me when she caught Rebecca and I laughing at Jennie's funeral.

After waiting until nearly all the jurors have returned their expressions to the unbiased, objective visages they've witnessed being worn by TV jurors I then ask — my question directed to a female jury member bearing a striking resemblance to Nicole — "Do you think you would be capable of such inaction?"

The jury member, now looking at me with a suitably indignant expression, says, "No. Never. No," shaking her head for added emphasis.

"Why not?"

"Why not? Because I . . . I just couldn't. I would feel compelled to do something about it. I would at least try to stop it."

"And what if the person didn't want you to stop it? What if she wanted to do this?"

"Excuse me?"

"What if your sister came to you and said she wanted to commit suicide — what would you do?"

"It would be obvious to me that she wasn't in her right mind and needed help."

"So you would get her committed?"

"I would call someone, yes."

"What if she had a good reason for wanting to do it?"

"I don't think there could be a reason good enough for me to agree to allow my sister to kill herself."

"How about temporary sanity?"

"Excuse me?"

At this point in the questioning, I pause, noting that my 'temporary sanity' defence has piqued the attention of the jurors, the judge, and the courtroom audience.

"Question," I say, a few moments later, opening my arms and making a pacific gesture to indicate that I'm posing the question to all twelve jurors. "Would a sane person, a rational person, knowingly contaminate or bring harm to their own body or mind?"

All twelve heads shake. A few jurors mumble, "No."

"I agree," I say. "In fact, many psychiatrists believe that an indication of the presence of insanity is *knowingly* contaminating or bringing harm to one's own mind and body."

Inserting another pause at this point — to take a sip of water as well as to allow my previous statement to sink in — I smile to myself, already knowing that all twelve heads will soon be nodding in response to my next question, then shaking in response to the question after that, then shaking in response to the question after that, then remaining motionless, then . . .

"I'm sure all of you here are aware of the harmful effects of DDT, carbon monoxide, pesticides, methane, tobacco smoke, mercury," I say, after a few more self-contented moments have passed. "You're all aware of this, right?"

All twelve heads nod.

"Is there anyone here who isn't aware of this?"

All twelve heads shake.

"Now, in your estimation, would a sane person knowingly contaminate the air they were breathing, the foods they were eating, the water they were drinking, the soils they were using to grow food?"

All twelve heads shake.

"If this is the case, why is it we manufacture and drive gas-guzzling, super-polluting vehicles when we could use less harmful modes of transportation? Why do our factories continue to release toxic effluent into our fresh water sources? Why do we continue buying genetically modified foods treated with pesticides or meat that's been injected with steroids and growth hormones? Why do we continue to manufacture and consume cigarettes? Why, despite the fact that we know the harmful effects of these and hundreds of other substances do we continue to contaminate our bodies with them? Is it because we're all insane?"

All twelve heads remain motionless, the faces now wearing confused expressions.

"After all, by our agreed-upon definition of insanity we should all be deemed insane, right?"

Just as the jurors begin shifting uncomfortably in their seats, probably in response to realizing that I've effectively put them on trial, that I'm indicting them, their way of life, I say, using a considerably calmer, almost placating tone of voice, "Now, what if your sister told you she was *infected* — not with HIV or herpes or syphilis or the Ebola virus — but with the idea of acceptance? What if she told you that she was starting to accept the way the world was, starting to accept a world where we tell our kids we love them then knowingly feed them nutritionally bankrupt, pesticide-laden foods while allowing their minds to be polluted with thousands of graphically violent TV images; a world that allows foreign corporations under NAFTA to sue our country for their right to produce and contaminate our ecosystems with carcinogens; a world that allows governments to take steps each year to ensure that they fail to provide us with clean air, clean soils, clean water, and adequate housing; a world that sees virtual reality replacing actual community; a world where more and more of our lives are being mediated by electronic media — what if she told you she was starting to accept all this, what would you say then?"

After allowing a ten-second window of opportunity for someone to respond I continue.

"Does anyone here know what the word 'Yugen' means? No? Well, it's a Japanese word that means, 'an awareness of the Earth that triggers feelings too deep and mysterious for words.' Jennie Brassard, the defendant's sister, had an awareness of the Earth that triggered feelings too deep and mysterious for words. She was so in touch with the Earth that she could feel its pain, its misery, and after trying for many years to change our vision, our ideas of success, of what constituted a 'good life,' after spending years trying to make us realize the insanity of living and believing in our current vision — a vision that knowingly contaminated our minds and bodies — after trying to do all this she discovered that she herself had absorbed too much of this vision, had become saturated with it, to the point where she herself had now become a contaminant, able to infect others, and she didn't want that, she didn't want to be the cause. She didn't want to be the person responsible for infecting another person with the idea that this vision was okay and so her only salvation, her only sane course of action was to end her life and carry with her as much of the Earth's pain and suffering and misery as possible."

Another pause, this one briefer, perhaps only five seconds.

"This is what Jennie Brassard wanted. She did not want to be an accomplice, an advocate of this system. She did not want to accept the insanity of this system, this world. To force her to continue being a part of it, to have her committed to a psychiatric facility, would not only be cruel and inhumane, but the work of an insane mind. Her brother, the defendant, Mr. Ryan Brassard, did what any truly compassionate, sane, and rational human being would do — he allowed his sister to commit suicide."

Another pause, this time to take another sip of water before abruptly setting down my glass and wheeling around to face the jurors.

"And before you rush to judge, before you strike up the chorus of 'How could he do such a thing?' take a moment right now and think about all the really horrifying things that are going on right now in the world or in North America or in our country or in our city or in your neighbourhoods or even in your own homes and the fact that you're ignoring it, accepting it, allowing it to happen. When you reflect on this, I mean, really, really reflect on this, on how you can just accept it and not do anything about it, I'm not so sure how sane or normal you can say you are, nor how qualified you are to find the defendant guilty."

a hint

My phone — the Sony QuadraStation portable phone, not my Kyocera cellphone — rings, waking me from my dream.

It's Rebecca.

"Do you realize what time it is?" I ask her, slightly annoyed at not being able to hear the jury's verdict of 'Not Guilty.'

"My, my, aren't we touchy."

"It's 3:30 in the morning."

"Ya, like you were sleeping."

"As a matter of fact I was."

"Nice try. I'd lay ten to one odds you were either a) dreaming your parents were back together, b) defending yourself in court, c) screaming yourself awake, or d) a combination of all of the above."

I chastise myself for not being able to keep secrets from Rebecca.

"So which one was it?" she asks.

"B," I say, relenting, realizing that if I don't tell her she'll just turn our conversation into another pseudo-interrogation until she gets the truth out of me.

"Still defending yourself as admirably as ever?"

"Haven't lost a case yet," I say.

"Must've been another sympathetic jury."

I chuckle, then say, "So, how's life in a hotel?" trying to redirect her attention to another topic. "Room service treating you well?"

Using her 'As-if-I'd-ever-fall-for-something-as-obvious-as-that' tone, she says, "Nice attempt at the redirect," then, instead of answering my question, she says, "The reason I called was so you could ask me the question you've been wanting to ask me for the last couple of days."

"Excuse me?" I say, trying too hard to sound nonchalant, knowing exactly what question she's referring to, hating the fact that she knows me so well.

She laughs, says, "Is that the best you can do?" and then, without waiting for my response, adds, "The way I see it, you've got two choices, you can either continue trying to deny that you know exactly what question I'm referring to or you can ask it."

Sighing, I say, "Okay, which one were you?"

"Whatever are you referring to?"

I sigh again. "Rebecca, it's too late to be playing this game. You know what I'm talking about. Just tell me."

"Um, no, I'm sorry, I actually don't know what you're —"

"Okay, I'll rephrase my question then," I snap, interrupting her, annoyed at having to play along with her little game. "While I was having dinner at Rain on Friday night with Daphne, Eriq, Brad, and Nicole, I was wondering if you were in the restaurant the whole time and, if you were, if you wouldn't mind telling me which one of the other patrons was you."

"Much better," she says, laughing. "And for your efforts I'll reward you with a hint: chartreuse chemise."

"Really?"

"Uh-huh."

"That was you? With the auburn curls, black pantsuit, and open-toe leather T-strap heels?" realizing, after she says, "Uh-huh," that the probable reason she didn't leave me instructions regarding what I was supposed to do at Rain was because this was another one of her tests, to see what I'd do if left to my own devices, without her guidance, but instead of calling her on this, which I know would make her upset, I say, suddenly remembering the scene outside Fluid nightclub where the Aldo-shoed guy Rebecca was with was arguing with the bouncers about the dress code, "And who was the argumentative Aldo-shoed guy you were with?"

"Jealousy will get you everywhere."

"No, really, who was he?"

"A bellhop at The Royal York."

"You're kidding."

"What can I say, I'm a sucker for a man in uniform."

"If Daphne only knew."

"Speaking of which, how's our 'little project' coming along?"

"She's close."

"Close enough for you to give her my letter?"

"Maybe."

"Really?"

"You should've seen her yesterday," I say, finding it difficult to contain my enthusiasm. "I had her in tears."

"Daphne was *crying*?"

"Yep."

There's a pause before I hear Rebecca say, "Bloody hell," her tone suggesting she's legitimately impressed. "That's a first, isn't it?"

"Yep," I say, feeling more than a substantial twinge of pride at Rebecca's acknowledgement of my achievement. "And not only was she in tears yesterday but today Eriq said he was *worried* about her."

"About Daphne? Eriq?"

"Yep. He told me he's never seen Daphne like this — ever. He thinks she's become totally dependent on you."

There's another pause, this one slightly longer than the previous one, followed by the sound of Rebecca chuckling, and it's just as I'm picturing her standing there with a self-congratulatory smirk on her face that she says, "And *you* thought it couldn't be done," to which I say, "Not true. I said I *doubted* it could be done," to which she replies, "Ya right, whatever," before adding, "And exactly how many times in the last two months have you said that Daphne was too strong, that I'd picked too formidable an obstacle? Ten times? Twenty? And do you happen to remember what I told you each time? I said that this was going to be a *process*, that you had to think in terms of a long-running TV series, not some slick, instant gratification, everything-is-wrapped-up-in-ninety-eight-minutes cheesy Holly-wood movie. Remember me saying that? Remember me saying that if we stick with it long enough we'll get to her, that by putting her into various scenes and exposing her to all sorts of scenarios, we'll be able to find out things about her that she doesn't even know exist and that with the help of the rest of the gang we'll discover her weaknesses, begin to exploit them until she wears down and finally cracks? Remember me saying that? And now look how close this is to happening. From a totally independent, 'I-don't-need-anyone-to-make-me-happy' woman eight months ago to actual tears and being completely dependent on me today."

After another two- or three-second pause, she laughs, says, "Bloody hell, I'm good," then asks, "So, what did it? Was it the part about being on a respirator in North Dakota or was it when you told her that I was off looking for my perfect place?"

"Quid pro quo," I say, feeling more than slightly miffed at Rebecca for taking all the credit for what has happened with Daphne.

"Well, well, well," she says after a moment or two, "I see someone's thinking he deserves something for all the work he's done. Oh, alright, what do you want?"

"Where's this 'Perfect Place' of yours?"

"Uh-uh. I'm not telling you that."

"Why not?"

"I'm just not. Next question."

"That's the only one worth anything."

"No. That's just the only one you're aware of being worth anything. There are many more things I'm sure you'd like to know. Answers to questions you haven't even thought to ask."

"Such as?"

"I'll give you another hint: vanilla . . . cinnamon . . . lavender . . . CK One . . . mandarin . . . curry . . . apple . . . cherry . . . Chanel No.5 —"

"You were *on* the subway on Friday afternoon?"

"As a matter of fact, I was."

"And you . . . you saw . . ."

"Yes, I saw you sitting there pretending to read my diary, eavesdropping on those two women."

"Where were you?"

"Standing with my back to you on the other side of the aisle, probably only about six or seven feet away."

"What were you wearing?"

"Sorry, can't tell you that."

"Did you get off at the same stop as me?"

"Nope. I stayed on."

"And?"

"And I made a date with the woman dating all the *f-r-e-a-k-*shows — emphasis hers, of course."

"Bullshit."

"No. Trueshit. Why do you think I didn't call you until now?"

"You mean you were actually out on a date with that woman?"

"Not a date-date. We just went out."

"Where?"

"A bar, Easy & The Fifth. I told her I wanted to see where she met most of her *freak*shows."

"Rebecca, you're some piece of talent."

"Hey, I'm not the talent. I'm the one running the show. Remember that."

"Only for one more episode," I counter, "and then *I'll* be the one running the show: writing, directing, producing, *and* starring. Heck, I may even decide to edit you right out of the trilogy."

"Ryan, are you familiar with the expression, 'Hell hath no fury like a woman scorned?'"

"Hey, like you said on page 142 of your diary, 'when you hand over the direction and production responsibilities to someone else, you have to expect some changes to be made.'"

I can feel her anger, her hostility through the phone and tell myself to wait five more seconds to allow the possibility of what I've just said to rampage through her cranium before saying, 'Gotcha!' and telling her that I was just joking, but after only two seconds she says, her tone precise, confident, foreshadowing yet another victory, "By the way, who were you serenading last night?"

"What?"

"I was missing my own bed and thought I'd stop by the apartment."

"You were *in* the apartment last night?"

"Yes, but only for a few minutes. I do so enjoy watching you sleep — I mean, dream-slash-scream yourself awake."

"Bullshit. You weren't there."

"No. Trueshit. In fact, I heard you talking in your sleep, pleading for your parents to understand that it wasn't your fault, blaming the whole thing on me again. I swear, if I just had your subconscious to go by, I'd say you didn't like me all that much."

As I imagine Rebecca standing in the doorway eavesdropping on me, listening to me talking in my sleep, watching me scream myself awake, I feel my grip on the portable phone tightening, my jaw clenching, my teeth starting to gnash — and I know I'm about to say something I'm sure she'll make me regret when I suddenly remember the TV being on that night and ask, "By any chance, did you happen to turn on the TV and forget to turn it off before you left that night?"

"No," she says matter-of-factly. "That is, I didn't *forget* to turn it off. I left it on intentionally so you'd drive yourself nuts trying to remember whether or not you forgot to turn it off before going to bed. Did it work?"

After counting to five I hear myself saying, "Rebecca, without a doubt, you've got to be the —"

"Sweetest woman you've ever laid your eyes on?" she says, interrupting me, replacing the words, 'most psychotic, manipulative fucking bitch I've ever met,' about to leap out of my mouth.

the Beaches boardwalk, Edna

My cellphone rings and it's Daphne; she's in the Beaches just outside Licks restaurant on Queen Street and wants to come over to get away from, quote, "The herds of stupid fucking yuppies and yuppie wannabes clogging the sidewalks," endquote.

I've just left The Suicide Loft about ten minutes ago where I'd been waiting for the same woman who missed the appointment last night to show up for the appointment she made this morning. She called at 7:30 a.m. to say that she'd be at The Loft at 9:00 a.m. and after waiting for her until 10:05, I decided to shower, change, and leave.

I quickly tell Daphne that I'm in my apartment, in the hallway of my apartment, actually, en route to the lake where I'd planned to take a stroll along the boardwalk to take advantage of the warm weather before having brunch at Brasa, but that I'd be willing to make a detour and meet her at Mac's convenience store at Queen and Hammersmith Avenue if she wanted to join me.

She's wearing patchouli this morning, perhaps hoping to run into Rebecca, and, after saying 'Hi,' and telling me I look like shit, that she swears I'm either on heroin or I could use about a month of sleep, I start babbling on and on about absolutely nothing like some sleep-deprived heroin addict until she finally asks me if I wouldn't mind not talking so much and after saying a few more completely inane things we walk the rest of the way to the boardwalk without saying a word to each other.

The warm weather and clear sky has more than quadrupled the boardwalk traffic and, in lieu of our silence, I spend my time mentally filming the dozens of inline skaters and cyclists, the hordes of young mothers and fathers pushing baby carriages, the hundreds of runners, the one person (wearing a wet suit) swimming in Lake Ontario, the two guys laughing and giving each other 'Oh my God, would you look at that' expressions every few strides in response to the two bikini-clad women they've been following for last 30 seconds.

While passing the park, two young girls — twins — dressed to look like Britney Spears, whip past us, squealing and screeching like prepubescent media whores, chasing a camcorder attached to a teenage boy, the two of them becoming instantly telegenic once in front of it, as though the earth beneath their feet had suddenly become a stage and a director shouted, 'ACTION!'

A few minutes later, just as we're passing the Beaches swimming pool, two people vacate a bench just in front of us and we decide to sit down and watch some beach volleyball for a while.

I was here the summer before at the Pro Beach Volleyball tournament and saw the Canadians Mark Heese and John Childs almost beat the Brazilians in the championship game. I mention this to Daphne, but she doesn't seem interested, she's busy staring at Lake Ontario.

"You know what I feel like doing?" Daphne asks me as a group of young neo-hippies with bare feet, cigarettes, flared jeans, and tie-dyed T-shirts parade past us like '60s caricatures.

"No," I say, "what do you feel like doing?"

"I feel like walking into the water. Walking right out into that fucking lake and never coming back, just like Edna Pontellier."

The mention of Edna Pontellier's name sends a sensuous spasm through me, immediately discharging the image of Rebecca reading Chopin's *The Awakening*, alone in her room on her sixteenth birthday, of her describing in her diary how she ached to join Edna, to rush into the water with her and for a moment I substitute Daphne for Edna and see Daphne and Rebecca holding hands by the water's edge, their naked bodies silhouetted against the afternoon sky, momentarily embracing each other in a passionate kiss before wading into the water, and it's just as I get to the scene where, once again wrapped in each other's arms, they begin to sink in blissful surrender, that a kid kicks open the lid of an empty box of Labatt's Blue sitting beside our bench, releasing a small swarm of wasps and flies that causes the boy to yelp and start running in the direction of the Beaches swimming pool.

After watching the boy nearly trip over a skinny middle-aged Italian man sunbathing in a navy blue Speedo, I ask Daphne, "Who's Edna Pontellier?"

Daphne sighs, deeply, almost groaning. "Forget it," she says, her face dropping forward into her hands.

seth

"Hi, Daphne."

A guy, slightly younger than me, I'd say twenty-five, maybe twenty-six, and wearing Gap cargo shorts is now standing in front of us, his eyes riveted on Daphne who a moment earlier — at the sound of hearing her name — had quickly lifted her face out of her hands, her eyes expectant, her expression hopeful, but who is now staring at the guy with more than mild disbelief, as though her past is flashing before her eyes.

"Hi," she says, her voice barely audible, uncharacteristically squeakish, before relowering her head, her face now pale, completely drained of colour.

"Hi, I'm Seth," he says, offering me his hand.

"Ryan," I say, shaking hands with him. "Nice to meet you."

For the next few seconds he stands there, staring at the top of Daphne's bowed head, then looks at me, smiling awkwardly, noticeably uncomfortable, as though he's forgotten his next line and is waiting for me to give it to him but I continue regarding him with mild curiosity, waiting for him to say something, which he finally does.

"So, you guys just enjoying the action?"

I defer to Daphne, allowing her time to respond, but she remains on MUTE long enough for me to consider saying something like, 'Ya, it sucks they're not having the Pro Beach tournament here this year,' but before I do Seth says, "Well, I'm kind of in a hurry. It was nice meeting you Ryan. Nice to see you again Daph. I guess I'll see ya later."

"See ya," I say, waving, and when he's almost out of earshot Daphne says, "Jerk," the bitterness now in her voice somewhat incompatible with the image of her staring at Seth in disbelief only a few seconds earlier.

After noticing Seth pause in mid-stride a split second after Daphne called him a 'Jerk,' looking as though he might turn around and come back, he shakes his head and continues walking and I say, "Now what in God's great Earth would make you go and say a thing like that about such a nice, polite young man as Seth?" still watching him weaving his way through the boardwalk traffic.

"Maybe because he only dates women that resemble actresses."

I chuckle. "Whatever."

"Don't believe me? One of my friends went out with him."

"Who?"

"Never mind who. She looked like Courteney Cox — that's why he went out with her. She told me the guy's bedroom was covered in framed photographs of Neve Campbell, Brooke Burke, Katie Holmes, Denise Richards, Courteney Cox, Angelina Jolie, Winona Ryder — every good-looking actress."

I'm about to tell her that Brooke Burke is not an actress, that she's merely the host of the *Wild On* vacation series, but Daphne only pauses for a second before saying, "But that's not even really why I think he's a jerk."

"And why do you think he's a jerk?"

"Because he calls his girlfriends by the name of the actress he thinks they look like. He called the girl he dated before my friend 'Neve' because she looked like Neve Campbell and he called my friend 'Court' all the time because she looked like Courteney Cox."

"As if."

"I'm serious."

"Really?"

She nods.

"Well," I say, "I'll admit, that is a little bizarre. In fact, it's bizarre enough that the next time I see your friend Seth I think I'll tell him as much."

"Don't bother. If I even hear you've talked to that creep I swear I'll *disown* you," she says, then, abruptly turning to look in the direction Seth took, her eyes scanning the crowd for him, she adds, "I wonder what he's doing down here in the Beaches?"

"I invited him," I say matter-of-factly and when Daphne looks at me suspiciously, I continue. "I met him a while back — months ago, in February — and when I bumped into him this morning again and told him I was on my way to meet my friend Daphne, he said he knew you and would love to see you again."

For a moment I think I may have gone too far, revealed too much, but then, after I say, "We were actually talking in The Natural Health Food Store when you called a while ago," she says, "Nice try, Ryan. You said you were in the hallway of your apartment on your way to the lake, when I called you, remember?"

"That's just where I *said* I was," I say. "It wasn't where I *really* was."

"Is that so? Well, if that was the case, why didn't you just show up at Mac's with him then?"

"It would've ruined the effect. You would've seen the two of us coming and been able to prepare yourself. Instead I told him he should follow us, wait until we were sitting on a bench for a few minutes and then —"

"And how did you know we were going to be sitting on a bench or that there'd even be a bench empty?"

"Well, to be perfectly honest, *that* I didn't know. I just lucked out."

"You're so full of shit, you know that, Ryan?"

"Not always. Anyway, I told him that once you and I have been sitting on the bench for a few minutes, he should come strolling by and say, 'Hey, Daph, long time no see,' in a sort of sexy-slash-soothing voice so you —"

She laughs, says, "In case you forgot, he said, 'Hi, Daphne,' and he sure didn't use 'a sort of sexy-slash-soothing voice' either. He said it like he was scared shitless."

"Ya, I know. He's not such a good actor, is he? Oh well, maybe with a little coaching, a few acting lessons, he'll be able to get into his character better and —"

"Ryan, I'm getting bored of this."

"Of what?"

"Of this little game of yours."

"It's not a game, it's the truth."

"It's boring."

"How can the truth be boring? How can knowing what's really going on ever be considered —"

"Ryan. Please. Shut. The. Hell. Up."

brasa, pre-food order

Since our arrival at Brasa on Queen Street three minutes ago, Nicole has been scrutinizing Daphne's attire, the corner of her lip slowly curling, possibly indicating disapproval, possibly confusion.

"Where did you get your clothes," she finally says to Daphne, her tone more curious than either disapproving or confused. "The Salvation Army?"

Daphne nods, then, in a flat, matter-of-fact tone, says, "Except for the sandals. I made them myself."

Nicole, who is wearing a lilac twill mini-dress, a leather trimmed tapestry clutch purse, leather peep-toe Mary Jane heels from Me Too Shoes, Clinique Happy perfume spray and her Victoria Secret bra inserts, stares at Daphne's sandals for approximately ten seconds and then says, "You're serious? You really *made* them?"

"Sì, yo los nice a mano. Idiota."

"Excuse me?"

"She said, 'Yes, my dear, I made them by hand,'" Eriq says while gazing at a rather attractive woman in her mid to late forties waiting to be seated in the Just Desserts café beside us.

"Oh," Nicole says, hesitantly, her eyes flitting back and forth between Daphne and Eriq, unsure of whether or not to believe Eriq's translation.

Whenever Daphne wants to silence Nicole she speaks Spanish to her. Or German. Daphne speaks four languages; five if you count sign language.

Nicole, although she took French in high school, only speaks one point three languages, maybe only one point two.

"I like them," Nicole says, sincerely, still looking at Daphne's sandals.

"Thrilled you approve," Daphne replies snottily.

Daphne and Nicole met about eight years ago on Koh Phangan island in Thailand during a Full Moon Party on Hadd Rin beach and somehow, in their drugged-out euphoria, discovered they were both from Toronto and ended up spending the next six months travelling together through Indonesia, Malaysia, and Australia. Something must've happened to them since that trip, though; you don't spend half a year travelling with someone and then a few years later end up hating each other without something happening.

I'm now busy looking at the mini-bazaar going on across the street in front of the Bellefair United Church, smiling when I notice the sign on the wall promising the church 'ministers all who worship here,' recalling the expression on my uncle's face during my sister's visitation when literally dozens of people came up to us, to my mother and father, and told us how much my sister had helped them, calling her a saviour, a saint, that she was their salvation, that without her in their lives they probably wouldn't be here right now, my uncle looking at these people like they were deranged and delusional for revering a person who had just taken her own life, wondering why so many of them were telling my parents that they would continue doing *her work*.

'What *work*?' he asked my parents, my parents asked me, all three of them looking at me, confused.

I shrugged my shoulders.

'Your sister Jennie was a . . . a garbage collector. Are all these people her co-workers?' my mother asked me. 'Or are they —'

"Whose idea was it to come here?" Daphne asks, displacing the memory.

"Mine," Nicole confesses immediately.

"And why?"

It's something Nicole wants to do — experience as many restaurants as possible in her life and, although she maintains it's because she wants to experience the food and the atmosphere before they move or go out of business, it's probably just to say she's been there, in case anyone important ever asks.

"Who knows? By this time next year Brasa could be gone," Nicole says.

"Well, whoopdee-fucking-doo, who cares if it's gone by this time next —"

"Is anyone ordering food?" Eriq asks, interrupting Daphne.

"Not for me, thanks," Nicole replies quickly.

"Christ. You mean you drag the rest of us here and you're not even going to eat? What's the matter, afraid of your purging reflex kicking in?"

"I ate before I came," Nicole says.

"What? A calorie-reduced, low-fat rice cake at 7:30 this morning?"

As Nicole is saying, "I'm saving my appetite for Brad's dinner," I subtly kick Daphne under the table and when she says, "Hey, who did that?" I pretend it was an accident, apologize, then ask Brad, "What's on the menu for tonight, big guy?"

"It's a surprise," he says, letting me know by the look he's now giving me that I should keep it that way.

"My money's on another *Morningside Cookbook* creation," I say, smiling.

"You mean *imitation*," Daphne says bitterly and before anyone can respond to her comment a waitress appears at our table, a young girl, probably no more than twenty-one, wearing cork-soled clogs, a Gap jean skirt, a blue cotton halter top and so much foundation and lilac blush that I actually hope Daphne will say something, something like, 'Christ, could you ever use a make-under!' but instead, she orders a triple scotch with two ice cubes and a Long Island iced tea.

"I had no idea this was going to be a liquid brunch," Eriq says, smiling approvingly at Daphne before ordering a Heineken.

After the waitress takes the rest of our orders — a cranberry juice for me, a glass of Alianca Bairrada Reserva 1997 wine for Nicole, and an Evian water for Brad — my attention falls back to the street, to the cars, the café, the people, the stores — Pier 1, grabbajabba, The Sunset Grill, the space where one of my favourite book/magazine stores used to be before it burned down, the — and suddenly, as though someone just changed the channel on the TV I was watching, I no longer see streetcars and SUVs and cars and shops and boutiques and cafés lined up along Queen Street but a completely different world, one where the transportation networks are all underground, where Queen Street, Toronto, Ontario, Canada, North America, The World, is connected by vast underground subway systems while on top, at ground level, there's nothing but grass and trees and shrubs and flowers and meandering cobblestone paths and no one wants to go anywhere to 'Get away from it all' anymore because they're surrounded by the natural world every second and for a moment I think I'm having a great idea, a revolutionary idea, an idea whose time has come, but then I remember all I've done is made another one of Eriq's short stories — 'The Un-paving of North America' — into a mental movie.

"Qu'est-ce que tu pense, Ryan?"

"He's probably thinking, 'Why is Brad asking me this inane question using a horribly anglicized French accent?'" Daphne says.

"Actually, I was thinking about traffic," I say.

"The movie?"

"Oh for Christ's sake, Brad," Daphne says, her irritated tone causing Brad to look at me, hoping I was referring to the movie but when I shake my head he says, "Well then, what about traffic?"

"Nothing really," I lie, and then, while looking directly at Brad say, "I was just wondering how a new BMW would look among all this traffic here in the Beaches."

"You're buying a car?" Nicole says, surprised.

"Not a car," I say, still looking at Brad, "*a* BMW. There's a difference."

Brad's eyes suddenly narrow, zooming in on me, and I can see he's trying to determine if, while I was at his house yesterday and the phone rang and after he answered it, mouthing the words, 'It's my father — business stuff,' and retreated upstairs, if I, in the two minutes or so he was gone, had enough time to

– slip into his study,

– notice the April edition of *Stuff* on his desk (the magazine already open to page 12 and displaying the BMW Q6.S bicycle circled in red ink with the word 'SOLD!' written on it in Brad's handwriting),

– read the fax confirming Mr. Brad Wellington's purchase of a new BMW Q6.S bicycle on May 25th *(Shipment due by no later than June 10th)*, and

– get back to the kitchen looking (when Brad returned from his phone call) like I hadn't moved an inch from the kitchen.

"Bullshit, Ryan," Daphne says, glaring at me. "You're not buying a Beamer."

"I might. I'm seriously considering it."

"Really?" Eriq says, leaning slightly forward in his chair, more than mildly intrigued. "What kind of BMW?"

When I say, after subtly re-adjusting my gaze, focusing once again on Brad's face, "The Q6.S," I actually see Brad's pupils dilate a second or two before his face flushes, resurfacing his slightly tanned skin in a bright red hue and when he begins shifting uncomfortably in his chair I return my gaze to Eriq who is now wearing an expression like he's never heard of the BMW Q6.S.

"Never heard of it," Eriq says.

"It's brand new," I say. "Just off the assembly line."

"Expensive?"

"No, not really. A lot less than you'd expect from a BMW and it's really good on — hey, speaking of expensive," I say, interrupting myself to point out the fact that there's an Audi now stopped in traffic directly in front of the café.

"Now *that's* a car," Eriq says.

"*That*," I say, "is the new Audi TT 225 Roadster. All $90,000 of it."

Eriq whistles. "It looks fast."

"Zero to one hundred kilometres an hour in just over six seconds," I say, looking at Eriq and after he whistles again, Daphne says, "Ya? Well right now it's gridlocked between a Grand Prix and a Nissan Pathfinder and all three of them are using our lungs as air-filters."

When I turn to look at the Roadster again something about the car in front of it — the Grand Prix — strikes me as familiar and after zooming in on the driver I notice it's the same woman from Starbucks, the one whose car keys Daphne stole, and I immediately cross my fingers on both hands hoping, praying the woman will notice Daphne.

"Just once," Daphne says, scowling as her eyes scrounge the traffic along Queen Street. "Just once I'd like to see a car manufacturer make a commercial with this scene instead of some Audi Roadster or Grand Prix zipping along an empty road at one hundred miles an hour or a Pathfinder or Lincoln Navigator ploughing through some untrammelled wilderness. Just once I'd like to see them make a commercial that shows what's really going to happen when you buy one of their cars — that you'll spend ninety percent of your time jammed in gridlock, staring at bumpers."

"Please," Eriq says, gesturing to the rest of the patrons on the patio, "you're depressing the car owners."

"*Depressing*? You know what depressing is? *Depressing* is that something like 45,000 people die each year in North America because of auto accidents — almost the equivalent of an Oklahoma City bombing *every two days* or the entire number of Vietnam War deaths *every single year* — yet there are no monuments being built, no days of mourning or remembrance scheduled. *Depressing* is the fact that each year over two hundred million gallons of motor oil are poured down drains or into landfills in North America, more than seventeen times the amount of oil that spilled from the Exxon Valdez, yet there's no public outcry, no fines levied. *Depressing* is the fact that each year more and more of our continent's natural habitats get coated with asphalt as more and more streets and highways and parking lots are built and expanded. *Depressing* is —"

"Your presentation," Eriq says, interrupting her.

"My what?"

"Your presentation. The way you deliver your message. It's depressing."

"Is that so?"

"Anyone can be heard," Eriq says. "Even the crazies on the corners get heard, but if you want people to actually listen, you have to present it better. You have to make it more appetizing, more palatable, more —"

"The truth isn't a garnish."

"No, but it sometimes works better if it is," Eriq says and then, after a slight pause during which it looks as though he's trying to think of a suitable example to illustrate his point, he says, "Take, for example, the nouvelle cuisine dining experience. Chefs can get people to eat anything nowadays as long as it *sounds* appetizing and *presents* well," and then, affecting a Parisian accent, he says, 'Mesdemoiselles and messieurs, for tonight's specials we have zee lightly braised slices of New Jersey Long Tailed Rat served on a bed of organic worms delicately sautéed in a pecan sauce and bathed in puréed mountain goat bladder. Also we have zee . . ."

As Eriq continues reciting his faux nouvelle cuisine menu to Daphne, I'm reminded of another one of his short stories, 'Stop the Inanity,' where the protagonist (Suzanne Pouter) is forever shouting at people to listen to her and pouting when they don't and it's only when a secondary character suggests that she change her approach, alter her presentation and the way she delivers her material, that people begin listening to her.

"Presentation is everything," Eriq is now saying. "Even if you're speaking the truth — especially if you're speaking the type of truth that few people want to hear."

"And what do you suggest I do, hand out appetizers or product samples while I'm talking or maybe I'll —?"

"Start handing out Eco-Tickets," I suggest, the suggestion automatically causing Eriq to shoot me a 'Don't say another damn word Ryan,' expression (which I ignore), deciding to focus on Nicole and Brad (who are both giving me 'I'm somewhat intrigued' expressions).

"Eco-Tickets?" Brad says. "What's an Eco-Ticket?"

"I read this short story once," I say, smiling at Eriq when his shoe kicks my shin under the table, "the author and title of which elude me now, but it was about this guy who prints up hundreds of these tickets, these Eco-Tickets that say something like, 'I'm sorry to have to be the one to tell you this but you've been charged with driving a carbon monoxide/carbon dioxide/nitrogen oxide/sulphur dioxide–producing, ozone-depleting, natural habitat–destroying, species-killing vehicle. The fine for doing so is $50. Please make your cheque or money order payable to Friends of the Earth, or Greenpeace, or Earthroots, or the World Watch Institute, or the respiratory wing of any hospital in the city,' and then he goes out and puts them on people's cars all over the city."

"And how is this so different from what I'm doing?" Daphne asks.

"It's a different presentation of the same material," Eriq says, a few seconds later, reluctantly coming to the defence of his idea, his character. "This guy, whoever he is, instead of going around yelling at people or smashing cars or bludgeoning them with a long list of facts, tries to get them thinking about what they're really doing every time they use their vehicle."

"Ya, well, I'm not here to sugar-coat the truth or present it on nifty pieces of paper."

I smile. "Unfortunately, life does not always imitate art."

"Screw you, Ryan," Daphne snaps, and before I can think of an equally witty response, Eriq says, "Before you get any higher on that horse of yours, Daphne, let me remind you that you too have a vehicle."

"A scooter."

"It's still an internal combustion engine that uses gas and oil and gives off carbon monoxide and pollutes the env —"

"It's a bloody Vespa, not an SUV."

"Now that sounds like something David Suzuki might say," Eriq says.

"Oh, I just love David," Nicole coos, her entire face suddenly coming alive at the sound of Suzuki's name.

Ever since 'The Photograph' came out — the one where Suzuki is naked except for the fig leaf — Nicole's been a fan. She's even attended a couple of his lectures and bought three of his books — all three of them autographed which, in her mind, was enough contact for her to begin calling him by his first name.

"David Suzuki is one of the world's biggest hypocrites," Eriq says with barely a trace of emotion.

"No, he's not," Nicole says earnestly.

Eriq smiles. "I heard a talk he gave a few years back where he said the carrying capacity of the Earth for airplane flights is roughly the equivalent of one forty-five-minute flight per person per lifetime. By how many minutes do you think he's exceeded his per person per lifetime limit? A thousand? Five thousand?"

"But David has to get the word out somehow," Nicole counters.

"Yes, but if in getting the word out he uses methods that actually *harm* the environment, isn't that hypocritical, Nicole?"

Nicole's face scrunches, her fingertips begin lightly daubing her forehead; she's probably trying to come up with a plausible explanation for Suzuki's actions.

Eriq smiles at her. "Nicole, the guy has admitted to flying thousands of times more than he should have. He also owns and drives a car. Hell, I've even —"

"But this is the first *new* car he's bought in thirty-five years," Nicole says.

"Yes, but he still *had* a car even though he knew of its harmful effects, right?"

"But it was *used*," Nicole says, her tone almost pleading.

"Which meant it was probably a *very* good polluter," Eriq says.

Nicole lets out a long sigh, momentarily deflated, then, suddenly perking up, she says quickly, smiling triumphantly, "His new car is a *hybrid*. It uses *half* the amount of fuel."

Eriq chuckles. "It's not just the fuel, Nicole," he says, his voice still exceedingly calm, reassuring, almost benevolent. "It's the space, the land, all of which are being destroyed because of the roads, the infrastructure, the parking lots required by cars. Whether they're hybrid or not, cars are still gobbling up all our green spaces. And if David is genuinely concerned about how destructive gas and oil and cars are, how they endanger our lives and the lives of thousands of other species, then *any* kind of car is bad and he shouldn't be supporting this type of transportation."

Her smile gone, Nicole starts to say something, then stops, the corners of her mouth collapsing, at which point Eriq says,

"The fact is he's implicating himself in the whole 'Do as I say, not as I do' thing which people, especially young people, pick up on right away. Young people have built-in hypocrisy detectors. They know when you're bullshitting them, when you're a walking contradiction."

"But *everyone* has contradictions," Nicole says. "I don't know a single person who doesn't. We're all striving towards an ideal, but we also live in the world and so we have to make compromis —"

"Oh, for Christ's sake, Nicorette," Daphne snaps, "What ideal are you striving towards, the perfect excuse? As soon as someone mentions things like responsibility and accountability people like you pull out a long list of excuses to justify their behaviour and —"

"Then why haven't you given up your Vespa?" Brad asks, cutting her off. "Like Eriq said, *it* burns fossil fuels too."

"Ya, about one-hundredth of what your fiancée's Nissan Pathfinder or your Lincoln Navigator burns, Beamer Boy. For Christ's sake, instead of badgering me about my Vespa why don't you at least downsize your four-wheeled planet stomper?"

"Maybe because I'm not the one badgering people about the harmful effects of owning and operating a vehicle," Brad says, surprising everyone with his firm tone.

"Brad has a point," Eriq says after a few moments. "Like Suzuki, you can't very well criticize something that, by your actions, you're condoning. That is unless," he says, turning his gaze on Daphne, "like Suzuki, you want to be known as a hypocrite," and, at this moment, just as Daphne is opening her mouth to say something, our waitress arrives with our drink order and Daphne actually snatches the drink off the serving tray and swallows a large gulp before the waitress has time to give Daphne a suitably indignant expression.

the (real) nature of things

"I think we need to kill off guys like David Suzuki," Eriq says after the waitress has departed.

"What?" Nicole says. "You want to kill David?"

"Metaphorically speaking."

"Oh," Nicole says, nodding her head as though she understands what Eriq means but then, halfway through her third nod, the look of understanding changes to one of slight confusion and she says, "Why?"

"Because he's a horrible role model."

"No he's not."

"Sure he is. Not only does he give people the idea that it's okay to say one thing and do another, he ends up making people feel powerless."

"How?"

"Right now Suzuki is seen as one of the 'Great Leaders' of the environmental movement and the rest of us — because we don't have a foundation named after us, because we don't have our own TV show, because we don't write books, because we don't fly around the world giving lectures — the rest of us end up thinking we're nothing compared to him and so we just sit back and wait for the Almighty David to do something. By not killing himself off, he perpetuates the myth of the Great Leader, the myth that he can singlehandedly save the world, that he will lead his people out of the asphalt jungle and deliver them into the promised land."

"But if *he* doesn't do it, who will?" Nicole whines.

"That's just my point. As long as we're busy paying homage and sending money and empowering one person, as long as we're believing in The Power of David, we won't take any action, because the great and almighty Mr. Suzuki is on the case and who are we compared to him? By virtue of his stature, his presence, he mutes both the voices and the motivation of others — the voices and motivation of the people actually living in the endangered habitats of the world."

"So you're saying he should quit?" Nicole says.

"Not on a personal level," Eriq says, "just on a mythological level. I want him to admit that the answers don't reside with him, that the world's future, the protection of the world's biosphere and ecological systems are not up to him, but are up to *all* of us, that *we* should be writing the books, giving the seminars, creating the dialogue, and doing the work, instead of one man flying all over the world preaching to us."

"But isn't that what Suzuki's saying?" Brad says. "Isn't that what he tells people all the time?"

"Actions speak louder than words. And, as far as I can see, Suzuki's just filling the airwaves with his voice. Besides, how can you fix a system by working within the system and playing by its rules? Unless, of course, you like the system and you like the rules."

"Are you suggesting he's doing this on purpose?"

"Who knows?" Eriq says, shrugging. "Maybe he likes his position, his authority, the power and influence and celebrity he has and doesn't want to give it up? I mean, if he was serious about cleaning up our mental and physical environment would he have a TV show that mimics the jazzed up, faster-than-thought presentation of material he says he deplores? Would he continue flying all over the world or own a car — even if it is a hybrid — when he knows the damage it does?"

"But, but," Nicole starts to say.

"But what? The truth is Mr. Buff Geneticist, the King of the Environmental Movement, Mr. David Suzuki doesn't want to lose his celebrity status, his power. I mean, he's already said that the person he'd like to see take over his TV show is his own daughter."

"Heredity. Now that's the *real* nature of things," Daphne says.

brasa, post-food order

"You shouldn't have ordered that," Nicole says to Daphne, referring to the slice of cheesecake Daphne just ordered from the waitress. "It's full of fat."

"Well, fortunately, unlike you, I actually consume more than two hundred calories a day so that my metabolism isn't so low that my body has to immediately convert everything I eat to fat."

"All I'm saying is that what you ordered is full of fat — and not the good kind."

"Then what should I have ordered Nicole, The Brunch of Anorexics — *nothing*?"

"I'm *not* anorexic."

"Didn't we already have this discussion?" Eriq says, yawning loudly and then, while I'm watching him yawning and listening to Daphne and Nicole bicker about what foods are fattening, what causes fat to accumulate in the body, the illnesses associated with the over-storage of fat cells in the body, I find myself thinking of the movie *Seven* and how Kevin Spacey's character forced that obese guy to eat himself to death and I spend some time thinking about the possibility of becoming so obese that I end up having a massive heart attack, and as I'm considering this as a possible method of suicide, thinking that perhaps I'm too vain to get really fat, I realize that nowadays, at least here in North America, fat people are the majority and I start imagining a revolution of fat, sedentary people, hundreds, thousands — hundreds of thousands — of fat, sedentary people carrying placards saying, 'Obese and sedentary people of the world unite!,' envisioning myself as the leader of a worldwide movement to deny thin people or athletic people access to restaurants, theatres, malls, nightclubs, first-class transportation —

"Do you think we really need to dethrone guys like Suzuki

first," Brad says, interrupting my thoughts, "or, do you think other people, people like us, can do —"

"Speaking of discussions we've already had," Daphne says, interrupting Brad, and then, turning to me, she says, "Don't you have an ABI term for this, Ryan — when someone can't let go of something?"

Ignoring her, I urge Brad to continue, saying, "People like us can do . . . what?"

"I don't know, maybe we . . . maybe the five of us . . . maybe we can . . . we need to . . ."

"Can you maybe pick a thought and finish it?" Daphne asks, annoyed.

"Well," Brad says, hesitantly, "maybe it's just a matter of getting people to come together and so we should —"

Eriq's chuckling interrupts Brad. "'Just a matter of getting people to come together?'" Eriq says, cocking an eyebrow at Brad. "Getting people to come together, as Noam Chomsky found out, takes more than just a little work. In fact, I'm sure Noam would agree it requires slightly more than a miracle."

"Why?"

"Why? Because most of us lead such diverging, atomized, insular lives that we barely say 'Hi' to our neighbours, let alone knowing them well enough to discuss politics or economics or feeling comfortable enough to suggest they devote what little free time and energy they have to a particular issue."

"Well, what if we start small, then? What if we —"

"Small isn't going to cut it. Like Chomsky's been saying for years in response to people asking him, 'How can we effect real change?,' 'The only way to really change things is by getting people to come together in large numbers.'"

"What kind of numbers are we talking about?"

Eriq pauses for a second or two, massaging his stubble-free chin, then, nodding his head as though he's settled on an appropriate number, says, "I'd say a million Canadians marching on Parliament Hill along with ten million Americans marching on Capitol Hill and all eleven million saying 'We're not going anywhere until this issue is resolved' ought to do it."

"Okay, and what if that happened?" Brad says, his tone fringed with excitement. "What if we started something that resulted in this actually —"

Eriq's chuckling again interrupts Brad, only this time the image I get while watching Eriq chuckling is of the main character in Eriq's short story, 'What Issue?,' the one who chuckles at the naïve idealism of one of his friends, and then, using the same ironic tone of voice the main character used, Eriq actually repeats, verbatim, what the character said, by saying to Brad, "Before we jump ahead of ourselves and start imagining an eleven million person march and CNN, the BBC, and CBC reporting that Washington and Ottawa have given in to our demands, let's take a moment and ask ourselves what issue is going to unite people, what issue is going to get one million Canadians and ten million Americans off their collective couches and march on our federal government buildings on the same day?"

"War," I say, reflexively giving the same response as the character in Eriq's story gave, believing now — as I did when I first read it — that it's a fairly accurate answer, seeing as how national suicide rates usually drop during times of war because it unites people in a common cause.

"What?" Eriq says, continuing the story's dialogue.

"War," I say. "It's the only real galvanizing issue nowadays. It's the only thing that could bring that many people together."

"You think Vietnam was a galvanizing moment for Americans?" Eriq challenges.

"I meant *planetary* war," I say.

Eriq gives me an amused look. "You mean like aliens invading earth?"

"If someone uses the movie *Independence Day* as an example I swear I'll stab them with my fork," Daphne threatens, interrupting our screenplay and returning the dialogue to real life.

Nicole sighs loudly and says, "Can we *please* talk about something else?"

"No, we cannot talk about something else," Daphne says, snapping the words at Nicole like a whip, then, turning back to us, she says, "Eriq's right. It's impossible to bring people together."

"It *is* possible," Brad says, his voice taking on a strained, almost entreating tone. "If people could just stop seeing each other as threats. Look at Toronto, it's a beautiful city, it's safe, there are tons of examples of people living close to each other, keeping in touch —"

"I thought you hated living in Toronto," Nicole says, crossing her arms, her tone borderline whiny, probably in response to Brad's decision to continue discussing our present topic.

"Sometimes I do, hon," he replies, placing his hand tenderly on her right knee. "I hate the traffic, the congestion, the smog alerts — but I certainly don't hate the city or the people or the potential we —"

"Oh, for Christ's sake!" Daphne says, suddenly jabbing her fork in Brad's direction, nearly stabbing him in the chin with it. "The only reason you don't hate the city or the people, Beamer Boy, is because you've never had to actually *deal* with the city or the people. You grew up in Vancouver — in North Van — not exactly an area renowned for its destitution, you went to private school, then to university, then *toured* Australia for two and a half years before going back home to North Van for a year and then, after informing Beamer Boy Senior you were accepted into the same law school as he was, he *buys* you a fortified mansion in the Annex where you've been living — alone — for the last five years."

"I think we're a little off-topic here," Brad says, shifting uncomfortably in his chair while glancing around at the other patrons, perhaps noticing, as I have, that several other conversations have been preempted by the drama at our table.

"Who gives a damn if we're off-topic?" Daphne says. "We're not in school. Besides, since when are you so concerned about bringing people together and making a difference in —"

The look that Brad is now giving Daphne — a look I've never seen him give anyone before, a look like she's just crossed a boundary of some sort, a look that would indicate Brad's about to tell her and the rest of us why he's so concerned about bringing people together and making a difference in their lives — causes her to actually stop talking, her expression to change, and she becomes — for Daphne, anyway — sheepish.

"So," I say after no one's said anything for a few seconds. "What *is* the topic then, Brad?"

"The topic," Brad says, the look already gone, "is getting people to come together. If people are given the opportunity to see that it's okay, that they *can* trust each other, that someone isn't going to automatically mug them or murder them if they decide to help, to lend their hand or their home —"

"Blah, blah, blah," Eriq says, waving Brad's rhetoric aside with a smile. "Just make sure the revolution or the rally or whatever you're calling it isn't the same night as a Stanley Cup playoff game."

"Or an NBA playoff game," I add.

"Or," Eriq says, "the same night as *Ally McBeal* or *Survivor* or *ER* or on a weekday afternoon — *Oprah*, 4:00 p.m."

"And, above all," I say, raising my voice and my right arm, my hand clenched in a tight fist, "make damn sure the revolution is *not* televised. Because as soon as it's on TV, people will tune in instead of marching on."

Eriq and Daphne laugh and Eriq says, "Ya, if you want to see a real revolution, if you want to see a million person march on

Parliament Hill or a ten million person march on Capitol Hill, take people's TV sets away from them. They'll be up in arms in a day."

"Amen," I say.

eriq's principles

Eriq and I are now walking west on Queen Street, towards Woodbine Avenue; he's on his way to visit someone, a quote-unquote, 'self-proclaimed trysexual man,' who lives in the new housing development at Greenwood raceway.

   Five minutes ago,
– Nicole left Brasa in near tears (because of Daphne),
– Brad, after quickly pulling $50 from his gazelle skin wallet and dropping it on the table, followed her like an obedient dog,
– Daphne told us we could all to go to hell, and
– Eriq, after paying for the bill with Brad's $50, my $20, and his $5 tip, asked me to join him for a walk because he needed my advice on something.

Eriq is wearing Energy cologne by Paco Rabanne, beige loafers, a beige jersey tanktop, and a cream-coloured lacquered-wool two-button suit from Helmut Lang that he told me is in the Spring/Summer edition of *FHM* magazine.

   For the last thirty seconds or so I've been telling Eriq about Martinique, an island in the French West Indies, where he's thinking about going for a few months this winter to try and write the novel he's been trying to write for years. I spent two months in Martinique, in a campsite just outside the town of St.

Anne, and three sentences into describing my visit to Les Salines, a nude beach that's very popular with the gay crowd, I sense Eriq isn't really listening to me anymore, that he's distracted and a moment later I realize the distraction is himself. He's busy window shopping for his reflection.

After Eriq admires himself in three successive shop windows we get stuck in a clot of slow-moving pedestrians at the corner of Queen and Waverley and I watch as he scans the crowd to see if anyone notices him.

When no one does, he lets out a long sigh, says, "Why do I even bother?" and after we walk around to the front of the crowd and continue walking west, he starts telling me about some woman he met at the gym who's invited him out for a drink tonight.

"She's only thirty-one, though," he says after checking himself out in another shop window, his tone discouraged.

Although he's bisexual, Eriq has never really enjoyed the company of younger women — especially young, straight women. He says he finds their dreams of a brilliant career, a fabulous marriage, a luxurious honeymoon in the Greek Islands, two perfect children, two BMWs, and one really large house, thoroughly nauseating.

"Who is she?" I ask.

"Well, at this point, the 'She' in question shall remain nameless. She's been pestering me for almost a month to have a drink with her though and today I finally relented and accepted her offer. I think the only reason I said yes is because I've been single for over a month now."

"Single? Are you serious?" I ask, feeling both surprised and slighted that he's kept this a secret from me for this long.

Eriq nods.

"But what happened to . . . to what's-his-name?" I ask, referring to the forty-something Bay Street exec Eriq's been with for the last year and a half.

"He traded me in for a new model — literally," Eriq says sullenly. "Two months ago this kid was just another nineteen-year-old dishwasher. Two months from now he'll probably be on every billboard in Toronto."

"That sucks."

Eriq shrugs. "Men are men," he says matter-of-factly. "Whether straight, gay, or bi, they're always on the prowl for the next youngest, prettiest thing."

"But you look great," I say, meaning it. "You look like you're twenty-two — twenty-four tops."

"Thanks. But it doesn't matter. They've been carding me."

"Bullshit."

"I'm serious. In the last month alone I've had half a dozen men ask to see my ID. As soon as I show them it's like, 'Sorry, you're too old.'"

"Sounds like you need to get yourself some fake ID."

He laughs, half-heartily, then, after I ask where he's living and he tells me he's renting a room in The Sheraton, he grows silent, his attention slipping away, the way it does sometimes when he's busy writing in his head. A block later he re-appears.

"You know, the truth is, I don't even really mind. I'm tired of being beautiful," he says, his voice trailing off, and then, a few seconds later, adding, "Do you have any idea how difficult it is to be beautiful? The manicures, pedicures, facials, tanning creams, moisturizers, exfoliants, the dieting, the work-outs, the —"

"'Burdened Beauty,'" I say, referring to his short story by the same name.

"Exactly. And the effort required to carry that burden is becoming too much for me."

"Time to pass the torch?"

"In a manner of speaking," he says, adding, a few moments later, "The only problem is I'm good at it."

"At what?"

"Being beautiful. Much better than I am at being a writer."

"Maybe you shouldn't give it up then," I say, recalling Rebecca's directive regarding Eriq — keep him focused on his looks, keep his vanity thriving, that if he ceases to be concerned about his physical appearance it may change the entire dynamic of the gang. "Maybe you should wait a while — until you're confident your writing is as good?"

After he shrugs and says, "Maybe," I mention the woman — the thirty-one-year-old — this time asking for more details, realizing that all this time on his own lately probably isn't good for him, that he needs someone to admire him, to make him want to spend time on himself again, and he tells me he met her two months ago, at Premier Fitness, that they've been talking quite a bit, especially since what's-his-name dumped him.

"She's quite attractive," Eriq tells me, "very down-to-earth, intelligent, easy to talk to. She's even an editor."

"An editor? Well, that sounds, well, promising, doesn't it?"

"I already have an editor."

"Who?"

"You."

I laugh. "Eriq, I'm not even in the same vicinity as being your editor."

"Okay, editor-in-training."

I laugh again. "Not even close. I'm just the guy who corrects your typos while transferring your manuscript from your handwriting to a word processor."

"You're more than that."

"Oh ya. I also print and bind the manuscripts after typing them."

This time he laughs. "I mean more than that."

"Eriq, everything I know about writing I get from you. You need someone who actually knows something about writing.

Maybe you should meet with this woman, give her a chance."

"Maybe," he says. "Maybe I will . . . it's just that she's too, too —"

"I know, too young, but —"

"No," he says, cutting me off, but not rudely, "that's not it. She's too determined to . . . ," and even though he doesn't finish his sentence I'm fairly certain I know what he's referring to.

"Who knows," I say, "maybe she doesn't want what the average, single, thirty-one-year-old woman wants? Maybe she doesn't want kids or —"

"Three."

"What?"

"She wants three kids. Four maximum, two minimum. She doesn't want just one because she was an only child and hated growing up without any brothers or sisters. She doesn't want more than four because more than four would be too much of a financial burden."

"How do you know all this?"

"I told her I wanted kids."

"So you lied to her?"

"You know as well as I do that if I told her I didn't want any kids she would've said she didn't either, that she didn't have the time or that at one point in her life she thought she wanted kids but now, with the way things are today, who would want to bring another life into this world? And then, once we were dating, once we'd moved in together, she'd start trying to change my mind."

"How many kids did you say you wanted?"

"I said it didn't really matter — two minimum, more would be fine — however many my wife wanted."

"Your wife? So you told her you wanted to get married too?"

"Of course. It's the only way to be sure."

"Of what?"

"That she wanted to get married."

Silence for a few more strides.

"Well, why don't you just use this attractive, intelligent, down-to-earth editor for a while?" I suggest. "She can help you with your writing, maybe even hook you up with a publisher or something?"

He shakes his head. "No. I don't think I can do it."

I look at him, cocking my left eyebrow in an attempt to give him the impression that I'm thinking, 'Ya right, whatever, Eriq.'

"I'm serious," he says, smiling at my expression but sounding serious. "When it comes to my writing, the prostitution reflex goes right out the window."

"Are you trying to tell me you've never done this type of thing before?"

"Never."

"You've never just happened to mention your interest in writing to one of your . . . admirers?"

"Not once."

"And they've never offered to help you out in this regard?"

"They've never known I was even remotely interested in writing."

"Really?"

"I've told you before no one but you knows about my writing."

"I know. But I always figured that was just something you told me so I'd agree to type out your manuscripts."

"It wasn't. I'm certain if they knew, they would've helped. And it's not that I haven't had the opportunity. I've met plenty of people in the industry — writers, editors, publishers. I've even had sex with a few of them."

"And you've never been tempted to say something?"

"I've always wanted my writing to get me there, not my looks."

"Wow, that's really quite . . . I never knew you were so . . . so . . ."

"Principled?" he suggests.

"Ya, I guess," I say, then, after a few seconds, I ask him, "But how are you going to get there, let alone get a good night's sleep, if you never show anyone your writing?"

eriq's dilemma

"So, aside from attractive, down to earth, intelligent, easy to talk to but too young, family-oriented editors — have there been any other offers of companionship?"

We're standing in front of Book City now; Eriq is perusing the books perched in the window display while I'm busy watching a squirrel seated on the edge of a nearby garbage can frantically gnawing on a partially wrapped Fusion chocolate bar.

Eriq sighs in response to my question. "Ya. Some forty-seven-year-old guy has shown more than a passing interest. He has his own design firm; fairly rich, good looking."

"What's the catch?"

"The catch is the last two men I've been with have all dumped me for a younger version of me within two years. I'd give this guy a year, not even, before he does the same thing."

"You never know, he might be different."

"I don't think I want to find out."

"I've got an idea," I say, putting on one of Brad's shiny-happy-people-holding-hands expressions while pulling Eriq over to a nearby bench. "Let's sit down and take a few moments to describe your ideal mate or partner or whatever you want to call it. Let's pretend you're putting an ad in the classifieds for prospective candidates: what should their qualifications be?"

"Hmm," he hmms, beginning to pull on his chin, kneading and stretching his smooth, slightly faux tanned skin. "Let's see.

Okay, the successful candidate will be a woman —"

"A woman?" I say. "Really? That's . . . interesting," and then, noticing that Eriq is pretending to be annoyed that I've interrupted him, say, "Oh, I'm sorry, please, go on."

> *The successful candidate will be a wealthy woman with two, preferably three, expensive Mercedes/Jaguar/Lexus-type cars, a Rosedale or similar address, a second home — perhaps a condo in Florida or the Caribbean. She will hold a high-profile lawyer/surgeon/CEO-type job, something that will keep her occupied and out of the house most of the time. She will be well beyond child-bearing years. She will be divorced at least once, and have no desire to remarry. Rather than someone to father her children or get her to the altar again, she will be more interested in lustful companionship, in having someone to accompany her to dinner parties and the occasional business function, as well on vacations to the French Rivera and the Cayman Islands.*

"I see you've given this some thought already," I say after Eriq finishes.

"I've had some free time lately to think about it."

"She's not exactly your run-of-the-mill, everyday woman."

Eriq nods. "Definitely a rare breed. I'd even go so far as to say she's facing extinction. Unfortunately."

"I noticed she had to be wealthy."

He nods again. "I've realized that economic security is a necessity for me. I'm certain some people can write in squalor, that they actually thrive on economic adversity, but I'm not one of them. This is where I disagree with Faulkner when he says a writer can produce anywhere, under any sort of condition. I can't."

"Have you tried?"

"What do you think I'm doing now?"

"Staying at The Sheraton is not what I consider to be living in squalor."

"Compared to where I've been residing the last ten years it is."

"Do you think Daphne's a closet heterosexual?" I ask Eriq, suddenly, making him laugh.

We've been talking for the last few minutes about where I think Rebecca might be and after I suggested a few places — Holland, France, The Royal York Hotel, Wisconsin — I decided to ask him if he thought Daphne was a closet heterosexual.

"No," Eriq says, still chuckling, "I do not think Daphne is a closet heterosexual. Though I am curious as to why you think she is."

"Okay," I say and after holding up my left fist and uncoiling my thumb, explain, "One: Rebecca is gorgeous; (my index finger) two: she's got a fabulous body; (my middle finger) three: she's intelligent; (my ring finger) four: she's gay; *and* (my baby finger) five: she's wanted to fuck Daphne's brains out since they met. Yet, Daphne's never once made a move on her."

"How do you know?"

"Rebecca's told me."

"And just because Rebecca *told* you Daphne's never made a move on her, you think it's true?"

"Why wouldn't it be?"

Eriq leans close to me, whispers, "Maybe Rebecca doesn't want you to know."

"Why not?"

"Maybe because she doesn't want to hurt your feelings . . . or maybe she doesn't want to be part of your fantasy."

"My fantasy?"

"I see the way you look at the two of them. Tell me you haven't pictured them having sex."

"Maybe, but that's not the issue here. The issue here is a)

Rebecca's been after Daphne for months now, b) besides Rebecca, I can't ever recall seeing Daphne on a date with another woman or even hearing of her having been on one with another woman, c) I *can*, however, recall seeing and hearing of her being out on dates with several different guys, d) let's face it, in the *Vogue* sense of the word, Rebecca and Daphne are a perfect match — which is why, and I know you're going to accuse me of making a bit of a stretch here, but I think that a) plus b) plus c) plus d) equals e) — the e) being that Daphne is really a closet heterosexual who pretends to be gay but really it's just an act and every so often she can no longer stand it and has to go on a hetero sex binge . . . I'm serious!" I say, responding to the 'Ryan-Brassard-you-are-completely,-I-mean-*completely*-full-of-shit' expression Eriq is now giving me.

"Listen," I say, trying to sound as serious as possible, "you told me yourself the gay community is full of these stories: a guy who is supposed to be straight doesn't want his family or friends to find out he's gay so he goes on a trip every couple of months to Montreal or San Francisco or Brazil or Vancouver, has his fill — so to speak — and then comes back and tries to live the straight life for a while. What's so unbelievable about the reverse happening, about someone who is supposed to be gay and doesn't want her family or friends to find out she's really straight so she goes on these heterosexual binges and then pretends to live the gay life for a while?"

Eriq opens his mouth to speak, probably to tell me I'm full of shit, but says nothing, perhaps realizing my theory, though slightly skewed, sounds plausible, perhaps even likely — given the fact that I'm using his words to prove my theory — then, just as he's opening his mouth again to say something I say, "Then again, maybe she's just a recovering homosexual."

"A *what?*"

"A recovering homosexual. You know, like a recovering addict, only Daphne is someone who was once homosexual but has since given up the habit and is now trying to live a straight life."

Eriq is now laughing, hard. "Ryan, there is no such thing as a recovering homosexual."

"Ya, you're probably right," I say, nodding my head. Then, after a few moments, after I've waited for him to stop laughing, I say, no, I declare — my tone of voice excited yet assured — like something profound has just occurred to me, like what I'm about to say will be incontrovertible, "Daphne probably has Bipolar Bisexuality Disorder."

Eriq bursts out laughing again, tries to say something, can't because he's laughing too hard, tries again but only manages to say something like, 'Bi-bi, bi-pola, bi, sex, bi," and so, without waiting for him to stop laughing, I state — this time trying to sound as though I'm quoting directly from the Psychiatrist's DSM IV — "A person suffering from Bipolar Bisexuality Disorder is someone who experiences phases in their bisexuality. Similar to people diagnosed with bipolar disorder who experience phases of mania and then phases of depression, Daphne is most likely experiencing an 'Only a man can satisfy me' phase in her bisexuality. Next month she might swing back and be in an 'Only a woman can satisfy me' phase."

"Ryan, really," Eriq says, still laughing, though no longer hard enough not to construct a coherent sentence. "Where the hell do you get this stuff?"

"What stuff?"

"Bipolar Bisexuality Disorder. I mean, come on."

"What? You don't think it's true?"

"Daphne is *not*, I repeat, *not*, bisexual."

"Sure she is," I say, and then, pretending to get excited again, like I've just arrived at the Reebok Turning Point in our debate, I add, "I mean, she wears patchouli, doesn't she?"

"What does Daphne wearing patchouli have to do with this?"

"Everything. I mean, she probably wears patchouli for the same reason you either wear CK Be, Yardley Sandalwood, Vetyver by Jo Malone, or Energy by Paco Rabanne."

"And that is?"

"Because they're androgynous scents — they attract *everyone*."

As Eriq begins mulling this over, I am only able to prevent myself from laughing for five, possibly only four seconds and then, after the two of us have attracted the attention of nearly every pedestrian within a twenty-metre radius with our collective laughter, I ask Eriq, "Which one did you like the best — 'The Closet Heterosexual,' 'The Recovering Homosexual,' or 'The Bipolar Bisexuality Disorder'?"

"I'd have to go with the latter, though I did enjoy your closet heterosexual-binging theory as well."

"So, what do you think I should do?"

We've just arrived at Woodbine Avenue and are about to part.

"About what?"

"My current dilemma."

"Well it seems like your only two candidates at this point don't have the necessary qualifications, in which case, I'd suggest you play the field until you get some better offers."

"I don't think I can afford to."

"But I thought —"

"Trust me," he says and then, after making me promise not to tell anyone, he goes on to say he feels like one of those athletes who's lived the high life for ten years, spending his money like it was always going to be there, then suddenly suffered a career-ending injury and has nothing to show for it.

"Well, if that's the case, I'd say, go for it. I mean, at the very least she might be able to help you get one or both of your short story collections published and then you won't need anyone to patronize you any more."

Smiling weakly at my double entendre, he says, "Ya, I guess," and then, after shaking my hand, adds, "Thanks, Ryan," before asking me if I think everyone is still getting together tonight at Brad's.

"I think so," I say without thinking, then, after a moment or two of reflection, add, "I mean, I hope so. I'm not too sure about Daphne, but I'm going and I'm fairly certain Nicole is going to be there."

"Don't worry about Daphne," he says. "I'll give her a call and tell her not to show up, which will all but guarantee her being there."

I laugh, then say, "Hey, why don't you bring the new woman?"

"I don't think so. I wouldn't want her to get the wrong impression."

"Eriq," I say, smiling, "you're priceless."

"Not true," he says, shaking his head. "I have a price. Unfortunately it's come way down in the last few weeks."

"Let me know when it hits rock bottom," I call after him as he begins crossing the street, but the noise of a streetcar drowns out everything after the word 'me.'

nicole, theories

"Ryan! Over here!"

I was on my way back to my apartment from The Suicide Loft where I had two thirty-minute appointments, completely preoccupied with what the second client told me just before he left — that what I'm doing, the service I'm providing for him and others like him, is indispensable — which had the effect of making me feel pretty good, good enough, in fact, to entertain the idea of postponing my expiration date, giving myself a few more months or maybe even a year to see how things turn out, to see if I might actually start sleeping more than two or three hours a night, if I might actually dream of something other than Jennie and my inability to act, to save her life, and I was in the middle of these thoughts when I heard a car horn and, while trying to remain focused on what I was thinking about, managed to resist the temptation to look in the direction of the honking until hearing Nicole's voice calling my name between the fifth and sixth honks and when I looked in the direction of her voice saw her seated, alone, in her Nissan Pathfinder.

'Well, isn't this convenient,' I say to myself in response to the fact that Rebecca had already called for an update on brunch and after hearing what transpired at Brasa, told me I should contact Nicole a.s.a.p. to smooth things over with her before heading to Brad's to ask him some questions.

Smiling and waving at Nicole, I begin walking towards her thinking I can use this opportunity to not only smooth things over but also to find out more about her so-called 'ex-per-i-ment' and after I reach her and ask her where she's headed and she tells me home, I lie and (since Rebecca didn't want Nicole to know I was going to Brad's before the dinner party) tell her I'm heading to The Big Carrot, a large health food store on the Danforth, to pick up something for tonight's dinner, and before I can ask her for a ride she says, "Hop in, I'll give you a lift," clearing off the passenger seat by tossing the May issue of *Vanity Fair* on the dashboard and steering the packets and bags of just purchased items from Pier 1 and Overkill behind the passenger seat.

Once we're driving, slowly, along Queen (it's still stop and go), I ask her where Brad is, mentioning that after she left Brasa he declined an offer to go for a walk with me and Eriq because he needed to get a ride from her and she tells me, almost too matter-of-factly, that he does this quite often — uses her as an excuse — and when I say, "Really? Wow, that's a little odd, don't you think?" she just shrugs her shoulders and says, "Everyone has secrets," and I nod my head, reply, "Ya, I guess you're right," begin wondering if Brad even talked to her two nights ago when she stormed out of Rain, if she slept over at his place that night like he told me she did, but instead of asking her if she did I hear myself saying something completely different, something like, "You know, I don't think you should worry about what Daphne says too much. She's just going through a tough time right now."

"I agree," Nicole says, nodding her head. "She is going through a tough time. But I'm not worried about her. I just feel sorry for her."

"Feel sorry for her?" I say, barely managing to tone down the incredulity in my voice.

She nods.

"Why?"

Nicole pauses, bites her lip, does this twirly-whirly thing with her head as though the idea of whether or not she should tell me the reason why is spinning around inside her brain, then says, "When I met Daphne in Thailand I told her about this idea I had for my thesis and the idea was you select someone — usually someone who is really passionate about something — and then you try to get them to abandon or even despise what they're passionate about."

"That was your thesis?" I ask, trying to sound only mildly intrigued, to disguise the 'Holy shit, this is all starting to make sense' thought I'm now having as I recall the conversation I overheard on the streetcar over eight months ago between Seth and some other guy.

She nods. "Ya, that was it. I changed it, though."

"Why?"

"I don't know. I guess the truth is because Daphne actually started doing this when we got back from our trip. She said she wanted to help me with my thesis, that she'd be the experimenter and I could take notes, gather information. And it was really fun for a while because, of course, Daphne was incredible. I mean, with her looks and intelligence, in a matter of weeks — sometimes only a couple of days — she could change someone completely. It was amazing to watch. She had vegans eating meat, meat-eaters converting to veganism, health fitness gurus becoming couch potatoes, tree-hugging environmentalists buying cars, car lovers selling their prized automobiles, happily married men telling their wives they wanted a divorce, 'I swear to be single for the rest of my life' guys proposing to her. She was so persuasive."

I laugh. "Your thesis sounds like an urban legend," I say. "In fact, I think I may have even overheard some guy talking about it in a streetcar once."

"Well, in this case, the legend is true."

"So Daphne was pretty persuasive, was she?"

"Too persuasive. That was part of the problem. She became addicted to it. It became her obsession. She couldn't relate to people normally anymore. It was like everyone she met became a project to work on. She could never let them be. She always had to change them."

"Is that why you changed your thesis?"

"Partly," she says, nodding. "I thought if I changed my thesis Daphne would stop, but she didn't, which is one of the reasons we stopped going — hanging — out."

"And what's the other part?" I ask quickly, in hopes of making Nicole think I didn't notice her Freudian slip.

"Of what?"

"Of why you changed your thesis."

"Oh, right. The other part is because I was tired of seeing people devastated, seeing them abandon their passions, changing who they were for an illusion. Some of them ended up so hurt, so crushed, so humiliated because Daphne would usually call them on it. Like, after they'd given up their passion or their raison d'être or whatever, she'd look at them as though they were the most pathetic thing on the planet and then ask them how they could do what they did, how they could abandon their passion, how they could give up something so special, so important, in a matter of days?"

"She would say that?" I say, trying my best to sound surprised.

Nicole nods.

"Wow. That's pretty harsh."

Nicole sighs. "Ya, I know. I kept hoping there would be someone who wouldn't listen to her, who would tell her to go fuck herself, that if someone were to do this it might snap her out of it, but no one ever did, so she just kept right on going."

"So she's never met someone she couldn't change?"

"Not that I know of," and then, chuckling, but not in a 'I think this is funny' kind of way, she adds, "Of course, the ironic part is that the exact same thing is now happening to her."

"What do you mean?"

"Rebecca."

"What, you think Rebecca is doing the same thing to Daphne as Daphne did to all these other people?"

Nicole shrugs. "Whether it's intentional or not remains to be seen. But ever since our first dinner at Jump Café in December when I saw Daphne, saw how she acted towards Rebecca, I've thought, 'Oh my God, I don't believe it. It's happening to her. This is way too ironic.'"

I'm now thinking Brad may have a point about Nicole being perceptive and I want to find out more, to probe the extent of her suspicions of Rebecca but before I can ask her another question it suddenly dawns on me why Nicole continues to hang out with the group, why she puts up with Daphne's shit: she wants to see what happens when the experimenter becomes the experiment, she wants to be there when Daphne implodes, breaks down, runs out of the restaurant or café in tears, but even though I want to confirm this, to find out if this is the experiment that Brad was referring to, at the same time I don't want to appear too anxious so I allow myself to become distracted by the various scenes and mini-dramas playing out along Queen Street, framed in the small-screen passenger window and the larger screen front windshield of Nicole's Pathfinder.

After a few moments of this I spend some time counting the number of young and not-so-young mothers pushing baby carriages (ten, eleven, twelve), chuckling to myself when I recall Jo-Jo calling it an epidemic, then, while watching a young man pushing a stroller, I catch the reflection of Jennifer Aniston on the cover of *Vanity Fair* in the windshield and after grabbing the magazine and flipping to the article and looking at the photos, I ask Nicole why she's not like this around the others.

"Like what?"

"I don't know, you're just different right now."

She shrugs. "Different people bring out different sides of your personality."

"Meaning?"

"Meaning, if you're only with that person you'll act differently or say things you wouldn't say if you were with someone else or with a group of people."

"That makes sense, I guess."

"In some cases the difference is so great that even if family or close friends saw you, it would shock them."

I'm about to ask her to give me an i.e. when she says, "Take you and Eriq for example. When the two of you get together, just the two of you, I'm sure he tells you things he doesn't share with the rest of us, right?"

"You mean things like how he's really not bisexual," I say, zooming in on Nicole's face, gauging it for a reaction. "That he's, in fact, not only a closet *hetero*sexual but a writer and that right now, as we speak, he's debating whether or not to date a thirty-one-year-old editor in order to get his two as-yet-unpublished collections of short stories published?"

"Is that true?" she says, leaning over, her voice hushed, her tone conspiratorial.

"Who knows?" I say, laughing. "Maybe."

She laughs, slightly embarrassed that she wanted to believe me and then, a few moments later, adds, "You're right, who does know? I mean, the amount of stuff that goes unnoticed or undetected by the average person, even between family members and good friends, is mind-boggling, it's —"

She suddenly stops talking, taps her index finger on her forehead several times, then says, "'My experience is what I agree to attend to. Only those items I notice shape my mind.'"

"Freud?"

"Close. William James, the founder of modern psychology. If there's one thing I've learned from six years of psychology it's that you can never know everything about people, there are too many sides to them, they're far too complex to ever really figure out, especially for one person. I mean, look at serial killers. Their friends, family, neighbours — the people who are supposed to know them the best — always say stuff like, 'He was such a nice guy,' or, 'He wouldn't hurt a fly,' or, 'He was the boy next door.' And then the cops start finding body parts in the guy's freezer or in a big pot on his stove."

"Scary."

"It is. But it's because people only noticed, only attended to the person's most salient characteristics and the rest they ignored or didn't want to know existed. I mean if you were narrating some story and describing me, you might only want your audience to see a certain side of me, make them think that I'm a spoiled brat or a complete ditz or a neurotic mess — who knows, you may even invent all sorts of lies about me in an attempt to fool your audience, trick them into forming an image of what I'm like, of how I'll respond to certain situations, and then, when they actually see me or hear me talking — unbiased by your description — I might sound very different and the image of me they'll have had based on your words will be inconsistent with the real me and — well, it won't be my fault, it'll be your fault."

I smile, awkwardly, suddenly feeling obvious, exposed to Nicole's perceptions, thinking that Brad wasn't that far off at all, that my sister Jennie could read people too — the image of her abruptly opening her eyes while lying in the tub, her gaze absorbing the camcorder, Rebecca, the bathroom, before stating, "Everyone, everything, is part of the play going on inside me. I am the medium. Everyone else, everything else, is the message."

"Are you still going to Brad's for dinner tonight?" I ask.

"Changing the channel, are we?" she asks, smiling, and when I don't respond she says, "And just when things could've got a whole lot more interesting. Oh well. Maybe next time."

"Speaking of interesting," I say, abruptly turning down the volume on the CD player, and, even though all the windows are up, whispering, "Don't you ever wonder if Brad's really a serial killer?"

"What? Where did *that* come from?"

"It was the next line in the story?"

"What story?"

"The one I'm narrating right now."

"Oh, right. So what happens next?"

"Well, actually, after you said, 'Where did *that* come from?' I was supposed to say, 'I had a dream about it last night. I saw Brad going around the city and picking up people, street kids mostly, driving them back to his place, giving them a warm meal, maybe even letting them use the shower and giving them a fresh set of

261

clothes before killing them, chopping up their bodies, boiling them, putting the meat in those three giant freezers he has in the basement and then, every time he has us over for one of his dinners, taking out pieces of these murdered people and mixing it in with the food he feeds to us, sort of like they did in the movie *Fried Green Tomatoes*,' and then you would start laughing, just like you are right now, and say, 'Brad is *not* a serial killer. But, I mean, nice theory, Ryan,' and I'm supposed to be laughing too at this point which, as you can see, I am, and then I say, 'It is slightly absurd, isn't it?' before reaching over and turning up the volume on the CD player, like this, then raising my eyebrows, twice, like this, then smiling, like this, and saying, 'Still, it all fit together so well in my dream.'"

I didn't think I was going to be

I'm westbound on the Bloor Street subway line, on my way to Brad's to not only ask the questions Rebecca wanted answered, but also to a) see if he's received the BMW Q6.S yet and b) ask him more about Nicole and her experiment, and since the last stop I've been debating whether or not I should tell Rebecca that Daphne's idea of taking away people's raison d'être came from Nicole, that it was actually Nicole's thesis being played out in real life that I'd overheard on the streetcar over eight months ago and this leads me back to the scenes of
   – Seth on the streetcar telling some guy what had happened to him,
   – me following Seth into Second Cup on Queen West after he got off at his stop,
   – me ordering — like he did — a triple espresso,

– me waiting for him to be seated then asking if the seat beside him was taken (it wasn't),
– me sitting down, introducing myself, stating — after we'd shaken hands and he'd introduced himself as Seth — that I was certain I'd seen him before, asking (while snapping my fingers) if he was just on the 501 Neville Park streetcar and when he told me he was, confessing that I'd overheard part of his story before telling him that I'd had a similar experience with a woman a few years ago in a different city and wouldn't mind 'comparing notes,' so to speak, which was enough for him to begin retelling his story, for me to learn that this particular woman, aside from being very manipulative and seemingly put on the planet to stomp on his heart, was also incredibly beautiful, independently wealthy, fond of wearing patchouli, and volunteered two days a week at the city library. Ten minutes later, after giving me a few more details about the woman, he told me he was running late and had to get going so we exchanged phone numbers, shook hands, and five minutes after he walked out of Second Cup Rebecca walked in and I immediately told her I thought I'd (finally) found her 'Perfect Partner,' that she almost fit Rebecca's criteria to a 'T,' and these old scenes lead me to the scenes of Rebecca and I going to the city library, smelling the patchouli wafting about the book stacks, Rebecca passing me the poem by Baudelaire, Daphne snatching it off the table, Daphne and Rebecca having their R.S.V.P. chat, me getting Daphne's phone number and calling her five days later, inviting her to dinner with us that night at Jump Café, me hooking up with Seth a few weeks later, telling him that I had begun working on a 'little project' that may interest him, and it's just as I get to the scene where (after getting permission from Rebecca) I first divulged to Seth exactly what the 'little

project' was that I begin tracking the erratic movements of a tipped-over, semi-full can of Jolt Cola rolling around on the subway car floor, banging against the metal poles and sides of the car, the can's contents alternately gushing and dribbling out, as though it's been wounded, leaving behind a trail of dark, sugary, caffeinated blood, and when it dribbles across a scrap of newspaper near my left foot I zoom in on the scrap, reading that tomorrow morning, at 5:00 a.m., Timothy McVeigh will be executed by lethal injection and this, for obvious reasons, inspires me to get out Rebecca's diary and turn to the copy of my sister Jennie's poem about a classmate, who, after being school president and graduating with the highest marks in the history of our school (99.7%), and receiving academic scholarships to every university he'd applied to, returned home at Thanksgiving, told his parents he was quitting university, and then mailed this poem to a friend of Jennie's before blowing a hole through his head with his father's rifle:

Great Expectations

Their eyes are on me,
probing me for the aberration.
I remain inert,
waiting for them to finish their inspection.

It's my own fault.
I should've had something ready,
an alibi,
a prepared statement,
something to make it seem more logical,
to reassure them that I didn't think I was going to be
like this either.

*Perhaps I should've quit earlier
before the expectations set in,
before I achieved anything that might confine me later.*

*Right now, though, I need an escape route,
perhaps a trephined skull
to let out the guilt,
the remorse,
the resentment,
and the expectations that have been accumulating inside my
head for almost two decades. . . .*

you dropped something

I was on Brad's new bicycle, the Q6.S, zipping along the Danforth in the far left lane en route to The Big Carrot to pick up a few more things for tonight's dinner and after passing a silver Hyundai Accent that was probably doing about thirty-five kilometres per hour and marvelling at how easy this was, how I wasn't even really breaking a sweat, I remembered Brad telling me as I was leaving how incredibly light and fast the bike was — and it was just as I was passing a black Ford Focus that I saw Rebecca and Daphne chatting on the south sidewalk and, seeing as I've been more than a little sceptical given all the 'faux' sightings I've had in the last few days (coupled with the fact that my eyes were somewhat bleary from the wind), I took another, longer look after swiping away the wind-induced tears from my eyes which, after I realized it wasn't Rebecca and Jennie (of course) and returned my gaze to the road, gave me just enough time to swerve hard — to my left — to avoid the pothole directly in front of me, which caused me to lose control of Brad's bicycle and now I'm on my way down to meet the asphalt wearing only a pair of khaki shorts and a plain blue cotton T-shirt which, at my current speed, is not going to be enough to ward off a severe case of road rash but this is the least of my worries since, thanks to swerving to my left to avoid the pothole, I'm now falling into the oncoming lane of traffic and, by the time I've completed my first roll on the asphalt the massive delivery truck that is now only a few metres from my front tire will undoubtedly be driving over me and, well, if I fast-forward the action, I can tell you that I see myself getting thoroughly crushed by the huge truck tires, my blood and organs and the twelve ounces of Tropicana Orange Juice I drank at Brad's twenty minutes ago squirting out every orifice, and in the instant before all this happens what flashes into my mind is the fact that I wasn't able to remain death-free until my suicide, that the date, time, and method of my death was — in my case, anyway — not under my control and the truth is that I don't really mind, because I'll probably miss the uncertainty, the not-knowing, the unpredictability of everyday life more than having an antidote to it and even though I know you're probably waiting for me to say, 'Gotcha!' or to find out that it's only a dream or one of my unreliable narrations the truth is —

"You dropped something."

I hear a voice, young, female, and when I open my eyes I see a young girl, probably only eleven or twelve, wearing a navy blue sundress and faux black leather T-strap pumps.

"Excuse me?" I say, wondering where the hell I am — my head reeling with images of being crushed by the massive delivery truck — yet still able to recognize that she looks a lot like Jodie Foster in *Taxi Driver* and am about to tell her so when she says, "You dropped something," pointing to about a dozen of my business cards on the streetcar floor laying next to the frothing can of Jolt Cola.

brad's, pre-dinner party

When I get close to Brad's house I see a bunch of people — three, maybe four — walking into Brad's house and decide to stay where I am and wait a while to see if they come back out and when they don't come out after ten minutes I sneak up the driveway, using the Lincoln Navigator for cover and then walk past the side of the house and around back, trying to find an uncovered window to peep into but (as usual) all the shades are drawn and so I sit down at the side of the house, waiting, and after about twelve, maybe fourteen minutes, the door opens and I hear Brad's voice, then two or three other voices and after standing up and taking a few steps backward, I start walking forward, fast, turning the corner quickly and, when I see Brad standing in the doorway talking with the three dreadlocked kids — the ones from Queen West — I say, using a tone of voice that would suggest I haven't seen Brad in years but just happened to be walking through someone's backyard and it turned out to be his, "Bradley Wellington? Oh my God, is it really you?"

"Jesus Christ, Ryan!" Brad says, now in the process of dropping the batch of papers he was holding while the dreadlocked trio busy themselves trying to catch them. "You scared the shit out of me!"

I apologize for scaring him and after helping the kids pick up the pieces of paper which, upon closer inspection, I see are actually tickets, *Eco-Tickets*, fining people $50 for driving a carbon monoxide/carbon dioxide —

"What the hell are you doing here?" Brad says, snatching the ticket out of my hand, handing it and the rest of the ones he's picked up to the girl who quickly stuffs them inside the novel she's carrying — *The Great Gatsby* — before saying, "Adios, amigo," to Brad and walking down the front steps with the other two.

"You plan on answering the question?" Brad asks me.

"What question?" I say, watching the dreadlocked kids walking across the front lawn.

"What. Are. You. Doing. Here? Dinner isn't for another two and half hours."

"I know," I say, turning to Brad. "I just thought I'd stop by to see your . . . you know, we don't talk too much anymore and —"

I'm far too distracted to finish the thought.

"Why didn't you call first?" he asks.

"Because I . . . I did but there was no answer so I . . . Brad, what the hell were those three kids doing here?"

Instead of answering he invites me inside and tells me to meet him in the laundry room and as I'm walking through the front hallway and into the kitchen I not only notice that the house reeks of sandalwood, there's also a bearded man in his late thirties, possibly early forties sitting at the dining room table eating a bowl of ratatouille and wearing one of Brad's oversized sweatshirts, a pair of Brad's shorts, and a pair of Brad's Air Jordans.

"Hi," I say.

"Hello," the guy says, his voice garbled, as though being pulled through spit. "Want some soup?"

"Um . . ."

"There's plenty more in the pot," he garbles.

"No, no thanks. Maybe later," I say, before shaking my head and opening the door to the basement and walking into the laundry room.

A minute or so later Brad comes downstairs carrying a laundry bag and when he gets closer I ask him again what the hell is going on, what those kids are doing here, why they're carrying Eco-Tickets, who the hell the guy in the dining room is, and he puts the laundry bag down beside the washing machine and starts to say that the guy is a friend of his father's who's in town for a few days, then stops — probably because he knows I'm about to call him a lying sack of shit — and says, "I walk around the city and invite people back to the house."

"What?" I say, shaking my head. "What do you mean, *people?* What kind of people?"

"Street people — bums, squeegee kids, bag ladies."

"What for?"

He shrugs. "Wash their clothes, let them use the shower if they want, make them something to eat, give them some of my old clothes —"

"Fuck off," I say, not believing him, and when he starts pulling out dirty clothes from the laundry bag, clothes I can't ever imagine Brad wearing, I say, "Are you serious?"

He continues pulling the clothes out, opening the lid of the washing machine, placing the clothes gently inside, evenly distributing them. . . .

"Hello? Earth to Brad," I say, my tone suggesting I'd like him to respond to my previous question, preferably now, and after sighing heavily a few times and scratching his head, he says, "Listen, the thing is, no one knows about this, not even Nicole," and then proceeds to tell me he's been doing this for about a year now and he's built up a semi-regular clientele, the news travelling by word of mouth, "Like how hobos used to leave marks on a person's fence that would tell other hobos 'This house is a good place to get a free meal, or a change of clothes, or a bath or some money,'" and how during the average week anywhere from ten to fifteen people come over, some of them spending the night, all of them eating some food, lots of them sitting and talking with him, some of them using the place as their fixed address so they can get a job, social assistance, whatever, and how he almost told me yesterday when I saw the three dreadlocked kids walking down his driveway that he wasn't really on the throne when I called, that what he was really doing was spraying the place with vanilla to get rid of the sandalwood essential oil that all three of them wear, that the three of them have been staying over on

Friday nights, making brunch on Saturday mornings, that one of the guys is an amazing cook, and that they usually sit around eating, reading the newspaper, talking about books, that there's even an informal book club at the house and right now there's about a dozen or so people reading *The Great Gatsby* and —

"And no one knows about this?" I say, slightly — no, *overly* — sceptical.

He shakes his head. "No one."

"So you're saying that if I were to mention this to Nicole at our little dinner party tonight she wouldn't know what the hell I was talking about?"

"She wouldn't have a clue. Well, maybe a clue, but nowhere near what she expected."

"And you've never been caught?"

"Only once."

"By who?"

"My father."

"When?"

"A few months ago. I was here in the basement, in the laundry room, actually, just like now and I heard someone yelling, 'Get the fuck out of my house!' and I came running up the stairs just in time to see the two street kids I'd made a meal for bolting out the front door, and I ran after them to try and explain but by the time I got to the end of the driveway they were already halfway down the street and weren't stopping no matter what I said. Of course, when I got back in the house my old man was totally pissed off, completely off his rocker, demanding to know who the fuck those two kids were and when I told him they were a couple of street kids I was helping out he started yelling, 'For Christ's sakes! This isn't a halfway house or a youth hostel or a fucking city shelter, Bradley! This is my house! You hear me? *My house!* And I do not appreciate coming into *my* house and finding a couple of street kids sitting on *my* chairs at *my* dining room table, eating from *my* bowls and offering me food from *my* own goddamned fridge!'"

He pauses, looks at me, probably realizes that I want him to continue, that I'm wondering what happened next and, after taking a deep breath, he says, "Then my old man asked me if those were my basketball shoes he saw those two kids wearing and I told him they were and he asked me if I'd given them away or if they'd stolen them and I said I gave them away and my father starts yelling at me again, telling me that they cost him $120 a pair and I said, 'I thought you told me they were half price?' and he yells, 'They *were* half price! They were Air Jordans!' and I told him I'd give him the $240 and he said he didn't want the $240, that the reason he'd bought me the shoes in the first place was because he thought I liked Michael Jordan and now that they were re-issuing all his old shoes, it'd be cool to have them as part of a collection and that's when I said I thought it'd be better if someone used them but he didn't agree and so then I told him that I really didn't like Michael Jordan as much as he thought I did — especially after I found out that at one point Michael was getting more money for being the image that sells the shoes than the 100,000 Indonesian workers who actually made them — and my old man went ballistic on me, shouting, 'Don't you start in on me with all this left-wing, warm and fuzzy, the-Indonesian-workers-are-being-exploited crap!' and proceeds to give me a lecture on what industry and business and capitalism has done for the world, for our family — especially for me — and that if I want to be one of these overly concerned bleeding-heart liberals who denigrates the very system of economics that's enabled them to have a bleeding heart and be overly concerned in the first place, then he's going to kick me the hell out of the house, fire me, and write me out of the family will."

At this point Brad puts the story on PAUSE again and this time instead of waiting for him to hit PLAY, I prompt him to continue by saying "So, what did you say?"

"Well, part of me felt like telling him 'Go ahead, take it all, I don't want it,' part of me wanted to grab the Carlos Delgado autographed baseball bat and smash his fucking head in, and part of me realized that if I did either of those two I'd lose everything, including my ability to help people. I mean, you can't really help the poor and homeless when you're poor and homeless."

"So, what happened?"

"Well, five minutes later he apologized, telling me that the real reason he was so upset was because he was afraid for my safety, that even though he knew I meant well, he was afraid something bad might happen to me if I kept inviting strangers, especially strange kids, into the house which, of course, was pure bullshit. I know the truth was the idea of some bum who didn't have a job, who wasn't paying taxes, who wasn't contributing to the economy — the idea of this type of person having access to *his* house, sitting on *his* couch, using *his* TV, drove him insane. It's why he insisted on having blinds on every window in the house and insists I keep them closed all day. It's why there are two locks on the front door, two locks on the back door, two locks on the door leading to the basement, a lock on every bedroom door, and a house alarm. It's why all the basement and ground floor windows have safety bars on them. It's why he posted a sign on the front and back door that said, 'Did you remember to lock the doors and windows and set the alarm?' It's why he calls me every couple of days — to make sure the house is in one piece."

I'm still having a semi-difficult time believing Brad, still waiting for him to say, 'Gotcha!' to say that he and Nicole have known about *my* experiment ever since agreeing to meet me that first night at Jump Café and wanted to create more drama, more action in *my* life, but he doesn't, he just stands there with the same 'I'm-not-making-this-up' expression on his face and so I say, "What did you say after he apologized?"

"Nothing, really. What could I say? I could see his point. I used to have locks on practically everything too. I mean, in university I used to keep most of my food in my room under lock and key for shit sake."

(It's true, he did.)

"So what changed?"

"Honestly?" he asks and after I nod he delays his response for a good ten seconds before saying, "I ran into your sister last year, a couple months before she —"

"Jennie? You never told me this?"

"You were still living in Hamilton at the time. And we weren't really talking all that often. Anyway, I guess I was going through one of those existential, 'What's-the-meaning-of-life?' phases that everyone goes through and after I was done complaining about my life Jennie asked me to describe a moment, an incident, an encounter — something — that altered or at least made me *want* to alter the way I lived my life and after thinking about it I told her I felt that way after watching the movie *Schindler's List* a few years before, especially at the end of the movie when Oskar Schindler is saying he could've saved a lot more people by selling his ring or his watch and —"

"You told her that?" I ask, slightly surprised — not that Brad's inspiration for changing his life would come from a movie, but that he actually admitted it to Jennie, and is now admitting it to me.

"Ya."

"And what did Jennie say?"

"She asked me *how* the movie made me want to alter my life and I told her that it made me want to start helping people, made me wish I was in that war so I could do what Schindler did and then she asked me if, after watching the movie, I actually started helping people and I told her I hadn't and when she asked me why not, I told her it seemed impossible at the time, that I got distracted by other things, by Nicole asking me where we should go for dessert, what I had to do at the office the next day, the fact that I had to get the Navigator's transmission looked at. Besides, there wasn't a war going on at the moment so what could I do? And then she asked me what was really preventing me from helping people, and when I asked her what she meant by that, instead of answering my question she asked me to accompany her on a walk and so after she bought about a dozen muffins we left the shop and started walking. It was late January, fairly cold — not super cold but there was a lot of snow on the ground — and we kept seeing these people on the street — lying in bus shelters, on hot air grates, tucked into doorways or in the corners of subway stations — and your sister talked to all of them, she knew most of them by name and they knew her, and she introduced me to them, and after we'd walked for about two hours and I'd met about a dozen street people and Jennie had given them each a muffin and a couple of dollars, we ended up back in the coffee shop and she said something like, 'No one needs to go to war or be in a war to do heroic things; merely choosing to attend to the lives of those around you, choosing not to pass by them or sidestep them or ignore them, is heroic enough. And it doesn't matter where your inspiration comes from as long as it translates into action. And the moment you do act, the moment you go up to one of these people, invite them into your life, ask them what they need, offer them your time, your concern, your home, you'll know what's really been preventing you from helping them.'"

    Neither of us says anything for a few moments until I break the silence with, "Well, that certainly sounds like Jennie," and then, a few moments later, after Brad has nodded his head in agreement, I ask, "What happened after that?" and he chuckles — only not like he's happy, more like he's reliving a memory that's both disappointing and disgusting.

    "Well, on the drive home that night I probably saw another

five homeless people sitting out on the street and as I passed by each one I kept thinking I could stop right now and help them. I could just do it. I could radically alter my life, their lives, right now, right now. . . ."

At this point he stops talking, steps on a sock that's lying on the floor, flicks it across the room and when it collides with the wall he asks, "You want to know what I did instead?"

I nod.

"I booked a vacation to Cuba and got drunk and high every night for two weeks. That's what I did."

I think about the parallels, how a couple of weeks after watching Jennie's suicide I booked a week-long trip to Cancun and got drunk and high each day in an attempt to avoid the memory of what I didn't do.

"And you want to know what happened when I got back?"

I shrug. "Sure."

"Here's some irony for you. The day after I got home from Cuba, I was looking through the last two weeks of newspapers and I came across an article about a woman, a homeless woman, freezing to death in a bus shelter."

He flicks another sock across the room, watching it stop just shy of the wall.

"The woman was one of the people I saw as I was driving back home after talking with Jennie," he says, his face reddening, his jaw clenching and unclenching. "While I was lying on some beach in Cuba, one of the people I told myself I could help froze to death."

He sends another sock across the room and it crashes into the previous one, sandwiching it against the wall.

"How'd you know it was the same woman?" I ask, noticing his eyes are now glossy, filling with tears.

He shrugs. "The description, the location. Apparently she'd been using the same bus shelter for months and after reading the article in the paper I drove by it every night for almost a week and she was never there and . . ."

The next word ends somewhere in his throat and after waiting a suitable amount of time for him to recover I say, "So what changed?"

"Hmmm?"

"Well, something must've happened," I say, gesturing towards the laundry, then towards upstairs, in the direction of the bum sitting at the dining table. "I mean, to change the way you were acting."

He nods his head, wiping his eyes. "It was a combination of things I guess. The fact that I couldn't stop thinking about that woman freezing to death played a big part. Then there was Jennie's sui —, I mean, death. And there was this quote I read in an old *Ms.* magazine from this —"

"Wait a second," I say, interrupting him, needing clarification, but also thinking that the line of questioning I'm about to embark on may serve to lighten the mood. "You mean, *Ms.* magazine — as in the leading feminist magazine in the world?"

He nods.

"When . . . no, where . . . no, *why* were you reading *Ms.* magazine?"

"I can tell you the when, the where, even the why. The when was March 28 of last year, the where was at the corner of Bloor and Bathurst, the why was because I saw some woman earmarking the page before setting it down carefully on the sidewalk in mid-stride and when I picked it up and flipped to the earmarked page the first thing I saw was a quote from this Janice Sevre-Duszynska woman who was trying to be ordained a Roman Catholic priest and the quote was, 'When you come to a sense of an evolving truth and you don't act, you are committing a sin of omission and to me the last 100 years of human history is notorious for what people have failed to do.'"

"March 28? That's...."

"I know, Good Friday, the day Jennie died. It was actually only maybe an hour or so after I heard the news and I started thinking about all the people on the street, how they didn't have Jennie around anymore to help them, to give them a blanket or a hot drink or a muffin or a couple of dollars, and I couldn't get the images of Jennie helping them, of that woman freezing to death, and the quote in *Ms.* magazine out of my head, and I suddenly found myself shouting, 'That's it. I've had enough,' and I hopped in the Navigator and invited half a dozen street people back to my house."

"Wow," I say, surprised. "Holy shit, in fact. I mean, what was *that* like?"

He chuckles, a happy chuckle this time, like he's replaying a fond memory. "To tell you the truth, I was scared shitless. Every time I stopped and invited someone on the street back to my place, every time one of them got into the Navigator, I became more and more aware of the level of suspicion and distrust I had for them, how protective I was of myself, my wallet, my jacket, my shoes, how each day I tucked myself away in my car, my house, my office, peeking out at the rest of the world from behind locked doors or barred windows — which, of course, was exactly what Jennie was talking about when she said that the moment I went up to one of these people and invited them into my life, the moment I asked them what they needed, offered them my time, my concern, my home, I'd know what was really preventing me from helping them. And what was really preventing me from helping them was fear, most of it unfounded and media-generated, but the fear that at any moment someone — my neighbour, the mailwoman, a crack addict, a gangster, a juvenile delinquent, a homeless vagrant — might break into my car or house and stab me or steal my DVD player or my father's precious Carlos Delgado autographed baseball bat."

"Has anything been stolen?"

He smiles. "Of course. Not much, though. A lot less than I expected, actually. And to be honest, I don't blame anyone for doing it. I mean, most of the time they can't believe I'm doing this — they're always waiting for the catch or thinking that this is a 'One Time Only' deal and so they'll maybe take something that they can use or sell or trade, just in case it is. But most of them, once they realize that there's no catch and they can come by almost anytime, don't touch or take anything without asking."

"Anyone try and take the bat?"

He laughs. "Not yet. Though part of me wishes someone would," he says, and then, after the two of us have been standing in silence for almost a minute, I say, "So it was you who told them then, right?"

"Told who what?"

"Told all those homeless people that Jennie had died, when her funeral was, where it was being held — all that."

He nods.

"My parents and my uncle couldn't figure out who all these people were, all these people coming up to them and telling them that Jennie had been their salvation, that they vowed to continue doing her work."

He smiles. "Jennie inspired a lot of people. Tons of them. And she was right, you know, when she told me that it doesn't matter where the inspiration comes from, not when what you're doing involves helping others, possibly saving their life, or at the very least, making life a little more tolerable for them. . . ."

juice for life/food for thought

I'm on Bloor Street, walking west, my head still slightly reeling from the conversation with Brad, replaying the dialogue, the images of him inviting the homeless into his home because of my sister Jennie, and it's as I'm picturing all these homeless people eating, sleeping, and hanging out in Brad's house that I realize how difficult it must've been to keep this a secret from me, from Nicole, from everyone for more than a year, and I start thinking about all the times in the last year, including yesterday, that I told him he prepares way too much food for our dinner parties and how he just smiled and said, 'Well, I'm sure somebody'll eat it,' or how many times in the last year when I called him and either got his answering machine or he told me he already made plans with Nicole or said he wasn't feeling well ('Migraines again, bud') or told me he had to go out of town for the weekend with his father on a business trip — that instead of doing this what he was probably doing was helping/entertaining/feeding street people and, of course, right in the middle of these thoughts, gnawing away at me, is the realization that I should probably call Rebecca and tell her what I've learned so she can decide what should be done with this new material, how we're going to use it but, for some reason, perhaps because of what she did a couple nights ago — coming into the apartment, watching me while I was dreaming, leaving the TV on — I decide to hold off on telling her, decide that tonight I'll be the one determining what to do with the new material.

After walking past the Grassroots hemp store on Bloor, I cross the street, consider going into Book City (don't), then Seekers Books where Rebecca sometimes hangs out (don't), then Juice for Life (do), quickly bypassing the small line-up of people waiting behind the 'Please Wait to be Seated' sign posted near the entrance and walking quickly towards the back of the restaurant, towards the last booth, which, thankfully, is still empty.

I sit there for who knows how long, staring at the tabletop, trying to organize things, wondering how I'm going to incorporate this new material into the upcoming dinner scene.

'A challenge for any director,' Rebecca wrote on page 41 of her diary, 'is how to incorporate new material. Deciding what is relevant and what is extraneous, what is vital and what is useless, is as important as deciding when it will be introduced, how it will be used, to what end it —'

"Quelle surprise. Qu'est-ce qui se passe, mon ex-ami?"

It's Katelin.

Did I mention she's a Francophile?

Loves everything French.

I think I even told her once she suffered from conversion disorder because it seemed like all she wanted to do was convert the whole world to French.

When I don't answer her right away she says (probably thinking I'm waiting for her to speak English which is something I used to do occasionally — refusing to speak to her until she spoke English), "I can't believe this. One ex-boyfriend and one ex-friend in the same day."

"Qui est ton ex-copain?" I say.

"Ooh-la-la, merci," she says, smiling at hearing me speak French, then, en anglais, she whispers, "He's sitting right over there," gesturing towards the front of the restaurant. "The one wearing the beige baseball cap and the striped T-shirt."

When I look I see Seth, the guy I saw while watching volleyball in the Beaches today with Daphne, sitting alone at the front of the restaurant, his eyes trained on the entrance. It was his idea to meet here but he must not have seen me when he came in.

"You dated *him*?" I ask, remembering why Daphne hated Seth, replaying her version of him while looking at Katelin, studying her face, comparing it to the vast inventory of actresses stored in my mind, abruptly realizing — to my amazement — that Katelin actually looks quite a lot like Jada Pinkett-Smith, only smaller, more petite — if that's possible — and as I'm thinking about asking Katelin if Seth ever called her 'Jada,' or 'JP' or if he had pictures of her plastered all over his room, Katelin says, "Yes, I dated *him*. Why, is there something wrong with *him*?"

"What's his name?"

"Guess."

"What do you mean, guess? I haven't the —"

"Seth. His name is Seth."

"How long did you two date?"

"Too long."

"What's too long?"

"Long enough."

"Bad break-up?"

"Something like that?"

"When?"

"When what?"

"When did you guys go out, break-up —"

"In the past."

"What's with all the cryptic answers?"

"I have my reasons."

"And they are?"

She ignores my question, a smudge of irritation-slash-bitterness now on her face, modifying the playful expression she was wearing a second ago.

"So," she says after a few moments, the playful expression slowly returning, "what brings you to Juice for Life?"

I decide not to say any more about Seth until I can find a way to re-introduce him and say, after doing a quarter turn and leaning back against the restaurant wall, my right foot now on the bench of the booth, "Actually, I just had a really intriguing conversation with Brad."

"Really? Well, that doesn't surprise me," Katelin says, surprising me.

I'd been expecting her to say something like, 'Come on, it couldn't have been *that* intriguing if you were talking to Brad,' seeing as she was always saying how over-*normal*, borderline boring, she thought he was.

After a moment or two during which I consider asking her why it doesn't surprise her, another thought squeezes forward and I hear myself saying, "You ever think you know someone and then you learn something about them that makes you look at him like you might not really know him, that the way you've been relating to him, if you had known this, probably would've been a lot different, which, in turn, makes the way you've been relating to him feel like, I don't know, a lie?"

She looks directly into my eyes for a few seconds, as though searching for something, then nods her head, slowly and says, "Sure, I mean, like Joseph Campbell said, 'Lies are what the world lives on.'"

In the instant that follows I think about Eriq's secret, about Nicole saying 'Everyone's got a secret,' about Brad's secret and how when I asked him how come I never knew this stuff about him, he laughed and said, "To quote Kevin Smith in the movie *Chasing Amy*, 'What you don't know about me would just about fit into the Grand Canyon,'" about Katelin and how (during our thirteen-hour walk and talk the day after her appointment in The Suicide Loft) when I told her I loved design, especially advertising design, adding that a clever, hip ad design could make me buy something I didn't even need she told me she felt the *exact same way*, that her dream was to be a designer, that she was actually thinking of applying to Ryerson University for design or —

"Ya, I know, the world lives on lies," I say, interrupting my own train of thought, "but it's more than lies, it's, it's — hey, you want to sit down?"

"I can't. I'm working."

"You *work* here?"

"As if you didn't know that."

"I didn't. I swear."

"Whatever."

"No, really. I had no idea."

"Then why did you come in here?"

"To see Seth," I say, watching her eyes when I gesture towards Seth, who is still looking at the entrance.

"He's got some issues he wanted to discuss with me about some old girlfriend of his," I say, and when Katelin looks back at me, I notice that as soon as I mentioned the word 'girlfriend' the irritated-slash-bitter expression reappeared on her face. "In fact, now that I'm thinking about it, he was the one who said we should meet here, in Juice for Life, and — hey, you know what, it's all making sense now. He wanted to meet here so he could show me who he was going to be talking about —"

"Ryan," she snaps, the irritated-slash-bitter expression changing, mutating to something else, something closer to disgust, possibly revulsion, "Stop it. For once, I'd like to talk to you without you making up some stupid story, without you being a total —"

"Can I get a smoothie?" I say, cutting her off, neither liking her tone nor the fact that her voice level has risen an average of point three octaves for each word she's spoken after the word, 'Stop.' "A banana blueberry smoothie, please."

Before leaving she pulls a folded piece of paper from her back pocket and hands it to me. "I think you might enjoy it."

I watch her until she walks behind the counter and gives the smoothie order to the juice guy and then I get up to use the payphone and while listening to it ringing see Seth reach for his cellphone and when he answers it I tell him it's not a good time right now, I've got a dinner party to go to in a little while but maybe I can meet him later tonight, at Whiskey Saigon, at say, around 1:00 a.m., and then he hangs up and after I do the same, I see him get up, say "So long" to Katelin, and leave the restaurant.

Returning to my seat I again watch Katelin — this time for a few minutes — moving through the restaurant, through the busyness and confusion and parcels of conversation, reminding me of Jennie, on camera, saying how she often sat for hours in restaurants and cafés around Toronto, that there was something about the incessant movement of bodies, the collage of faces, the collision of conversations that made her feel vivid, alive, connected, the fragments of dialogue and images now lodged in her mind replaying for days afterwards, inspiring her poetry.

    I open the piece of paper and see that it's a poem entitled 'Deception Found.'

> *Each day I*
> *wear a stranger's face*
> *think a stranger's thoughts*
> *speak a stranger's ideas*
>
> *Each day I*
> *mute my face*
> *evict my thoughts*
> *silence my ideas*
>
> *Each day I watch —*
> *watch the part that really is me*
> *being razed,*
> *razed towards oblivion*
> *oblivious to everyone —*
> *everyone but me.*

Who am I?

This was why I was so attracted to Katelin initially: the fact that, like Jennie, she a) wrote poetry, b) lived a double life, a life few people knew about, and c) guarded the secrecy of that double life very well. Well, okay, maybe not *very* well.

Though Katelin never came back to The Suicide Loft, she did agree to come with me to dinner the following weekend at Jump Café. In fact, she made three appearances before telling me she'd had enough, that going to dinner with us was a euphemism for going into battle and she had no desire to be a part of our unarmed conflicts; she was disturbed by the speed with which everyone — especially Eriq and Daphne — could turn on each other, could go from friend to foe in a nanosecond, not to mention the feeling she got that the rest of us considered this to be normal, that we seemed to not only expect, but *enjoy* and be *comforted* by the conflict and hostility, that it seemed as though we liked the roles we played in this little drama series.

I tried persuading her to stay, telling her it was just a matter of time and exposure before she'd get used to it, that conflict can be fun, that, in my opinion, there's nothing more boring than sitting around with a bunch of people who agree with each other all the time, who just want to talk about how right or great they are without ever being challenged.

Of course, Katelin disagreed, stating she didn't want to get used to it, that she had no interest in building up an immunity to hostility, no desire to develop antibodies so she could someday regard this type of interaction as normal, adding that she'd much rather hang around people who aren't always challenging you and trying to make you feel stupid.

When Katelin returns with my smoothie, I hand her back her poem.

"I like it," I say, then ask, "Who's it about?"

"A friend of mine," she says, the lie flowing so easily, so effortlessly, so naturally, from her that it reminds me of why I invited her to dinner at Jump Café: she's such a good actress, which, if I remember correctly, made Rebecca slightly nervous, telling me once that, 'I never know if she's lying or telling the truth. She's difficult to read.'

"By the way," Katelin says, setting a few napkins on the table beside my smoothie, "is the gang still meeting, I mean, *clashing*, every weekend?"

I smile, nod, say, "Yep, we're still clashing away. In fact, we'll be clashing at Brad's house for dinner in about an hour."

"How wonderful."

"Care to join us?"

"I'd rather watch infomercials all evening," she says, then, as though she's just remembered something she's been wanting to ask me for a long time, she asks, "Are Brad and Nicole still together?"

I nod. "Still together, still engaged, and still scheduled to be married in three months."

"Well, I guess that makes sense," and before I can ask her why that makes sense, she asks, "And how about Eriq, is he still doing the same thing?"

"Ya," I say, "if by, 'still doing the same thing,' you mean being or attempting to be supported by wealthy patrons."

"I did."

I smile, anticipating Katelin's next question.

"And I take it you're still hanging out with *her*?" she asks, saying *'her'* like it's something thoroughly repugnant.

"You mean Daphne?"

"The one and only."

I nod. "Ya."

"Well, isn't that nice — the whole gang is still intact."

"Except for Rebecca."
"Why, is she playing Houdini again?"
I nod.
"How long?"
"Five weeks, two days, and counting."
"I'll bet Daphne's climbing the f-ing walls."
"Why do you say that?" I say, realizing as soon as I've said this that I sounded far too eager and when I see that twinkle in Katelin's eyes and she smiles like she's got me, I know that she knows something about me, something she won't tell me, and she says, "*You* must be having fun without her around, though."
"Why would you say that?"
"Uh, gee, I don't know. Probably because you get to run the show whenever she's not around."
"What are you talking —?"
"Are you forgetting I was there?" she says, interrupting me. "I saw the two of you in action. Whenever Rebecca was around you acted like you were her assistant or her understudy, but as soon as she was out of the picture you'd start acting totally different, like you were the one in charge."
"Are you feeling okay, Katelin?" I say, moving slightly forward in the booth, looking at her with a curious-slash-concerned expression, as though there might be something seriously wrong with her. "I mean, speaking of making up stupid stories. Where did you get your poetic licence from, the back of matchbox cover?"
"C'est la poêle qui se moque de la chaudron."
"Excuse me? I think I'm going to need a translation."
"You could always look it up, you know."
"It'd be easier if you told me."
"And where's the fun in that?" she says, and, her expression changing, she adds, "You know, it's too bad Seth had to leave."
"Why?"

"Daphne's his favourite topic."

"Daphne? What, are you serious? How do you know this?"

"I said he was my ex-boyfriend. I didn't say we weren't speaking."

"Oh, right," I say, and then, suddenly feeling squeamish, ask, "So, do you guys talk a lot?"

"Some."

"I guess he comes here quite often?"

"Actually, no, this was his first time."

"Really? Why do you think he was here?"

"I thought you said he was here to meet you?"

"I was just kidding."

"Really? Because just before he left he told me he was supposed to meet someone, but apparently the person called and cancelled."

"That's too bad," I say, trying to sound like I mean it.

Katelin smiles, almost laughs, then, looking at me with almost no identifiable emotion, asks, "So why are you still here?"

dinner conversation: no appetizers, just the main course

"Why, she's been in therapy, of course."

We've just retired to the living room after having dinner in the dining room, during which no one (despite what Katelin may have said) clashed once. It was, in fact, one of the most polite, civil (or, as Rebecca would say, *unfilmable*) dinner scenes I'd ever witnessed from the cast — definitely a scene in need of some direction — though it may have only seemed unfilmable because of what'd happened earlier with Brad. Everything has been a little anti-climatic since then (even seeing Katelin and Seth in Juice for Life), and instead of spending my time creating or encouraging friction or drama (like Rebecca would've insisted on, and I would've normally done) I was busy looking around and imagining homeless people sitting in my chair, eating out of my bowl, off my plate, using my fork, breathing the same air I was now breathing — remembering what the Top Five girl had said about how we're all connected, all part of one another — and as I was thinking all this, Eriq, after taking the cup of espresso Brad had just handed him, said, "So, what have you been doing the last couple of days, Nicole?" to which Daphne, answering for her, replied, "Why, she's been in therapy, of course," causing Eriq to nearly drop his espresso.

"As a matter of fact," Nicole says, ignoring Daphne, "I bought an easel yesterday and some art supplies. I'm thinking about doing some painting and sculpting in my spare time."

"For Christ's sake," Daphne says, frowning, "why?"

"I think it'll be a good hobby."

"You mean good therapy," Daphne snorts.

"No, I've always been interested in painting and sculpting and —"

"That's it!" Daphne interrupts, pounding her fist on the arm of the sofa as though she's just discovered something. "This new *hobby* of yours wouldn't happen to have anything to do with the fact that in the May edition of *Vanity Fair*, your idol, Mrs. Brad Pitt, said she likes to paint and sculpt in her spare time, would it?"

"I do *not* idolize Jennifer Aniston."

"That wasn't my question."

Daphne waits three, maybe three and a half seconds for a response from Nicole before saying, "Your silence is awfully incriminating."

"I'm *not* doing it because Jennifer Aniston does it."

"Right. Whatever. Let me guess — she *exposed* you to the idea and now you've become so inspired you've just got to try it, right?"

"What's wrong with that?"

"You're pathetic."

"Question," Brad says, looking directly at Daphne, his tone suggesting he's slightly annoyed. "Why is it alright for *you* to read articles in *Vanity Fair* or watch TV shows or movies but when someone else does it, you act as though the person committed one of the seven deadly sins?"

"Because, Beamer Boy, *I* don't *become* the movie or the TV show or the article in *Vanity Fair*."

"Neither is Nicole, she's merely inspired by the article."

"Bullshit, she's *imitating* the article."

Eriq laughs. "Imitation *is* the highest form of flattery."

"No," Daphne says, "imitation is the surest indication of *passivity*, of people too lazy to think and create for themselves."

"Imitation is perfectly natural," I say, disagreeing. "I mean, how do you think you learned to speak English or French — by imitating the sounds of your parents and the people around you. Besides, should it even matter where or who you get your inspiration from? I mean, whether it comes from reading an article in *Vanity Fair* or Timothy Findley or Shakespeare or watching a movie like *Thelma & Louise* or *Schindler's List* or just hanging out with your friends shouldn't matter. What should matter is what's being done with the inspiration. That's what counts."

"Well, I'm fairly certain that imitating — oh, excuse me, I meant to say, being *inspired* by — Jennifer Aniston isn't going to yield any earth-shattering changes in the way we think."

"How do you know that? I mean, really, you don't, right? You don't know that reading this article in *Vanity Fair* isn't going to inspire Nicole to begin painting or sculpting which, in turn, might get her interested enough in the arts to start supporting them — just like you don't know that reading a book by Timothy Findley isn't going to inspire someone to become a writer or watching a movie like *Schindler's List* isn't going to inspire someone to convert their home into a halfway house for homeless people or —"

"Or what if the article in *Vanity Fair* was put there just to get people to buy their magazine and look at all the pretty ads?" Daphne says, and before I can formulate a rebuttal, she adds, "For Christ's sake, why can't we just admit what's really happening here: that just like almost everyone else on this bloody planet, Nicole's infected with this overwhelming compulsion, this obsession to copy and clone whichever 'star' happens to be en vogue this month and that her so-called *inspiration* from *Vanity Fair*, from Mrs. Brad Pitt, will die a quick death and the easel and paint will sit in her basement for years and never be used?"

"Here, here," Eriq says, pounding the arm of the couch, before adding, ignoring the finger Daphne is now giving him, "And while we're at it, why don't we also admit that imitating is easier or, as Ryan put it, perfectly natural? Why are we wasting all this effort trying to be original when, like the good book says, there's nothing new under the sun?"

"The good book?" I say, frowning. "You mean, *The Sound and the Fury*?"

Eriq shakes his head, smiling at my reference. "The Old Testament. Ecclesiastes. Chapter 2, verse 12."

"What are you saying?" Daphne asks, glaring at Eriq.

"I'm saying, why bother wasting all this time trying to create, innovate, invent, revolutionize, and be original when you can just sit back, go with the flow, and reap the benefits of other people's efforts?"

"But," Brad says, now scratching the back of his head, "what if you don't agree with the *results* of other people's efforts? What if you don't agree with what they've created or invented?

Shouldn't you at least make an effort to change them, to suggest other ways?"

Eriq smiles. "Unlike my stepsister over there," he says, pointing at Daphne, "I grew out of my passion for revolution, for trying to change things, and decided years ago to adopt a more *laissez-faire* attitude to things."

"You mean, *lazy frère* attitude," Daphne says, and then, after a sip of cappuccino, she relaxes her posture, sinking back into the loveseat and adds, "Spoken like someone who's never had to struggle for anything in his life."

Eriq, now wearing an 'I'm up for this debate' expression, sniffs the air a couple of times before saying, "Est-ce que le parfum de l'envie que je sens?"

"You're confusing envy with indignation," Daphne snaps, sitting forward again.

"Indignation?" Eriq says, smiling, mildly amused. "How can *you*, Daphne, of all people, be indignant? You lead every bit as privileged a life as I do."

"Hey, I *earned* my money."

"No, *my* father invested $10,000 for you on your eighteenth birthday and *his* investment broker turned it into half a million within ten years."

"Well, don't blame me if *you* decided to take the ten grand and spend it on clothes rather than have *our* father invest it. Besides, I've done my fair share of work."

Eriq gives Daphne a 'you can't be serious' expression, then says, "I wouldn't consider you and a bunch of your Platinum Visa friends renting condos and tipping the wait staff in the Caribbean and South America doing your fair share of work," putting finger quotation marks around 'fair share of work.'

"We did more than that. We helped create jobs, helped them earn a living, helped them —"

Daphne is interrupted by Eriq's laughter.

"Come on Daphne, what you *did* — whether you want to admit it or not — was go around endorsing the vision of turning every country *not* in North America or Western Europe into feudalistic resorts for the credit card generation. What you did was help turn the countries of the Caribbean and South America into country *clubs*, into amusement and theme parks for the rich. What you *did* was impregnate the people of these countries with the idea that the only way to 'Get a Life' is to think of their own culture, their own language, their own customs and traditions as second-rate, as nothing more than a tourist attraction and that the only path to success is to turn their country into miniature versions of America and then join America in finding some other, less developed country to exploit. If you really wanted to help these people you'd have stayed home and watched *Lonely Planet* on the Outdoor Life Network — it would've been a helluva lot more environmentally friendly not to mention —"

"For starters," Daphne says, cutting him off, "*I* didn't create this vision. *I* didn't impregnate anyone with *my* idea of success. This vision, this idea of success was there long before I visited these countries. Secondly, I *always* made sure I paid *more* than I had to for food and accommodation — even when I knew they were overcharging to begin with."

Eriq smiles. "How incredibly magnanimous of you," he says. "But I'm not so sure that putting a few bucks in someone's pocket qualifies you for 'Good Samaritan of the Millennium.' Besides, it's a small price to pay for forcing these countries to bend over and take it up the ass for the last five or six hundred years."

"Hey, at least I'm in a position to help and be magnanimous. At least I'm in a position to put money *in* people's pockets instead of taking it *out* of their pockets. And as for bending over and taking it up the ass, isn't that exactly what you do to ensure you get your free handout every month?"

"Daphne's right," Brad says, immediately whipping the room into silence, giving me time to notice that Nicole's mouth is actually hanging open and both Eriq and Daphne are staring at Brad wearing   stunned-slash-flabbergasted-slash-'Holy-shit-I-never-thought-I'd-ever-see-the-day,' expressions.

"I think as long as you're in a position to help people you should help them," Brad says, timidly, slightly embarrassed by the overwhelming silence.

Eriq recovers first, his tone uncharacteristically hostile — especially since he's replying to Brad, whom he usually doesn't get angry with — which makes me wonder if he's maybe just pissed off at Daphne's 'free handout' comment or the fact that he doesn't have any free handouts at the moment or that he's having to resort to doing something he doesn't like in order to get a handout or if he's just decided to adopt the same hostile tone of voice that the antagonist in his short story, 'Conversation Pieces,' uses when he says the following words, "You know, Brad, when I look at someone like yourself, I can't help but think you've got more than enough resources at your disposal to make a real difference in people's lives, yet, as far as I can tell, you're not using them to help others, are you?"

talking cure

The anticipation is nearly killing me.

I've been waiting, semi-patiently, for about ten seconds now for Brad to hit Eriq with the truth, to smack him (and Daphne) with the ultimate punchline, to deliver the words, "As a matter of fact, I am helping people — lots of them," but he doesn't. Even after I urge him (with my eyes) while mouthing the words,

'Tell him,' Brad continues to just sit there on MUTE until Eriq says, "You know, with a house this size and your fondness for cooking, I could see you really —" he pauses here, surveys the rest of us, then says, "Oh hell, fuck it. Why don't *all* of us combine our resources and really make a difference? With Brad's house, his passion for cooking, and his knowledge of law combined with Daphne's. . . ."

While Eriq inventories our resources I realize that what's really happening here is, just like the antagonist in 'Conversation Pieces,' Eriq is putting us to the test, trying to determine if we're just like the rest of the characters in the story, if we're capable of feeling a sense of accomplishment from merely *talking* about all the things we *could* do, while at the same time juxtaposing this with memories of Tolstoy, of how Tolstoy never talked about doing something he wasn't already doing, of how whenever Tolstoy came across a sound idea he would put it into practice, incorporate the idea into his everyday life, *before* discussing it with others, how he believed that talking about something got in the way of actually doing it, that talking often became a substitute for acting and that more often than not the ideas that could really help people, the ideas that could make a difference in their lives never really became anything more than just a *conversation piece,* something nice to discuss during dinner or, in our case, after dinner.

When Eriq has finished his inventory and no one has responded to his proposal of combining our resources and really making a difference, he says, his expression morphing from seriousness to 'Relax, I'm just joking,' "I think it could really work. I mean, instead of us meeting every Friday at Jump Café and seeing who can outwit and outhurt who, we could take the money we'd normally spend at the restaurant, load up Nicole's SUV with groceries, cook a massive meal here at Brad's house, then drive around the city and serve it to all the homeless and hungry, and then, since hell has now frozen over anyway, we could buy everyone a pair of skates and go for a nice, long. . . ."

beamer boy's new beamer

"Why the hell didn't you say anything?"

– Eriq just left for his date with the too-young editor at Easy & The Fifth,

– Daphne and Nicole are still in the living room, ignoring each other, and

– Brad and I are in the kitchen, cleaning up.

Despite my question and the insistent, 'I'd appreciate having my question answered right away,' tone I used, Brad continues cleaning off the dinner plates, slowly scraping the food into the wastebasket, then thoroughly rinsing off each plate before carefully placing it in the dishwasher.

"Hello? Earth to Wellington? Come in Wellington."

He sighs. "Have you ever heard of the French saying, 'Une hirondelle ne fait pas le printemps'?"

"Nope," I say, shaking my head.

"'One sparrow does not a spring make.' It means that just because you see one sparrow, doesn't mean spring is here."

"Ya, I already figured out the translation, I'm just wondering what this has to do with you not telling Eriq and the others about what you've been doing for more than a year."

"Well, fourteen months does not a philanthropist make."

"Ya, but at least you're doing *something*. And you've been doing it for a while now. Fourteen months is long enough to make a statement."

"I don't know. Maybe if I was sitting up in a tree like Julia Hill or something a little more dramatic it would've been —"

"A little more dramatic? Are you kidding? Brad, it would've been perfect. I mean, the way Eriq was talking to you, the way both he and Daphne were looking at you. It couldn't have been written any better. It would've been the perfect Kodak moment, the —"

"Well, I don't know about that. Besides, I'm kind of glad it stayed a secret. I mean, at first, when I'd been doing it for a few weeks I felt like telling people — you, Nicole, even Eriq and Daphne — but I didn't because for the first time in a long time I felt like I wasn't doing something just for effect, like it was an act. It felt real, like it was the right thing to do. And I felt like if I said something, I'd come across as a poser, as someone who's like, 'Hey, look at me, look at what I'm doing. See what a wonderful person I am?' Of course, I have to admit, it also felt kind of cool to hide it from everyone, to know that I was doing something that none of you knew about, you know?" and as soon as he says this I know exactly what he means because I feel the same way about The Suicide Loft; there's something comforting-slash-thrilling-slash-satisfying in doing something that no one else knows about.

I watch Brad scraping, rinsing, and putting the dishes into the dishwasher for a while and then, as he's closing the dishwasher and pushing the 'water miser' button, he asks, "What the hell was up Eriq's ass tonight?"

After raising an eyebrow at Brad in response to his choice of words in the above question, I'm tempted to say that the reason Eriq's acting this way is because things aren't going well with his patron-seeking but instead I decide to go with a shrug and, "I don't know. Maybe he was just trying to stir the pot. I think he likes doing that."

Brad sighs. "You know, I wish he'd spend less time stirring the pot and more time using *his* resources. I mean, I don't mean to badmouth the guy but it's just that he's so smart and so talented and he knows so much about so many issues that if he just cared more I'm sure *he* could make a serious difference in people's lives."

"He cares," I say reflexively, thinking of Eriq's short stories and the depth of concern displayed by his characters (and him), then catch myself, "I mean, I'm guessing he does. Hell, for all we know, he might be more concerned about these issues than he lets on."

"I guess," Brad says, giving me a playful shot in the shoulder and adding, "Anyway, thanks for not mentioning anything about what you saw this afternoon. I thought for sure you were going to say something."

"I was tempted, trust me."

"Hey, let's leave the rest of the clean-up for a bit," he says, "I want to show you something," and after we've walked down to the basement, past the three large freezers, I see a very expensive-looking mountain bike leaning against the wall and when I get closer I see that it's a BMW, a BMW Q6.S.

"Holy shit, there it is. The Q6.S."

He nods. "Ya, I guess it wasn't really a surprise to you, though, huh — Sir Snoop-A-Lot?" he says, nudging me.

I laugh, replaying the image of me sneaking into his den, seeing the sales receipt and then the *Stuff* magazine open to the page displaying the bicycle.

"Look at this machine," I say, straddling it, admiring its sleek, sexy contours. "It's fucking impressive."

"It's so impressive I think I'm going to get rid of the Navigator."

"What? Why? It's just a bicycle."

"Hey, it's not just a bicycle, it's a BMW. There's a difference," he says, reiterating one of my Brasa comments and after I say, "Touché," he says, "The truth is Daphne was right. I need to scale down my four-wheel planet stomper. I'm thinking about trading it in for something smaller. I'd still like to have a vehicle.

It's kind of handy for going around and picking up people or dropping them off and for getting supplies and things."

"You should have one then."

"Ya, I probably will," he says, and then, after I've picked up the bike a few times and commented on its light weight, I say, "Hey, I was meaning to ask you before — that guy, at the dinner table this afternoon —"

"You recognized him?"

"Sort of."

"Follow me."

We walk over to the laundry room and he shows me the beige silk suit — the Reese's Peanut Butter Cup stains still on it.

"To be dropped off at the dry cleaner's tomorrow morning," Brad says, smiling.

"So it *was* him," I say.

"He's got you to thank," Brad says. "I picked him up right where you said you saw him — just outside Osgoode Hall on Queen Street."

"And what about the other three, the kids in dreads?"

"I've known them for a while now — almost a year, in fact. They help me out with a lot of stuff. They're the ones who told me about the camaraderie of street people, how it's like a family, how a lot of them would rather live on the street with their street family than at home with their real family. . . ."

eriq, no woman's land

"Rebecca's the last thing she needs," Eriq says, bitterly.

It's just after midnight and I'm on Yonge Street now, walking towards downtown with Eriq, admiring the ongoing orgy of cold neon erupting from rooftops, window displays, and the sides of buildings, their screaming messages deafening my eyes.

Eriq cellphoned me thirty minutes ago to tell me he'd ended his date with the too-young editor early and wanted to hook up and since meeting him outside the Gloucester nearly fifteen minutes ago we've been passing commentary on Brad's dinner party (both of us); on Brad's hypocrisy (Eriq); on the fact that Brad's maybe not a hypocrite, that maybe he's actually doing something (me); that there's no way Brad is doing something (Eriq); that maybe he is because (as Nicole said this afternoon) there's lots we don't know about one another (me). Ya, like what? (Eriq.) Like for instance, neither Brad or Nicole or Daphne knows you write — never mind that your characters, which are often just thinly disguised versions of yourself, are constantly struggling with the same issues we discuss whenever the five of us get together — so maybe there's something about Brad that neither Nicole or Daphne or you know about? (Me.) And this got us talking about all the things we actually know for sure about each other and at one point I said that if there's one thing I know about Daphne it's that she needs Rebecca and Eriq looked at me like I was retarded and said, bitterly, "Rebecca's the last thing she needs."

At this moment, Yonge Street is festering with traffic.

Anonymous faces, framed in open car windows, occasionally shout/jeer/taunt, trying to find a receptacle for their angst, a sufficient reaction to interrupt their tedium. Most of the sidewalk herd know better, however, and continue facing front, their expressions blank, sealed for protection.

"Why?"

"Why what?" Eriq says after a few moments.

"Why is Rebecca the last thing Daphne needs?"

He doesn't respond right away, looking like he's collecting his thoughts, then mumbles, "Just a sec, I'm collecting my thoughts," before asking me, "Have I ever written anything about Rebecca?" and when I give him a 'What are you talking about?' expression, he rephrases his question, asking me, if, to my knowledge, I have noticed a character in any of his short stories who is based — in whole or in part — on Rebecca?"

"No," I say, shaking my head after conducting a thorough mental inventory of Eriq's stories. "I don't think so."

"Don't you find that just a little odd? After all, I'm certain you've seen yourself in print, as well as Brad, Daphne, Nicole, and myself."

"True."

"So why do you think I've never written Rebecca, never used her as a blueprint for one of my characters?"

I shrug.

"Because I've never been able to get a firm grasp on her. Even when she's hanging out with us it seems like she's not really there. I've tried writing her about a dozen times but every time I think I'm getting close to putting her in print I end up losing all sense of her character; she either morphs into someone else or she just vanishes completely and. . . ."

His words trail off, possibly interrupted by the sight of the guy riding the gold moose outside the Zanzibar across the street. Native and wearing a pair of bright orange overalls and work boots, the guy is singing a significantly shorter, modified version of 'O Canada,' — 'O Canada, your home *on* my native land, you stand on guard against the likes of me' — over and over while shaking his fists defiantly at pedestrians and passing vehicles.

A few moments later I consider telling Eriq that if he knew Rebecca better, knew her the way I do, had the *Insider's Report* so to speak, he'd have a better idea of who she is and he'd probably be able to write her but then, reconsidering, I decide to play out another line of argument and say, "So, what you're really saying is that Rebecca has a really strong shadow side?"

"Ya, I suppose you could say. . . ."

I allow Eriq some time to amend his sentence fragment but when he still hasn't said anything after ten seconds I say, "I thought you said having a shadow side always makes for the most interesting characters. In fact, I think it was the first time Rebecca and I met you at the International Festival of Authors and the three of us were talking about writing, you told us that having a shadow side makes for an interesting character."

"That's true. But with Rebecca it's a little beyond that. With her it's almost as though her shadow side is so dominant it makes her virtually impregnable. In fact, if I really think about it, it's almost as if she doesn't exist, like she's an invention or a figment of someone's imagination who refuses to let her be seen, to let her be known. I mean, at some point light should fall on a person's shadow side and reveal something of the character's true essence. Readers don't mind being kept in the dark or having to wear a blindfold for a while, as long as they feel confident that at some point the blindfold will be taken off or at least that they'll be afforded a peek or two and be able to more fully appreciate and understand the character. When this doesn't happen, when the shadow side isn't illuminated, when the character's motivation and hence the character remains a complete mystery, readers become lost. And that's what's happened to Daphne. She's become lost. Lost in no-woman's land."

A white Pontiac Sunbird has just pulled up beside us, moving at our pace, and one of the five girls in the car — the borderline obese, blond-haired one in the back seat closest the passenger side window, says, in a throaty, sexy voice, "Hey boys, wanna get laid?" and after Eriq tells them to go back to their cribs and suck on their soothers, all five of them tell us to go fuck ourselves before screeching away from the curb and when they're out of sight, I ask Eriq, "So, what do you think Daphne should do?"

"I think she should get rid of her."

"What?!"

"I don't mean kill her," he says, laughing at my reaction. "I mean, Rebecca is Daphne's kryptonite. Every time Daphne sees Rebecca she gets weaker and weaker, and not in a good way."

"Whatever," I say, giving Eriq a 'You can't be serious' expression. "Daphne lights up like a Christmas tree when she sees Rebecca. I mean, to quote you again, whenever Rebecca's around she wears that nauseating *Better Than Chocolate* expression."

"If I were Daphne, I'd stick to chocolate. It'd be a heckuva lot healthier for her."

A few strides later I say, "If Rebecca's so unhealthy, why doesn't Daphne just forget about her then?"

"For the same reason I can't stop trying to write Rebecca. No matter how impossible it is, I still want to try to write her. And, in the same way that I want to contain and capture Rebecca in print, Daphne wants to do this with her in real life."

"Have you told Daphne this?"

"A couple of times."

"And?"

"And what do you think? She reacted like I expected her to react — like she's reacted her whole life when someone's given her advice — she told me to fuck off and mind my own business."

"You don't like her, do you?"

"Who?"

"Rebecca."

"I don't really trust anyone I can't write. It's just the way I am. And in that way, I think Daphne and I are the same. We don't operate very well in uncertainty. We like to know what's going on behind the scenes at all times. It's why we're both so attracted to books: because once they're written you can no longer manipulate them. You know exactly where the characters are going, what they're doing, why they're doing it, how they're going to react. They're decided, choices have been made, things have happened — past tense, case closed, the end."

daphne's visions

I'm now on Bay Street, it's windier here, the tall buildings pirating the wind, creating mammoth conduits. A tiny tornado hatches in the TD alcove, sucking up an Eatmore wrapper along with dozens of stray bank statements, whirling them into a frenzy and, for a moment, I replace them with the sight of dozens of executives jumping from the office windows above until recalling, as soon as I hear the first one splat on the sidewalk, that there was only one — *one* — documented case of a Wall Street employee jumping from his office window in 1929.

Ten minutes later I'm in line at Whiskey Saigon, am probably about thirty seconds from being let in, when Daphne calls me, says she's got to meet me, that she needs to talk.
"I keep thinking I see her," she tells me over the phone. "At the subway station, on streetcars, in bookstores, walking along the street, in my dreams, everywhere. I think I'm going mad."
There is a brief moment during which I consider saying, 'Welcome to the club,' or 'You've got to learn to deal with it, Daph' and then telling her how many times in the last week alone that I think I've seen my dead sister Jennie walking around Toronto and when Daphne says, "Do you know where Rebecca is? If you know where she is you should tell me, Ryan. I really need to know," I tell her I don't but she doesn't believe me.

"I know you know, Ryan. You've got to know."

"I'm sorry, Daph, I don't —"

"Fuck!" she screams, "I can't live like this anymore!"

A second later I'm listening to a dial tone and after calling Daphne back five times without reaching her, I start to get concerned and so I call her apartment thinking (even though the number that came up on my call display was her cell number) she may be in her apartment but there's no answer there so I leave her a message to call me when she gets in no matter what the time, and then, in a mild panic because, of course, I'm imagining Daphne committing suicide without Rebecca and Rebecca going completely psycho, I call Rebecca — four times — but she's not answering either, so I leave a message on her cellphone voicemail, telling her to call me, that something's up and we need to talk — right away.

you dropped something

"Hey, check this out."

I'm on the 501 Neville Park streetcar, on my way home after deciding not to go to Whiskey Saigon.

A guy, a bum — the same bum who was sitting on the sidewalk outside Milestones café the other day — has just pulled a piece of paper from his pocket and said, "Hey, check this out," to another bum sitting in the seat across the aisle.

"I picked this up on Queen Street," the bum is now saying to the other bum. "I saw some kids putting them on the windshields of cars. By the end of the night every car I saw had one. Listen to this. It says, 'You have been charged with driving a carbon monoxide/carbon dioxide/nitrogen oxide/sulphur dioxide–producing, ozone-depleting, natural habitat–destroying, species-killing vehicle.'"

"Whas the fine?" the other bum slurs.

"Fifty dollars. And it says 'Please make cheque or money order payable to Friends of the Earth, Greenpeace, Earthroots, World Watch Institute, Earth First!, or the respiratory wing of any hospital in your city.'"

"Fuckin' Greenpeace assholes," the other bum says. "What'd they look like?"

"Who?"

"The kids who was handing them out."

"Oh. There were three of them. Two guys and a girl and all of them had dreadlocks."

"Ya, I've seen 'em, those three. I've seen 'em sittin' with a sign saying they want money for buyin' pot."

"I saw the girl give one to a cop outside Montana's."

"What'd the cop do?"

"He just looked at the ticket and started laughing."

"Fuckin' cops."

A few minutes later, after the bums get off the streetcar, I close my eyes and replay one of the sessions I had at The Suicide Loft this afternoon: it's the session with the young guy who's been coming to see me every two weeks for the last four months. He looks like a young Robert Redford, except for his eyes. His eyes make him look a lot older, like they've seen more than the average twenty-four-year-old guy, like they've witnessed something too horrible to ever forget, which they have.

For the past six months the two of us have been constructing a sort of photo/pictorial album of what he's gone/going through, with me taking pictures as he draws what he's thinking and feeling. Because he won't actually tell me anything — in fact, aside from making an appointment over the phone and saying 'Hello' when he came for his interview, I've never heard him speak — my challenge has been to figure out what's happened to him, what he's done/is doing that is creating so much pain and anguish in his everyday life.

What I've pieced together before today was that he was involved in some sort of accident where a young woman died in a fall during Spring Break at a party in Florida, that it was at least partially his fault, that he's never spoken about it to anyone. Today I learned that she fell from a sixth-floor balcony and that he visits her grave every month.

the top five kids

"If you could have sex with any Canadian, who would your Top Five be?"

For the last twenty, maybe twenty-five minutes, I've been sitting in the rocking chair, rewinding and replaying everything that's happened today, everything I've discovered about Eriq, Nicole, Brad — even Katelin — wondering how much of it, if any, I was going to share with Rebecca, trying to imagine what she'd do with the information, knowing for a fact that she wouldn't want Brad and Eriq to find out that they've actually got a lot in common, and for some reason, just like Eriq proposed at dinner a few hours ago, I started toying with the idea of bringing everyone together, combining our resources to really make a difference — maybe even bringing Jo-Jo into the mix — and just when I got to the part where I'd brought everyone together at Brad's and we'd decided to carry on with Jennie's work Rebecca suddenly charged onto the scene and started taking the gang in a completely different direction and because I needed something to divert my attention away from wanting to wring

Rebecca's neck, I was actually just about to turn on the TV when I heard the voice of one of the Top Five kids (which couldn't have been better timing seeing as they usually reserve their lighter Top Five Lists for their Sunday night talks), which was precisely what I was in the mood for.

"Sex? With any Canadian?"
"Any Canadian."
"Should we narrow the field?"
"Umm . . . sure, okay. Let's confine it to . . . the entertainment industry."
"Define entertainment."
"Musicians, writers, actors, athletes, talk show hosts, journalists, politicians."
"Politicians? They're not entertainers."
"Come on. Look at Sheila Copps or Jean Chrétien — are you telling me they're *not* entertaining?"
"Alright. But we're just talking sex, right, not a friendship or an intimate relationship?"
"Just sex."
"Okay, if it's just sex, my Top Five would be Erica Ehm, Natalie Furtado, Pamela Wallin —"
"Pamela Wallin?"
"She's sexy. I mean, every time I see her I just want to —"
"That's . . . that's, I don't know what that is. What's the opposite of pedophilia, *old*ophilia? That's what you are, you're an *old*ophiliac."
"She's not *that* old."
"She's like what, fifty?"
"So?"
"So, that's like almost three times your age."
"Hey, you're the one who picked the category."
"Okay, who else?"

"Alright, rounding out my Top Five would be Wendy Mesley and then maybe, I don't know, Kim Campbell? No, just kidding. Let's see, probably . . . is 'Jewel' Canadian?"

"American."

"Okay, then I'd have to go with Rita McNeil."

"Rita McNeil? You mean that really, really, really —"

"Yes. *That* Rita McNeil."

"So you're telling me you'd rather have sex with Rita McNeil than Pamela Anderson?"

"I don't think Pamela Anderson would make it into my Top Fifty. Your turn."

"Okay, and these are in no particular order of preference, but I'd have to go with Keanu Reeves because he was an absolute god in *The Matrix*. Vince Carter for reasons we don't need to get into right now. Rick Mercer because he's cute and funny and witty. Leonard Cohen because he's —"

"Speaking of oldophilia, Cohen's way older than Pamela Wallin."

"Ya, but it's okay because I'm female."

"Oh, I see. The old reverse double standard."

"Hey, we women need all the reverse double standards we can get."

"Whatever. Why Cohen?"

"Because he's probably got the sexiest voice and the sexiest aura on the planet, and rounding out my Top Five would be Bif Naked."

"Are you serious? I didn't know you would, you know, do that."

"Normally I wouldn't. But in Bif's case, I think I'd make an exception."

Silence, the sound of a car going by, then, "Alright, how about the 'Top Five Canadians in the Entertainment Industry you'd want to have a *friendship* with'?"

"No sex?"

"No sex. Just friends."

"Hmmm. Margaret Atwood, Mia Kirshner, Barbara Gowdy, Naomi Klein, and Barbara Amiel, though, I'm pretty sure I'd like to have a more *intimate relationship* with Mia and Barbara Amiel —"

"That'll be our next category."

"Can I carry people over from this category?"

"No carry-overs."

"Okay, in that case, I'll take out Mia Kirshner and Barbara Amiel — and maybe Naomi Klein — naw, she's already happily married so —"

"I'm pretty sure Barbara Amiel is married too."

"Ya, but happily? I mean, really, just how much fun do you think ol' Conrad is in the sack?"

"I'll bet he's a stallion."

"Well, I guess I know who's going to make *your* Top Five Intimate Relationships. Anyway, instead of Mia and Barbara, I'll substitute Christie Blatchford and Wendy Wolfe, the entertainment reporter. You?"

"My Top Five Friendships would be Brian Mulroney, Al —"

"Brian Mulroney? Why?"

"Free Trade. NAFTA. I want to know what the hell he was thinking when he signed that agreement despite something like seventy-five percent of Canadians opposing it. Next would be Alan Fotheringham, then Farley Mowat, Ron MacLean, and then Evan Solomon — no, wait, Avi Lewis. I'm saving Evan for the Intimate Relationship category."

"Well then, without further ado, the moment we've all been waiting for — your Top Five Canadians in the Entertainment Industry you'd like to have an Intimate Relationship with."

"Hey, wanna do this last Top Five down at the beach? We can lie on the sand, listen to the waves, stare at the stars and —"

"Set the scene?"

"Exactly."

"Sure. You wanna stop by Grover's house first and see if he wants to join us?"

"Nah. Let's just you and me go."

"Okay."

hell freezes over

A week has almost passed and it's now Friday evening and I'm over at Brad's house
 – walking (through the front hallway),
 – waving (at Jo-Jo, the dreadlocked trio, and several other street people sitting in the living room earnestly discussing *The Great Gatsby*),
 – pausing (to watch Eriq in Brad's den, printing up another batch of Eco-Tickets),
 – observing (Brad in the kitchen cooking what looks to be enough food to feed about fifty people with the pseudo-help of Nicole, who is asking the silk-suit smeared with Reese's Peanut Butter Cups guy where he buys his clothes),
 – coming to a full stop (when I see Rebecca and Daphne in the dining room), and
 – asking (Rebecca, with a surprised-slash-annoyed expression on my face), "What are you doing here?"

"What do you mean, Ryan?" Daphne says, replying for Rebecca. "This was her idea."

"*Her* idea?"

"Ya. She thought it'd be great if we brought everyone together, use everyone's resources to do some good. Isn't it amazing?"

"Daphne, what are you talking about? This was *my* idea."

"I don't think so, Ryan. I mean, Rebecca's been back for almost a week now. She told us how she was in the U.S. and saw these people just like us who had all these resources available to them and who decided to make a difference in people's lives by reaching out to them and welcoming them into their homes and cooking meals for them and —"

"No, no, no!" I shout, wondering if and when I let this all slip to Rebecca, how she got access to it, if she's in my head, "I was the one who told her about all this, about Brad and Eriq and —"

At this point, I notice the rest of the gang has drifted into the dining room and are now wearing puzzled, borderline indignant expressions.

"Ryan," Eriq says, his eyes filled with a mixture of pity and annoyance, "why are you doing this?"

"I'm serious, Eriq. It was my idea. Really. I mean, you originally proposed it but I was the one who put it into action. You've got to believe me."

"Typical," Nicole says.

"No kidding," Daphne says. "It's bad enough that he's always trying to be like Rebecca. Now he's actually trying to take credit for her ideas."

"You guys don't understand. It was my idea. Rebecca's never wanted you guys to be like this. She's the one who's orchestrated the animosity between everyone, who's encouraged all the arguments and the —"

"Ryan, really. What's the matter with you? Are you feeling alright? Maybe we should call a doctor or something. I mean, look at him. He looks absolutely dreadful. Brad, be a dear and see if your family doctor can make a house call," and just as Brad moves towards the phone it starts ringing and after simultaneously preventing Brad from picking it up and reaching for it myself I notice it looks exactly like my portable Sony Quadra-

Station phone — which it is — and I realize that I'm not in Brad's house talking with Rebecca, I'm in my apartment, in Rebecca's bed, reaching for my phone. . . .

good news, bad news

"Which do you want first?" I say to Rebecca, my head not completely clear of the dream I was having moments earlier, especially the feeling of how callous and condescending everyone was towards me, how they all thought it was Rebecca's idea to bring everyone together.

"Give me the good news first."

"Okay, Nicole and Eriq both think you're the last person Daphne should be with."

"Really?"

"Uh-huh."

"Did either of them tell Daphne that?"

"Eriq said he did, twice."

"Wow. That is good news. Daphne'll do the opposite of whatever Eriq thinks she should do. What's the bad news?"

"I think Daphne's close. Maybe too close. She called me a while ago and I think she might have cracked."

"What? What happened?"

"She told me she can't live like this anymore and then hung up and I tried calling her back about a dozen times but couldn't reach her so I ended up leaving a message at her apartment to call me as soon as she got in."

"And?"

"And what?"

"Has she called?"

"Not yet."

"Shit. You better call her again and tell her about the letter."

"I'll call her right now."

"Okay. And listen, Ryan. If you talk to her, see what kind of mood she's in first and if she's the same as she was a while ago tell her you've got a letter from me at your place for her, then call me right back. If you don't talk to her, leave another message for her to call you as soon as she gets your message and when she calls, call me back, okay?"

"Got it. I'll see ya later."

"Oh, one more thing. What exactly do you and Eriq have against girls in white Pontiac Sunbirds trying to pick you up on Yonge Street?"

"Were you following me again?"

"Tout le temps, mon cousin, tout le temps."

"And you wonder why I always feel like I'm being watched."

the audience is watching

"Why are you making it into a made-for-TV documentary?"

To be perfectly honest, I don't know how this happened so quickly. I don't know how we got everything arranged in such a short time, how it all fell together . . . and I especially don't know why I agreed to do it here — in The Suicide Loft — which I told Rebecca from the beginning was off limits, but this turned out to be her 'Perfect Place' and her 'Perfect Partner' (Daphne) is beside her now and the two of them are hooked up to portable I.V.s, the I.V. bags bulging with a lethal mix of saline, morphine, and potassium chloride. Their final solution.

"Simple," Daphne says, looking directly into Cam 2. "Something's not real unless it's on TV."

"Don't you think that's a pretty twisted view of reality?" I ask, reading the question from the cue cards being held by Seth.

"Define reality," Rebecca says.

"Not TV."

"Really? Ever heard of Jerzy Kosinski? No? Well, he's an author . . . *was* an author, actually — he committed suicide a few years ago — but that's not important. What's important is that he did this experiment where he staged a fight scene between himself and someone else in a room full of children. The moment the fight started it began being played on a big screen in the room and you know what happened? Almost all the kids chose to watch the fight on the screen."

"*That's* disturbing."

"No, *that's* reality."

"Your reality, maybe, but not everyone's. There's a lot of people out there who could never do something like that."

"Really? Well, the next time you're in a room full of people engaged in conversation, flick on the TV and see how long it takes for everyone to stop talking to each other and start watching the TV."

"That's different. I'm not arguing that if a bunch of people are in a room and someone turned on the TV people wouldn't end up watching TV. What I'm saying is, in my opinion, there would be a lot of people who couldn't just sit there watching a TV screen while someone was getting beat up in the same room. They'd have to do something about it."

She laughs, turns her gaze slightly away from the camera lens and, looking directly at me, says, "You'd be surprised what some people are capable of watching without doing something about it — isn't that right, Ryan?"

jo-jo, the burdened beauty

"I've got to meet him."

It's Jo-Jo; she just called me, pulling me out of my dream. I'm still lying in Rebecca's bed, waiting for Daphne to call me so I can tell her that Rebecca has sent her a letter.

When the phone rang, the first three rings were incorporated into my dream and I saw Rebecca glaring at me, giving me a 'Why the hell didn't you turn off your cellphone?' look and it wasn't until she threatened to yank the I.V. out of her arm and crush my goddamn phone that I answered it and realized I'd been dreaming again.

"Got to meet who?" I ask Jo-Jo.

"Your writer friend."

"Why?"

"He's changed my life — with one story. What the hell have I been thinking all this time? Trying to Evian-drink, diet, and protein shake my way back to my twenties. It's complete nonsense. I've been acting like an idiot. I've always said I'm a woman who prides herself on knowing exactly what she has time for, and I don't have time for this anymore."

"Let me guess, 'Burdened Beauty'?"

"Yes. It was so beautiful, so painful, so wonderful to read. My heart nearly broke witnessing this young man's beauty fading, becoming more and more difficult to maintain, yet seeing him cling to it all the more desperately, eventually seeking solace in his writing, hoping that what will endure are the beauty of his characters, of his words. Oh Ryan, I've got to meet this poor boy. I've got to help him."

"Jo-Jo, I'll see what I can do."

"Promise?"

"Yes."

"When, today?"

"Well, I'm pretty busy today —"

"Tomorrow?"

"I'll talk to him soon and see if I can arrange a rendezvous, okay?"

seth's final interview

"Come on, man, tell him the story, Seth."

I've been sitting on the patio at The Black Bull restaurant on Queen West two tables away from Seth and his two friends, eavesdropping on their conversation for the last ten, maybe eleven, minutes.

Seth left me three messages in the last two hours, each time telling me he wanted to make sure everything was okay, that he was concerned about our mix-ups and my no-shows. The third and final message, the one I listened to just before meeting Eriq at Pages bookstore, said that he'd be hanging out on the patio at The Black Bull restaurant for lunch with a couple of friends and if I wanted to hook up with him afterwards he'd wait for me there. I wasn't really in the mood to talk to Seth but thought it might be a good opportunity to do some eavesdropping on him so after putting on a fairly simple, yet effective, disguise that consisted of a wig, a Yankees baseball cap, and a pair of Ray-Bans, I walked over to the Black Bull.

He and his friends showed up together a few minutes after I was seated, and Seth, with his back to me, is now listening to one of his friends trying to get Seth to tell the other friend the exact same story I overheard Seth telling the guy on the streetcar just over eight months ago.

"Naw," Seth says, "it's boring."

"No it's not, it's like one of the best stories I've ever heard, man."

"You probably wouldn't feel that way if it happened to you."

"Come on, just tell it."

"You really want to hear it?"

"Yes."

"Long or short version?"

"It's up to you man, it's your story."

"Okay. Let's see . . . okay, I was going out with this girl who I'll refer to as Kathy —"

"Aw, man, how come you won't ever use her real name?"

"Hey, like you said, it's my story. My story, my rules."

"Okay, okay, go on."

"Her name was *Kathy* and we'd been dating for a while, almost nine months and I was totally stoked about her, in love, the whole bit, and we were all set to go on a trip to Portugal because she was totally messed up about this design program she was taking at university and didn't know what she wanted to do only that she didn't want to continue taking design and so I suggested she quit, take a break and because she always wanted to go to Portugal and I have an aunt who lives in Portugal who's told me about a million times that me and a friend can stay with her for as long as we like for free I tell Kathy we should go to Portugal for the winter — maybe the rest of our lives — and she agrees and it's like two minutes, fuck, not even two minutes, maybe twenty seconds after I pick up the airline tickets at The Flight Centre on Yonge Street that I meet her."

"Who — Kathy?"

"No, Danielle who —"

"Whose name has also been changed?"

"Right. She — *Danielle* — had been in The Flight Centre, at the wicket beside me, asking the salesclerk if her sister had recently bought a ticket here and they told her they couldn't give out that kind of information because her name didn't match Danielle's and even though she showed them her wedding ring and said that that was why her name was different and that all she really wanted to know was where her sister was or when she was coming back or at the very least if she'd purchased a one-way or a return ticket because she'd left behind her seven-year-old son who's been crying almost non-stop for the past eight days because the boy already lost his father in a car accident last year and now his mother has just up and left . . . anyway, they still wouldn't give her the info so she grabbed a handful of brochures, chucked them into the air, called the salesclerk a fucking idiot and ran out of the building and about half a block later I saw her sitting on some steps and when she saw me she smiled like she recognized me and asked me to help her up, which I did and when she saw the airline tickets in my hand she asked me who they were for, telling me how lucky I was to be going, that she's been to Portugal and loved it there and then asks me if I wouldn't mind going with her to The St. Lawrence Market — just for a walk, to have some company, someone to talk to, so I go with her and the walk turns into lunch and lunch turns into an all-afternoon conversation during which she tells me she's not really married, she's actually a lesbian and currently in between girlfriends, and then the afternoon conversation turns into dinner back at her place, and before long she goes into this whole *Chasing Amy* routine and starts telling me she's never felt this way, this kind of connection, this close to someone — especially with a guy — this fast and then starts telling me she has to have me, that she'll do whatever it takes to have me —"

"No way — she was a dyke?"

"I don't know, maybe."

"So what happened?"

"What happened? What happened was after about three days

of the most incredible sex and conversation I ever remember having, I told my girlfriend Kathy that it was over, that I'd met someone else, and I got her tickets changed into Danielle's name and when we were sitting in the airport, actually in the tunnel after getting our tickets checked, Danielle stopped and looked at me like I was the most pathetic thing on the planet and then asked me how I could do what I did, how I could dump my girlfriend, abandon her; what possessed me to give up someone so special, so important — in a matter of a couple of days?"

"Holy fuck, she really said that?"

"Pretty much word for word."

"Then what happened?"

"What do you mean?"

"I mean, did you go?"

"Go where?"

"Portugal?"

"Hell no."

"Why not?"

"Because I was too fucking stunned to move or speak or do anything except watch her board the plane, is why."

"You mean you didn't even go with her?"

"No."

"Did she visit your aunt?"

"Hell no."

"What'd she do then?"

"I have no idea."

"And what about all that shit about being a lesbian and all that *Chasing Amy* shit or whatever — what was that all about?"

"Again, no idea. I think she's either an actress or a —"

"An actress? You never said you thought she was an actress before."

"I know, but a little while ago I saw a movie — what the hell was the name of it again — I forget, but it's got Dennis Quaid in it, and he plays this guy who's taking these acting classes and as part of the classes he's got to go out into bars and make up all these stories about his life and someone else from his class watches him to see if the people he's telling the stories to actually end up believing him."

"Does he screw anyone?"

"No. Which is why I think this Danielle woman might just be some married chick whose husband goes out of town a lot and every once in a while she gets bored and decides to have sex with a perfect stranger for a few days until he thinks he's in love with her and promises that he'll never leave her and then, twenty seconds before boarding a plane to Portugal or something she realizes she can't go through with it."

"Ya, but what about all that stuff in The Flight Centre, like her throwing that temper tantrum and talking about her sister and then her telling you she was a lesbian —"

"Well, who knows? Who knows what the real story is? I mean, maybe the sister is really her husband's secretary who she suspected was having an affair with him or maybe she just says she's a lesbian to get a guy turned on?"

"My head's reeling."

"The possibilities are endless."

"No kidding. People are fucked up, man."

"Have you even seen her since then?"

"Once."

"No way, really? You've actually seen her? Where?"

"In the Beaches, a couple days ago, along the boardwalk. She was sitting on a bench with some guy."

"Her husband?"

"No. They weren't together."

"What'd you say?"

"Nothing much — what could I say?"

"I would've called her a fucking bitch or demanded an explanation or something."

"Ya, well, I thought about it. Part of me really wanted to. But another part said, 'Why bother?' I mean, what's done is done."

"I guess."

"Listen guys, I should probably get going. It was cool running into you again."

Seth, a.k.a., the man behind Cam 3

While watching Seth walking out of The Black Bull patio and crossing Queen Street, I make a call on my cellphone and after the second ring see Seth stop in front of the Peter Pan Bistro, dig into his front pocket, pull out his cellphone, answer it and a few seconds later, nod his head while saying, "Okay, okay, I understand," then hang up and continue to walk down Peter Street before making a left on Richmond.

"What's the second question?"

No longer wearing my disguise, I am now standing with Seth across the street from where they film episodes of *The Lofters* and it's probably been two minutes since Seth gave me an answer to my first question, reassuring me that he did not tell Katelin anything, that he would never say anything to her about what it was we were planning. Never.

"What?"

"You said you had a couple of questions to ask me."

"Oh ya, right. The second question is, do you only date women who resemble actresses?"

"What?"

"Daphne said you had all these framed photos of people like Katie Holmes and Brooke Burke and Courtney Cox and that you only ever dated women who looked like actresses — that you even called your girlfriends by the names of the actresses they looked like."

"What a bloody liar," Seth says, shaking his head, looking quite pissed off. "She's probably confusing me with the framed Polaroids she has of all these people on *her* walls. The one she took of me was at the moment — the exact moment — when I got off the phone with Katelin after telling her I was in love with someone else, that I was cancelling our trip to Portugal. Daphne said she wanted to capture the moment. I wouldn't be surprised if all those photos on her walls are of the moments she's fucked people over."

"It's what I've been saying to you all along," I'm now telling Seth, calmly, reassuringly, as we're walking in front of The Princess of Wales Theatre, trying to assuage his concern that things are taking too long. "This is a process. This sort of thing doesn't just happen overnight. You have to think in terms of a long-running TV series — not some slick, instant gratification, everything-is-wrapped-up-in-ninety-eight-minutes cheesy Hollywood movie. You have to be patient. I mean, this isn't some improvisational piece where we can just wing it. Something like this requires some serious planning. I mean, think of all the variables involved with getting Daphne to willingly agree to a suicide pact and for the two of them to commit suicide while —" and here I pause for a second or two to give the next five words more weight, "you and I film it?"

"You mean you're going to let *me* help you film it?"

I nod.

"So I'm not just going to be in the next room watching it on a TV monitor?"

I shake my head. "Only for the last couple of scenes. For the rest you'll be handling Cam 3."

"What changed your mind?"

"Let's just say, it was something I heard you say."

"When? You mean, in the Beaches — to Daphne? That was horrible. I've got to be the world's shittiest actor."

"No, that wasn't it. And as for the acting, we'll work on it. You just have to learn to control your emotions. Like I said before, the trick is to get rid of yourself, what you — Seth Jackson — are actually feeling and thinking so that you're free to insert any feeling and thought in its place and become virtually any character at the drop of a hat."

"I know, I know. It's just. . . ."

"Don't worry. I guarantee with a little practice, you'll get the hang of it."

"I hope so," he says, shaking his head, looking doubtful.

"You will," I say, and then, giving him a playful punch in the shoulder. "Remember, De Niro wasn't built in a day."

He laughs and I smile, pat him on the back, and then, tapping the non-existent watch on my left wrist say, "Listen, I've got to go. I'm going to be late for a rendezvous but before I take off, I just want to apologize again for all the mix-ups and no-shows."

"Don't worry about it," he says, sincerely. "If things work out like you say they're going to, I won't mind at all."

even better than the real thing

My ex-friend Katelin wanted to meet me for a semi-late lunch and I suggested we dine at The Salad King and since she's late, I'm busy replaying the dialogue between Brad and myself that occurred a few minutes ago: him wondering why I wanted him to meet me at Sen5es at 8:15 p.m. tomorrow night; me refusing to tell him, saying that it could possibly have something to do with him having some assistance with his 'Good Samaritan' work (which led me to the image of the bearded silk suit-wearing guy slurping ratatouille in Brad's dining room before our dinner party last night and wondering if, right now, Brad was on his way to the dry cleaner's to get the Reese's Peanut Butter Cup stains out). And then I'm back to thinking about Eriq and Brad and how I've decided to go against Rebecca's script and let the two of them know they have more in common than they think, making a mental note to give Eriq a call after I'm finished having lunch with Katelin and ask him to meet me somewhere tomorrow, maybe The World's Biggest Bookstore, where I'll then convince him to meet me at Sen5es on Bloor West at 8:30 p.m. — and it's just as I'm wondering whether or not I should tell Eriq about Jo-Jo, unsure if it will add or take away from the drama of Eriq discovering that he and Brad have more in common than anyone would've guessed, that I notice a very thin young couple in their early twenties watching a heavyset couple in their mid to late thirties smiling and laughing and talking boisterously while eating.

"Let's promise each other we'll never get like that, okay?" the thin guy says to the thin girl.

"I promise."

"Me too."

They look at each other, smile, take a sip of their water.

"Wouldn't it be great to stay exactly as we are at this very moment?" the thin girl asks.

The thin guy nods.

"If I could just suspend time," the thin girl says, "I wouldn't want to change a thing. This is exactly how I'd want things to be, wouldn't you?"

When the thin guy nods again I decide to make a quick call

to Eriq to set things up for tomorrow's rendezvous at The World's Biggest Bookstore and am about to do so when —

"Désolé, mon ex-ami," I hear Katelin say from somewhere behind me and then, after popping a bubble in my ear, she plunks down on the chair across from me. "My mother called and needed to talk. She said to say 'Hi.'"

I hit the END button on my cellphone and put it back in my front pocket.

"Il n'y a pas de quoi," I say. "Et, dit bonjour à ta mère pour moi."

Katelin smiles. "I *so* like it when you speak French to me."

"Enough to remove the 'ex' from 'friend' when you refer to me?"

"*That*," she says, raising her left eyebrow, "remains to be seen."

I smile, try to raise an eyebrow, the left one, but only manage to furrow both brows and she laughs at my attempt then asks, "So, how was dinner last night?"

"Intriguing," I say, before adding, "Borderline overwhelming, actually."

"Really? Care to elaborate?"

"Ya, sure. I've been wanting to tell someone this because pretty much all I've been thinking about since yesterday afternoon is that. . . ."

I pause here, something preventing me from continuing, from telling her that since yesterday afternoon my life feels as though it's been on fast-forward, that it's been like watching a movie or reading a novel where in the last ten minutes of the movie or the last twenty or thirty pages of the novel all these things are revealed that just throw you for an enormous loop, things you hadn't really counted on and I've just been trying to make sense of it all, and instead of telling her this, I change it to, "All I've been thinking about is that it was quite an intriguing evening."

She looks at me as if there's more, as though I haven't told her what I'd intended and when I don't say anything more, she asks, "That's it?"

"Ya, I think so."

She gives me a disbelieving look then says, "Ryan, I know there's more — at least something more than, 'it was quite an intriguing, borderline overwhelming evening.'"

"No, really, that's pretty much it. I guess I made it sound like it was more than it actually was. Sorry if that was the case."

"And you accuse *me* of being cryptic?"

When I don't say anything she rolls her eyes, shakes her head, half-laughs, and then, after blowing a bubble and bursting it loudly, says, "Okay, Mr. Secretive, if you won't tell me what's really on *your* mind, I'll tell you something that's been on my mind for several months now, okay?"

"Shoot."

"Remember when I said the reason I was going to stop hanging around with 'the gang' was because I despised Daphne and didn't really like Eriq all that much either?"

"Ya."

"Well, you want to know what really did it for me? I mean, aside from Daphne and Eriq?"

I shrug, say, "Sure."

"Nicole, Brad — and *you*."

At this moment I tell myself I require a different expression than the one I'm currently wearing, something to suit the occasion, and I consciously mould my face into an expression of mild intrigue, bordering on confusion, before responding with, "Really? Why Nicole and Brad — and *me?*"

"Hmm. . . ." She hmms, smiling, as though she's savouring the moment, as though she's been thinking of this moment for several months now and doesn't want to rush into it, wants to make it last. "I think I'll start with Nicole first. I met her one night out on the street pretending to be a bag lady."

I look at her, my facial expression now suggesting she can't be serious.

"I'm serious," Katelin says. "She told me she was trying to *experience* what it was like to be a street person."

If this was anyone else besides Katelin I would probably give her a different response, say something like, 'Really? Wow, that's totally bizarre, huh?' using an 'I'm-totally-fascinated-please-tell-me-more' tone, but it's Katelin so I say, "Ya, right, whatever, nice try," using an 'I-don't-believe-you-so-you-might-as-well-stop-trying-to-bullshit-me' tone because I know this will get her riled up — enough to stop savouring or stretching out the moment and answer my questions quickly.

"Ryan, I'm serious," she says, sternly.

"When?" I say, using the same tone.

"When what?"

"When did you see her pretending to be a bum?"

"In March, late March — when she was supposed to be on vacation, remember? She told everyone she was taking off for three weeks to some resort and —"

"And she was completely tanned when she got back."

"She was going to a tanning studio every other day —"

"Where?"

"Where what? Where was the tanning studio?"

"No. Where was she pretending to be a bum?"

"Near High Park."

"Why?"

"Because she figured none of us would see her since none of us live around there or have any reason to be in that neighbourhood."

I give Katelin a doubting gaze. "She *actually* told you that?"

"Yes, Ryan, she *actually* told me that."

"And why were *you* there?"

"I was visiting my aunt, on Grenadier Avenue."

"And what, you just *happened* to bump into her?"

"Yes."

Katelin's forehead is creased with frustration.

"I saw this bag lady sitting on the sidewalk and I asked her if I could get her something to eat and that's when I noticed it was Nicole. At first she tried ignoring me, waving me away, pretending she didn't understand what I was saying, but then I took out my cellphone and started dialling your number, telling her what I was doing and that I was going to ask you to call Brad and for the two of you to come down and see who I just ran into, and then she asked me to stop, but I said I wasn't going to unless she promised to tell me what the hell was going on and after I promised her I wouldn't call you or tell you or anyone else anything about this we went into a nearby restaurant and she told me she'd been doing it for just over a week by this point and was planning to do it for another week."

I allow my gaze to drift off, settle on a corner of the restaurant, at the point where the walls and ceiling intersect, then begin slowly nodding my head, counting the seconds off in my head until a sufficient amount of time has passed that would let her think I've pondered the possibility, then I abruptly cut back to her, drawing in close, my eyes focusing, scrutinizing her like I'm attempting to divine the truth until she finally asks me, "What are you doing?"

"I'm wondering if you're full of shit?"

"Ryan, I'm telling you the truth. Nicole is completely, I mean, completely and totally off her rocker. You wouldn't believe the stuff she's done. Apparently she gets off on using herself — her body — as some kind of testing facility. That night, when I saw her on the street, she told me she's been a stripper, an escort, done every kind of drug imaginable — including roofies, on purpose. She said she even got pregnant a few years ago and had an abortion just to know what it felt —"

I flash Katelin a look that suggests I think she's gone too far, that her story has just crossed the boundary of believability, and she says, her tone of voice suggesting she's more than slightly annoyed by my response, "Ryan, I am *not* making this up. You know her wrists, her scars? She told me she did that so she'd know what it was like to attempt suicide, to feel her blood, her life, flowing out of her. I mean, how twisted do you have to be in order to slit your own wrists and risk killing yourself just for the *experience*?"

At this point I'm seriously considering telling Katelin she's full of shit, am in fact going to, when the idea that she could be joking, that at any moment she's going to say, 'Gotcha!' slices into my brain and before she can say another word, I ask, "You sure she wasn't just acting?"

"Acting? No. Why would she be acting?"

"Maybe she was bored and wanted to liven things up?"

"What?"

"Ya, who knows? Maybe her life needed a little more drama, a little more action so she made up this story. *Or*," I say, sounding excited, as though I've just hit upon a brilliantly plausible explanation, "maybe she's doing it to cope with the things going on in her life," before adding after a slight pause, "People do it all the time."

"Do what all the time, lie?"

"Hey, you said it yourself, 'The world lives on lies.'"

"That was Joseph Campbell."

"Ya, but you believe him, right?"

"So?"

"So, you ever think the reason the world lives on lies might be because everyone's reality is too mundane or horrible or overstimulating or panic-inducing or regrettable for them, that everyone feels like they need to get the hell out of their so-called life and so they end up inventing a false persona, sometimes a whole new life for themselves?"

"Who? Who does this?"

"Well, in this case, Nicole."

"Ryan, Nicole wasn't lying or creating a false persona. She wasn't acting."

"How do you know?" I ask. "Did you go back the next day to see if she was there?"

"No, I didn't —"

"Well then, how do you know she wasn't just playing a joke on you or going to a costume party?"

She clenches her jaw, takes a deep breath, lets it out, then says, "As I was about to say, I didn't go back the next day because the next day I saw Brad and since at the time I was thinking 'Nicole is completely nuts' which automatically gives me a 'Get out of your promise to Nicole to not tell anyone guilt-free' card, I told Brad everything and you know what he said?"

I shrug, casually. "Shoot."

"He said, 'Are you sure? I mean, are you positive it was her?' and when I said that yes, I was positive it was her, you know what he did? He got this really weird, almost, I don't know, *appreciative* smile on his face like . . . like as if he'd suspected it all along and just had it confirmed and when I told him I could show him where I'd seen her, where she probably was right now, he said, 'No, no, that's okay. She'll be fine,' and then made me promise not to tell anyone — not even you."

I remain on MUTE for a good thirty, maybe thirty-five seconds, enough time for Katelin to sigh and say, "Well?"

"Well what?"

"Well, aren't you going to say something?"

"What's there to say?"

"I don't know, maybe that you're surprised? Shocked?"

"Why? Should I be?"

"Yes."

"Well, I'm not. In fact, I think it's normal."

"*Normal?* How can *this* be normal?"

"Listen, Katelin. Actors play different characters all the time, right? George Clooney played an ER doctor, Sarah Michelle Gellar plays a vampire slayer, Gillian Anderson plays an FBI agent, Michael Richards played Kramer, Chuck Norris plays a Texas Ranger, James Gandolfini plays a mobster — what's the big deal if Nicole Chambers plays a bum and Brad Wellington plays the boyfriend mildly intrigued that his girlfriend is playing a bum?"

"The big deal, Ryan, is that Brad and Nicole are *not* actors and they weren't acting."

"Hey, like Shakespeare said, 'All the world's a stage and all the people actors.'"

"Life is not a play, Ryan. And Brad and Nicole are not actors."

"The play's the thing, Katelin."

"Ryan, stop it, life is *not* a play."

"No, you're right. Sometimes it's a TV show, sometimes it's a movie, sometimes it's a documentary, sometimes a docudrama, sometimes it's a commercial or a billboard in Times Square or —" I stop, noticing she looks like she's about to leave and, changing my tone, making it sound warmer, less condescending, say, "Okay, look at yourself, Katelin, you act differently when you're at work than when you're with me, right?"

"So?"

"So, which one is the act and which is the *real* you?"

"That's totally different. I *know* you."

"Sure, but they're still different roles, right? I mean, when you go into work you switch into your 'waitress' role, when you go out with your friends you switch into your 'friend' role, when you're having sex maybe you switch into your 'dominatrix' role — who knows? The point is, sometimes, everyday roles are either too much or not enough for some people so they need to take on other roles, assume other identities and —" at this point I decide to test her, thinking back to our original thirteen-hour walk and talk, hearing her giving me a completely different version of herself than she had the day before at The Suicide Loft — "and I mean, haven't you ever wanted to be someone else? Haven't you ever pretended to be someone you're not?"

She pauses, looks as though she's mulling over the question. "No. Never. Why would I?"

"Well, like I just said," I say, smiling, admiring her ability to lie without betraying the lie, "maybe you're not satisfied with your life, maybe you're bored and want some added spice or adventure — or maybe you'd do it just to deal with life in general, to get you through the day, to help you cope with things that have happened to you?"

"Is that why you *act* the way you do?"

"Excuse me?" I say, trying to sound surprised, confused.

"You always act as though you're being filmed, like someone's following you around with a camera. I always feel like you're acting, like you're hiding something. Everything about you feels so calculated, as though everything you say, even your expressions and your emotions, comes from a script or a screenplay or something."

"You know," I say, trying to appear as serious as possible, "I once heard of a guy who was filmed watching his sister commit suicide."

"What?"

"Ya, the guy was actually sitting in the bedroom being filmed watching his sister on a TV monitor slicing her wrists in the bathroom only ten feet away."

"Ryan, why are you telling me this?"

Ignoring her question, I continue speaking.

"He said the only way he could do it was by pretending he was an actor doing a scene and this particular scene had him watching his sister killing herself."

"That's sick."

I shrug.

"Sometimes pretending or playing a role is more real than reality, in fact, sometimes we don't know we're doing it or that we're even capable of doing it, it just happens, subconsciously — we slip into these different roles, adopt different character types, almost as though we suffer from multiple personality disorders. Winona Ryder once said she feels like she has an identity crisis every day because of all the roles she's played; she said she doesn't know who she is from one day to the next. It's the same with this guy who watched his sister kill herself. He said he felt like he was in a TV studio or on a movie set; the director asked him to get into make-up, gave him his lines, told him where to sit, what to do, and before long he found himself completely immersed in his character. He said he was just playing another role — the role of 'brother watching sister committing suicide' — and that when it was over he didn't really know if it had actually happened, if the whole thing had been an act, if his sister was really just acting too. As it turned out, she wasn't acting and he said it was at that precise moment that he realized life had become so fiction-like and fiction so lifelike that soon none of us will be able to distinguish between the act and reality."

Katelin is looking at me with a blend of disgust and disbelief and after shaking her head she says, conclusively, "I'll *always* be able to know the difference."

It's at this point (despite what Katelin just said about my emotions being an act) that I feel myself becoming slightly annoyed with Katelin, which is too bad, because she's not overacting; in fact, she's probably the best actor aside from Rebecca and myself that I know and to someone else she'd be more than convincing, but because I already know the truth, because I already know she's so into the character she's playing right now she's unable to distinguish between her act and reality, she's not going to be able to convince me of anything, and part of me wants to tell her this, to tell her to stop the act, stop pretending to be indignant and self-righteous, that it's me, Ryan, she's talking to, not some naïve, you-can-pull-the-wool-over-my-eyes idiot, but another part, Rebecca's part, tells me to let her continue, to let Katelin dig herself deeper into her character, into the role she's created for herself, to see what happens, and so I say, "Katelin, let me ask you something — who is the poem really about?"

"What poem?"

"The poem you showed me in Juice for Life yesterday."

"It's about a friend."

"You sure it's not about you?"

"Yes, Ryan, I'm sure."

"So you're saying you've never once pretended to be someone else, you've never once intentionally presented a side of yourself to someone and then a completely different side to another person?"

"Never."

She's delivered her last three lines with such believability that I'm actually cringing, my stomach muscles tightening with envy-slash-admiration.

"You know, Katelin," I say, smiling, "you are definitely one of the most intriguing people I know."

"Is that why you invited me to hang out with 'the gang' — because you found me intriguing?"

I nod. "As a matter of fact, yes. I thought you'd liven things up, make 'the gang,' as you call it, more interesting, more entertaining — and you did."

"Are you listening to yourself?"

"What?"

"You're talking as if I was an actress hired for a few cameo appearances on your TV show in an effort to boost ratings."

"What's wrong with that?"

"What's wrong with that? What's wrong is it's a pretty warped way of treating people."

"I think it's fairly normal."

"Stop saying that, Ryan. It's not normal. It can't be. I mean, don't you see that? Don't you have any real emotions?"

"Hey, like Andy Warhol said, 'Once you see emotions from a certain angle you can never think of them as real again.'"

She is now looking at me as though I'm completely off my rocker and so, even though I kind of like the sensation of Katelin thinking I'm crazy, I say, in an effort to redirect her, to make her feel more at ease, "You said earlier that the reason you stopped hanging around 'the gang' was because of Brad, Nicole, and *me*. So what's the *me* part?"

"I think you already know the *you* part."

"Humour me."

"It's not really all that funny."

"Come on," I say, giving her a playful nudge, "you know what I mean."

"Actually, I don't. I don't know anything you mean and *you* — more than anyone — should know that this is possible."

I laugh.

"Why *me* more than anyone?"

"Because you, more than anyone, know that people may not appear exactly as shown."

"'May not appear exactly as shown'? And what's that supposed to mean?"

She rolls her eyes. "This is hardly the time to plead ignorance, Mr. Double Identity."

When I give her a 'What-are-you-talking-about?' expression, she gives me a 'Do-I-have-to-spell-it-out-for-you?' expression, then says, "Have you ever wondered why I never went back to The Suicide Loft?"

Whoa.

Quick fade on Cam 2, please, quick fade, Cam 2. . . . Hello? Cam 2? I need a quick fade right —

"You said you invited me to dinner that night at Jump Café to liven things up, to make it more entertaining," Katelin is now saying. "Of course, the entertainment was in seeing my reaction to eventually discovering that it was Daphne who made Seth cancel our trip to Portugal, that it was Daphne who made him break up with me. And you weren't lying yesterday when you said you were at Juice for Life to see Seth, were you?"

Goddamn it Cam 2, I need a quick fade —

"What are you trying to do, get him to join your infamous gang? Or is he going to be just like you? Is he going to be your understudy?"

Fuck the quick fade Cam 2, I need a full cut — right fucking now for Christ's —

"For your information, Ryan, the poem is about you. It's about your lies, about you living a double life. The reason I never said anything that day in The Salad King was because I was curious to see if you were going to say you'd seen me the day before during our interview at The Suicide Loft. When you didn't and you started telling me all this b.s. about your life and didn't even mention that you ran The Loft, I decided right there to start telling *you* a bunch of b.s. figuring that sooner or later you'd say something but you didn't and then when you invited me to dinner at Jump Café and I realized what you and Rebecca were up to, I couldn't believe the two of you could be so cold, so unfeeling, so calculating, so evil, so —"

It's about bloody time, Cam 2.

full confession

As I'm wondering how to incorporate this new material, how I'm going to manage the variables this new information might possibly unleash, I suddenly realize what Brad meant by Marcel Proust's quote that 'the real voyage of discovery is not in seeing new things, but seeing with new eyes,' because right now I'm seeing things through Katelin's eyes and it's not exactly a pretty picture, and it's as I'm blinking and rubbing my eyes in an attempt to get rid of this P.O.V. that I begin to feel faint, the blood leaving my head, the sounds in The Salad King — of the fat couple's laughter, the thin couple's conversation, the hissing frying pans — fading into the background, and just before I'm about to pass out, in a desperate attempt to remain conscious I run out of The Salad King and into the phone booth across the street and begin dialling, hoping to talk to someone, anyone, in order to —

"Yes? Hello? Is everything okay?"

"No, not really," I say, noticing, despite the fact that I can barely breathe, how soft, friendly, and consoling her voice is — the perfect voice for a suicide hotline.

"Are you thinking of committing suicide?" she asks without hesitation.

"Yes."

"How long have you felt this way?"

"Um . . . I . . . I don't know," I say, having difficulty concentrating, distracted by the blitzkrieg of thoughts and feelings being produced by Katelin's still extremely vivid P.O.V. "A long time. Over a year."

"Is there something making you think of doing it?"

Despite my inner turmoil I realize that what she's now doing is attempting to place something between me and my intent to commit suicide by having me focus on what is causing the stress and/or depression in my life. It's an effective tactic.

"I'm tired," I hear myself saying after she again asks — her voice softer and more consoling this time — what is making me think of committing suicide. "Tired of living a lie."

"What lie are you living?"

"My whole life."

"Your whole life is a lie?"

"Well, no, not my whole life — just the last fourteen months of it."

"And what have you been doing for the last fourteen months?"

"Adopting a completely different persona."

"And what's been happening as result of you doing this?"

"Well, things aren't going so great. Especially lately."

"And do you think this different persona is the source of your problem?"

She's good at her job. Of course I know they've trained her to ask these sorts of questions, questions that will give her some indication of where I'm at and how she should deal with me. Plus, the longer I stay on the phone — and alive — the more chance I have of coming to my senses, deciding that everything is okay, thanking her for being a lifesaver — literally — and going on with my life.

"I don't know whether it's the source," I say. "But it's definitely a problem. A big problem."

"And what do you think would happen if you got rid of this different persona and returned to who you were before?"

"I'd probably kill myself inside of five minutes."

"And why do you think you'd do that?"

"Because my only salvation these past fourteen months, the only way I've been able to put up with myself is by adopting this persona, and that's because the person I was before — the real me — is so repulsed by what I did, so consumed by guilt and remorse, that each time I return to who I was before for longer than a few minutes, I end up wanting to blow my bloody brains out!"

The men playing chess on the outdoor tables are now staring at me, not only because I've been shouting my response but also because I've been punctuating my confession with punches to the phone booth.

"Hello? Are you still there?" I say into the receiver while surveying the now bleeding knuckles on my right hand.

"I'm sorry, yes, I'm right here. I was . . . I was just wondering if there was someone — a friend, a family member, a co-worker — who you could talk to, someone who you trust and care about who would support you in your efforts to be the real you?"

Now she's trying to get me to devalue my suicidal thoughts by heightening the value or meaning of something else — in this case my current relationships — which is one of the reasons Jennie decided to kill herself when she did. She didn't want to begin to devalue the atrocities she witnessed everyday, lose the shock response, the sadness of seeing a homeless person sleeping in the alcove of a bank or on the steps of City Hall; she didn't want to find meaning in an SUV, in having the right clothes, a condo, a fabulous lifestyle. She also knew from the outset that this was a losing battle, that sooner or later the shock, the sadness would diminish, that her sense of 'We've got to change the way things are right now!' would fade, that she would begin accepting the world around her, become adjusted to the atrocities she witnessed each day and resign herself to the idea that this is how things were. Which is why she vowed that as soon as this started to happen, she would commit suicide.

Despite knowing this I spend some time thinking of those people who would support my return to the real me, performing a quick inventory of what would be required of them if I did, wondering if I told Jo-Jo or Brad or Nicole or Daphne or Katelin or my parents or my uncle what I'd done fourteen months ago if they could merely add this tidbit of information to their list of 'Things I know about Ryan Brassard' — like maybe somewhere between 'He likes Golden Tofu Curry' and 'He used to skateboard,' they could insert, 'He watched his sister Jennie commit suicide without doing anything about it,' because if they could do this, then they'd probably be able to accept and maybe even understand the rest of the things I've done in the last fourteen months — the lies, the acting, the directing, the manipulating, and so on — and for a moment it all seems plausible, that maybe this woman on the suicide hotline is right, that maybe I should come clean, that maybe people can handle it? Besides, just like Jennie feared and the Top Five kid was saying last night, people are getting more and more immune to atrocity nowadays, to the point where they might not even think that what I've done is such a bad thing, and I've almost got myself convinced of this possibility when Katelin's P.O.V. flashes into my brain and I realize that no amount of 'talk therapy' — whether coming from some woman on a suicide hotline, myself, or anyone else — is going to ease my conscience, much the same way that a full confession won't bring me any closer to closure. . . .

voices

Less than an hour later I'm back at my apartment, rifling through Rebecca's trunk — the one with some of her old disguises — looking for the three old CN railroad spikes Rebecca's great-grandmother gave to her, and after I find them and grind them down to fine points and set the shafts of the spikes in metal sleeves I've fastened to the wooden floor beside her bed, I pop a couple of aspirins, three painkillers, and a handful of sleeping pills — chasing each of them with a shot of Crown Royal — and then, standing with my back against the wall, my eyes fixed on the thermostat on the opposite wall I start leaning forward, visualizing the sharpened railroad spikes piercing my skin, tearing through my intracostal ligaments, prying apart my ribs, and plunging into my left ventricle and aorta, and just as my body starts to pick up speed, falling forward with increasing momentum, I feel something hard slamming into me and end up crashing into the dresser before landing on the floor five or six feet away from the railroad spikes.

"Bloody hell!" I hear Rebecca shout. "I think I've dislocated my shoulder."

She's on the bed, body writhing, face contorted with pain, right hand gripping her left shoulder.

"And you wonder why I follow you around and sneak into the apartment sometimes?!" she shouts at me, sitting up, her eyes wild with anger. "Christ. Look at what you end up trying to do!"

"I can't take this anymore," I say, my throat tightening, my eyes filling with tears.

"Can't take what anymore?"

"I've . . . I've . . . I've started hallucinating. I'm hearing voices. Half the time I don't know whether I'm awake or asleep. And when I'm asleep all I do is dream about Jennie, about how I wasn't able to. . . ."

"Listen, Ryan," she says, the anger now gone from her voice, replaced by her pacifying-slash-persuasive tone, probably realizing that what I've just said coupled with the tears now streaming down my face is a fairly good indication that a) I'm being sincere, b) I'm close to losing it, and c) if she can't convince me to hang in there for a few more days, everything will be lost. "Ryan, you just have to —"

"Wait a second," I say, interrupting her. "Do you hear that?"

"What?"
"That voice."
"What voice?"
"It sounds like it's coming from —"
which is when I realize I'm still in the phone booth across from The Salad King, that I must've finally passed out or something because I'm slumped down on the floor of the booth, the telephone receiver dangling beside my head, the voice of the suicide hotline woman — no longer soft and consoling but rather piercing and urgent — demanding to know if I'm still there.

natasha

"Oh my God. This place is incredible!"

I'm in The Suicide Loft with Natasha — the person I had arranged to meet at Starbucks between 3:15 p.m. and 3:30 p.m.

After picking myself off the floor of the phone booth and pulling myself together by virtue of a not-so-abbreviated consultation with Rebecca's diary, I headed to Starbucks and met Natasha, who actually turned out to be the Sarah Polley lookalike, the one who works at Starbucks and whose voice kept me company while I rode home on the streetcar Friday night after having dinner at Rain, which was why her voice sounded so familiar to me when I called her that first time from the payphone and, after we talked for a few minutes about the whole 'coincidence versus fate' thing surrounding our meeting, she suddenly started talking about suicide, telling me that the way she used to want to die was freezing to death, that she'd always admired the Inuit's idea of how when they got older and thought they were a burden to their community they'd slip out at night and go for a walk and never come back and that when she lived on the street she often thought about not putting on her long underwear or throwing away her sleeping bag or avoiding a heating vent or shelter and when I'd asked her how she ended up on the street she told me that a few years ago she and her twin sister were at some wild beach party in a condo in Florida during Spring Break and her sister was doing all these crazy dance moves with some guy out on this large balcony when the two of them decided to re-enact the final dance scene in *Dirty Dancing* where Jennifer Grey runs and jumps into Patrick Swayze's arms and he hoists her above his head, only her sister and the guy she was dancing with were pretty drunk, which was probably why the guy lost his balance as he was hoisting her above his head and ended up tripping over a chaise lounge and falling on top of someone sitting against the balcony railing and from that moment on all Natasha said she remembered doing was watching the guy — first lying there on the concrete balcony floor laughing, probably because he thought that everything was fine, that her sister was just somewhere behind him, then noticing his laughter abruptly stop when he heard everyone screaming, then seeing him scramble to his feet, look over the railing at what everyone was pointing at, and start shouting, 'Oh my God. Oh my God,' over and over — and the whole time she was watching him do all this she was thinking how amazing his eyes were, that he was exactly her type, how he looked like a young Robert Redford and that, right up until her sister went flying over the railing and plummeted six stories to her death, she'd desperately wanted it to be her dancing with this guy instead of her sister . . . which was when I started shaking my head and muttered, 'Unbelievable,' and when she asked me what was 'Unbelievable' I paused for a long moment and, well, I don't know, maybe it was the fact that she could talk so openly about the subject of suicide, that it didn't seem to bother her at all; maybe it was the fact that she'd told me there'd been a time in her life when she used to think about committing suicide nearly every hour of every day; maybe it was the fact that when I asked her what had happened that made her stop thinking about it all the time she told me that she wanted to get to know me a bit better before she told me that; maybe it was the fact that part of me was still seeing things from Katelin's P.O.V., still replaying scenes and dialogue from my discussion with her and the suicide hotline woman and consequently wasn't thinking straight — whatever the reason, I ended up telling Natasha that I had something to show her, referring to the photo-pictorial album that the Robert Redford look-alike and I have been creating these past few months at The Suicide Loft.

I'm about to say something in response to her 'Oh my God, this place is incredible!' comment but just before her comment I pulled out the Robert Redford look-alike's album and it's now open in front of her and I notice she's no longer looking around with an, 'Oh my God, this place is incredible' expression on her face but rather is looking at me with an, 'Oh my God, this album, this place — you, are totally freaking me out' expression.

"Where? . . . Who? . . . How did you get these photos? And this drawing? This is a drawing of my sister's gravestone," she says, her eyes suddenly furtive, rapidly alternating between me and the album pages and because I want to get rid of the expression on her face and reassure her that everything is okay, that *I'm* okay, that I'm not some monster she needs to be afraid of — before I know what I'm doing I'm betraying the code of client confidentiality, telling her that I got the photos from the guy who had been dancing with her sister, that the drawings belong to him, that he's one of my clients, that The Loft is an alternative to people considering suicide, that I started it after my sister Jennie committed suicide, as a way to help people cope with . . .

and it's at this point in my explanation that I realize I'm crying, consciously crying — for the first time since Jennie's death — and instead of trying to stop the tears or excuse myself and go to the bathroom, I end up collapsing on the couch and the moment I feel Natasha's hands gently rubbing my back and her soothing voice say, "Hey, it's alright. It's okay," I start sobbing uncontrollably and all I feel like doing is telling her everything, wondering, hoping, that she could be the person to support me/accept me/understand me, understand why I sat there and watched my sister die, why I didn't intervene; understand that all I've thought about the past year or so is how I'm going to kill myself — and then, after I slobber, "I don't deserve to live," Natasha hugs me, tells me she knows how I feel, that she used to feel the same way, that she too felt responsible, standing there on the balcony, seeing her sister disappear over the railing and all she did was stand there, thinking about how hot the guy who inadvertently killed her sister was.

"The thing you have to realize," she's now saying, still hugging me, "is that it's not your fault. You can't blame yourself. You weren't there, you couldn't have done anything."

Her words of consolation rip right through me, causing me to break free of her hug in order to look at her, to see if what she's said was meant to hurt me, if, like Katelin, she knows more than she's letting on, if this is some sort of game and everyone's in on it except me, but when I look at her I see that she's merely trying to console me, and I break down again, lapsing once again into her grasp, this time wanting to scream, 'You don't understand! I *was* there! I was in the *very next room* the whole time. I could've easily stopped it. I *should've* stopped it. I mean, what kind of a sick, twisted, psychotic bastard watches his own sister take her life?'

Instead of this, though, I blather, "She's . . . she's not . . . she's not coming back," and then the realization that no matter how many languages we translate her suicide into, no matter how many networks decide to air it, no matter how many people talk about her, no matter how many times I dream I've saved her, no matter how many times I think I see her on the street, she won't be coming back — this realization rips my life apart and I burst into tears again.

"Oh, Ryan," Natasha says, squeezing me, starting to cry. "It's going to be alright. You're going to be alright."

"I just want it to end."

"It will. It'll get better. Trust me."

But how can it? I've done everything possible to make it go away, to make it better, I've tried everything but there's no escape, no exoneration, no sanctuary, just a continuous stream of reminders, flashbacks, nightmares, hallucinations, guilt, remorse, self-loathing, and . . . and . . . and maybe that's how it should be. Maybe I should never be free of these things. Maybe this is my penance for not doing anything to stop it.

It's only after she says, "Oh Ryan, you're being too hard on yourself," that I realize I've said the last few lines out loud and before I can think of what this means she says, "You have to let it go. You have to try and forgive yourself," which reminds me of Barry (the grief counsellor) and how he said the same thing to my parents which makes me think of them, of what I've put them through, compressing the last fourteen months of their lives into a fifteen-second montage of their daughter committing suicide, their son and niece laughing at the funeral, them feeling responsible for her death, their different ways of grieving, their separation and divorce, the fact that I've deprived them of knowing the real reason Jennie took her life, that I've toyed with them, watched and documented their mutual destruction as though I was making a made-for-TV movie — and it's after these fifteen seconds are up that I encounter the impossibility of taking Natasha's advice, of 'letting it go and forgiving myself' and continue crying.

a living hell

Although it feels like days, it's actually only a few hours later — five to be exact — and I'm in The Loft with Natasha and my parents with the intent of explaining everything to them in reverse, starting from the moment I met Natasha, and Natasha's been doing a really good job of telling them how I operate The Loft, as a tribute to Jennie, as a way of helping others find an alternative to suicide, that I've probably saved dozens of lives in the last ten months or so.

"What Ryan does for these people is quite extraordinary," she's now saying. "I mean, take, for instance, the man who accidentally killed my twin sister. Every other week Ryan helps this man by —" but before Natasha can say another word Rebecca walks into the living room and, looking directly at me, says, "Can someone please explain to me why it takes a tragedy to get people to act? I mean, why is it that someone always has to die before we do something?"

"Rebecca, what . . . why . . . what —"

At this point I notice Rebecca looking at me strangely, the expression on her face indicating that the words coming out of my mouth are all wrong, that I'm supposed to be saying something completely different and after five more seconds she drops her head, says, "Cut," then, after throwing her hands in the air and saying, "Bloody hell. I *knew* this would happen," she walks up to me and with her back to Natasha and my parents says, in a semi-hushed voice, "This is precisely why I was dead set against this so-called brilliant idea of yours. I said a live studio audience would be too disruptive, that they'd make us forget our lines but you insisted on them being here. You said they'd make Episode 2 more *authentic*. Well, they're here — and so far the only thing authentic about this episode is that you're fucking it up!"

It is just after Rebecca says, "They're seeing your work," that

I think she's lost it, gone mad; that is until she brushes past me saying, "Screw it. We'll just skip this scene. You can edit it out later," and after shrugging my shoulders and making a gesture to my parents and Natasha that suggests Rebecca is absolutely fucking bonkers and reassuring them that I have no idea what she's going on about, I turn around and see Daphne and Rebecca sitting side by side on two Henry Jacobus & Sons oak dining chairs hooked up to a dual I.V., their hands and feet bound to the chairs — except for Rebecca's right hand, which is about to inject, via syringe, potassium chloride into the main I.V. tube.

"Bloody hell, Ryan," Rebecca shouts at me, simultaneously squeezing the contents of the syringe into the I.V. and pointing to my right hand, "would you at least turn on the damn camcorder and start recording!"

"What?" I say, looking down at the portable phone in my right hand and thinking 'What the hell is Rebecca talking about?' before abruptly looking back at Rebecca and noticing her closing the valve on her I.V. tube.

"Hey! What are you doing?" I shout, watching the potassium chloride travelling quickly down Daphne's tube, into Daphne's left arm.

"What do you mean, 'What am I doing?'"

"You closed your valve!"

"So?"

"So?! This isn't what we planned. This isn't what we agreed on."

"Bloody hell," she says, already starting to disconnect the I.V. from her left arm. "You didn't really think I was going to kill myself and let you and your stupid little understudy handle things the rest of the way, did you? I mean, exactly how naïve are you?"

"Rebecca, you're . . . you're —"

"Getting pissed off that you haven't turned on the bloody camcorder yet, is what I am," she says and then, when I hear

Daphne whimpering, telling me to help her, that she doesn't want to die, her eyes gorged with terror and panic, I scream at Rebecca to stop it and she says, her arm now completely free of the I.V., "If you're so concerned about her, why haven't you stopped it yourself?"

"Rebecca, I'm serious. Stop it!"

"Ryan, either a) stop it yourself or b) shut the hell up, start recording, and zoom the fuck in on Daphne."

No sooner have I dialled 911 than I hear a stampede of footsteps and a cacophony of voices but for some reason it's not until I catch a glimpse of the action on one of the two TV monitors that I realize the cops and emergency response team are now on the scene, only instead of rushing to help Daphne and apprehend Rebecca, the half dozen cops are now pointing their guns at me and the two lead cops, bearing a striking resemblance to my parents, are saying, 'Please, Ryan, put down the weapon. Put down the weapon,' which is when I realize that instead of my Sony QuadraStation cordless phone I'm holding Rebecca's Sony Digital8 camcorder in my hand.

"We're not joking, Ryan. Put down the goddamn weapon!"

"No, wait! Please. Give him a chance."

It's Katelin, on the other TV monitor, pleading with the police.

"Please, Ryan," Katelin's now saying, turning away from the police and looking directly at me through the TV monitor. "Stop doing this to yourself. Stop treating your life like it's a movie."

In the background, just behind Katelin, I see Rebecca motioning to me and when I switch back to the first TV monitor I catch a close-up of Rebecca mouthing the words, 'Start recording. Now!' with an 'I'm-bloody-serious-Ryan' expression on her face and it's maybe half a second after I hit the REC button on the camcorder that I hear my mother say, "It's no use. He's gone. There's no bringing him back. He can't distinguish between the act and reality any more. We're going to have to do this the hard way," and the cops, including my parents, fire a volley of shots at the first TV monitor before turning their guns on the second TV monitor and it's as the air in the living room of The Loft fills with shrapnel from the exploding TV monitors that Katelin tries to grab the camcorder out of my hand, which is when I hear my portable phone ringing and I start shouting at the cops to stop shooting, at Katelin to let go, that can't all of you see I'm just holding a fucking portable phone in my hand you. Bunch. Of. Lunatics! and they all look at me, see that it's a portable phone, that it's ringing, and my mother says, 'Well, aren't you going to answer it?'

It's Rebecca.

"Bloody hell. That certainly took long enough. You weren't sleeping, I mean, having another nightmare or —"

"Tell me honestly," I say, cutting her off, my heart still pounding, the pillowcase already soaked with sweat. "Are you going to do it?"

"Do what?"

"Commit suicide."

"What are you talking about?"

"You know what I mean. Are you going to go through with it or do you just plan on letting Daphne kill herself while you watch?"

"Ryan, what, or should I say, *who*, has gotten into you?"

"No one."

"So you're just all fine and dandy one day and the next day you're asking me this question?"

"Rebecca, you know I haven't been fine and dandy for a while. Ever since . . . since . . . oh, why the hell did you stop me?"

"Stop you?"

"From killing myself last year when I was going to."

"Because you were being impulsive. You weren't seeing the big picture. You would've been just another ignorant suicide."

"Says who?"

"Says me — and you. In case you forgot, you agreed with me, remember? Besides, doing what we're doing now is much better, much —"

"Better? For who?"

"For all of us: you, me, Jennie."

"Jennie's dead."

"Ryan, please. Is there a point to all this drama?"

"Ya, there is. I don't think I can do it."

"Do what?"

"Give Daphne the letter."

There is a slight pause before Rebecca, using her 'I'm-sick-and-bloody-tired-of-your-whining' voice, says, "Ryan, we had a deal, you hear me? A deal. And it's too late to back out now. I need you to give her the letter."

"Rebecca, I'm serious. I really don't think I can do it."

"The hell you can't. I haven't spent eight months planning every last detail of this to have you back out now — especially now that we're so close."

"I feel like maybe we —"

"Ryan, listen to me!" she snaps, cutting me off. "I don't care what it is you're thinking or feeling. I need you to give her the goddamn letter. And so help me; if you don't, I'll make your life a living hell."

"It already is."

"Not in comparison to what I can make it. Trust me. You have no bloody idea, Ryan. No bloody idea."

rendezvous

"Cognitive dissonance."

"What?"

"It's called cognitive dissonance," I say, looking up from a copy of *Utne Reader*, "when you know you should be doing something but you don't do it."

It's just after 11:30 a.m. (Daphne still hasn't called me, despite me leaving four or five messages on her voicemail for her to do so) and Eriq and I are in The World's Biggest Bookstore browsing through magazines and for the last few minutes, ideas of how I was going to get Eriq to meet me at Sen5es tonight have been ping-ponging around inside my head until Eriq mentioned that he felt like he had to do more, that he's always felt like he should do more but hasn't, and I told him that the term to describe this was 'cognitive dissonance.'

"Maybe you just need a vacation?" I suggest, testing him, seeing if, like Brad and myself, he can be distracted by the prospect of a vacation.

"Ryan, I do not need a vacation. I've been on vacation for most of my adult life. The truth is, and God knows I hate to admit this, but Daphne's right. I'm not in a position to help anyone. It would be one thing if I was taking from the rich and giving to the poor but I'm just taking from the rich and. . . ."

Ten seconds later, when he still hasn't completed his sentence, I say, after having a mini-debate with myself and deciding that I will not inform Rebecca first of what I'm about to propose to Eriq, "What if I told you I had a potential candidate for you? Would that make you feel any better?"

"That depends," he says, giving me a sceptical look. "Who is it?"

"Someone."

"Man or woman?"

"Woman."

"How old?"

"She just celebrated her 42nd birthday."

"Divorced?"

"Two years."

"Children?"

"None. Doesn't want them. Never has."

"Wealthy?"

"Not obscenely."

"Second home?"

I nod. "A rental here in Toronto. But both houses are paid for and she makes a killing on the rent."

"Does she like to travel?"

"She's going to Europe this summer — Spain for the month of July and France for the month of August. She rents a small villa each year."

"Sounds promising. Is there a catch?"

"There is. She's currently only dating men under the age of twenty-five."

"Seriously?"

I nod. "Fortunately, she's willing to make an exception on your behalf."

"What? You've told her about me?"

"I've described you," I say and when he gives me a look as if to say, 'What did you tell her?' I tell him I may have mentioned something about his sexual prowess and after we both laugh, I add, "Oh ya, P.S., she loves writers. Apparently her dream is to have a writer-in-residence."

He laughs. "'A writer-in-residence.' She actually said that?"

I nod.

He chuckles then says, "Speaking of writing, where's my book? I thought you were going to give it to me at Brad's?"

"I lent it."

"To who?"

"To the woman we've just been discussing, actually."

"You *what?*"

"Hey, unlike the characters in your stories, sometimes us real folk don't do things you want them to. Besides, maybe it's time to shed some light on that shadow side of yours."

"That's easy for you to say — it's not *your* shadow side."

"Well, if it's any consolation," I say, pulling out Findley's *Stones* from my messenger bag that Jo-Jo gave me to give to Eriq, "she gave me something to give to you — as collateral," and I hand him the book.

"Hey, this is my . . ."

"Ya, I know — your favourite book. She told me your writing style reminded her of Findley's."

"Bullshit."

"I'm serious. She said it was really good writing. She used to be a manuscript reader or something when she lived in England. She said your style was similar to Findley's but your content was all your own, very unique, very real. She said she was blown away by 'Burdened Beauty.' Said it changed her life."

"Really?"

I nod. "Really."

"Hey, this book has been autographed by Findley."

"I know. She told me you can keep it if you like."

"Who *is* this woman?"

"A friend. So, you want me to set something up? I was thinking about inviting her to dinner this Friday at Rain."

"Rain?"

"Ya, I think Nicole wants to make Rain our new rendezvous spot instead of Jump Café. So what do you say, want me to invite her?"

"I don't know," he says and just when I think he's about to say 'Yes' I say, pulling a folded piece of paper from my back pocket and handing it to him, "While you're in your decision-making mode, I'll throw something else at you."

"What's this?"

"Have a look."

As he unfolds the piece of paper I zoom in on his face, watching his expression change from mild curiosity to recognition to confusion as he sees it's an Eco-Ticket, an exact physical replica of the idea he wrote about in 'Exhausted Air.'

"Where'd you get this?"

I tell him if he wants to know he'll meet me tonight at Sen5es restaurant on Bloor West at 8:30 p.m. with a copy of 'Exhausted Air' and when he insists on knowing where I got the ticket I just smile, thinking of the look on Brad's face when he realizes Eriq is the author of the Eco-Ticket idea and the look on Eriq's face when he realizes Brad is the one who made his idea a reality.

the no-show client finally shows

It's now 4:26 p.m.

Three hours and seventeen minutes have passed since Daphne (only two minutes after I left a voicemail message stating I had some good news for her) called me and we arranged to meet at my apartment.

Natasha and I are at The Loft now and even though she's just told me that she had an amazing talk with her mother and that I've helped her and her mother tremendously and that her mother invited me over for lunch tomorrow, I can't seem to shake the images of:

– Daphne standing in the entrance to my apartment on Queen Street slightly less than two hours ago, looking desperate, hopeful,

– me handing her the letter, telling her it came as part of a package that Rebecca had sent to me,
– Daphne hugging me, actually hugging me,
– me saying, 'Daph, there's something I should. . . .' the words stalling in my throat, thinking of Rebecca's threats to make my life a living hell if I didn't follow through with my end of the deal,
– Daphne saying, 'What is it, Ryan?,'
– me saying, 'Never mind,' and then, pointing at the letter, adding, 'I hope it's what you're looking for,'
– her smiling, hugging me again, and leaving, running down the hall, down the stairs, out of the apartment building, hopping back on her Vespa, and zipping across Queen Street, heading towards the lake, probably wanting to open it there.

"What's that?"

It's Natasha.

We're seated on the avonne bench and she's looking at me with an inquisitive expression on her face and it's not until I hear the intercom buzzer that I realize — simultaneously — that Natasha's question was in reference to the buzzer and that I had an appointment scheduled for 4:30 p.m.

Actually, it's not so much that I forgot, as it's that the person who made the appointment is the same woman who's been making and breaking appointments almost every day for the past two weeks. She called me as I was on the way to visit Seth at The Black Bull yesterday to say that she'd like to make an appointment for 4:30 p.m. and even though I'd lost track of the time it didn't really bother me all that much since I was fairly confident the woman was going to be a no-show again.

"I'm sorry. I completely forgot I had an appointment," I'm now saying to Natasha, distracted, trying to figure out what I'm going to do, where Natasha can go. "Can I get you to hide or, I mean, not hide but, well, the thing is, the sessions are supposed to be completely private and confidential and —"

"No problem. Where should I go?"

"Um, probably the office, if you don't mind?"

"Not at all," she says and after she's in the office and agrees not to come out or make a noise and I've told her I'll do my best to reschedule the appointment, I go back to the intercom and ask, "Can I help you?" and when I hear the woman say, "I have an appointment," the sound of her voice makes me decide to turn on the TV, punching the channel for the vestibule camera into the converter and when the screen lights up I see Daphne standing beside the intercom.

My eyes still on the TV screen, I push the TALK button on the intercom and say, "I'm sorry ma'am, I think you have the wrong address," disguising my real voice with a deep, Leonard Cohen–like voice — the same one I use whenever I call a random number on a payphone.

"I'm certain I don't," Daphne says. "I've called and confirmed the address several times in the last two or three weeks."

"This is just a residence, ma'am . . . I'm sorry."

I hear Daphne growl, see her gesture as though she's about to push the TALK button on the vestibule intercom again before throwing up her hands and storming out of the vestibule.

utterly boring

It was half an hour later when Seth called me.

He said he was riding the Queen streetcar when he saw Daphne get hit, twice — once by a van and then by the streetcar he was riding on — likening it to the part in *Meet Joe Black* when Brad Pitt gets hit by a car, is thrown into the air, and then is immediately hit by a van going the other way.

    The thing that struck me the most was Seth's voice, the way it trembled and twitched and cracked as he described Daphne's injuries, how the blood was leaking out of her ears, how her face — her *beautiful* (emphasis his) face — was full of cuts, how the one side of her head was caved in, how there were shards of glass and mirror lodged in her legs, how she started convulsing as the ambulance attendants were loading her onto the gurney, how the attendants refused to let him ride along in the ambulance with her but that they told him they were taking her to St. Michael's Hospital.

On my way to St. Michael's, I tried to imagine what had caused the accident and I started the scene off with Daphne down by the lake, finding a relatively secluded spot before opening the letter I'd given her and then beginning to read the enclosed screenplay, reading about Rebecca's lifelong search for a 'Perfect Partner,' about her finally discovering Daphne and quickly falling in love with her, about how much she wanted Daphne to be the one, how she wanted to die with Daphne, how it would devastate her if Daphne didn't want the same thing, and then, after learning that Rebecca had recently found her 'Perfect Place' and was ready to die — hopefully with Daphne — after learning of this, I imagined Daphne running back to her Vespa and zipping over to The Suicide Loft, desperate to talk with someone, hoping to make sense of what was going on, and then, after being turned away, she ended up driving like a madwoman in the direction of downtown, en route to the Starbucks on Queen West where Rebecca was waiting for her, waiting to hear if she was willing to join Rebecca in this final scene, if they were going to create the 'Perfect Moment' together. . . .

When I got to the hospital, Brad and Nicole and Seth were already in the waiting room and Brad and Nicole pounced on me as soon as they saw me, making statements and asking questions rapid-fire, perhaps figuring that since I'd done some work at St. Michael's with people who had suffered head traumas I would be able to give them an idea as to what was happening with Daphne.

"They say she has a massive head trauma."

"She had a seizure. I think they called it a 'grand mal.'"

"She's unconscious."

"She's in a coma right now."

"Do you think she'll be okay?"

"What are her chances of a full recovery?"

By this time I was already starting to feel dizzy — my forehead throbbing from the countless variables involved in Daphne's prognosis — my stomach churning from the antiseptic smell of the hospital.

"Do you think she'll survive?"

"I don't know. It's probably too early to tell," I responded, the whole time thinking that if Daphne's head injury was as severe as Seth had described, even if she did survive there would undoubtedly be profound changes — memory deficits, an impaired ability to reason, to debate, difficulties concentrating and acquiring new knowledge — things that made her distinctly Daphne, that gave her life meaning, that gave the rest of us so much entertainment and —

"Can you imagine Daphne being any different?" Brad said, as though reading my mind.

"It would be horrible," Nicole said.

"Boring," Brad said. "Utterly boring."

"She's the life of our group," Nicole added. "I mean, what would we do if she . . . if she. . . ."

"I thought . . . ," I started to say, then, as I watched Nicole collapse into Brad's arms, I stopped, realizing that despite Rebecca telling me over and over again that if the rest of the gang knew what we were planning they'd probably thank us; despite Daphne appearing to be the bane of everyone's existence, the truth was something completely different. The truth was Rebecca was wrong; the truth was the rest of the gang genuinely cared about Daphne; the truth was that once again I had failed to stand up to Rebecca and now Daphne was in the hospital, in the I.C.U. — and it was at this point that somewhere, very distant, I could hear someone, I think it was Seth, speaking, saying to the others, "I think he's going to faint."

herstory vs. mystory

But I didn't faint.
 I threw up.
 Twice.
 Then I started running.
 And it wasn't until I was nearly at the lake that I stopped, deciding to answer my cellphone which had been ringing on and off ever since I'd left St. Michael's and, after hearing Rebecca's voice on the other end, I heard myself explaining what had happened, that less than an hour after I'd given Daphne the letter she was struck by a van and a streetcar, was now in the I.C.U. at St. Michael's Hospital, in a coma, and would either die or survive with significant and irreparable brain damage.
 Of course, Rebecca didn't believe me at first — she thought I was b.s.ing her, concocting some borderline implausible story to try and get back at her for her being such a bitch to me last night but then, when I told her to call St. Michael's and find out for

herself, she said 'Bloody hell' in a tone that suggested she now believed me and after about a half dozen more 'Bloody hells,' a few 'Holy shits,' and one or two 'Damns,' she said, "Christ, what the bloody hell are we going to do now?"

"I know. We're screwed. I mean, we could get in a lot of —" is what I started to say, thinking that, like me, Rebecca was worried that if the police found the letter I'd given to Daphne it would more than likely arouse suspicion, which might lead to an investigation and result in Rebecca and me being arrested, but then, realizing the tone of Rebecca's voice didn't match what I thought she should be thinking, I abruptly stopped what I was saying and instead said, "Wait a sec, what did you mean when you said, 'what the bloody hell are we going to do now?'"

"Well, from the way you describe it, it sounds like Daphne's not going to recover, that even if she survives, she'll more than likely end up being a vegetable, right?"

"I guess."

"Well, there's no way I'm going to commit mutual suicide with a vegetable."

"Rebecca . . . what . . . why are you —"

"The plan was to get *Daphne* to agree to a mutual suicide. *Daphne*. Not some altered version of Daphne. Not some vegetable. I mean, where's the challenge in that?"

I remember standing there, less than a stone's throw from the lake, staring blankly at a capless 1 litre plastic Pepsi bottle housing a half smoked soggy cigar, wondering what the hell was going through Rebecca's mind, if she had any idea of what she was saying. "Rebecca . . . are you . . . are you listening to yourself?" I finally said. "I mean, don't you even care?"

"Of course I do. You don't think it *bothers* me that I've just wasted eight months of my life on her? Of course I care. But I mean, what's done is done. We can either sit here whining and complaining about it for *another* eight months or we can move on."

"Move on? What are you talking about? Move on to what?"

"To someone else. I was thinking the woman on the subway, remember her — the one who dated all the *freak*shows? I'm thinking she'd be a suitable replacement for us, not to mention a lot less —"

"Rebecca, stop it."

"Stop what?"

"For fuck sakes!" I shouted, abruptly punting the Pepsi bottle, watching it spinning through the air, spewing pieces of soggy cigar. "What's wrong with you? Don't you get it? It's over. Done. Finished. And so am I."

"Like bloody hell it is and like bloody hell *you* are. There's a lot more at stake here than just your little crisis of conscience. Besides, it's not like we were trying to persuade ten-year-old children to do this. Jennie was twenty-eight. Daphne is thirty. They were old enough to make their own decisions."

"Rebecca, please," I said, walking towards the downed Pepsi bottle. "What we did was . . . wrong. I mean, Daphne might . . . she might . . . die."

"Hey, that's not — I repeat, *not* — *our* fault. *We* didn't drive her Vespa into that van — *she* did. In fact, we may have even prolonged Daphne's life. For all we know, if it wasn't for us being in her life, she might've died months ago and never got a chance to be reconciled with Eriq and Nicole. Who knows? What you've got to realize is that not once did we force Daphne to do anything. It was *her* decision."

"But how?" I said, now standing over the Pepsi bottle, beginning to nudge it back and forth between my feet. "How could it be her decision when we've been manipulating her for the last eight months? You even said it yourself — you wanted to get her to question the validity of her existence, you wanted to change her destiny."

"Listen, if you're so determined to back out of our agreement and undermine everything we've done for the last year or so, then fine, go ahead and do it. The truth is, I'm sick and tired of trying to hold you to your word. In fact, that's it. As of right now, I'm going to start looking for someone else to help me. Maybe I'll give that understudy of yours — what's his name, Seth? Maybe I'll give Seth a call and see if he wants to help me."

It was at this point that two images appeared in my mind:
– the first image was of Seth in the hospital, slumped in a chair in the waiting area, sobbing uncontrollably, his eyes filled with fear-slash-remorse,
– the second image was of Seth after he'd spent a few weeks with Rebecca, after she'd taught him to control his feelings, to consider authentic emotional responses a weakness, to be as calculating as she'd taught me to be,
– and it was in the process of comparing these two images that something inside me snapped and I heard myself saying, "Leave. Seth. Alone," slowly, menacingly, through tightly clenched teeth. "He doesn't need you fucking with his head like you've been fucking with mine for the last fourteen months."

"Oh, bloody hell, Ryan! Listen, before you start rehearsing the 'it-was-all-her-fault-your-honour-she-fucked-with-my-head' speech, remember that you — just like Jennie and Daphne — had a choice. At any time during this whole thing you could've decided to do something different. I never once held a gun to anyone's head — including yours."

At this moment in our conversation, I remember feeling angry; so angry, in fact, that if I'd been speaking to Rebecca face to face I'm certain I would've been choking her while shouting the words, "Don't you get it, you fucking psychotic bitch! Daphne Garceau might die and you and I are responsible!" but, seeing as we were talking via our cellphones, I could only stomp on the Pepsi bottle while shouting the words, after which Rebecca said something about my calling her a fucking psychotic bitch which I didn't really catch because she was also laughing and then, after she stopped laughing, she asked, "How do you know?"

"How do I know what?" I snapped, the image of my hands clasped tightly around her neck still warbling through my mind.

"How do you know that Daphne might die. In fact, how do you even know Daphne is injured?"

"What the hell are you talking about?"

"Did you see her?"

"Who?"

"Daphne."

"What?"

"Bloody hell, Ryan. Do I have to spell it out for you? Did. You. Actually. See. Daphne. In. The. Hospital? Or did you just listen to Seth tell you some sob story about Daphne getting in an accident, about her being rushed to St. Michael's and then, when you arrived at the hospital, saw Nicole and Brad and Seth crying in the waiting area, telling you how much they loved her, how they couldn't imagine life without her, et cetera, et cetera?"

"What? How did you . . . ?"

"Ryan. Do you think for one second I was going to do something like this without knowing what you were made of?"

"What the? So, so what, you're saying that . . . wait a sec. Are you trying to tell me that this whole thing has been like a . . . a —"

"A rehearsal for the real thing? Yes."

"What-fucking-ever. If you think I'm —"

"It's the truth."

"Rebecca, if you think I'm naïve enough to believe that this whole thing has just been a rehearsal, you're even more psychotic than I thought you were."

"Well then, what's it going to take to convince you? How about we start with Seth, your quote, unquote, 'understudy.' Where did you first see him?"

At this point, I considered giving the Pepsi bottle another kick but instead collapsed on the lawn, my mind struggling to inventory the possible reasons for Rebecca's present behaviour, straining to figure out where she was coming from, what angle she was playing. "Listen Rebecca," I said after a few moments, "if you're trying to get me to forget about what's just happened to Daphne or make me feel better about it by concocting one of your little impromptu screenplays, don't bother, okay? I'm not interested."

"You first met Seth on the Queen streetcar, right?"

"That's it. I'm hanging up now, Rebecca."

"No you're not."

"Oh yes I am."

"I know I've got your interest."

"Not anymore you don't."

"So you're telling me you're not even mildly intrigued by me telling you that this has just been a rehearsal?"

"Rebecca, I'm neither intrigued nor in the mood for another one of your bullshit screenplays."

"It's not bullshit. This one's a work of art — trust me."

"Rebecca, I'll never trust another word that comes out of your —"

"Listen, I'll make you a deal; just play along with me for twenty minutes or so and after that, if you still feel that what I'm saying is bullshit, I promise I won't ever bother you again, okay?"

"Sorry, too late, gotta go, see —"

"All I want is one little twenty-minute scene."

"Forget it."

"Come on, it'll be the easiest scene you've ever done. I don't need any emotional outbursts, no tears or gestures or facial expressions or asides about what you happen to be thinking or feeling while either of us are talking — I just want dialogue. Pure, unadulterated dialogue."

"I said forget it."

"Bloody hell, Ryan. It's not like I'm asking you to do something extraordinary here. You won't even have to say much. I'll do most of the talking. You just have to listen — and maybe ask the odd question or dish out a sarcastic comment here and there just to keep things going."

"I can't believe I'm still talking to you."

"Well, maybe the reason you're still talking to me is because you want to do this scene every bit as much as I do — just like I know that one of the reasons you're reluctant to do it is because for the first time in eight months you don't know how it's going to turn out, you don't have the script in front of you — and all I can say about that is if you do this right, if you just sit there and listen and respond the way you think a character in this situation would respond given what I'm telling you, I guarantee you it'll be the easiest and the best scene you've ever done."

"For fuck sakes," I shouted while pounding my right fist repeatedly into the lawn beside me, creating several fist-sized divets. "This can't be happening."

"Well, it is. But what's crucial is finding out why this is happening? Which is what this scene will do. Now, please, Ryan, let's just do this scene, okay? It all starts with you answering the following question: you first met Seth on the Queen streetcar, right? . . . Good, good, I like the dramatic pause, it's creating a nice effect . . . and your answer should come right about —"

"Yes."

"Excellent. Thank you. So you first met Seth on the Queen streetcar and he was carrying a black briefcase, wearing a beige Hugo Boss trenchcoat over his charcoal grey Ralph Lauren suit, and was on his way to work in the financial district on Bay Street, right?"

"Yes."

"Well, what if I told you that Seth lives nowhere near the

Beaches and doesn't work on Bay Street, but that he actually owns a house in Rosedale, lives off his trust fund, and that prior to taking the Queen streetcar at 7:30 a.m. that morning, he hadn't been on a streetcar since he was fourteen."

"I would say you're full of shit."

"Of course you would. But what if I also told you that if you examine the details a little closer you would perhaps find it more than slightly ironic that Seth just *happened* to be on the same streetcar on the same morning I asked you to meet me at Second Cup on Queen West at 8:00 a.m. — *and* that the moment I hung up after calling you on your cellphone and telling you I'd be about an hour late, you started hearing some guy telling his friend about this woman named Daphne — describing, in the process, my 'Perfect Partner' — and that this guy just *happened* to get off at the same stop you were getting off at, walk into the same coffee shop you were going to, and then, after introducing himself as Seth, just *happened* to tell you all the pertinent details about this Daphne woman, including where she volunteered, before suddenly realizing, roughly five minutes before I showed up, that he was running late, but that he'd love to exchange phone numbers and keep in touch. I mean, don't you find all of this just slightly ironic?"

"So you're saying that Seth's not really who I think he is, that he's really like, what? *Your* understudy?"

"Partner, actually. He's the front man, the liaison between . . . well, anyway, let's just say he's not who you think he is. And he certainly isn't the guy you thought you 'discovered' on the streetcar confessing his sordid little tale about Katelin and Daphne or, as he referred to them when he was being watched by you on the patio at The Black Bull restaurant yesterday, 'Kathy' and 'Danielle.'"

"So if Seth's your partner, that makes Katelin . . . ?"

"She's also a partner."

"Okay, now I *know* you're full of shit."

"Really? How's that?"

"I can believe you being able to convince Seth to tell you everything he and I have talked about, but I know Katelin would never listen to you. She loathes you as much as I do. Besides, I know things about her that you couldn't possibly know."

"Well, before we go any further, let's make sure we're both talking about the same Katelin, okay? The Katelin I'm talking about not only bears a striking resemblance to Jada Pinkett-Smith and loves everything French, she also visited you at The Suicide Loft one day, then — coincidentally, of course — just happened to be in the very same section of HMV as you the following day and, after luring you into The Salad King, asked you to sit with her, telling you she didn't want to eat alone before going into this long-winded explanation of why she didn't want to eat alone, which turned into a thirteen-hour conversation during which you undoubtedly got the impression she had a split personality because what she'd told you the day before at The Suicide Loft didn't exactly match what she was telling you during your thirteen-hour conversation. Now, are we talking about the same Katelin? Hello? Earth to Ryan? You still there? I take it by your silence that we're talking about the same Katelin. Well, to be fair, you're probably right about her loathing me and not listening to me. If you recall, I think I told you she made me slightly nervous, which is actually the truth. Katelin's a little *too* fond of improv for my liking, which was why she stopped coming to our little soirées at Jump Café; I couldn't really trust her to stick with the script. In fact, I had some serious reservations about using her again but, in retrospect, I'm glad I decided to listen to Seth and let her have another couple of cameos. She ended up doing some great work, especially in that final Salad King scene when she was telling you about Nicole and her experiments which, by the way —"

"Which, I suppose, you're going to tell me are all b.s. too, right?"

"Actually, no. Oddly enough, that's true. Nicole's really done all of those things. In fact, that's how she came to be part of the group. Someone told Seth about this woman who was so desperate to be an actress that she was going around doing all this really extreme getting-into-character stuff — sort of like how De Niro gained all that weight for *Raging Bull* or Tom Hanks lost a ton of weight and grew a big beard for *Cast Away* — only this woman was going around getting pregnant, becoming a call girl, a stripper, even slicing her wrists, just so she would know what it was like to be this type of character. It was a little too extreme for my tastes, but Seth seemed to think she'd work out fine, and she did. I mean, she certainly had you convinced she was a Prozac-popping, psychiatrist-seeing airhead, albeit with a more than slightly bizarre shadow side."

"So where does that leave —"

"Brad? Glad you asked. Brad's actually been playing many roles — a few of them authentic, a couple of them phoney, and one of them you definitely have no clue about. The authentic ones are that he's a lawyer in his father's firm, he's fond of designer clothing, organic food, and Peter Gzowski's *Morningside Cookbook* — and he's been your friend since university. The phoney ones are that he's been helping street people for the last year and that he's getting married to Nicole in three months. The truth is Brad pretty much detests street people, which is the real reason he was fumigating his place with vanilla-scented spray that day you came over. And as for him being engaged to Nicole, well, that's pretty much impossible seeing as he's —"

"Wait a second. Are you saying that those three dreadlocked kids and the guy with the silk suit eating leftover ratatouille in Brad's dining room are your partners too?"

"No. Much to Brad's displeasure, they're the real deal. Tough to fake homelessness. Of course, as Brad already mentioned, they have you to thank for at least giving them a couple of home-cooked meals and some new clothes that, even though they were last year's style, nearly killed Brad to part with. He's such a packrat. He keeps everything. In fact, during one of our rehearsal sessions at his place he was telling the rest of the gang how —"

"'*The rest of the gang*'? Are you saying everyone else knows about this — about you filming Jennie and the idea for the trilogy and —"

"Hell no. Only Seth knows about that . . . and Brad, of course but he's —"

"Brad?"

"Well, ya, but it's not —"

"Rebecca, what the hell is wrong with you?"

"It's not a problem, Ryan. Trust me."

"Not a problem? Are you insane? How can you telling Brad about filming Jennie and the trilogy not be a —"

"Ryan, it's not what you think. Trust me, everything is —"

"Stop using that word!"

"What word?"

"'Trust.' How the fuck am I supposed to trust you?"

"If you just relax and listen to me for a few minutes, everything will make sense. I —"

"How can this ever make sense? You're insane, you're —"

"Ryan, I am *not* insane. And it *will* make sense if you just let me explain. But before I even start to explain, I'm going to warn you it probably won't be the most coherent explanation I've ever given, which is why you've got to promise you won't interrupt me the moment you think something doesn't add up, okay? The truth is, I actually thought I'd have more time to think about what I'm about to tell you but since we've been speeding things up lately I really haven't had . . . anyway, enough preamble, here's the deal: one year ago today, we — and when I say we, I mean, Brad, Seth, Daphne, Katelin, Nicole, and myself — we all enrolled in this acting school called Act 5, Scene 5 and —"

"So now you're saying that all of you were friends before you and I brought everyone together six months ago at Jump Café?"

"No, not really. Well . . . actually, can you ask me that question again a little later? I think I just got things sorted out in my head and I'm afraid if I don't get it out right away I'll end up confusing you even more."

"Hey, I'm just responding the way I think a character would respond given what you're telling me."

"Cute. And the sarcastic tone was a nice added touch. Anyway, as I was about to say, it all started when Seth came over to Brad's house and showed the two of us this brochure for an acting school called Act 5, Scene 5 that one of his parents' friends, this really eccentric film financier, gave him the night before. Seth was all nervous and excited because he'd been telling Brad and me for weeks about this rumour travelling around his parents' social circle about a really exclusive, edgy, innovative, one-of-a-kind acting school that supposedly guaranteed graduates a leading role in a TV series. Of course, Brad and I didn't pay much attention to it, telling Seth that it was probably just an urban myth or another one of his fantasies about how the three of us could get on TV — until Seth showed up that day at Brad's house and the three of us sat there reading this brochure that basically said: 'Act 5, Scene 5 is the most revolutionary, avant-garde acting school of the new millennium. Simultaneously combining acting lessons and auditions by having aspiring actors perform in unfilmed, real-life, sometimes scripted, sometimes improvisational scenes while being covertly viewed and assessed by a variety of personnel from the TV industry and —'"

"And exactly how does this relate to —"

"Wait, I'm not done. 'Similar to Language Immersion

Programs, students of Act 5, Scene 5 are thoroughly immersed in all facets of the acting experience — acting, writing, directing, producing, financing — and must be completely committed and available 24-7 for a period of one year. Upon graduating, in addition to receiving hundreds of hours of invaluable acting experience and countless feedback sessions from industry professionals, students are not only guaranteed a leading role in an upcoming made-for-TV movie or miniseries, they will also meet the brainchild behind Act 5, Scene 5 — the person responsible for creating the characters they've played and writing the scenes they've acted in for the past year. And all this for the bargain basement tuition fee of $25,000.'"

"$25,000? You spent that much money on . . . actually, you know what? I don't give a shit. I just want to know how this relates to —"

"Bloody hell, Ryan. Relax. I'm getting to it. Remember what you told Daphne a few days ago about *Thelma & Louise* and how if you just saw the final scene in isolation it wouldn't make any sense? Well, this is the same thing. I can't just blurt out the punchlines; they need to have some context or else nothing is going to make sense. Trust me, even with the context you're going to have trouble believing me. Anyway, Brad, Seth, and I decided to enrol in the school and about a week or so after we'd sent in our post-dated cheques, we received a package in the mail containing a cellphone and a set of twenty scenes and a week later we acted in our first scene, which is when we met Daphne and Katelin and Nicole, who turned out to be the only other people enrolled in the school."

"So how did you . . . ? This doesn't make any sense. How did you know where to meet or who was involved? Where was the school? Who contacted you? Why were the cheques post-dated? Who —"

"Okay, hold on, slow down. The cheques were post-dated for one month after our first scene to allow us to determine if we liked what the school had to offer. If we weren't satisfied, we could quit and we wouldn't be charged anything. Exactly thirty days from the day of our first scene, the cheques would be cashed. If the cheque bounced, it would result in an automatic expulsion and a lawsuit. Of course, we all stayed beyond the thirty days and none of our cheques bounced. Now, as for how we knew where to meet and who was involved, like I said, after we were accepted into the school, we each received a package in the mail containing about twenty scenes. For each of these scenes there was a date, a time, a script, and a location. The scene might entail well-defined characters following an excruciatingly detailed storyline or it might entail nothing more than a general discussion of an issue from the perspective of a few roughly defined characters. Scenes could last anywhere from a minute to a couple of hours and may involve only one of us or all six of us. As for where the school was, it was anywhere the scenes took place — in a restaurant, on the streetcar, in a bus shelter, in a mall, in a café, in a taxi, at a baseball game, on the street — wherever. And as for someone from the school contacting us, that occurred via the cellphones we each received with our original package which we were instructed to carry with us only when we were going to do a scene."

"They gave you cellphones?"

"Ya. But they weren't normal cellphones. They were designed to only receive calls."

"What do you mean?"

"Just that. You couldn't dial out because they were equipped with only two buttons — an answer button and a hang-up button. There were no number pads. They also only had a 'vibrate' mode. Anyway, during the first month, I received six calls on my Act 5, Scene 5 cellphone. The first three were from an acting coach, the fourth and fifth were from a talent scout, and the sixth was from a director. The calls always came within fifteen minutes after I finished a particular scene and the person would spend no less than five minutes and no more than ten discussing my performance, giving me tips and/or compliments on everything from my facial expressions, gestures, body language, tone of voice, cadence, accent, and word speed to my wardrobe and hairstyle — basically anything that either made or might've made my performance more or less convincing. To be honest, initially I found it slightly nerve-wracking knowing that some director or casting agent might be watching me and calling me afterwards to give me their appraisal of my performance but by the end of the second week, I was used to it and would actually get these incredible rushes of anticipatory excitement whenever I felt I'd given a good performance and thought I might receive a call. Of course, I'm sure you can relate to this feeling."

"Really? And how's that?"

"Well, I mean, all you have to do is think of the scene in your apartment with Daphne a few days ago when you thought it was your performance that made her cry. I know that scene made you feel pretty good. Now imagine how much better it would've felt if you knew a talent scout was watching and assessing you and afterwards he contacted you and told you how impressed or blown away he was by your performance. Which is why we all loved it so —"

"Is this a good time to ask if all of you were already friends before we started getting everyone together at Jump Café six months ago?"

"Okay, Mr. Impatience, the truth is, all of us weren't really friends. Daphne and Seth and Katelin had taken acting lessons at another school together a couple years ago but they weren't what you would consider friends or even acquaintances, really. And, like I said, Seth heard about Nicole through the acting grapevine. As for Brad, Seth, and I . . . well, ya, we were friends beforehand but I'd never seen Daphne or Katelin or Nicole before our first scene together for Act 5, Scene 5."

"But you obviously became friends once this Act 5, Scene 5 thing started."

"Actually, we didn't. And that was because part of our admission to the school entailed signing contracts prohibiting us from discussing any aspect of Act 5, Scene 5 with anyone, including each other or even to be seen with each other outside of our rehearsals or our particular scenes. The school had a 'zero tolerance' rule about this and warned us that a breach of this aspect of our contract would result in immediate expulsion. They even went so far as to hire people to periodically try and get information out of us but none of us cracked."

"How do you know?"

"Know what?"

"If none of you could speak with each other, how did you know no one cracked?"

"Because five weeks after the school started we found out the whole thing was a scam."

"What?"

"Remember how I said we received a package in the mail containing roughly twenty scenes and that for each scene there was a date, a time, a script, and a location? Well, as it turned out, the final scene in the package didn't come with a script — just a date, a time, and a location: a restaurant called Scaramouche. And so there we were, all six of us, sitting at our reserved table in Scaramouche, making small talk, casually surveying the other patrons to see if anyone was watching us, wondering if this was some sort of test and we were being evaluated, and just when Brad suggested we order some food some guy dressed in an Armani business suit presented himself at our table and informed us an envelope had arrived in the restaurant's mail that day preceded by a phone call instructing that it be dropped off at our table fifteen minutes after all six of us were seated —

and then he handed the envelope to Seth. The envelope was addressed to 'The Cast,' c/o Scaramouche and had no return address and after the Armani suit guy responded 'I'm sorry, I don't,' then, 'Again, I'm sorry, I don't,' and then, 'Once again, I'm sorry, I can't help you,' in response to Brad asking him if he knew who had sent the letter, if he knew who made the phone call, and if he knew who booked their reservation. After the Armani suit guy departed, we exchanged a few puzzled looks and then Seth opened the envelope. Inside he found a note with the words, 'Dear cast of Act 5, Scene 5, Answer them — preferably in unison,' written on it, followed by a very bizarre-looking, completely illegible signature. Thirty seconds later, after we'd exchanged about a dozen more puzzled looks, a few shrugs, and a couple, 'What the hell does this mean?' comments, our Act 5, Scene 5 cellphones started vibrating and, like the note said, we answered them — in unison — and listened to some guy informing us that the acting school was a farce, that all the so-called *industry* people — the directors, acting coaches, and talent scouts — who had contacted us and commented on our performances were phoney too and then, after referring us to a passage from Shakespeare's *Macbeth*, Act 5, Scene 5, the guy reassured us that this wasn't a joke or a test or an experiment or part of the curriculum, that this is just what happens to stupid people who are willing to do anything to be on TV."

"This really happened?"

"Yes, it did. And I don't really appreciate the more than slightly elated-slash-satisfied tone of voice you used to ask me that question."

"So everyone lost $25,000?"

"Ditto, regarding the tone of voice, and yes, all six of us lost $25,000. And none of us could believe it. We just sat there, completely stunned, wondering what we should do, who we should report this to, and I remember asking Brad, since he was the lawyer, if we could sue them — which everyone was for — but Brad said that since we had no idea who the brainchild behind Act 5, Scene 5 was, since we'd never met him or her or even had a contact number, since we'd received all our communication via one-way cellphones or by mail with no return address, it basically made it impossible to sue 'them' because we really had no idea who 'them' was. About two seconds later, I suggested we could maybe trace the cellphones, find out where they were manufactured, who bought them, who the numbers belonged to but Brad and Seth — and Katelin, actually — said they'd already tried that and came up with nothing. Zilch. Of course, Nicole wanted to sue them anyway — even if we couldn't find them — stating that any publicity is good publicity and it might get us noticed by some real people in the acting industry, which is when Seth interjected and said that even though he, like the rest of us, had lost a ton of money, the truth was he didn't really care about the money as much as he cared about the lost opportunity to not only improve his acting ability but also gain experience in the areas of directing and producing and financing, which is what he was really interested in. And then he started telling us how much Katelin and Brad and Nicole and Daphne and I had improved our acting ability in only one month, and how he could only imagine how good we would've been if we'd had another eleven months to work on it which resulted in —"

"Okay, for the last time. How the hell does this relate to me?"

"Earth to Ryan, ever heard of the word patience? I'm getting there. Now, how the hell this relates to you is that Seth wasn't just being nice — the month with the phoney acting school *had* made us all better actors, much better. I mean, you should've seen Daphne during our first scene together. She was horrible. Absolutely horrible. But after a month with the phoney acting school, she was getting to be pretty good. And when I compare her to how she is now, bloody hell — what a difference. I mean, just think of some of the performances you've witnessed from Daphne in the past few days. Remember the scene in Starbucks on Friday afternoon when she stole that woman's car keys? And then a few minutes later in the scene in front of Peter Pan Bistro where she was screaming at everyone like a bloody lunatic, or even some of the improv work she did — like that scene in the apartment when you handed her Josh Sebring's business card and how she was able to convince you Josh was just a bullshit artist and not really a producer for an indie film company based in Montreal — which he is, by the way. She was incredible in that scene. She should get an Emmy or an Oscar for her work in the last few days. Everyone should. In fact, I'm getting goosebumps just thinking about how convincing they all were and how —"

"Am I supposed to be pretending to want to know all this?"

"Okay, Mr. Sarcasm. What would *you* like to know?"

"Well, for starters, I'd like to know if anyone ever found out who the brainchild behind Act 5, Scene 5 was?"

"As a matter of fact, yes. I did. And so did Seth, of course, being that he's been Brad's boyfriend for almost seven years, which —"

"Hold up. Rewind. What did you just say?"

"Exactly what I tried to tell you earlier — that the reason Brad is not getting married to Nicole in three months is because he's really gay and —"

"Oh, for fuck sakes, Rebecca."

"I'm not making this up, Ryan. It's the truth. He just came out of the closet last year, which is the real reason he has you call him before you visit — in case his boyfriend is over . . . well, that and the fact that we have most of our rehearsals at his place and because I usually stay at his place whenever I quote-unquote, 'go away as part of our plan to drive Daphne nuts.'"

"Rebecca, do have any idea how full of shit I think you are right now?"

"So? I really don't care if you don't believe me. The fact that Brad is gay isn't really the important part of the explanation, anyway."

"Really? And exactly what is the important part?"

"The important part involves the role I said you definitely had no clue that Brad was playing."

"Which is?"

"Well, aside from the roles I already told you Brad was playing he was also . . . actually, you know something, before I say another word, I should explain a few things. And before I explain a few things I should probably warn you that what I'm about to tell you may seem even more far-fetched than the stuff I've already told you so you have to promise me you'll hear me out, okay? Ryan?"

"Any chance of you putting this far-fetched explanation of yours on fast-forward?"

"I'll try. Now, do you promise to hear me out?"

"Whatever. Go on."

"I'll take that as a 'Yes.' Anyway, remember when Jennie and I were like nineteen and we came over to your student house when you were in university and asked if you had any quote, unquote, 'hot roommates,' and you laughed and told us you had the perfect guy for us and then started telling us about this guy from B.C. named Brad who never went out, was a total clean freak, spent all his time in his room, and went to his grandparents' place north of Toronto nearly every weekend so he could concentrate on his studies? And remember when Jennie and I said he sounded like a complete geek you told us you actually felt kind of sorry for him and said you were going to befriend him and try and get him a personality and a life before he graduated and then the three of us decided we'd start that night and so we dragged him out to a nightclub . . . remember all that? Well, what you don't know about that night is that when you and Jennie were at the bar getting us drinks, Brad leaned over and said something about how the true voyage of discovery is not in seeing new lands, but in seeing with new eyes, and then asked me if I'd like to start seeing with new eyes. Of course, right away, all these warning lights were going off and I was sitting there thinking, 'Psycho. Serial killer. Lunatic,' but then he starts telling me how the past few years of his life have been so mundane, so boring, so *disastrously dull* that he's been forced to imagine it differently, to see with new eyes, and that how he's done this is by changing the lens through which he looks at the world to one that automatically modifies his life, as well as the lives of other people, replacing them with more tolerable ones, ones that are more colourful, more entertaining, and that after a while he started bringing the modified versions of his life, as well as the lives of his parents, his friends, his acquaintances — everyone — out of his imagination and into his real life, re-inventing them on almost a daily basis until the lines between the stories and the reality blurred and became virtually indistinguish — why are you laughing?"

"Because this is the exact same thing that you wrote in —"

"My diary? Ya, I know. Page 4. They were Brad's words, not mine. Anyway, at this point, I was more than slightly intrigued by Brad and so just before you guys got back with our drinks I accepted his offer to see through new eyes and we arranged a time and a place to meet the following weekend and instead of going to his grandparents' place like he told you he was, we ended up renting a car, driving to Montreal, and spending the next two days and nights pretending to be anyone but who we really were. And Ryan, it was in-fucking-credible. We must have made up at least two dozen different impromptu screenplays that weekend. I never had so much fun. And Brad was amazing. You wouldn't believe how gifted he was at improv, even back then. He could make up a story or a character sketch of the two of us so quickly, so easily, and so convincingly, it just boggled my mind. He was, without a doubt, the most creative, intelligent, fascinating person I'd ever met. And when I compared the person I saw in Montreal to how you described him to Jennie and I when we were at your student house, I couldn't believe the difference. It was as though you had no idea who he really was, that there was this side to him you never knew existed. I mean, it was like when you and I were at the International Festival of Authors listening to Eriq describe a riveting character, listening to him tell us that the best characters, the most memorable characters, are the ones who have a shadow side, a side full of hidden, often quirky details, usually inconsistent with other parts of their character, which ends up distinguishing them from the rest of the herd. That's Brad. Of course, I realize to you Brad always appeared to be — how did you put it — a pathetic, boring loser? But believe me, Ryan, he's just the opposite. *I* didn't know he was gay and that he and Seth had been together for seven years until just last year, and I've been best friends with him for almost ten years now. He had everyone, including me, convinced he was straight and that Seth was just a good buddy. And the only reason I found out was because they told me. Otherwise I probably would've never known. That guy's got a shadow side the size of the Grand Canyon. I mean, there's so much to him that it's like . . . it's like — it's like I told Eriq that night at the Festival of Authors about Brad having this risky-slash-adventurous-slash-cerebral side that no one else knows about. Of course, you just thought it was something I was making up to get Eriq to meet us for dinner at Jump Café, which it was, but it was also the truth. Only the risky-slash-adventurous-slash-cerebral stuff wasn't bungee-jumping and parasailing and cliff diving and being a super jock, it was all this extreme, improvisational acting he was doing. Bloody hell, Ryan, you should've seen what we ended up doing some weekends or during the Christmas and summer holidays; it was unreal. And Brad kept upping the ante, getting more and more into his characters, taking more risks, to the point where some of the things he was doing ended up making Nicole's experiments seem like child's play. I remember thinking a few years ago that he had a death wish and one day, when I told him that I thought he was going too far, that he might get killed acting out one of his 'impromptu screenplays,' he just looked at me and said, 'Hey, like Freud said, "Life is impoverished when the highest stake in the game of living, life itself, is not risked."' Which, if you remember, is exactly what I told Eriq that night at —"

"Is Eriq . . . is he a —"

"What? A partner? No. He's not. He doesn't have a clue about any of this."

"What about Jo-Jo?"

"She's not a partner either. And I can sense you're getting a wee bit paranoid, starting to doubt everyone, right? Well, don't worry. There are tons of people — like Eriq, Jo-Jo, your new friend Natasha, and everyone else besides Katelin who visited The Loft — who have no clue about any of this stuff."

"How do I know? After all, it does seem a little ironic that Jo-Jo showed up at that intersection in Hamilton when she did, asking to give me a ride home, talking about her plan to kill herself, and then, after I told her all about Jennie, my own plan to kill myself, your intervention, my research on suicide, and my dream of opening a place in Toronto for the suicidal-at-heart — things which only you knew about — she suddenly revealed to me that she's from Toronto, has a vacant apartment in her house, and might even be willing to help finance the construction of my dream and . . . now why the hell are *you* laughing?"

"Because that *is* kind of ironic. But, the truth is, I had nothing to do with Jo-Jo and whatever the two of you have done."

"And I guess I'm just supposed to believe you're not lying to me?"

"Yes."

"Speaking of irony."

"I'm not lying, Ryan."

"How do I know? I mean, really? How do I know Eriq isn't really just another aspiring actor like the others and that him telling me he doesn't like you and that he thinks you're slightly evil a couple nights ago wasn't just a way for him to extract information from me as to how I really feel about you?"

"Was he at the hospital?"

"What?"

"Was Eriq at St. Michael's?"

"No."

"Why not?"

"Who knows? Maybe it's all part of this impromptu screenplay of yours, so you can get me to think I'm completely nuts and —"

"Come on, Ryan. Snap out of it. Stop holding onto what you hope this all is and concentrate on the big picture, on what it was Brad and Seth and I were trying to —"

"How the hell could Eriq not know that Daphne was just playing some part?"

"Easy. They've been estranged for years. Until eight months ago they hadn't spoken to one another in more than five years."

"And you're telling me that Daphne agreed to do this? To her own brother?"

"Half-brother. And if you're wondering how she could do what she did to Eriq, well, I mean, we're both aware of a lot worse things one sibling has done to another."

"Fuck you, Rebecca. You're such a —"

"Sorry, you're right. I apologize. That wasn't called for. The truth is, it was actually Daphne's idea to get Eriq to join our cast."

"Whatever."

"I'm serious. Just let me hit the REWIND button once again and I'll explain. Okay, so there we all are at Scaramouche, we've just had our bitch session, we've talked about the futility of suing a non-existent school, we're still more than slightly stinging from the reality that we were stupid enough to spend $25,000 for the chance to be on TV — and now we're in the midst of trying to make ourselves feel better by giving each other compliments on the improvements in our acting abilities when suddenly Seth suggests we make Act 5, Scene 5 a reality. Of course, all of us give him a look like he's nuts but he insists he's serious, that we could use the school as a vehicle not only for continuing to improve our acting, but for getting ourselves a role in a made-for-TV movie or miniseries, just like the school's brochure had originally promised. 'Think about it, guys,' he said. 'The idea is sound. We already proved the school works. It dramatically improved our acting in only one month. And since before tonight we'd already planned on spending another eleven months involved in this project, why not continue it?' He then told us that his parents knew loads of people in the TV industry and that he was sure he could get at least one of them involved with the project, which is when he told us that the truth was he was more interested in the direction, production, and financial end of the acting business anyway and that maybe, if we pooled our resources, improvised a little, it could work — which is when Brad admitted that while he enjoyed acting, his real passion lay in writing and then Daphne and Nicole said that they were only really interested in acting and Katelin and I said we were both passionate about acting and directing, which is when Brad smacked his hand down on the table and said that maybe Seth was onto something, maybe we had all the necessary resources right here at this very table to continue Act 5, Scene 5 on our own and the next thing I knew, we were all back at Brad's house generating character sketches and storylines and scenes and locations and how we were going to market ourselves and who would be responsible for what, and by the end of the evening we had recommitted ourselves to the project for the remaining eleven months. Brad even made up contracts that same night which we all signed, stating that we agreed to not only stick together for eleven months but that we wouldn't discuss anything about Act 5, Scene 5 with anyone outside our group for a period of ten years, just like the original contract had specified and —"

"Pardon the interruption, but aren't the twenty minutes up yet?"

"Not yet, but seeing as you're in such a rush to get to the ending, I'll hit the fast-forward button now and tell you that after a month or so of writing, directing, producing, and acting in our own scenes, things got a little stale and predictable and we realized we needed to spice things up a bit so we had a bit of a brainstorming session on how to do this and Seth came up with the idea of getting other people involved in the scenes, people who weren't actors, who had no idea about Act 5, Scene 5 or what we were doing, explaining that this would provide us with all sorts of uncontrolled variables and unpredictability and would really test us as actors and directors. As it turned out, it was a brilliant idea as week after week we invited strangers out to dinner or brunch with us and challenged ourselves to convince these people of increasingly bizarre tales. For example, during one dinner scene around Labour Day last year we convinced a young, recently engaged couple who Daphne had met at Holt Renfrew that Brad was Vince Carter's lover, Nicole used to be a man, and Katelin was a devote member of the KKK. It was insane. We must've started at least one hundred rumours. I remember one night, at this really ritzy party Nicole got us invited to, we actually had people convinced that Daphne slept with Paul Bernardo a few months before he . . . actually, I should jump in here and let you know that what was also happening while all this stuff with Act 5, Scene 5 was going on was you moving to

Toronto and setting up The Suicide Loft at Jo-Jo's place, me moving in with you, and us starting the search for my 'Perfect Partner' which, in case you were wondering, is actually crucial info because after a couple months of Brad, Seth, Katelin, Daphne, Nicole, and me writing and acting in these increasingly bizarre skits to see what we could convince people of — but roughly a week before you discovered Seth on the Queen streetcar — Seth presented us with a couple of twists to our current Act 5, Scene 5 skits. We were all assembled at Brad's house for one of our rehearsals when he made his presentation, gladly confessing the twists weren't actually his idea but that they came directly from one of his parents' friends, a (drum roll please) TV executive who had expressed considerable interest in Act 5, Scene 5. The TV exec said he really liked the whole concept of Act 5, Scene 5 but felt that what would make this project unique is if, instead of spending a couple of hours convincing a different set of strangers every weekend to believe some borderline unbelievable story, we involved people we already knew — friends, relatives, co-workers — in a story that was developed over a much longer time period. In fact, the TV exec told Seth that if we could a) generate solid ideas for a potential storyline as well as detailed descriptions of some interesting characters, b) establish at least one regular event and location — preferably dinner at a classy restaurant — where our performances could be unobtrusively observed, c) find a minimum of two pseudo-outsiders whom we already knew and whom we could incorporate into our story, and d) commit to a minimum of six months, the exec was certain he could get a few people from the industry to covertly tune in every week and watch our scenes, follow our story, assess character and plot development as well as evaluate our acting, writing, directing, and producing skills and, if we were good enough, maybe even offer us roles in an upcoming TV movie or series. Of course, when we heard this we nearly exploded from excitement and after about ten or fifteen minutes of carrying on like a bunch of idiots we started brainstorming. The first thing we realized we needed would be the pseudo-outsiders who were going to be involved. First off, we agreed we should only have two outsiders involved, believing that any more would create too many variables. Secondly, we felt that the only way it was going to work was if the outsiders were a) available, b) relatives or friends we hadn't had much contact with for a few years, otherwise they'd know something was up, and c) more than mildly interesting if the story was to incorporate or revolve around them. It was at this point that Daphne suggested Eriq, her half-brother, would be a suitable candidate, telling us she hadn't talked to him in more than five years and hardly at all in almost ten years. When she told us he lived in Toronto, was probably available, and described what he was like, we all agreed he was more than mildly interesting. After a few bogus candidates from Brad and Seth, I suggested you, telling everyone that not only were you my cousin and had been Brad's roommate in university, but that you were new to Toronto, were interested in acting and filmmaking, and had recently discovered your sister's dead body in the bathtub after she committed suicide which resulted in you opening up this totally unique place called The Suicide Loft here in Toronto."

"I can't believe —"

"Needless to say, you were a shoo-in."

"You fucking psychotic bitch."

"Stop jumping to conclusions. I'm not finished explaining everything. Anyway, once we made contact with you and Eriq and had our two outsiders, we started working on ideas for a storyline and after a week we'd generated about six or seven really solid ideas that we gave to Seth to give to the TV exec and the one the exec ended up liking the most was Seth and Brad's idea of using you as the central character in an effort to explore the whole suicide angle. The idea that Brad and Seth had for this particular storyline was that I had always been obsessed with suicide, had, in fact — ever since reading Kate Chopin's *The Awakening*— always wanted to commit suicide and that when my cousin Jennie did it, I was immediately resolved to do it. The only obstacle in my path, however, was that I didn't want to do it alone. I wanted to commit simultaneous suicide with someone I was in love with. Of course, according to Brad and Seth's storyline, this was going to be more than mildly difficult, and not just because I needed to find someone willing to commit suicide with me. For one thing, I couldn't fall in love with just anyone. She had to be a woman. And she had to be beautiful. Really beautiful. And intelligent. And very independent. And wealthy. And successful. And last, but not least, she had to possess a burning desire to live. In short, she had to possess all those qualities that would make it seem as though she was too formidable an obstacle to overcome. Which is where you, Mr. Ryan Brassard, came in. Utilizing your personal fascination with suicide, I would reveal to you my lifelong desire to commit suicide. I would let you know by virtue of personal stories and access to my diary that from the age of sixteen or seventeen I'd always been in search of a perfect place to die — and a perfect partner to die with. I would use whatever arguments were necessary to convince you of the merits of suicide and to get you to assist me in my quest to not only find my 'Perfect Partner,' but to convince her to commit suicide with me. Of course, in order to make this whole experience more palatable for you, I would play on your interest in acting and filmmaking and present this as a real-life screenplay, an opportunity for you to test your acting, writing, and directing skills. It didn't just have to be about finding me a perfect partner, we could also involve other people, maybe people related to my potential perfect partner or perhaps even friends of ours, and see where we could take them. Is this beginning to sound familiar? Anyway, after the storyline was settled, the six of us came up with a regular event and location — dinner every Friday night at Jump Café — as well as a couple of alternative events and locations — such as brunch at some other restaurant or café on Saturday and dinner at Brad's house every other Sunday, and then we came up with some rough character sketches for each of us, such as Nicole and Brad being engaged; Nicole being a Prozac-popping, neurotic mess; Brad being this real simple, anal guy; Daphne and Nicole having a history, maybe even a sexual history; Daphne being this really beautiful, wealthy, intelligent woman — which she is, as well as an independently minded person with an unyielding zest for life. Of course, that's why she ended up being my 'Perfect Partner,' which is exactly what you thought was actually happening, that Daphne was my 'Perfect Partner' and that you and I had assembled this gang of *faux friends* in order to convince her to commit suicide with me, which is precisely what Katelin and Daphne and Nicole were thinking too, only they thought it was just part of the script for Act 5, Scene 5, which it was, but underneath all this, underneath what you thought was happening and what Katelin, Daphne, and Nicole thought was happening, what was *really* happening was an opportunity to see what you were made of, to see if you'd actually follow through with our agreement and — what's so funny?"

"You mean other than the fact that you actually expect me to believe all this."

"Well, what's your alternative?"

"My alternative is to once again tell you you're full of shit. All this crap about a phoney acting school and everyone being an actor is so farfetched you should've just left it on the shelf marked 'Bullshit Screenplays That Never Found An Audience.' I mean, come on, Rebecca, all this cloak and dagger stuff with certain people thinking this was happening while other people thought something else was happening — it's not only absurd, it's also way too elaborate and involves way too much planning to pull off. Not only that, even if you did manage to pull it off, it's not even close to being worth it just to see if I would follow through on our agreement? I mean, why would you go through all this trouble just for that?"

"Just for that? Ah, hello. Earth to Ryan bloody Brassard. As you were so fond of reminding *me* practically every other day during the last eight months — this isn't some game we're playing here. We're trying to convince another human being to *willingly* commit suicide with me, which isn't all that far removed from murder. And seeing as I have no intention of ending up in jail, I had to be more than a little cautious about who I wanted involved in this project. And, more to the point, I had to be certain about you. I mean, face it, Ryan, you're not exactly the most stable person on the planet. Between your dreams, your guilty conscience, your never-ending suicidal ideations, and, more recently, your hallucinations and public displays of what appears to be your rapidly approaching breakdown, you don't exactly inspire a lot of confidence. But you're also the one in possession of the videotapes, the ones that have me unmasking myself beside Jennie's dead body and so, seeing as I really had no choice but to involve you, the only thing I could do was determine how far you were willing to go and what you were willing to do."

"Okay, that's it, time's up. I'll talk to you —"

"Oh, come on, Ryan. I can understand you being upset and a little sceptical — okay, a *lot* sceptical. And I know the whole idea of it being the rest of the gang who was doing the majority of the acting and directing and you and Eriq were the ones who were actually being duped doesn't sit well with you. I can understand all that, really, I can because —"

"How?"

"What?"

"How can you understand the feeling of being duped when apparently you're the one who's been doing all the duping?"

"I was about to tell you how — oh, you should see my arms right now, they're completely covered in goosebumps from the anticipation. I was about to tell you something that only Brad, Seth, and I know — and that's that it was actually Brad who came up with the original idea of Act 5, Scene 5. He was the brainchild behind the acting school. It wasn't phoney after all."

"What?"

"I told you he was the most creative, intelligent person I knew. He duped everyone, including me. For the first month of Act 5, Scene 5, Seth was the only other person who knew. The rest of us — me, Katelin, Nicole, and Daphne — thought it was a legit school. Amazing, huh? Brad planned everything from Seth telling me and Brad about a rumour of a really innovative acting school making its way around his parents' social circle, to the brochure describing the acting school, to the people he enrolled in the school, to the original package of twenty scenes, to the one-way cellphones, to the Armani suit guy presenting himself and handing us the envelope at Scaramouche, to Seth suggesting that we continue Act 5, Scene 5, to Seth telling us that some TV exec was interested in our project and that if we used people we knew, had a regular location and a solid storyline, and were committed for a period of no less than six months — he would get industry people to come check us out and even hire us if we were —"

"This is eff, you, see, kay, ee, dee."

"From a certain angle, maybe. From another, it's a brilliant work of art. Of course, only Seth and I know that Act 5, Scene 5 was Brad's idea, just like only Seth and Brad and I know about us filming Jennie and —"

"Wait a second. So after the first month Brad told you Act 5, Scene 5 was his idea?"

"Ya. See, Brad's always known about my passion for suicide. Since that first weekend in Montreal almost ten years ago he's known about this and so when he and Seth heard about Jennie wanting to commit suicide, Seth suggested I convince her to let me film it and that afterwards he and Brad would film me committing suicide with my 'Perfect Partner.' Of course, as it turned out, you came back to the house to get your lift ticket and discovered what Jennie and I were doing and so I had to improvise and got you involved and promised to give you the tapes and then a few weeks later you called me and told me that that was it, that you were sending the tapes to your parents and then going up north and killing yourself and so I called Brad in a panic and it was his idea for me to go over to your place right away and explain things to you, that I wasn't there to prevent you from killing yourself, I was just there to get you thinking about suicide differently, that if you went through with this now you'd be an 'ignorant suicide,' that it would make more sense to study it, to explore which of the hundred thousand exits best suited your personality. And then he told me to give you my diary to clarify things further, to help you deal with Jennie's death and to see things from a completely different vantage point. And then, a few weeks later, just before you moved to Toronto, Brad came up with the idea for the trilogy, of getting you to agree to you and I working on Episode 1 — Jennie's suicide — together, while you operated The Loft and helped me find my 'Perfect Partner' so that you and your eventual understudy, Seth, could film Episode 2 — my suicide — which would enable *you* to finally commit suicide, if that's what you really wanted. If it wasn't, it wouldn't matter anyway because I would already be dead when the tapes of me unmasking myself beside Jennie's dead body came out. So there you have it. It was Brad who was the mastermind. He was the brainchild behind Act 5, Scene 5, which, aside from seeing if he could pull something like this off, he created to a) prevent you from prematurely killing yourself and sending the tapes to your parents, b) show you and me how convincing something like this can be, and c) help me make sure you'd go through with it, that when you and I really did find someone who wanted to kill herself with me, you wouldn't back out. And now that you know all this, maybe it's time we all got together and —"

"For fuck sakes. If you think for one second I'm going to get together with . . . with —"

"The quote, unquote 'cast of faux friends' we've assembled? Don't worry. You won't have to. Though they don't know it yet, Nicole, Daphne, and Katelin have all been offered acting jobs in an upcoming made-for-TV movie, which is why we've really been speeding things up, especially during the past day or so, to get to some sort of resolution one way or another so we can tell them the good news. Besides, the eleven months are up today anyway, so they're no longer bound by their contracts. Of course, Seth and Brad will have to be involved no matter what. After all, the trilogy is really Brad's idea, not to mention the fact that after we're both gone, he and Seth are the ones who will make certain the tapes get to all the TV stations and —"

"This is . . . this is just . . . just —"

"That's pretty much how I feel whenever I think about it. But you know what else is indescribable? You. Really. I mean that. You've been nothing short of fabulous during this entire final scene. I don't think even Brad could've written it any better. Of course, there's still something that needs to be done to kind of tie up all the loose ends."

"Rebecca . . . this is too . . . this is . . . what loose ends?"

"We'd like you to go back to St. Michael's where Seth and Brad and Nicole and Daphne and I'll be waiting for you in the lobby. By this time Katelin should be there too and Seth will give you five packages addressed to Katelin, Nicole, Daphne, Brad, and me. After handing them the packages, tell Daphne — who's been instructed to give you back the letter, unopened, that you gave her at the apartment — to hang onto the letter for a bit longer and at this point, Seth will inform us that you're the CEO and brainchild of Act 5, Scene 5, that you set the whole thing up, had Seth suggest we continue with the project, use our own resources, that this was all part of the curriculum, to see how dedicated everyone was, to see what we were capable of, blah, blah, blah, which is when Brad and I are going to start saying stuff like, 'Ya, right, whatever. What a load of b.s.,' at which point you'll take out your cellphone and dial the number Seth will have just handed you and when it starts ringing all five packages that you handed each of us will start vibrating and we'll tear open our packages and find the same style cellphones as we were given one year ago, as well as copies of our original contract highlighting the section regarding our agreement to never discuss any aspect of Act 5, Scene 5 with each other or anyone else for a period of ten years, as well as a graduation certificate from Act 5, Scene 5, with a very bizarre, completely illegible signature on it which, upon closer inspection and help from Seth will reveal that it's actually your name. As soon as this happens, Brad and I are going to start saying we can't believe it was you — his best friend, my own cousin — who was actually pulling all the strings, who set this whole thing up, and then we'll turn on Seth and start in on him, calling him a sneaky bastard for planting the idea of continuing Act 5, Scene 5 that night at Scaramouche and then later on how he got us to believe that he had a TV executive interested in what we were doing and that if we took the TV exec's suggestion about involving people we knew, he would get other people from the industry involved, and I can guarantee you that once Katelin, Daphne, and Nicole hear all this, once it sinks in that Seth was the front man and you were the main man — and that instead of them duping you, it was actually you duping them — they'll be totally blown away. I'm sure they'll have a million questions for you, most of which Seth will answer for you, but one thing you should do is remind us that our original contracts are still valid, that confidentiality is still the primary concern, that everyone involved in this project — from us to the casting agents, acting coaches, directors, talent scouts, and TV executives — everyone wants Act 5, Scene 5 kept a secret. And then you can tell us that, as promised in the original brochure, you have some good news for us — and at this point, Seth will hand everyone except Daphne another envelope and you'll ask us to open the envelopes and instruct Daphne to open the envelope you had asked her to hang onto for a bit longer and instead of finding a copy of the 'Perfect Moment' screenplay enclosed in her envelope — which is what you and everyone else thought was in there — she'll find what the rest of us will find: an offer to have a leading role in an upcoming made-for-TV movie. Of course, my offer and Brad's offer are bogus, but the offers to Katelin, Daphne, and Nicole are legitimate. The TV executive really exists, and all those people who originally contacted us were actually talent scouts and acting coaches and directors. When we receive the news of getting roles, be prepared to receive a major ass-kissing from all of us. It'll be the usual b.s. about how grateful we were for the opportunity to be involved in the school, being able to work with you, for giving us our start, et cetera, et cetera. So just do your best to play along and. . . ."

It was somewhere around this point that I started laughing, and in case you're wondering why, it was because a) I started thinking about cause and effect, how if Jennie had committed suicide alone and left behind a letter and her journal like she'd originally intended, if she hadn't let Rebecca convince her that filming it was a better idea, if I had called the police or a doctor or someone else that night, my life would've been a whole lot different at this moment, but as Rebecca wrote (on page 23 of her diary), 'The smallest decision, the slightest action or inaction, can change the course of his/her/our/their/my/yourstory'; b) I was also thinking about Daphne and Seth and Katelin and Nicole and Rebecca and Brad and what the Top Five kid said about being duped and how it almost didn't pay to care about anyone anymore because more often than not the person you care about turns out to be a way different person than the one you cared about; and c) I realized that this, like a lot of other things in the past few days, more than likely wasn't happening, that I was probably dreaming again and would soon wake up and realize I was still in my apartment or The Loft or a phone booth or a streetcar, and so I just started laughing and after Rebecca asked me three, maybe four times what was so funny and why I was laughing so hard, instead of answering her, I did what anyone would do under the circumstances, I decided to play along.

"Sorry about that," I said, trying to sound as though I meant it. "I'm just a little . . . it's okay now . . . So, anyway, what happens now?"

"Ryan? What's going on?"

"Nothing. I'm fine."

"Are you okay?"

"Couldn't be better."

"You haven't completely lost it, have you?"

"Au contraire, mon ami. Like you said, from a certain angle it's a brilliant work of art and I can either spend the next eight months moaning that it was at my expense or I can move on, right?"

"You sure you're okay?"

"I'm fine. So, what happens now?"

"Well, we need to find a replacement for Daphne. Someone real, of course."

"And who did you have in mind again? The woman who dated all the *freak*shows?"

"She's definitely on the list."

"So there are others?"

"Of course. There's a hostess at Rain. There's two girls from the white Pontiac from the other night. There's this woman from . . ." and as Rebecca continued talking I started thinking that if this *were* a movie what the audience would be hearing through the cinema's sound system at this moment would be a voiceover, that while Rebecca continued inventorying her list of prospective 'Perfect Partners,' the audience — instead of watching Rebecca talking into her cellphone — would be watching the following scenes:

Scene 1: me back at The Loft, destroying all Jennie's suicide tapes and letters and journals except for the originals and three copies,

Scene 2: me making up several packages containing a copy of Jennie's suicide letter, her journal, her diary, and the videos, addressing one to my parents, one to Eriq, and one to the police, and then FedExing the packages,

Scene 3 (which would really be a montage of images cutting back and forth between):

– me stuffing my duffel bag full of suicide paraphernalia — sleeping pills, potassium chloride, ground-up cherry and apple seeds, muscle relaxants, aspirin, a bottle of Crown Royal, the samurai sword, and my grandfather's 12-gauge shotgun;

– my parents and Eriq and the police receiving the FedEx packages;

– me getting on a bus bound for Lake Superior;

– my parents watching the video — watching me watching Jennie die, seeing Rebecca sitting on the tub beside Jennie's lifeless body, holding Cam 2, unmasking herself,

wiping off her make-up, taking off her wig, removing her disguise and revealing who she really is;
– me renting a canoe and, after FedExing another package to Eriq, throwing my duffel bag into the front of the canoe, pushing off from shore, and starting to paddle out into the lake;
– my mother calling the police;
– Rebecca being put into custody;
– Eriq (and Jo-Jo, as per my request) sitting in The Suicide Loft watching the video on my 2001 Sony 32" widescreen TV;
– me about a mile or so from shore, my legs bound together with rope, a large rock tied to the end of the rope, swallowing spoonfuls of ground-up cherry and apple seeds, chasing it with dozens of sleeping pills, muscles relaxants, and swigs of whiskey and potassium chloride;
– Rebecca being charged with — hell, whatever they charge someone who videotapes her own cousin killing herself;
– Eriq opening the second FedEx package containing my journal — bound in a blue felt cover — describing the last fourteen months and highlighting the last few days of my life, hoping he might be able to turn it into a mildly amusing story;
– me lifting the rock and gently lowering it into the water before picking up the samurai sword, placing the point against my stomach, then inserting the barrel of the shotgun into my mouth and, while falling forward into the water, simultaneously thrusting the sword into my abdomen and pulling the shotgun's trigger;
– the audience knowing, finally, that this is one instance where things appear exactly — I repeat, *exactly* — as they are shown.

Acknowledgements

Special thanks to:

Jack David, for saying yes.

Jen Hale, for all that you've done, but especially for your contagious enthusiasm.

Joy & Nadine, for your efforts — both now and down the road.

Shelley & Joan, for always being there.

Brian & Nikki & Craig & Jay & Carolyn & Kris & Mark & Myle & Henry & the Apples — Sonia, Barney, Heather, and Derek, for providing timely sanctuary.

Linda, for your awe.

Maureen, for helping me through the really difficult times.

Toronto & Apples Acres, for your inspiration.

Shannon, for starting a new chapter in my life.

— Gordon j.h. Leenders
thesuicideloft@hotmail.com

Gordon j.h. Leenders lives in Hamilton, Ontario. He holds a B.P.E. and a B.Ed. and a diploma in Outdoor and Experiential Education, and has been working as a cognitive rehabilitation therapist for five years. *May Not Appear Exactly As Shown* is his first book.